2024

Not Like In The Movies

THE JOURNALS OF ELIJAH BROWNE

A JACK WALSH NOVEL

BOB PIERCE

ILLUSTRATIONS AND PHOTOS BY THE AUTHOR

Published by Bob Pierce

MILTON, VERMONT

Published by Bob Pierce
73 Milton Falls Court
Milton, Vermont 05468

BobsAwesomeBooks@gmail.com

Printed in the United States of America.

CreateSpace printed version ISBN-13: 978-1499786910
ISBN-10: 1499786913
Title ID: 4840473

BOB PIERCE
design

Dedications

First and foremost, I want to dedicate this book to the Lord who gave me the idea and the inspiration to write it through interruptions, distractions, health challenges and economic setbacks. May those who read it find the inspirations that I did and the truths that I'd learned.

Secondly, this tome is dedicated to my wife, Stephanie, who has been by my side now for over twenty-five years and without whom these creative ventures would not be possible.

Also, to my friend and frequent inspiration, Pastor Kirk Weed with whom I have spent many long and engaging conversations about theology and the Christian life.

And to the late Reverend Earl McNair who, in his last years and at a very old age, still enthusiastically inspired me to see the pricelessness of life and the infinate possibilities of encouraging and inspiring others. I do so miss our time together.

FORWARD

We live in a very tumultuous time. Even a cursory scan of the headlines reveals a litany of evils, corruption and oppression in every corner of every community in all the world. In the day-to-day lives of Americans, we are seeing out-of-control government spending sending taxes to soaring heights making it harder and harder for average citizens to make ends meet; the cost of healthcare drifting farther and farther beyond reach; moral decay that is fast-approaching (and some would say, long past) the tipping point and people in our nation have become increasingly more hopeless, Godless and pessimistic about the future. The American dream seems to be nearly deceased.

But unknown to most, and certainly to the average citizen who endures the daily rigors of their work-a-day lives and anesthetizes their minds with hours of television, social media and web-surfing, is a much more sinister and global movement of powers that are intent on world control.

Right under our collective noses.

Organizations both secretive and overt are, and have been, working throughout banking, government, international finance, religious orders, military and politics to influence and, ultimately, take control of a new world order of their crafting. While we concern ourselves with the latest bus drivers' strike, they are manipulating the World Bank to maneuver funds in the billions and even trillions of dollars. While we're keeping track of the World Series, they are staging coups and propping up co-operative governments in third-world countries. While we are sitting at our kitchen tables, scratching our heads and trying to figure out how to stretch our shrinking paychecks to cover all of the bills spread out before us each month, they are infiltrating stock markets, investment firms, presidential cabinets and the Pentagon with their members to inject their influence in the broadest and most intrusive scope possible.

And whenever we hear anything about it, we just write it off as the unbelievable prattling of paranoid conspiracy theorists. But what if it were all true?

What if there were such organizations as The Trilateral Commission, Skull And Bones, The Illuminati, The Freemasons, The Templars and The Lámdearg? What if these groups really were working to bring about a one-world government with a one-world economy; a sort of blend of communism and fascism that would feed off of the working masses around the world.

Kind of makes our concerns about the twenty-five cent jump in the price at the pump seem rather trivial.

And what if someone, some average Joe, happens to stumble on something that might upset these groups and their world agenda — even if it were just a ripple in their overall schemes? What if he wasn't ready to just roll over and give in to them? And what if he found a few — just a few — people that he could trust to watch his back? In some small way, that person would be a hero; unsung, uncelebrated, unknown, but nevertheless a hero.

Follow Jack Walsh on just such an adventure from the innocent discovery of a set of ancient volumes to the unabashed determination to fight back against the evil that pursues them and save the life of one good man — and the discoveries that he and his companions make about themselves along the way. When you turn this page, you will be stepping onto the roller coaster with your E-ticket in hand... enjoy the ride!

— *Bob Pierce*

Cast of Characters

Jack Walsh
Jaded detective novelist and former jaded newspaper journalist.

Jacob Goodspeed
Director of the Montgomery, Vermont, Historical Society.

Agent Meagan Flynn
Bad-ass C.I.A. babe and director of the Dublin field office.

Special Agent George Walker
F.B.I. agent from the New York City office.

Eamon O'Neill
Leader of the Lámdearg and heir to the Throne of Erin.

Emilio Moretti
Illuminati operations leader and procurement specialist.

Cardinal Innicus de Recalde
Illuminati Grand Inquisitor.

Jenny
Bartender, waitress and manager of Dino's Bar & Grille.

Gideon Erdan
Leader of the Mossad (supposedly) commando squad.

Gregor Ivanovich
Grand Master of The Poor Knights of Antioch.

Pope Linus II
The Pope.

major players
You Can't Tell The Players Without A Program

This book brings into play a number of secret societies, religious orders and law enforcement agencies (some, a blend of various categories), many of which are fairly well-known and others are not; so to make things a little clearer for you, my beloved reader, here is a brief explanation of each of the groups that are mentioned in the story.

The Central Intelligence Agency (C.I.A.) — The American international intelligence agency whose mission is to gather intelligence and use covert tactics to assert the interests of the U.S. throughout the world. Much of this activity is unknown and unseen through espionage, but much is also very much overt through military action and manipulation of political and economic influences. Surveillance and infiltration are common tactics, but violent actions — including assassinations — are also in their repertoire, often employing mercenaries and local insurgents. The agency is headquartered in Langley, Virginia with offices in most major U.S. cities and in locations around the world with an unknown number of employees, field operatives and associates. Most of their activities are shrouded from the public, and so, they are imminently suspect in the minds of most Americans and people throughout the world. They have worked in tandem with the American military in every action around the world since its founding after World War II and has provided priceless intelligence to commanders both in the field and stratagems behind the lines and in the Pentagon.

Centro Nationál de Inteligencia (C.N.I.) — The Spanish intelligence agency with is the central umbrella agency for their National Office for Security, National Cryptographic Center and National Office of Intelligence and Counterintelligence. It's headquartered in Madrid, Spain and operates under the authority of the Ministry for the Presidency. More of a law-enforcement agency than an intelligence agency, still it employs many of the same tactics and techniques to gather intelligence and monitor communications as other such agencies.

Direction de la Surveillance du Territoire (D.S.T.) — The French agency was formed in 1944 and played a number of pivotal roles during World War II and has since grown to be the nation's premier intelligence agency. Their stated jurisdiction is within its own national borders, but their reach is far beyond that having operations worldwide. During the Cold War, they were instrumental in exposing over two hundred and fifty Russian K.G.B. agents stationed under legal cover in embassies around the world (all of which were arrested and executed). The agency is headquartered in Paris, France.

Direction Générale de la Sécurité Extérieure (D.G.S.E.) — A branch of the French Ministry of Defense, this is a covert operative agency whose jurisdiction is outside of the borders of France. The agency has been racked with scandal and missteps, one of the most notorious was their sinking of Greenpeace's Rainbow Warrior with the loss of one of the ship's hands in a port in New Zealand. The agency is headquartered in Paris, France.

Federal Bureau of Investigation (F.B.I.) — America's national investigative agency is chartered for domestic investigations of cases with multi-state or inter-state jurisdiction. The agency maintains field offices in over fifty countries and attaché offices in over sixty U.S. embassies with headquarters in the J. Edgar Hoover Building in Washington, D.C.

GCHQ Bude — A satellite listening station operated by the British Signals Intelligence Service, located on the site of a World War II air base near Morwenstow in Cornwall County, England, on the Atlantic coastline. Its location is strategically significant as that is the point at which transAtlantic telecommunications cables come ashore from North America. The agency monitors international communications both by hardwire cables and by satellite from this installation, including internet, cell and other media. They have been accused of industrial espionage and listening in on domestic communications. Recent revelations revealed an operation called Tempora which gives the agency the authority to collect and store all communications, domestic and international for analysis. The Bude installation is part of an international network that includes locations throughout Europe, Asia and North America — including Washington, D.C.

The Illuminati — The name is notorious and often confused with assorted other organizations throughout history that have adopted it, but the original organization was founded by Ignatious de Loyola as an offshoot of the Jesuit Order. Often referred to as the Vatican's "hit squad" or "enforcers," it has been instrumental in numerous persecutions, inquisitions and massacres in the name of both advancing the Roman Catholic religion and squelching the advancement of Protestantism throughout Europe and the world. The organization is headquartered in the Vatican in Rome, Italy and is known officially as the Holy Church Office. Their tactics of the past, even as recently as the mid 20th century, have been brutal and violent, but in recent years have become, generally, more covert and subtle.

Interpol — Headquartered in Lyon, France, is an international law-enforcement agency that works in conjunction with national law-enforcement agencies in 190 member countries around the world. Their stated purpose is to enhance the resources of these various agencies within the parameters of their national laws and international law. They offer these member countries investigative support, intelligence, training and access to cutting-edge technologies on a global scale.

Irish Republican Army (I.R.A.) — Their origins are shrouded in history mostly because of their terrorist nature which tends to shun any sort of records. The tensions between the native Irish and the so-called plantionists has brewed for centuries, but the Vatican-sanctioned massacre of 1641 added a deeper division making it not just a political conflict, but a religious one as well. When the "troubles" began in the mid 1960s, the original Irish Republican Army was formed in 1969 with support from Libyan terrorist groups and various American organizations. After the climactic "Bloody Sunday" in 1975, the British government launched a concerted campaign to put down the group until a cease-fire was called. A prominent leader of the I.R.A., Gerry Adams, formed the Sinn Féin political party, became its president and to this day had maintained an uneasy peace (see Sinn Féin below). Despite this new era of peace, there are still some terrorist factions that operate essentially autonomously insisting that violence is the only answer to their demands for independence; one of these groups is the shadowy Sons of Erin.

The Order of the Jesuits (The Society of Jesus) — Ostensibly a religious order of the Roman Catholic Church, it was founded in 1534 in Paris by the son of a Basque arisocrat, Ignatius (Inigo Lopez) de Loyola. Loyola formed the Jesuit Order after his ordination as priest by Pope Paul III and the order was given sanction by the Vatican in 1540. The order has a three-fold mission: the founding of Catholic schools, the conversion of non-Christians (non-Catholics) and the obliteration of Protestantism — all of which on a global basis. These goals have led the order to the implementation of many very controversial methodologies throughout history including torture and mass murder. They instigated the massacres in Paris in 1572 (the St. Bartholemew's Day Massacre), Venice, Italy in 1542, The Netherlands in 1543 and 1544, Ireland in 1641, widespread persecutions and executions throughout Scotland, England, Ireland, Germany and Europe throughout the mid sixteenth and seventeenth centuries, the Spanish and European Inquisitions of the seventeenth and eighteenth centuries and numerous others, many of which in collaboration with various organizations such as the Freemasons, the Nazi Party (the Ustashi), the Irish Republican Army and their own Illuminati, Knights of Columbus and assorted sub-orders throughout the world. Their tactics and operations have grown with the advancements of technology and politics throughout the years. The Vatican maintains political embassies throughout the world and welcomes ambassadors from many nations to their own embassies in Rome through which much of the Jesuit mission is orchestrated. Known as a religious and educational organization, their covert operations and violent past are much ignored or forgotten today, but their mission remains unchanged.

The Knights of Columbus (K of C) — Originally founded as a strictly American order of the Roman Catholic Church, the K of C was founded in 1882 by Fr. Michael McGivney in New Haven, Connecticut. The order's original stated purpose was to be a benevolent society for the influx of Catholic immigrants then pouring in from Ireland into America. By the beginning of the 20th century, membership mushroomed to tens of thousands with chapters opening across the country, Canada, and Europe. The order embarked on an acquisition of assets on a grand scale — including Yankee Stadium — and the establishment of a multi-billion dollar insurance and investment enterprise along with numerous other financial endeavors. Their economic and political influence grew exponentially throughout the latter years of the century. Their critics have consistently accused the order of being an influence of the Vatican to gain control of the U.S. government and its economy on behalf of the church. Because much of these accusations come from organizations like the Ku Klux Klan, they have generally been easy for the order to simply brush aside as these groups have very little credibility in the American mainstream.

The Lámdearg (The Red Hand) — The name is Gaelic and

dates back to the earliest history of Ireland and the establishment of its first royal family, the O'Neills. Legend holds that a dispute arose about who would inherit the kingdom of Ulster as the reigning monarch had no heir. A boat race between two brothers of the Uí Néill clan was held and it was agreed that, whomever first "touched their hand to the shore of Ireland" would be its next king. Near the end of the race, one brother, Niall, was losing by a short, but insurmountable, length and so severed his right hand and flung it to the shore thereby being the first to set his hand upon the shore of Ireland. The O'Neill clan became the ruling family of Ireland with Niall as its king and to this day their symbol, the Red Hand, appears on coats of arms, municipal logos, shops, tourist traps and businesses throughout Ulster County and Northern Ireland. It also appears on the official (though outlawed by the British) flag of Northern Ireland. Today the royal family of O'Neill exists in a sort of home exile, honored and regarded by the inhabitants of Northern Ireland (especially those of many generations) and is paid homage and tribute. After thousands of years, the Lámdearg has established itself as sort of a blend of political power, economic manipulator and organized crime with influence, investments and operations around the globe. They are intrenched into virtually every Fortune 500 company in the world, governments and intelligence agencies in numerous countries, all reporting back to their headquarters in Coleraine, Northern Ireland. The royal lineage continues to exercise its power locally and plans for the one day return of the O'Niell clan to the legitimate throne of Ireland.

MI5 — Made famous in numerous spy movies, MI5 is officially referred to as The Security Service. The agency operates within the jurisdiction of British borders, much like the American F.B.I., and is headquartered in London with a satellite in County Down, Northern Ireland. Their jurisdiction is stated as being strictly domestic, but their investigative activities often extend far beyond British borders to regions throughout the world where British rule once reached and their influence and interests continue to this day.

Mossad — Israel's national intelligence agency based in Tel Aviv; it is the central coordinating agency that specializes in counter-intelligence and counter-terrorism operations. They are one of the most secretive organizations of its kind in the world and reputably the most highly-trained and intensely devoted to their mission. Their known tactics include intelligence gathering, commando and insurgent operations and espionage. They operate all over the world in the interests of protecting Israeli citizens and jews of any nationality anywhere in the world. The agency's leadership reports directly to the Israeli prime minister.

National Security Agency (N.S.A.) — Formed in 1952 at the height of the Cold War, the agency is an arm of the U.S. Department of Defense (technically a military agency, not an intelligence agency) and is based in Fort Meade, Maryland. Its directors are typically military and it operates under the auspices of the Pentagon. Much of its operations have been historically classified, but recent developments have brought much of their activities to light. Chartered for international intelligence gathering through the monitoring of telecommunications, their reach has exploded along with the modern digital age. They tap into satellite communications (through which almost all long-distance phone communication travels), internet (through the U.S. Cyber Command), cell phone, radio, cable and land communications, much of it today includes a large amount of domestic transmissions as well. Their jurisdiction was greatly expanded after the 9/11 attacks and the implementation of the Patriot Act. They operate massive listening stations throughout the world, the largest of which is located in Bluffdale, Utah in the Wasatch Mountains.

The Poor Knights of Antioch (The Knights Templar, or Templars) — The Templars (who were originally called the Poor

Knights of the Temple of Solomon of Jerusalem) were established during the first Crusades around 1119 as a sort of armed escort service for pilgrims to the Holy Land who had to travel dangerous roads through Saracen lands to reach Jerusalem from their Mediterranean landings some dozen miles away to the west. In time, they took on a more inclusive role in the military operations of the Crusades. During the Third Crusade, around 1178, a few Templar scouts were exploring the occupied city of Antioch and discovered a small band of warrior monks of an order formed by Empress Helena of Constantinople some six hundred years earlier to shield the discovery by the Vatican of John the Revelator whom she had found in her quest for relics in the Holy Land. The ravages of the Saracen wars had taken their toll on these monks and their order was decimated so the Templars formed a new, secret sect based in Antioch, divorced from the Vatican, and sworn to the protection of John and his secret. When the Crusades ended and the church disbanded the Templars, arresting thousands and seeking to confiscate the Templar treasures, this small band in Antioch severed themselves completely from Rome, fled north into the Balkans with John and the vast majority of the treasures. Today they continue their sworn quest to protect John and also to administer the Templar Trusts (under numerous names in several countries) which are today headquartered in Geneva and hold investments and assets estimated to be in multiple trillions of dollars.

Sinn Féin — A political/diplomatic arm of the Irish Republican Army (I.R.A., see above) formed to end the so-called "troubles" that racked Northern Ireland for decades with reciprocal militant and terrorist attacks by various factions in the streets of its major cities. The British government tried in vain to put down the unrest with military force but, ultimately, Gerry Adams, a prominent member of the I.R.A., proposed a political solution which has been effective now for several decades. Sinn Féin is headquartered in Ulster and is a semi-autonomous governing body subordinate to the British rule of the island. Due to it's phenomenal success, the British government mostly gives Adams (who has been its only president since its founding) free rein in most local matters.

Skull and Bones — On the surface, a college fraternity on the campus of Yale University in New Haven, Connecticut. Its name referring to the supposed possession by the group of the skeletal remains of the Native American warrior chief, Geronimo. The order was founded in 1832 by William Huntington Russell and Alphonso Taft. The order boasts as some of its alum such notables as presidents William Howard Taft (son of one of the order's founders), George Herbert Walker Bush and his son George Walker Bush along with William F. Buckley, Senator and Secretary of State John Kerry, James Jesus Angleton (who established the Central Intelligence Agency of which George H.W. Bush would become director), Henry Luce (founder and publisher of Time, Life, Fortune and Sports Illustrated magazines), Howard Stanely (co-founder of Morgan Stanley) along with many influential members of finance, industry, politics and intelligence. Their list of members is public record, but the society itself is cloaked in secrecy. Their headquarters, called The Tomb, is an imposing structure in New Haven, on the Yale campus. The order is thought to be instrumental in orchestrating international economics and politics, its alumni and members being fiercely loyal and intimately coordinated in their agenda for a singular world order.

The Sons of Erin — A loosely-associated branch of the Irish Republican Army that is not content with the diplomatic efforts of Sinn Féin and maintain an insurgent presence in Northern Ireland, particularly in Ulster County. They continue an underground campaign of violence, still intent on a Catholic purging of Protestants and are often called upon by the Vatican to enact small, strategic operations throughout the United Kingdom.

THE
JOURNALS
OF
ELIJAH BROWNE

Bob Pierce

table of contents

Bob Pierce

introduction

My name is Jonathan Bartholemew. I'm a novelist, you probably know me as Jack Walsh and may well be familiar with my crime/suspense novels like *The Lion's Claw, Midnight in Kiev* and my latest, *The Twelfth of Darkness*. The nom-du-plur was my publisher's idea. He said that my real name was way too long, besides, "Walsh" can be in much larger letters across the front cover of a six-inch-wide paperback novel. Such are the nuances of the publishing business.

All of my novels thus far have been fictions, some have borrowed from some historical events and some were based on things I'd read in the news, but by and large, they'd been entirely made up in my own imagination. Not so this book. The events that you will read about in this novel actually happened with little or no embellishment and, frankly, if I hadn't experienced them personally, I'd have a really difficult time believing anyone who might relate them to me over a drink or

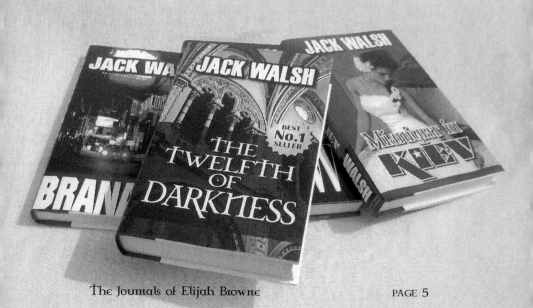

two (or even three).

As a writer in my particular genre, I've done a lot of research into secret societies and conspiracy theories, all of which are great fodder for suspense yarns. Just include the name "Freemasons" somewhere and you're almost guaranteed a best-seller. But as the events of this adventure began to unravel, I realized that much of what I'd assumed was just the unbelievable paranoid rantings of the fringe-factor, had a lot of truth in them.

An awful lot.

The story sort of gets its start when my dad passed away about twelve years ago. In his retirement years, he began work on our genealogy, researching both his side of our family tree and my mother's side. In deteriorating health, he spent about a decade house-bound on oxygen and, so, did the vast majority of his research through letter-writing and phone calls (though never long-distance). He refused to get a computer and was unable to travel, so those were his only options.

When he passed away, my mother essentially purged the house of much of his things. I got a few mementoes and, in one of my visits, she asked me if I wanted all of his genealogical materials. Apparently noone else in the family showed any interest and she knew how much work went into it all; she'd hoped that someone else would at least care enough about our family history to preserve that work, whether anyone ever continued the research or not. I really had no intention of pursuing it myself, but being a writer, I could relate to the body of work that it represented and relented — at the very least, I could store it until someone else in the family stepped forward to pick up on the project.

I frankly had no inkling of just how much material there was. She led me into a spare bedroom that had been his den at one time and pointed to three copy-paper cartons, a metal file box and a pile of what appeared to be photo albums stacked along the wall. Really? He did *all of that* from the sofa in ten years? Suddenly, I wasn't so sure that I actually did have room to store it all, but I had made a commitment, so I loaded it up in my car to bring back to my home in Vermont.

Well, since that day, my career as an author had taken off and I'd been able to move out of my little condo into a pretty nice old home on a hill overlooking the city of St. Albans. As the movers packed things up and asked me which room in the new place I wanted everything put in, I labeled all of the boxes of my dad's genealogy papers "office" so that they'd be out somewhere where I could easily access them (honestly, my curiosity was getting tickled and I didn't want them just stuffed into a shelf in the basement and forgotten).

As I was putting things away into my new bookshelves, I designated a whole section for all of the genealogical stuff so that it would be out of the moving boxes and in a place where I could idly pluck a few papers or a notebook down to flip through. Maybe someday I'd get serious about this but, for the time being, it would just be a "someday" project.

I discovered in this idle perusing that my dad had actually succeeded in tracing our lineage on his side of the family all the way back to England and found a few branches over the years that led to two American presidents and a number of other interesting characters but for Mom's side, he'd only been able to reach back a few generations. One thing that I found was that a long-held family belief about the origins of my maternal grandparents was, in fact, false.

I grew up hearing stories that my grandmother, Dorothea Browne, and my grandfather, Frank Walsh, had both emigrated to America from County Cork in southern Ireland — from different towns and at different times — meeting one another here in America and settling in New Haven, Connecticut.

Wrong.

Dorothea Browne was born in the small northern Vermont town of Montgomery. Her father lived there and her mother was from the town of Swanton to the west. Perhaps a previous generation may have come from Ireland. My grandfather Walsh's heredity had, thus far, eluded my father's efforts. I thought this to be quite interesting, but I just put the papers back onto the shelf until a few years later, when Mom passed away.

That was two summers ago, and this is where the story really gets started in earnest. After the funeral in Connecticut, I returned home to Vermont and in a melancholy moment, took down that notebook with my father's notes on the Browne family. I became quite fascinated and decided to pay a visit to Montgomery, it's only a few towns east of where I live. I contacted the Historical Society there by e-mail and got a response from its director, Jacob Goodspeed. He told me of a boarding house that was once owned by the Browne family at around the time of my grandmother's birth and invited me to come and delve into the stacks of records that he had in the Historical Society's archives to see if I could ascertain anything more. I eagerly accepted that invite and drove out to the little town a few weeks later.

Montgomery is a town that had once been a thriving mill town, situated on a criss-crossing labyrinth of rivers flowing down the mountains that surround the valley in which it sits, it once hosted a number of mills and was a major manufacturing and milling center. With so many rivers lacing through it, the town had — and to this day still has — the distinction of having the most covered bridges of any town, many of which are still in daily use. But today the mills are closed, most are gone altogether. The major industry in the town now is tourism, for the covered bridges in the warm weather months, and the skiers from nearby Jay Peak in the winter. The town has one inn, two restaurants, a few bars, a grocery store and a few mom-and-pop businesses scattered between its three crossroads.

At one time, despite its small population, the town had numerous churches, far more per capita than I'd expect to find in a town that size. Today, though, only two are still houses of worship, others are private homes and one had been donated by the Episcopalian church to the town to house its Histori-cal Society and now serves as its headquarters, museum and archive. It's now called Pratt Hall and the interior is still well preserved, particularly, the tall, intricate stained glass windows that flank its sides and form an awe-inspiring backdrop for its former alter platform.

In the months of my genealogical research, I'd gotten to be pretty good friends with Jacob Goodspeed, an amiable re-tiree from the IBM plant in nearby Essex Junction with a wry sense of humor and a gift for sarcasm. He always seems to be in a good (almost jovial) mood. One cannot help but enjoy his company. His normal garb featured a plaid shirt (flannel in the cool weather) and a pair of beige chinos kept in place by a pair of suspenders. A big fan of movies and local lore, he would frequently brace his trousers with a mis-matched pair of sus-penders one of which a bright red and the other a bright green, a nod to a hugely-popular Canadian comedian who goes by the moniker "Red Green" and sports such attire. Jacob is such a fan of Red Green that he is a charter member of the Possum Lodge, a fictitious men's lodge that, according to the comedian, exists in the rural Canadian wilderness, some great distance north of Toronto in the presumedly-fictitious town of Possum Lake.

Often, if I were in town around mid-day, we would walk up the street to Dino's Bar and Grille for lunch. Even during the ski season it's pretty quiet there in the middle of the day and typically one would only find the owner (who would generally be busy in his office or somewhere in the back room at that time) and the attractive young bartender, Jenny, who would double as waitress and chef until the rest of the staff would be-gin arriving for the busy evening hours. Jacob and I had spent many enjoyable hours sitting in the nearly-deserted dining room, listening to the music we'd punched-up on the jukebox and enjoying the pub cuisine and amiable conversation.

During these months, Jacob mentioned to me a set of co-lonial-era journals that he had stored in the back of the vault.

They'd been discovered in a hidden cavity in an old desk that was part of a collection of furniture and other artifacts donated to the Historical Society by the Smith family who were the last owners of the boarding house that he'd told me about; they donated the building to the Nazarene Church to be used as a combination sanctuary and parsonage in the 1954. He was in the process of cataloging the Society's entire collection on the computer so that they could publish a listing online and hadn't yet gotten to the older items in the huge, walk-in vault. I wasn't allowed to take the books out of the building or photocopy them, but I was free to inspect them on their library table and handle them with cotton gloves. The bright light of the copy machine might damage them, but I was allowed to photograph the pages with a digital camera, as long as I didn't use a flash.

There were three leather-and-canvas-bound volumes in dry, deteriorating condition. They were filled with ledger pages with the business finances of Elijah Browne's boarding house. There were also notes here and there written in the margins or, in some cases, across broad sections of the pages. About three quarters of the way through the first book those notes began to tell a most amazing story. Even for a devout conspiracy-theorist like myself, what I read as I worked my way through the three books was astounding. If it were true — any of it — it was positively explosive and surely there would be those even today who would do anything, even kill, to get their hands on them.

As the months went by and I was able to read through more and more of the journals, I became increasingly concerned for Jacob's safety and that of the little town. Who knows to what extreme someone might go to get possession of those books for their own dark purposes or to prevent their becoming publicized and to silence those of us who knew of their existence or their contents. But, before I had a chance to sit down and have a serious talk with Jacob about it all, our adventure abruptly began.

ᴛʜε cαʟm
ʙεꜰοʀε ᴛʜε sᴛοʀm

Pratt Hall was at one time in the little town's history, St. Bartholomew's Episcopal church. Famous for its colorful and intricate stained-glass windows, it stands today on Main Street across from the Black Lantern Inn in Montgomery, Vermont. Its years of service as a place of worship are long-since passed, the building now serves as the home of the Montgomery Historical Society which has restored it to its once-proud and beautiful state and secured it a place on the list of National Historical Sites as the bronze plaque beside its cathedral-shaped double front doors today attests.

On a quiet Thursday morning, a solitary soul toiled in the dim interior, familiar to these environs. The church pews that once filled the sanctuary floor had been removed some years before and the open space is now often used to host community events, meetings and displays of the Historical Society's collection of relics, documents and artifacts that help to tell the rich story of the town of Montgomery. On that cool spring morning, the cloud-diffused sunshine shone through the tall stained glass panes and cast distended trapezoids of colorful light across the bare wood floor, draping themselves over anything that might be set upon it. The projected shafts of light illuminated particles of dust that drifted through the room from one window to another, catching first one filtered color of sunlight and then another as the rising and circulating warm air from the building's heating system caused them to swirl en-masse in a continual, flowing dance around the dark space. In the middle of the room was the unfinished display of many of the historical society's collection for Civil War artifacts still under construction by the volunteers who were planning another work night on that next Friday evening to complete the project so that others could begin to put the items and their identifying tags into place the following week.

A serene and idyllic moment is space and time. The calm before the storm.

At the far end of the room was the raised, carpet-covered platform that once served as the site of the preacher's podium and the church's small choir, backed by more stained glass windows that towered above and created a spectacular backdrop for anyone or anything that ever stood upon that stage. Today, those windows are the backdrop for the desk of one Jacob Goodspeed, the tall, thin, gray-haired director of the Historical Society who was alternately working on and cursing at the modern desk-top computer that sat upon his antique desk, arranged at an angle to one side of the platform. The computer was a necessary evil of the job and, so, was nicknamed by Goodspeed "The Beast." Despite having been an engineer at IBM before his retirement, he lacked patience for most anything technological in these, his supposed golden years. He refuses to get a cell phone, for example, preferring to use a "real" phone and would rather write and mail an actual ink-and-paper letter to someone in lieu of using e-mail or social media.

His self-appointed task which he'd toiled at off-and-on for the three years that he'd thus far been director, was to make a comprehensive catalogue of the Society's entire collection. The computer would give them a permanent and searchable listing that researchers could refer to and volunteers could use to keep track of the inventory and it could also be posted on their

Bob Pierce

website so that people like me who are doing research from a distance would be able to look through it on line. But first, someone had to input all of it into the cantankerous machine and that task fell to him alone. The suggestion of the society's board of directors that he recruit volunteers or interns to help with the daunting project was rejected with his assertion that it would take infinitely longer to train them than the time he might save and, besides, they'd never understand his unique system so he'd likely have to re-do everything that they'd accomplish anyway. His cluttered desk was stacked with papers clipped into small bundles and notes on small scraps lest his aging memory neglect some fleeting thought. Baskets of papers and other small piles on the floor encircled the chair that he sat on. The only space on the surface of the old desk that was not carpeted with paper was that on which the computer monitor and keyboard sat and the green-shaded brass lamp beside them. Not even his coffee mug was so honored, having to find a perch upon an expendable piece of paper to Goodspeed's left as the computer mouse rested upon stacks of paper to his right.

From his vantage point, he could look across the former sanctuary and see the front entry doors directly in front of him at the opposite end. The oaken floors spread out in orderly stripes, reaching to the oak baseboards and wainscoting along the walls, capped with red walnut chair rails. The walls above, painted in a light, neutral color, drew the eye to the dark horizontal lines of walnut that rimmed around the perimeter of the room, encircled the six stained glass windows on either side and finally wrapped around the sharp corners of the front entry way and terminated at the frame that surrounded the double doors at the front of the building. But on that morning, he was far too busy, and far too frustrated with the project he was working on to be enticed by the warm, classic view. As he frowned and growled at the computer screen, he was unaware that the front door had opened and shut and a lone figure had quietly entered the room. His attention was suddenly wrested away when he heard the old oak floor boards creaking and echoing in the cavernous empty space, and then the man spoke with a somewhat familiar voice and a decidedly northern-New England accent.

"Jacob Goodspeed?" he queried.

Jacob lifted his face from his work and peered around the side of the monitor, slipping his narrow reading glasses down his nose to get a more focused view. He stroked has long brush of a mustache and squinted to see the figure half in the shadows and half in the brilliant, stark sunlight, and replied, "yes, can I help you?"

The man walked slowly across the room, approaching where Goodspeed was seated. He watched as the man got closer and then rose to his feet.

"My name is Ernie Fuller, from Richford."

"Fuller...sure, you own the garage up there by the border, right,?" he removed his reading glasses and set them down on the cluttered desk and then walked out from behind it to greet his unexpected visitor. He approached the edge of the carpet-covered platform where a pair of steps led down to the wooden main floor.

Fuller continued as Jacob approached him, "this town, Mr. Goodspeed, has a very unique history, shared by only a handful of others around the world."

"Does it now?" Jacob extended his right hand to shake hands with the man who regarded the gesture for an apprehensive moment before reaching out his own hand in greeting.

"I am here to retrieve some documents from your town's earliest past."

"Retrieve? What do you mean?"

Fuller returned his hand to his side and, looking down, smoothed out the fabric of his coat with a diversionary, brushing swipe. He looked around the room and began to slowly wander, looking at the ornate windows, he was clearly uncomfortable. "Do you believe, Mr. Goodspeed, that there are things that should be kept secret for the best interest of the public? Things that, if known, could cause chaos, economic and societal disaster?"

Standing near the unfinished Civil War display as he watched the man with rapt attention, Jecob set himself down on a stool left by one of the volunteer workers and replied, "I'm not sure how to answer that. Look around you, Mr. Fuller; this is a place of information, much of it otherwise lost to time and revealed only to those who take the time to come here and uncover it for themselves. I guess I'd have to say that, no, I don't think any information should be kept from the public. Let them decide for themselves what's in their own best interest — if they even care."

Fuller stopped his pacing and turned to look at Jacob with a sly smile, "I would expect an answer like that from the man who curates an historical society collection."

"What is it that you want? You're starting to get on my nerves."

"I am here for the journals."

"Journals? What journals?" Goodspeed rose to his feet and began to slowly glide back toward his desk on the raised platform in the back.

"The journals of Elijah Browne."

"Don't know any Elijah Browne," Goodspeed replied as he reached the steps to the platform. That was a lie, of course, I'd been there on numerous occasions over the previous months studying those very volumes. He was trying to buy some time; he may appear to be a most affable and jolly sort of fellow, but Jacob Goodspeed was a real Vermonter and one not to be trifled with when backed into a corner.

"Elijah Browne lived here in your town shortly after it had been founded after the Revolution. You're the director of this historical society, aren't you? You don't know about this man?"

"A lot of people have lived in this town since then, Mr.

Fuller. I've only been here myself for about ten years. I don't even know the guy who lives four doors down the street from me — how can you expect me to know someone who lived here two hundred years ago?" He stood beside his desk and, with his left hand, he reached down and hooked the tips of two fingers under the porcelain knob of the top drawer.

Fuller slowly walked up to the edge of the platform, looking up at Jacob, "Your diverting tactics are a waste of both of our time. You know exactly what I am talking about."

Jacob slowly began to draw open the drawer, hoping that his sinister guest would not notice what he was doing, but it was really impossible for him to be very covert so close-up. Fuller was not sleited at all and warned him as he slowly reached his hand into the opening of his coat, "whatever you have in that desk drawer, Mr. Goodspeed, I suggest you leave right where it is."

He froze with the drawer open a few inches. He looked down and could see the wooden grip of his thirty-eight caliber revolver glinting in the sliver of light allowed through the narrow opening. He raised his hand and looked up at Fuller who waved to him with his free hand to step away from the desk. He stepped to one side and said, "I can't let you have those books; they were donated to the Historical Society and are part of its collection. If you'd like to make an appointment, I can let you examine them here in our library, but I can't let them out of the building."

"You don't understand, sir. I am not here to examine them, I'm not doing research, I am here to take them to a safe place."

"They're already in a safe place."

"Safe from thieves, perhaps, but not safe from history."

"You're talking in circles, friend. What does a guy like you want with these books anyway? How would they be any safer in a gas station than they already are in my climate-controlled, fireproof vault?"

"They won't be stored there, you can rest assured."

Just at that moment I happened into the situation, arriving for my pre-arranged lunch date with Jacob. As I walked into the room from behind Fuller, I asked, "So where *would* you store them? New Haven? Rome? Or would you just burn them and be rid of them altogether?"

Jacob looked past Fuller who turned to watch me approach from behind him, carrying my twelve-gauge Mossburg which I coincidentally happened to have in my car with me. I didn't have any shells with me, though, but he didn't know that. Fuller just smiled and responded, "very good, Mr. Walsh," and slowly removed his hand from under his coat.

Jacob looked down at me, as I trained the muzzle of the shotgun on Fuller with a look of concern, "you know this man, Jack?"

"I know who he is and, it would seem, he knows who I am, but no, we aren't actually acquainted." I paused a few feet from Fuller and leveled the barrel of the gun at him and added, "besides, he was just leaving. Weren't you?"

"Not without the journals," he insisted, raising his hands.

"Look, you're just gonna have to get it into your skull that you are not leaving with them — ever. They stay right where they are. Kabeesh?"

Fuller looked up at Jacob who by then had retrieved his pistol and held it at the ready, pointed in his general direction. "Do you have any idea who you are dealing with? You have no hope of prevailing."

"You're still not getting those books, Mr. Fuller, so you might as well just be on your way and crawl back to Richford where you came from," having an ally with a shotgun in the room helped encourage Jacob's heightened level of bravado.

Fuller lowered his hands, still keeping them in clear view, and turned toward the door. He was fully cognizant of the guns pointed squarely at his back as he walked slowly away. He approached the front doors and reached out to grasp the handle of one of them, unlatching it and pulling it open a few inches before pausing and looking back at the two of us.

"I came to civilly ask for the journals. We thought that it was only right to be respectful, at least at first. What happens next is your own choice — remember that." Then he turned and walked out. I followed him to the sidewalk and watched as he got into his car and drove away, back in the direction of Enosburgh.

As I stood on the front porch of Pratt Hall, watching the rusted green Subaru Outback disappear around the bend of Main Street, Goodspeed came up from behind me, "Jack, what are you doing here?"

Confident that the sinister visitor had, in fact, gone, I ushered Jacob back into the building, closing the door behind us, "we're doing lunch — remember?"

"Oh, right. Hey, you never did answer me; how do you know Fuller?"

"I don't know him personally, but I know that he's 'K of C' and after having read those journals, it only seems natural that the Vatican would be sniffing around once word of their whereabouts got out."

"I haven't told anyone about them."

"Neither have I, but we haven't exactly been secretive about them, either. We've talked about them over lunch at Dino's without any concern about who might be around. We've talked here in the building, too, walking down the street; anyone could have overheard us and, if the right people — meaning, of course, the 'wrong' people — heard us, word could get back to all sorts of nasty folks."

"Nasty?"

"People who would be willing to kill either of us for them."

"That qualifies; that's pretty nasty."

"How long had Fuller been here by the time I got here."

"He got here about fifteen minutes ago."

"Well, I don't think he'll be back. They'll send others."

"Oh? There's more?"

I just smiled and changed the subject, "what about that lunch? I'm famished."

"Don't have to twist my arm. Let me shut down the Beast and turn off some lights. Just give me five minutes."

"You got it."

* * * * *

Dino's Bar and Grille, named by its owner after a Thin Lizzy song, is located on the commercial crossroads of Montgomery Center on the opposite corner from the Shur-Fine supermarket and across from the Baptist church. Lunchtime on a weekday afternoon is usually pretty quiet. Aside from Jenny the bartender, the owner and the cook, it was not unusual for there to be nobody at the tables in the small dining room so it lent itself to privacy, and for such a meeting, it was perfect.

The entry door on the side of the building leads patrons in through the bar. It's a shabby, but clean space festooned with all sorts of skiing posters and memorabilia. Some old wooden skis mounted on the walls formed big "X"s with photos and glowing neon beer signs interspersed around them and, in the back corner, a pay phone. In the age of cell phones proliferating even in that rural berg, the old pay phone probably didn't get much use any more, but the phone numbers and notes written on and scratched into the wall all around it are still an iconic part of the local decor.

The two of us walked in through the side door and were met by a most attractive young auburn-haired woman, Jenny, who was behind the bar setting out glasses that had just come out of the dishwasher in the kitchen, taking them from the large plastic trays and placing them into the overhead racks and shelves under the bar, preparing for the rush of late-spring skiers that would later flood into the little town from Jay Peak right around sunset. She smiled and directed us into the dining room and told us to sit anywhere.

We gravitated to a table near the juke box at the opposite end of the room and sat down facing the door to keep an eye on whoever might come or go while we were enjoying our lunches. In just a few minutes, Jenny brought a couple of photocopied menus and asked if either of us would like anything to drink while we made up our minds about lunch.

"Oh, I'll just have a Diet Coke," I said.

Jacob ordered a Diet Dr. Pepper which is not on the menu, but because he's a regular, she kept behind the bar just for him. The cheerful young lady jotted down our drink orders on her pad, stuffed it into the back pocket of her tight-fitting jeans, and turned to fetch our drinks from the bar.

Jacob smiled and watched attentively as she walked away across the dining room. I was about to open the conversation that I had asked him to join me at this quiet hideaway for when I noticed that his attention was fixated elsewhere. Glancing in the direction that he seemed to be gazing, I realized what he was so focused on. I just shook my head and whispered, "dirty old man."

"Huh? What?" Jacob snapped his face around to look at me, his face somewhat flush.

"I said 'you're drooling'."

He grabbed his napkin and quickly wiped his mouth, realizing that I was pulling his leg. He just snickered and set the napkin back down on the table as he stroked his mustache back into shape.

"She could be your granddaughter, you know."

"I know. I may be getting old, but I'm not dead, Jack."

We both had a good chuckle and then I settled in to talk turkey with him, "look, Jacob, this is serious."

"Sure, I got 'ya."

"Do you have any idea what's actually in those journals?"

"No, not really. I mean, when you first found them in the back of the vault, I looked at the first couple of pages and saw the name 'Elijah Browne' and saw lots of columns of figures

Bob Pierce

and notes inside. I knew he ran a boarding house in town and assumed the books were just the ledgers and notes from years of running his business."

"I've read them from cover to cover. The first one has some notes in it about how Elijah was approached by a stranger from Europe to be the liaison for a religious order and helped them build a monastery up on the hill outside of the village and then be the go-between for them. He did it for years, in fact, his son Elisha took over the family business when he died and continued working for these guys. Those columns of figures you saw were lumber, food, medicine and other supplies that Elijah got for them over the years."

"Sounds creepy, who were these guys?"

"I did a little research. The group was called 'The Order of The Poor Knights of Antioch.' They were Templars."

"Templars? Like Masons?"

"No, those guys came along later, they got nothing to do with the original Templars from the Crusades."

"So that's all in the first book? What's in the other ones?"

"Stuff that will blow the history books apart."

"What?"

Just then, Jenny returned with our sodas and set them down with cocktail napkins under each one to keep the condensation from the glasses from making a mess on the table. She set her tray into the crook of her arm to use as a hard surface to write against and put her order pad down on it, "you boys ready to order lunch?"

I looked over at Jacob and snickered, "I haven't even looked at the menu, we've been talking so much. You know what you want?"

"Yeah, I'll have your mushroom-bacon cheeseburger — well-done."

"Fries?"

"Of course."

She scribbled down Jacob's order and then turned to me

and asked what I'd like.

"Uuhh, I was in here a few months ago and you guys made a really great Reuben for me, I think it was a special. Can I order that?"

"Sure. You want fries, too?"

"Yeah, fries. That'll be good."

"Okay, I'll get your orders in right away. The cook is here today so we'll get these right out for you."

"Thanks," I said as she turned and walked away.

Before I could lose Jacob's attention to the waitress' undulating gate again, I reengaged the conversation with him; he was instantly attentive.

"Elijah wrote in these journals some notes from conversations he had with a mysterious old man who lived in that mansion who he was convinced was the Apostle John from the Bible."

"John? From the Bible? That's *nuts*. He'd have to be, what, about eighteen hundred years old by then."

"I know, but what if it's true?"

"*You're* nuts."

"Look, I'm no expert, but just check out what Jesus says at the end of the book of John. Peter asks Jesus some snarky thing about John and he snaps back to him to mind his own business and says 'what does it matter to you if he remains until I return?' That's the whole idea with Christianity, right? That Jesus is gonna come back some day? And that hasn't happened yet, so..."

"So John would still be around? Waiting?"

"And he has seen it all. Can you imagine what kind of impact that would have on religions and countries and economies around the world."

"This is pretty heavy," Jacob took a sip of his Dr. Pepper and looked at me with a countenance of deep concern.

"The monastery burned down when they all left in the late eighteen hundreds with everything they left behind inside, nothing left but ashes. They even dug up their dead and brought them with them. There's no evidence of them ever having been here except for those journals. There's probably a lot of people that would want to get their hands on those books."

"What are you thinking."

"Well, if the Templars are protecting John, they'd want to get the books to keep his secret. What if there were other people who would want to *publish* what's in there?"

"And what about the Knights of Columbus, the Vatican?"

"They'd kill us for those books in a heartbeat. They've done a whole lot worse over the years, that's for sure. The K of C are the least of our worries with them, though. They'll be sending their Illuminati; they've got all kinds of covert groups all over the world."

Jacob slouched back in his chair, mindlessly stroking his brushy, gray mustache and just stared blankly out the window to the quiet streets of Montgomery's little village. Outside he could see a white-bearded man in a filthy baseball cap and overalls carrying a bag of groceries from the Shur-Fine store across the way getting into his pickup truck. A young couple walked past the window holding hands; he knew them all. They were his neighbors in that tiny berg and they were all perfectly oblivious to all of this; he couldn't imagine that such a quiet place where people lived such simple lives could be turned upside down with such a deadly controversy. He turned again and looked at me, "so what're we gonna do?"

October twelfth, 1788

A dark stranger with an eastern European accent this day came hither by the liv'ry stables for to speak with me. Vicar McGlynn directed him to see me; said he was with a religious order from Europe and that his name was Bro. Vadim, wanted to establish local representative to helps build monastery on North Hill. Sayeth they are not papists.

NOBODY HERE BUT US CHICKENS

It was about midnight, I had long-since turned in and was sound asleep when the phone on the night stand beside my bed rang. At first, I didn't really hear it, I thought it was part of a dream that I was having but eventually it roused me from my sleep. With my eyes still shut, I groped with annoyance in the darkness and eventually my open palm found the receiver and my fingers just instinctively wrapped around it. I rolled over in bed onto my back and raised the phone to my face and groaned, "Hello?"

A voice on the other end of the line spoke in a thick accent. It sounded eastern-European or maybe Germanic, it was such a bad connection that it was hard to tell. He asked me if I was, in fact, me. My suspicions were immediately raised, so I answered his question with one of my own and asked who he was.

"I am looking for Mr. Jack Walsh," he said with a notable edge, then reiterated, "are you Jack Walsh?"

"Yes I am. Do you have any idea what time it is?"

"Here it is mid-day."

"Where is 'here'?"

"That is not important."

"Well it's bloody important here — here. Here it's the middle of the bloody night!" I sat up in bed and reached for the lamp on the night stand and flicked it on, "what do you want?"

"Mr. Walsh, we understand that you are in possession of certain documents. I am hoping to arrange with you their return."

"Who, exactly, is 'we'?"

"I cannot say, especially not over the telephone there may be others listening. Just understand that we are an international organization, very old and very powerful."

"The Mafia?!" I said sarcastically, but almost as soon as the words had left my mouth, I realized that I was wrong and suddenly it dawned on me — the man's accent, it rang familiar from my research that I was doing for my next book. I lowered my voice to a near whisper, "you're with the Order, aren't you?" I had no idea who it was I was talking about, but it sounded pretty ominous. I was surprised, though, at the response I got.

"If you know anything about our Order, Mr. Walsh, then you know I cannot confirm that."

"Of course not, how silly of me. So, what documents are you talking about? I don't have any documents that you people could possibly be interested in."

"We know you are writing a book. I would very much like to dissuade you from doing so. But that discussion is for another day, for now, I need to recover Elijah Browne's journals. Do you have them?"

The fact of the matter was that I had no intention of writing any sort of book based on those journals, I was only looking them over to research my own genealogy, Elijah Browne was my great, great (there may be another 'great' or two in there somewhere) grandfather. I had to buy some time, so I whipped up a quick story to put the man on the phone onto a rabbit trail to somewhere else.

"No, I don't have Browne's journals. I had them sent to Yale University, to their carbon dating lab, to be analyzed. They've had them now for a few weeks; they told me it would take a couple of months." I knew that mentioning "Yale" would put the man on the phone into a quick tizzie.

"Yale University. That is in the city of New Haven, is it not?"

"Yes, as a matter of fact, it is."

"That was a very dangerous thing to do, Mr. Browne. Did you tell anyone that you were doing that?"

"Well, just the guy at the Historical Society. I had to tell him, they belong to them."

"The Knights of Columbus is headquartered in New Haven. If they get word that the journals are there they will stop at nothing to retrieve them."

"Well, don't you have people there, too? At Yale?"

"What do you know of this?"

"I'm a bit of a conspiracy-theory buff, I know a little about a lot of things. There's an unmarked door on campus, leads to a secret hall they call 'the Tomb'. Most people believe it's just a harmless, if not particularly creepy, fraternity. Yet several of our presidents have been members of this so-called fraternity. They knew, didn't they?" There was silence on the line for a few minutes. "Hello?"

"I am here."

"That's what they are there for, isn't it? To keep an eye on the Knights? To monitor the Vatican's influence in the U.S.?"

"This needs to be kept very quiet. If a confrontation were to take place between these groups, blood would run through the streets of that city. You have no idea what you are dealing with, or who else might get involved."

"Oh, I'm pretty sure I do. And I think you'd best wrap up this call and dial up your friends in the Elm City and give them the heads up as quickly as you can. You can thank me later."

"*Thank* you? Are you *insane*?!"

"You're welcome, have a nice evening."

I pushed the receiver button to hang up the phone. I knew that the more-or-less diplomatic visit from the local Knights of Columbus lodge earlier that day was just the tip of the iceberg.

I knew that they, and others, would be ramping up their efforts — I just didn't think it would be so soon. I quickly dialed the phone to contact Jacob to warn him.

"Mmmmm…hello?"

"Jacob? It's Jack."

"Jack? Jack? Do have any idea what time it is?"

"Yeah, Jacob, I do. I wouldn't be calling at this hour if it wasn't important."

"Well, then, what's so important?"

"I just got a call from someone that I think is with the Templars."

"The journals?"

"Yeah. I told him they were in Connecticut, I'm not sure if he bought that or not, it was pretty clumsy but I think I may have bought us a little bit of time — very little. I'm not sure that either of our phones may be tapped, but we've gotta do something right now — tonight."

"Tonight? Jack, I'm in bed; do you have any idea what time it is?"

"Yeah, Jacob, get it together, man. You've gotta get the journals and hide them tonight."

"Hide them? They're locked up safe and sound in my vault."

"Safe and sound, you think? Tell me, if you were some sort of international secret society spook and you rolled into sleepy Montgomery, where do you think you'd look first for those books?"

"Uuuuhh, the vault?"

"And do you think these guys might have the sophistication to get into your vault?"

"I don't know, do you?"

"Yeah, Jacob, and they could do an awful lot of damage in the process. You get those journals and hide them someplace where you'd think nobody would ever look for them and then pack a bag. I'll pick you up in ninety minutes."

Bob Pierce

"Pick me up? Where are we going?"

"I don't know yet. We'll start at the airport and see where we end up from there."

"You're insane, Jack, you know that."

"I know, but so far it's working for me — you're the second one to tell me that tonight. I'll see you around two o'clock!"

I hung up the phone and got dressed, then I grabbed a couple of shirts, clean socks and underwear, my razor and toothbrush and stuffed them all into my backpack. I've done so much impromptu traveling researching my books, that I've gotten pretty good at throwing a quick bag together and hitting the road. I got to Jacob's house just a little after two Friday morning. I pulled up in front of the modest house that Jacob Goodspeed called home on a side street in Montgomery Center. Jacob was waiting inside and when he saw my headlights sweep across the front of his house, he slipped quietly outside without turning on his porch light lest he attract any undue attention to our nocturnal rendezvous from his neighbors (it's a very small town and people in very small towns love to talk).

He walked up to the car and opened the door to the back seat and tossed in his backpack, then slipped into the passenger seat up front. I pushed the gearshift lever into first gear and we began our hour-and-a-half-long ride to Burlington International Airport.

We had suddenly been thrown into a desperate situation together, but when we had first met just a couple of months before, it was a much more business-like relationship. I sort of felt guilty, dragging Jacob into this whole mess. When I had first contacted him at Pratt Hall asking questions about my grandmother, he did a little digging for me and found that Elijah Browne had run a boarding house in town, and guessed that, when my great-grandfather, Albert, had moved to town with his new bride, he had returned to take over the business which eventually grew from a boarding house to a stage stop doing a brisk business with travellers between New York's Champlain

Valley and the mill towns of New Hampshire and the Connecticut River Valley. He discovered that there were a number of old documents in the Historical Society's collection, many of them dating back to the time of the Revolutionary War, when the town was first incorporated, and encouraged me to come out and check them out, that's when I discovered the journals.

Shortly after the turn of the twentieth century, the Browne estate had sold the building that once was the boarding house (there were no longer any Brownes left in the area and the house had been abandoned for several years) the Smith family. It remained empty for many years until the remaining family members, by then all living in other parts of the country, decided to donate the building to be used as a church. First, however, they had to hoe out all the old furniture and junk that had been left behind, having accumulated for generations. In a back corner of the living room was an old secretary's desk. It was the desk that Elijah Browne and, subsequently, his son Elisha had used to run their businesses. Bills were paid, letters written, and guests' registries were kept in the various cubbies, compartments and drawers of the very plain, utilitarian piece of furniture. The old desk had seen many, many years of service and neglect and, by the time the building's new owners had found it, it looked it.

But the director of the Historical Society at that time asked to have anything that they intended to discard offered to their collection and that desk, along with a few other pieces of furniture and boxes of old papers were donated. When Jacob took over the post of director, he found the desk in storage and decided to have it restored to use it as his own, so he brought it to a furniture expert who began work on the desk by disassembling it and that's when he discovered a secret cavity in the back of the desk with three old, leather-bound journal books hidden inside.

When Jacob went to pick up the finished desk, the restorer handed him the journals in a brown paper bag along with a few other odds and ends that he'd found inside the drawers like old business cards and a glass inkwell encrusted with lampblack ink that had fallen into the interior parts of the desk's framework.

The journals were dusted off and stacked in the back of the vault while the other items were boxed and stored with the rest of the society's collection. A few years later, I stumbled on the books and spent some time reading them, that's when I realized just what they were.

As we drove down the dark, unilluminated interstate, I told Jacob that I was sorry that this whole thing was causing such an upheaval in his otherwise quiet, rural life.

"No worries, Jack," he said. "I've been spending so much time bent over that God-awful computer that this will be a nice diversion."

"Okay, Jacob. I just hope this little diversion doesn't get us killed."

"So you think the guy on the phone was a Templar?"

"He never said so, I was just guessing."

"It wasn't Ernie Fuller, was it?"

"No, I'm sure it wasn't. Even if Ernie tried to fake the accent, his voice was just too different. But I'll tell ya', when I suggested that the guy was somehow associated with the Skull and Bones, he started getting really agitated. Seems I've struck a nerve."

"Really? You think that these Templars are somehow in bed with the Skull and Bones?"

"Well, on one level it sort of makes sense, but honestly, it was a flyer, just trying to throw out a diversion to buy us some time to get outta Dodge."

I pulled the car into the airport's parking garage, not knowing when I might be back to reclaim it, then we grabbed our bags and walked to the terminal with no idea where we were going yet. It was still early morning, around four o'clock, and was still quite dark out. As we walked across the pedestrian bridge from the garage, Jacob said, "Jack, I'm not feeling very comfortable with this."

"I know, neither am I. I like to plan things out before I do anything, but if we don't know what we're doing, it's all that much unlikely that anyone else will figure it out."

"I guess that makes sense ... I guess."

We rode the escalator down to the main terminal area and the long row of airline check-in counters. At that hour, there were very few travelers in the terminal building yet, we stood and studied the list of flights on the large, black screen above our heads as if we were in a fast-food restaurant trying to decide what to order for lunch.

"How about Arizona?" Jacob asked, subconsciously stroking his mustache as he studied the various options.

"That would be good. I was thinking farther, though. How about Seattle?"

"I hear it rains there all the time."

"That's just an old wives' tale."

"Well, okay. I guess."

We got into line with our backpacks and shuffled ahead, one space at a time, until we finally reached the counter. The woman behind the window asked to see our reservations, presuming we'd conveniently made previous arrangements on the internet and printed out confirmation numbers at one of their convenient kiosks.

"We want two tickets to Seattle, please," I said.

"Excuse me?" the woman replied.

"Seattle. Two, please."

"Do you have a reservation? A confirmation number?"

"No, we just want to buy our tickets here, now."

The woman looked perplexed and then turned and waved for a supervisor to come and help her.

"Is there a problem?" he asked.

"These two men want to fly to Seattle but they don't have a reservation. I don't know what to do. Can we do that?"

"Well, if there are seats available there's no reason why not."

The woman then began typing frantically on her computer terminal, painfully aware of the line of people beginning to gather up behind us. With her supervisor's coaching over her shoulder, she would type and wait, type and wait, type and wait, until finally she announced that she could put us on a plane in Burlington to John F. Kennedy airport in New York where we would conveniently catch a plane to Chicago and then connect to Seattle from there. But the flight from Chicago would not leave until the next morning.

"We don't have that kind of time," I replied. I turned to Jacob and asked, "anywhere else work for you?"

Jacob looked back up at the big board and pondered for a moment, "how about Phoenix?"

"I think that will work," I said and then turned to the woman behind the counter and her supervisor and asked if she could book us through to Phoenix to arrive the same day.

She looked at the two of us as though we were just a little bit crazy (a reaction that we were going to have to get used to in this little adventure, so we'd discover), but nevertheless, she continued trying to make the connecting flights work. Finally, to the relief of those waiting in the lengthening line behind us, she announced that she could get us conveniently to Phoenix that day through New York and Memphis. I laid my credit card down on the counter and said "let's do it!"

With boarding passes in hand, we made our way to the T.S.A. security line, placing our bags into the convenient gray plastic tubs along with our belts, shoes and all the contents of our pockets. After the rather unusual scenario of our impromptu ticket purchase (apparently the ticket agents somehow warned them that we were coming), the T.S.A. agents paid particular attention to us and, after having walked through the scanner, we were each patted down for our safety and convenience before being allowed to continue to the waiting area.

Jacob hadn't flown in many years, the whole new security process caught him off guard. But I encouraged him to just "go with the flow" and with very little delay, we were through the line and walked to the conveniently-located metal benches so that we could return our belts, wallets and other personal items to their respective places about our bodies and put our shoes back on, though Jacob had to leave his toothpaste, mouthwash and shaving cream behind, not knowing that there was a limit on the size of the containers he was allowed to take or that he had to put them into zip-lock bags. I told him not to worry, we could get replacements at a gift shop or a pharmacy in Phoenix when we got there.

Once we found the gate from which our plane would board, Jacob bought a couple of cups of coffee from a conveniently-located kiosk and we settled in for the half-hour wait. The time went by quickly enough.

At just about a quarter to six, the gate attendant stepped up to the microphone and announced that everyone in group one would begin to board in just a few minutes and to please get into the proper, conveniently-labeled line. Buying our tickets on the fly at the last minute, we were most definitely not in the first group, nor any other group that might receive any special consideration on that flight, so we just stood back and bade our time until the attendant announced, "everyone else."

"That's us," I quipped to Jacob.

"Everyone else? That's us?"

"Blending in, my friend. Blending in. It works, just go with it."

Carrying our backpacks, we stepped up to the door that led down to the jetway and out to the plane. Only two or three others were behind us. We got onto the crowded plane and found our respective seats, separated from one another by half the plane's length. Every seat was taken; not unusual as just about every flight to just about anywhere flying out of Burlington connects through either Newark, New Jersey or JFK in

New York. Jacob found himself sitting next to a young mother with an unruly child whom he found great enjoyment in relating with, while I sat next to a businessman in a tweed suit jacket who had stuffed a trench coat into the overhead compartment next to his briefcase.

The flight took off in the beginning glows of morning dawn and arrived in New York in a little less than an hour without incident or drama. As we got off the plane, we walked out onto the tarmac and into a long tented corridor that conveniently sheilded us from the harsh, cold wind. I stood off to one side to wait for Jacob to catch up with me, then we walked together with the flow of the rest of the crowd into the warmth of the terminal building to get our bearings and see where we had to be to catch the next connection on our westward trek.

As we stood checking our boarding passes, comparing them to the oh-so-convenient video screen listing all of the day's arrivals and departures, I noticed out of the corner of my eye, the businessman that had sat next to me on the plane. He was standing with his back to a wall, near a trash receptacle and seemed to be looking in our general direction. The man just seemed to be hanging around with his trench coat draped over his arm, he didn't seem to be checking to see where he needed to be going or rushing off to get to another gate like all of the other passengers that came in with us were doing. He just cooly, expressionlessly, stood there, occasionally checking his watch as though he kept forgetting what time it said just a few short minutes before.

"That guy makes me nervous," I intimated to Jacob.

"What guy? The guy you rode next to over there?" We both stood by the video screen and looked right at the guy, there was no ambiguity to our attentions.

"Yeah. You think I'm being paranoid, don't you?"

"Some great statesman once said that, if you think people are out to get you, it isn't being paranoid if they actually are."

"Who said that?"

"I don't know. It was either Will Rogers or Rush Limbaugh, I can't remember."

"Well, in this case, I think it's just the better part of prudence to start putting some real estate between us and him."

"You think he's alone?"

"So far, anyway."

"What d'you got in mind?"

"Let's go get a latte."

"A latte?" He shrugged his shoulders, "okay, I'm in."

We stepped out together and drifted into the crowd flowing along the open space that formed a defacto corridor leading from gate to gate inside the terminal building between the inner storefronts and the outer banks of seats for waiting passengers, walking past the man with the trench coat and beyond. As we got past the next gate, Jacob turned to look and see if the man was following. I grabbed his elbow and yanked him back around.

"Don't look!"

"How do we know if he's following us?"

"Oh, we know he's following us, besides, see those big convex mirrors?" I nodded upward as we passed one of several large, circular mirrors conveniently hanging from the ceiling. Jacob rolled his eyes upward to get a quick glance without turning his head.

"Oh, yeah, great idea. And the glass in the shop windows and the chrome on these kiosks. Look for reflections."

"Got the idea when I wrote *Moscow Sunset* a few years ago."

"Walsh...Jack Walsh," Jacob tried his best Sean Connary accent. "Shaken, not stirred!"

"Whatever..." I stopped and grabbed Jacob's arm and yanked him into a Hudson News shop and quickly led him around to the inside corner where we could hide behind a display of paperback novels and watch through the unobstrocted portions of glass in the front window as the crowd walked past.

In fairly short order, the man with the trench coat walked by without a glance toward us and continued along with the flow of the crowd. I looked up and saw that Jacob was at the check-out counter buying a pack of M&Ms and a book.

"Look, Jack, they've got your book here. Our next connection is a long one so I figured I'd get some 'Ms' and a book. *The Twelfth of Darkness*, what does that mean?"

"It means we've gotta get going or we'll miss that flight." My voice was showing a subconscious edge of impatience, but, still, I waited for the few minutes it took for my traveling companion to make his purchase and cheerfully thank the clerk.

We turned back the way we came when we walked out the front door of the shop and made our way to a convenient courtesy desk. When we stepped up to the desk, I asked Jacob for his boarding passes and then told the young man behind the desk that we needed to take a different flight and asked that we be rebooked from JFK to San Diego instead of Phoenix. The attendant, without making eye contact, conveniently took our respective passes and began typing on a computer terminal in front of him. After a few minutes, he asked, "I can connect you through Atlanta, then Phoenix. Is that okay?"

"But we were going directly to Phoenix from here to begin with. Why do we now have to go to Atlanta?" It seemed a little strange to me.

"That's the only way I can get you San Diego, sir," the man had no expression in his voice. It was really weird, a monotone like some sort of cyborg.

"Okay, whatever works. That will be fine."

"I see you two don't have seats together on the reservations you already have, is that still okay?"

"I've got a good book to read," Jacob replied; "that'll be fine."

I turned to the attendant and nodded, "yeah, that's fine."

"Okay." After a few more minutes of computer clicks, the attendant turned to retrieve the new boarding passes from a printer, conveniently located within arm's reach on a counter behind him and then turned and handed them to us. "Your flight from here will conveniently leave from gate twenty-three in..." he glanced down at his watch, "...about forty-five minutes."

"Thank you."

"Yeah, thanks." We gathered up our new boarding passes and walked away, back into the flow of the crowd.

We stopped at a bakery that we'd stumbled on and each got a muffin and coffee since neither of us had had breakfast yet and still had a long, long way yet to go. By the time we got to gate twenty-three, a small crowd had gathered there to wait for the plane to Atlanta. We double-checked the convenient video listing and saw that it was still expected to leave on time, so we sat on the floor with a group of bohemian college students along the wall, behind the other travelers sitting in the rows of chairs, to stay as much out of sight as possible.

"This reminds me of my college days," Jacob mused as he peeled the paper wrapper off of his blueberry muffin.

"Really? Howso?"

"A few buddies and I tramped across Europe in the summer between our junior and senior years. All we had was what we could stuff into our backpacks." He smiled and picked up his pack, "in fact, this is the same one. Son of a gun."

"Son of a gun," I repeated with a chuckle.

In the din of voices, public address announcements and the phrenetic swirl of humanity all around us, the two of us sat on the dirty carpet and ate our muffins and sipped our coffees until our flight was announced to board. We gulped down the last of our coffees and gathered up our trash while we waited for the last call and then got to our feet and walked to the gate. As we walked around the rows of chairs to get in line, Jacob noticed the man with the trench coat out of the corner of his eye.

"Is that him?" he asked as quietly as he could without drawing any attention.

Bob Pierce

"It is. Don't run, just keep walking."

"What if he follows us?"

"He doesn't have time to get a ticket, we'll be in the air before he can change his flight."

We walked past the counter, scanning our boarding passes on the convenient reader window as we did, and then walked out to the plane that waited on the tarmac for the last of its passengers for the flight to Atlanta. The man with the trench coat never moved from where he stood, he just watched us intently as we disappeared through the door and down the stairs.

Repeating the routine that we'd just done in Vermont, we squeezed through the crowd choking the aisle of the narrow plane to find our respective seats. We each stuffed our backpacks into the convenient overhead compartments and sat down, clipping our seat belts in preparation for take off. On that flight, I was seated next to a young coed student who spent most of the flight working on a laptop computer on her folddown tray. Jacob found himself next to a rotund salesman of shower curtain rings dressed in plaid and the pair struck up a boistrous conversation that lasted the entire flight and annoyed all who sat near them. It seems that Jacob Goodspeed can make friends with just about anybody from any walk of life and have a good time wherever he goes. I don't think he ever got to read a single page of *The Twelfth of Darkness*, and I don't think he cared a lick. I just had to smile to myself.

Once in Atlanta, we had to run to catch the next connection. Normally a frustrating situation, but it also meant that if someone were looking to follow us in that airport, they'd have a really tough time keeping up. The flight to Phoenix, again, was uneventful. The plane, however, was a somewhat larger craft, conveniently affording more leg and elbow room. Jacob tipped his seat back and caught a quick nap, I, however, was much too wired to be able to close my eyes (I don't sleep well on planes or trains, anyway). That flight, the longest leg of our intended journey, gave Jacob an opportunity to read partway through my novel. He'd never read any of my books before, he seemed to be engrossed. When the plane landed and rolled to the terminal and all of the passengers got to their feet to wait in the aisles to disembark, Jacob was still in his seat with his nose in the pages of the paperback novel. Not until the passenger who sat next to him by the window barked at him to get up and get going did he put the book away and get to his feet.

Once off the plane in Phoenix, we had a couple of hours before we had to catch the next, and final, connection to San Diego. We found the gate from which we would be leaving and then located a Starbuck's counter nearby and got a couple of coffees and scones and returned to the seats conveniently aligned by the boarding gate for a quick snack and the short wait for the announcement to board the plane. We weren't so concerned about being followed there, but still, I kept a wary eye out, studying the crowd all around us. We had chosen seats to wait in with our backs to the wall so that we could watch each and every face that drifted into the waiting area for the same flight, but I felt confident of our safety as we sipped our drinks and noshed our scones.

Though we were comfortable that we were safe – for the time being, anyway – we still waited for all of the other passengers to board so that we could be sure that we were not being followed. For one last time, we repeated our then-familiar routine of squeezing onto the crowded plane, stuffing our bags into the overhead compartments and finding our respective seats to meet the passengers that we'd be spending the next couple of hours with – for better or for worse.

Again, I tried to catch some sleep on the plane but it was a futile effort and a relatively short flight, anyway. Before we knew it, the stewardess was announcing that we were on the final approach to San Diego. Jacob peered out the window at the brown, desert mountains below, dotted with patches of green here and there around scattered clusters of development. We propped our seats back into their upright positions and folded our trays and waited for that impact of the landing gear hitting the asphalt of the runway and the violent desceleration as the plane conveniently slowed to a stop at the far end of the runway and then taxied to the terminal.

The passengers waited impatiently as the plane rolled slowly across the airport and approached the terminal building. As it rolled up to the jetway and the brakes finally brought the craft to a stop, the clanking of seatbelt buckles being undone and the murmur of voices talking on cell phones announcing their respective arrivals to friends and relatives who were waiting for them filled the cabin.

We each got up from our seats and retrieved our respective bags from the overhead storage compartments and waited with the rest of the passengers for the door to be opened and the jetway to be fitted to the side of the plane. In short order, the stewardess signaled that it was okay to disembark and the passengers began to file out and snake their way down the corridor and out into the expanse of the terminal building to be bathed in the bright southern California sunshine pouring in through the tall windows. The warmth was a welcome change from the chilly, spring temperatures of the northeast and the brightness of the sunlight was so much more intense. Jacob peeled off his windbreaker and stuffed it into his backpack. I took the cue and did likewise. In the warm San Diego sun, we didn't need any jackets.

We walked across the large, open space of the terminal building, past the baggage-claim conveyors. Near the doors to the sidewalk were racks of tourist literature. We stopped to take a look at potential hiding places and find some city maps to help us find our way around in a strange environment. We each grabbed a few flyers and then walked out to the sidewalk in front of the building.

"I love palm trees," Jacob noted as we walked out into the air and looked around the area around the airport. Tall palm trees and short, stubby ones dotted all over the landscape with unusual flowers and tall grasses in artistically-arranged clusters gave even such an urban location the look of tropical paradise to a pair of Vermont yankees.

"We need to figure out what we're going to do next," I said matter-of-factly as we stood there on the sidewalk, shuffling through the various rack cards and brochures.

"Well, I'm hungry." Jacob said as he turnd his gaze from the swaying palm frons to talk with me. "I had a blueberry muffin – or at least most of one – in New York at seven this morning. Since then it's been a scone in Phoenix, airline pretzels and coffee" he looked at his watch, "it's four-thirty in the afternoon."

"Actually, my friend, it's one-thirty. Three hours' difference."

"No wonder I'm starved. We missed dinner and now it's almost lunch time! I gotta get some real food; let's find a decent restaurant."

"Not a bad idea." I just had to smile, it's all I could do because there was no way I could follow his logic. All he knew was that he was hungry — whichever meal we might engage.

"Any ideas?"

"Well, we're in a strange city. Usually the best thing to do is head downtown. We can figure it out from there."

"Good idea. Let's grab a cab."

Jacob unzipped the outer pouch on his backpack and we stuffed all of the literature into it and zipped it back up. We walked out to the curb and, as we did, a young man in a blue vest stepped out in front of us and waved to a line of colorful cars waiting several feet up the driveway and the driver of the car in the front of the line climbed into the driver's seat and rolled the car forward to pick up his fare.

The young man in the vest reached out and pulled open the door to the back seat and the we climbed in. "Downtown!" was the only direction we gave to the driver and, in a moment, we were heading out the long, curved road to Harbor Drive and then east to San Diego's Gaslamp District. As the cab wove through the traffic along the coastline, we checked out the scenery and gazed out over the water at the hundreds of yachts and sailboats docked in the many marinas that lined the shore. Masts of tall ships were visible through the towering palm trees and, in the distance, the distinctive shapes of naval warships and at least one aircraft carrier.

The cab made its way to the tourist-filled streets of the Gaslamp District; San Diego's historic section of town packed tightly with ornate, brick buildings housing restaurants, bars and shops catering to tourists and baseball fans who flock to and from Petco Stadium on the periphery of the district, home to the San Diego Padres.

As the traffic got to be so congested that the cab was spending far more time stationary than in motion, I just paid the driver and we got out and blended into the thick pedestrian traffic flowing around the sidewalks, swirling around the classic old buildings. When we got to the corner, we stopped and surveyed our surroundings. Goodspeed noticed a nice-looking restaurant across the street with lots of dark wood, glass and gleaming brass.

"That looks like a pretty good place. Look, there's a menu in the window, let's go check it out."

I looked across the street through the choking crowd, and then looked up the road. "Doesn't it seem to be strange?"

"Strange? What do you mean?"

"There's a bazillion people on the street and they all seem to be moving in the same direction, like a hoard of zombies in some sort of science fiction movie. You notice that?"

Jacob stood with me on the sidewalk as the flow of humanity diverted around us, all appearing to be headed in the same direction just as I had observed. "Where do you think they're going?"

"I don't know, but if we want to blend in here, we might want to find out."

"But, what about dinner? Or lunch? Need I remind you, I haven't had anything to eat since that muffin at J.F.K. – I'm starved!"

"We'll get something in a few minutes, let's check this out first."

"Don't make me regret this."

"Oh, don't worry, I'm sure we both will before the night is out."

We followed the flow of foot traffic down the crowded sidewalk and around the corner and noticed, at the end of the block, the imposing structure with a large red, white and blue sign identifying it as the Petco Stadium.

"Didn't the cabbie say that there was a game tonight?"

I just grinned and then looked at Jacob, "how about hot dogs for dinner while we take in a game?"

"Blending in, eh?"

"In that crowd? We'll be positively invisible for nine innings."

"Not a bad idea, I guess. Let's go."

We bought our tickets and went into the stadium and found a hot dog counter to grab some dogs, fries and beers (first priority at that moment) and then located our seats in one of the upper rows along the third base line. Considering we just spontaneously showed up there, the seats weren't all that bad. We got comfortable and, even though neither one of us are baseball fans (and had very little understanding of the game that we were watching) we were actually having a good time. We seemed to forget — for a little while anyway — that we were being hunted. The man in the trench coat was a vague memory while we sipped our beers, munched our hot dogs and cheered for both teams because we couldn't agree which one was our favorite.

We got caught up in the revelry of the crowd, cheering and jeering the accomplishments and failures of each player. We had fun trying to pronounce some of the players' names and laughed when the video cameras showed kissing couples on the big screens between innings. By the sixth inning, we had gotten so wrapped up in the fun of the moment that we hadn't spent a second talking about what we might do when the game was finally over which was, as we'd planned, part of what we were going to do while we were so cleverly hiding in plain sight. Jacob got to his feet as the visiting team finally went down for the last time and the home team was about to get up to bat. He announced that he was still hungry and was going to make a quick run to the refreshment counter for a couple more hot dogs.

"Weiners," I corrected.

"Weiners? I thought that was a kind of dog."

"No, no. Hot dogs out here are called wieners. You wanna blend in, you gotta sound like a local."

"A local? Compared to where we came from, this is *another planet*. I don't think we're gonna blend in very well."

"The land of fruits and nuts, my friend."

"I'll try my best — you want anything while I'm up there?"

"Ha, ha! No. No that's okay, I'm all set, thanks."

"Okay, I'll be back in a few minutes."

I turned to once again watch the ball game down on the field as Jacob climbed the concrete steps to the upper walkway and the concessions counters but, as he reached the upper-most steps, he realized that the beer he'd had with his first wiener had caused an urgency and he needed to find a men's room before getting in line for his next snack.

Upon his emerging from the busy men's room, he noticed that the traffic of people had greatly increased. He made his way back to the concessions stand and got in line for his next helping of California wieners. As he stood there, shuffling forward one step at a time, he glanced around at his surroundings and the people. He had never been to California before and had never been in a professional sports stadium, either. Centennial

Field, where he'd gone on a couple of occasions to see minor league games with the Lake Monsters in Burlington, was nothing like Petco Stadium.

As he glanced around, he happened to notice two men standing near the wall and off to the side of the large counter that he was approaching to order his dogs. They were dressed in dark suits, white shirts and ties. They wore sunglasses and had coiled wires protruding from their respective left ears. They stood there sullenly surveying the crowd. They stood out amongst the t-shirt-and-ball-cap-clad crowd like a pair of sore thumbs.

He tried to reason to himself who these two might be and what they might be there for and came to the only reasonable conclusion that they were there looking for the two of us. He kept glancing over at them for fleeting glances to see if they were looking at him, but it seemed that they hadn't noticed him in the thickening crowd yet. He felt safe and secure. Enough so that he felt emboldened to do something arguably stupid.

He stepped out of line, just a step to his right, so that he stood between two of the lines and turned to face the two men who stood about fifty feet away. He looked directly at them and gently stroked his mustache. One of the men panned his glance around and caught a glimpse through the confusion of faces, one face leering directly back at him. He locked his gaze on Jacob and reached out to poke his partner to get his attention; when he turned, the man pointed out the tall man with the mustache in the crowd.

For a few long moments, the three of them leered at each other and the crowd obliviously flowed around them. Then, as the concessions lines moved forward and they lost sight of Jacob for a moment, he disappeared. They quickly moved forward and spread out into the crowd to see if they could locate him. In the mean time, Jacob had ducked down a bit and slipped through the crowd to a door marked "Employees Only" and found himself in a long, cinder-block-lined hallway. He was alone as the big steel door shut behind him and the sound echoed its reverberations down the long corridor's length and back again.

There was only one direction to go from there, so he ventured down the long, curving hallway that wrapped around the periphery of the stadium, deep within the bowels of the structure until he came to a doorway that, in turn, led to a stairwell. Ever vigilant of the possibility of being followed, every stadium employee that he'd encountered he studied with a wary eye as they'd pass. He walked purposefully, knowing that if he looked like he belonged and knew where he was going, others would believe it and be less likely to confront him.

When he came out of the door at the bottom of the stairwell, he found himself in another masonry hallway, but this one was much wider and painted in the team colors of white and blue. About thirty feet to his right, he could see the bright sunlight shining in from the field illuminate a segment of the hall, so he turned and walked in that direction. Just before he reached the tunnel to the field, he came upon an open archway and a baffle that led him into a locker room.

It was a much bigger space than he'd expected, with rows of open alcoves and shelves, each of which with a number above it and a locker next to it. The open area between the facing lockers was rowed with long wooden benches. Everything he touched and every move he made caused a distinct echo in the room. An opening at one end of the room led to the showers and another to a couple of offices. When he finished exploring, and not finding another way out, he returned to the locker room. He was headed toward the baffle and back out to the hallway, when he heard someone come into the room, already talking.

"Hey, Ted! Ted! It's almost the seventh inning!" A short, very nervous man in a blue polo shirt and carrying a clipboard came walking into the room.

Jacob panicked. He looked around for somewhere to hide

quickly, but found himself cornered. Hanging on a rack against the wall was the costume for the team's mascot, the famed San Diego Chicken. He quickly reached up and grabbed the head off of the shelf at the top of the rack and slipped it on just as the man rounded the corner and saw him standing there.

"Oh, good, you're here," he looked back down at his clipboard, turned on his heel and began walking back out — still talking, "you've got about ten minutes to get out there! Better hustle!"

Jacob found himself standing alone with the mascot costume and realized that the crowd was expecting the Chicken for the seventh-inning-stretch and Ted, whoever he was, was nowhere to be found. As he removed the chicken head, he smiled to himself, sizing up the costume on the hook.

"Not exactly 'blending in,' but I just can't resist," he reasoned as he took down the various elements of the suit and put them on. The fans would not be disappointed, the Chicken would appear that afternoon.

Walking in the big, floppy chicken feet was a bit awkward, but he made his way out to the hallway and followed the light to the tunnel that led out to the field, coming out of the tunnel next to the dugout on the first base line. The crowd spotted him and began to cheer. The players were just leaving the field and the nervous man with the clipboard, who stood just outside the tunnel opening, waved him out.

Without a clue what he was doing, Jacob — the Chicken — walked out onto the field trying to look as confident in what he was doing as possible, waving to the crowd. Ted was obviously a somewhat shorter man than Jacob, but nobody seemed to notice (or care) about the gaps between the different parts of the costume. The fans cheered as they rose to their feet, many of which taking advantage of the break in the action to seek out a rest room or flag down another beer vendor.

I stood up, too, and arched my back, pressing in on it with both hands and then looked around for my companion.

Bob Pierce

Jacob had gone for hot dogs and still hadn't returned. When I looked up the stairs, I could see that they were choked with people and figured that he'd just gotten hung up trying to press through the crowds, so I turned back to watch the antics of the famous San Diego Chicken musing to myself that the Chicken seemed a lot taller in person than he did in any videos I'd seen on television.

Jacob walked out to the pitcher's mound, jumping up and down and waving to the crowd as he did. Then, he stood with his big, yellow chicken feet on the rubber strip and scratched at the ground as he'd seen so many chickens on the farms back home in Vermont do. He then turned sideways and cupped his hands together, pressed to his chest and peered at home plate over his shoulder. He had recalled a pantomime bit that he'd seen Jonathan Winters do once of a pitcher and thought he'd try and imitate that. Jacob Goodspeed, however, was no Jonathan Winters. The crowd booed him and jeered at him and yelled to him to get off the field as he clumsily went through his antics.

The painfully bad pantomime lasted for a torturous three or four minutes when, suddenly, the Chicken stopped and stood on the mound with his big chicken feet spread apart, his yellow-gloved hands balled into fists and pressed against his hips and his long tail feathers flailing in the breeze behind him. He leered at the tunnel opening that he'd just come out of. From my perspective across the field, I could see two figures in dark suits and sun glasses standing just inside of the tunnel entrance, out of view of most of the crowd. Just at that moment, the Chicken reached up with one hand and brushed his beak just as so often seen Jacob unconsciously stoke his mustache.

"Oh, crud," I whispered to myself.

Then the Chicken squatted down and reached out his two hands, beckoning the men in black with his waving fingers, enticing them to come out onto the field. Those seated along the first base line couldn't see the two men, but as they edged out closer to the field, the rest of the fans started to and began yelling to the men to go out and get the Chicken.

Jacob then turned his back on the pair and bent over, wiggling his butt and his tail feathers at them and then jumped back around and taunted them some more. The announcer, ad-libbing on the public address system, got into the act suggesting that the two men were agents "K" and "M" (neither of them could be "J" since they were both white) and they were there to get the Chicken; adding that he'd always personally suspected that the famous Chicken was not of this world.

I grabbed our backpacks and ran down to the railing at the edge of the field. Before a security guard could stop me, I threw the packs over the railing and leapt over and onto the dirt strip at the edge of the grass. I quickly grabbed the straps of the packs and began running to my friend's rescue, though I didn't have a clue what I was doing (but that was okay, neither did anyone else). I didn't know who they were but I knew they weren't actors doing this for the entertainment of the fans.

The two men in black stayed back in the shadows of the tunnel entrance as the crowd got louder and louder until Jacob's taunting finally motivated one of them to storm out onto the field. The crowd jeered him with renewed enthusiasm. Those who could not see the two men before that moment suddenly got into the spirit and the volume of the cheering and yelling rose all the more as the one man walked out into view with a stomping, angry gait.

The man walked up to the pitcher's mound and the Chicken took a comic boxer's stance, rotating his fists in the air like Moe Howard might have, bouncing on the balls of his big yellow chicken-feet around in circles around the sinister man who kept reaching out, trying to grab him as he turned around in circles, following after the goofy bird.

I ran across the grass between the pitcher's mound and home plate, dropping the two packs and picking up a bat as I reached the opening to the tunnel. The second man had drawn his pistol and was holding it hidden under his folded arms, when he saw me running toward him with the bat in in hands, ready to take a swipe at him, he snapped his hand around and pointed the gun at me. I swung the bat as I ran in a desperate move to swat the gun out of the man's hand and, when the bat made contact, the gun went off as it got smacked by the bat and slammed against the concrete.

The gunshot rang out throughout the stadium and many frightened people screamed in fear and began rushing for the exits, but the quick-thinking announcer assured the crowd that it was all part of the act. The stadium's security guards were not so convinced and began quickly making their way to the field. I swung the bat a second time and connected with the man's gut, knocking the wind out of him and laying him out flat in the tunnel entrance. The crowd went wild. Then I turned to help my friend, the dubious Chicken.

Thus far, the first man had not drawn his weapon, instead choosing to take down the unarmed Chicken with his bare hands, but Jacob knew just enough of martial arts techniques to be dangerous (as much to himself as to any adversary), even in the awkward costume, and kept just out of the man's reach, landing the occasional punch while dancing all around the infield.

I came up from behind the man in the suit and swung the bat once again, hitting him across the right shoulder blade. The man twisted in pain and turned around as I was already swinging with a follow-up to the mid-section. The man doubled over upon the impact and tried to turn away and, when he did, the Chicken connected with a right cross to his jaw and the man in the suit fell to the ground like a limp sack of potatoes, lying spread-eagle on his back on the lush, manicured grass.

The crowd went crazy. They screamed and cheered their Chicken. They hadn't seen anything like that since he'd beat up Barney the purple dinosaur some years before. It was intoxicating and Jacob put his fists in the air like Rocky Balboa and bounded up and down on the pitcher's mound while the announcer played "Eye Of The Tiger" on the public address speakers.

I grabbed my friend the Chicken by his bright yellow-fethered sleeve and tried to snap him back to reality.

"Jacob! What the heck are you doing!? We gotta get out of here!"

Jacob stopped his bounding and turned to me and nodded. He waved to the crowd and we ran to scoop up our backpacks and duck into the tunnel on the third base side of the field, away from the gathering crowd of light-blue-shirted security uniforms at the opposite side. We ran down to the hallway as Jacob tried to strip off the costume and get back down to his street clothes as fast as he could while we kept moving. He left a trail of yellow-fethered costume bits behind us as we made our way toward any door that had the word "exit" anywhere near it.

Once the big yellow chicken feet were off, and he was back down to his sneakers, we were able to move much faster. We finally found a door that led out to an open lot behind the stadium lined with green dumpsters and employees' parked cars. We slung our packs over our shoulders and nonchalantly strolled out through the chain-link gate to J Street.

March twenty-third, 1789

Berton Lebeau of Richford north walketh the land with me and Vadim this day. Hired Burton to do survey and to stake out the property for monastery buildings. Need to have land cleared, a well dug. Shall send a note to Peter Blakeslee on the morrow.

September second, 1790

Went to North Hill with Bro. Vadim and Burton
Lebeau to inspect progress of construction of monastery
buildings. Timbers are in place and walls are being
put up. Millworke is to be delivered within the
week. Fireplaces and chimneys are nearly completed.
Expect to be able to close roof and walls by winter
to worke inside.

no funny business,
i know karate

San Diego's Gaslamp District is normally a really busy place, especially in the evenings, and on that particular evening, with baseball fans starting to drift out of the stadium in the last innings of the game, the streets and sidewalks were filling up and becoming all the more crowded. Jacob and I made our way through the crowd, trying to go with the flow of the pedestrian current along J Street behind the stadium for a couple of blocks, until we reached the intersection of Fifth Avenue. We paused for a moment, looking up at the street sign on the pole, and then smiled at each other. Something familiar, if not just in name, from our part of the world. We crossed the intersection and began walking north, up the hill. The farther we got from the blocks immediately adjacent to the stadium, the more the crowd around us thinned.

Jacob looked down at his watch in the light of one of the many classic gas lamps that flickered along the way and, to his shock, it read after eleven o'clock.

"Is that our time or local time?" I asked.

"Oh, good question. It's what, three hours difference?"

"Yeah, turn it back three hours. It's earlier here."

"So, it's about twenty after eight."

"Right."

Jacob slowed his pace as he trained his attention on pulling out the stem on his watch and spinning the hands back three hours. Once he pushed the knob back in, he looked up again and caught up with me.

"You know, I never did get that hot dog."

"What, are you still hungry?"

"Are you kidding? It's been a really long day and we still need to find a place to stay tonight. I don't wanna spend it sleeping on a park bench somewhere."

"I hear that."

"This place coming up is nice," an unfamiliar voice from behind us offered.

"Huh? What?" Jacob looked back over his shoulder at the faces following behind us on the sidewalk.

"Don't turn around, Mr. Goodspeed."

Of course, that admonition almost assured his doing exactly that. Just as he turned his body and began walking slowly backwards to get a closer look, he recognized the man walking directly behind us and blurted out, "oh, it's you..." before tripping on his sneakers. I noticed him stumble out of the corner of my eye and turned quickly to grab his arm and keep him from falling backwards onto the concrete.

"I told you not to turn around because I didn't want you to trip and fall, Mr. Goodspeed. You really need to trust people more, you know."

"Trust? You're the guy on the plane. The one with the trench coat."

"Yeah, why should we trust you?" I added as I helped steady my septuagenarian friend. The three of us stopped walking and stepped off to the side by one of the gas lamp poles to get out of the way of the foot traffic on the sidewalk.

"I probably should have introduced myself earlier, but we had to be sure you two were who we thought you were. That took a little time."

"Who, exactly, is 'we'?"

"I'm sorry; F.B.I., my name is Special Agent Walker," he reached out his hand toward me in greeting.

"You'll understand why I don't shake your hand," I just kept my hands at my side while Jacob slipped his into the pockets of his windbreaker.

"I suppose. Hey, let me buy you guys dinner, we can talk. As I said, this place up here is really good."

Jacob looked up the block and saw a sign on the next building, "'Croce's'?"

"It's a little away from the stadium so it's a lot quieter, they've got live music every night and the food is excellent. Can I talk you into it?"

I looked over at Jacob and smiled, "I guess we can trust him *that* much, anyway."

Jacob looked at the agent and said, "Okay, I guess we'll let you buy us dinner. But no funny business, I know karate."

"Yes, I know. I watched you two beat the snot out of those two guys back at the stadium — and in a chicken suit no less. I was impressed."

"You're just yankin' my chain."

"No, seriously. I can only imagine how much that suit restricted your movements, and you still laid them both out. I'm not sure that I'd be able to do as well."

Jacob smiled and looked over at me, "I think I like this guy."

"Yeah, well, let's go eat. I'll let you know how I feel about him later."

Agent Walker waved his hand and smiled as if to say "okay, let's go" and the three of us walked up to the door of Croce's restaurant where the hostess seated us at a table along the wall, not far from the stage and brought us three menus and wine lists.

The restaurant was fairly busy that night, but not packed full and the young woman with the Martin guitar sitting on a stool at the microphone on stage helped to make the atmosphere all the more mellow and comfortable.

Without a word, we sat at the table and perused the menus. Jacob, thinking that he might not get a real meal again for another few days, figured he'd best take advantage of the situation and ordered as much as he thought he could eat in one sitting. I wasn't being so calculated.

When the waitress came to ask for our drink orders, Jacob ordered a draft beer, I ordered a Bourbon and Special Agent Walker ordered a cola. Upon hearing that, I suspected that Walker was on duty, so I changed my order to a glass of water with lime.

The waitress thanked us and then turned to go and gather our respective orders; when she did, I leaned over the table and discreetly asked Walker to see his identification.

"Maybe you should do that *after* he pays for dinner," Jacob suggested.

"Oh, it's okay." Walker reached into the inside breast pocket of his tweed jacket and produced a leather folder which he flipped open with his thumb. On one side was his gleaming polished gold F.B.I. badge and on the other was his identification card with his photo. I read the name on it quietly, out loud,

"Special Agent George H. Walker." I then looked up at his face with an intense look as I sat back again in my chair.

"Everything okay?" Walker asked as he put his I.D. folder away.

"Who were those guys at the stadium? Your people?" I asked.

"No, they weren't with the Agency."

"That's not what I asked."

"What are you talking about, Jack?" Jacob interrupted.

Walker quickly replied, "I'm not sure, but I have my suspicions who they were. We've been monitoring the local Knights of Columbus and the Jesuit university and we've been hearing some very interesting chatter."

"Illuminati." I said quietly.

"We think so. There's a Jesuit school here in San Diego, in the Old Town section, with a campus that we are reasonably certain is a regional headquarters for them."

"San Diego and New Haven. Near, but not in, Los Angeles and New York."

"That's the idea. Hard for such a big organization to fly *totally* under the radar, makes them a little tougher to find — that is, if you even know to look for them in the first place."

"Most people just write off the Illuminati as the fabrication of conspiracy theorists and Hollywood."

"Yeah, that helps too. Not to mention that there are a few organizations around who use the same name. Makes it more of a shell game."

"But that's not who we're talking about here, right? We're talking Ignatius DeLoyola. *Those* guys, right?"

"Yeah, those guys. You ready to trust me now?"

"Look, guys, I feel like I'm a little out of the loop here," Jacob interrupted. "Who are these guys you're talking about? Are they dangerous?"

"Dangerous? I'd say so," Walker replied.

"*Really* dangerous," I added.

"Like the guys who threatened Jack on the phone this morning?"

"Not exactly," Walker interrupted. "Those guys were Templars. Make no mistake, they *will* kill you because they believe their mission is timeless and more important than any individual life; either of you two, to put a finer point on it. But they will do everything they can before resorting to that because that would attract far too much attention. Gregor Ivanovich is the guy who called you, Mr. Walsh. We think he's their Grand Master right now, a real cold character. He's got a few notches in his belt already — that we know of. If it came down to it, yeah, he'd kill you without a thought. But that would be a last resort."

"So, Jack, I'm thinkin' it's probably a good thing to have

an F.B.I. agent as a friend about now. What do you think?"

"He's not a lucky rabbit's foot, you know."

"I know, but he *does* have a gun. And an expense account."

"Our tax dollars at work, I suppose. I'm kinda looking at this dinner as sort of a tax refund."

"Look guys, I'm planning to stay with you until this is over," Walker injected. "The F.B.I. is here to serve citizens like you. Understand that this situation has international implications and, if we start getting involved with other governments, not only are you going to be running into a quagmire of diplomatic relations, you're likely going to be playing dodge-ball with the C.I.A., N.S.A. and the State Department. They have a way of making people like you disappear."

"That's not good."

"No, Mr. Goodspeed, it's not. Do you think the two of you can trust me for a few days?"

"No funny business?"

"No funny business, I assure you."

"Okay," Jacob reached his hand across the table and shook with Walker.

When Walker then extended his hand to me, I reluctantly reached out and gripped it and squeezed tightly and growled, "nothing funny about it."

"No, Mr. Walsh, nothing funny at all."

* * * * *

After dinner, we left the restaurant and continued walking up Fifth Avenue toward Broadway. Walker told us that the F.B.I. maintained a safe house at a nearby hotel, the U.S. Grant, and we were welcome to stay there as long as we needed to.

"So you can keep an eye on us?" I accused.

"No, not exactly. Just to make it easier to keep the bad guys away from you. It's an environment that we have pretty good control of. Anywhere else, you're wide open to any sort of random exposure."

"Jack, I really need to crash, man," Jacob pleaded.

"Yeah, I know. It's been a really long day. This isn't some flea-bag motel like in the movies, is it?"

"You tell me," We paused at the corner and Walker pointed a block up the street from where we stood at the corner of Broadway. In the dark, the imposing U.S. Grant was dramatically illuminated in all its classic elegance and grandeur.

"Wow," Jacob whispered.

"Okay — yeah — nice place. I think we'll take you up on your offer."

"Great, let's get you two checked in so you can get some sleep tonight."

We walked up to the tall, glass doors and into the lobby. Walker talked with the desk clerk who called for a supervisor who, in turn, registered the two of us anonymously into one of the suites held by the Bureau in its block of standing reservations on the fifth floor. We just stood amongst the ornate columns and crisply-covered stuffed chairs in the lobby, trying to be as inconspicuous as we could while we waited for Walker to return from the counter with our room key-cards.

We rode the elevator together up to the fifth floor and Walker led us to our door.

"If you need anything, I'm staying two doors down."

"Anything?" Jacob asked.

"Well, the hotel does have room service and there's a mini-bar in the room. I meant that, if you feel threatened and need me for *that* sort of thing you can come bang on my door or call my room."

"Okay. Then I guess this is 'good night.' Thanks again, we really appreciate it."

"No problem, gentlemen. We'll meet up at breakfast down stairs in the cafe tomorrow morning. Say, eight?"

"Is that eight o'clock Vermont time or eight o'clock San Diego time?" Jacob asked, still trying to sort out an oppressive case of jet-lag.

"Local time, Mr. Goodspeed."

"Great, I'd love to sleep in a little."

"Good. I'll see you then." He handed us our room key-card and walked down to his own door while we swiped the card in the lock and pushed open the door.

When we walked in and flipped on the light switch by the door, we found ourselves standing in an elegant room of shiny black enameled furniture with a comfortable-looking sofa and stuffed chair upholstered in an eggshell-white brocade fabric trimmed with dark brown piping. Through an archway in the center of an open dividing wall was the bedroom with two very inviting queen-size beds. The walls were festooned with strange-looking mural that looked like pirates or something that neither of us could (or cared to) identify.

Jacob dropped his backpack onto a chair next to one of the beds and yawned broadly, "this is great, I can't wait to just flop out on this and get comfortably unconscious."

"Let's go check out the bar."

"The bar? Are you kidding me?"

"Just one quick drink, c'mon, it'll be fun."

"I don't think I've got even that much energy left in me, Jack."

"I insist. You'll thank me later."

Jacob just stood there and watched me walk back out to the living area. He stared blankly for a moment and then shrugged his shoulders and followed.

The bar at the U.S. Grant is just as elegant as any other part of the historic hotel. When we walked in, there was a man in a tuxedo sitting at a baby grand piano at the opposite end of the room playing something very classic-sounding and making for a very pleasant ambiance. Much of the patronage were dressed in suits and smart-looking dresses and were gathered in little groups or pairs, anchored to the various tables or the seats at the bar.

We walked in and found a couple of seats at one of the tall bar tables with equally tall stools. A barmaid was at our table the instant we sat down and we both ordered decaffeinated coffee.

Jacob looked around at the room and took in the atmosphere for a moment. "This is nice. I'm sure, though, that I'd enjoy it a whole lot more if I weren't *so danged tired* and I didn't have people out there somewhere *trying to kill me!* Why are we here?"

"I wanted to fill you in on some of what's going on here, but I'm afraid our room might be bugged and I didn't want them to know that we suspect what we do."

"Bugged? C'mon, now you're really being paranoid."

"I don't think so, but either way, it always pays to play it safe, don't you think?"

"I'll give you that. You were right about us being followed on the plane in New York. So what's so all-fired important that you need to tell me tonight and can't wait until tomorrow — after a good night's sleep?"

"Well, first of all, this guy Walker. I don't think he's quite what he makes himself out to be."

"I got that vibe from you. I noticed that you're acting particularly suspicious around him. What's that all about?"

"I was wondering, why is the F.B.I. even interested in all of this? I mean, so far anyway, no crime has been committed. Right?"

"Yeah, I guess. But what about that Russian guy who threatened to kill you? Isn't that some sort of crime?"

"Maybe something for the local constable, but certainly not a federal crime. Nothing the F.B.I. should care about."

"I suppose. Just scary words from a creepy-sounding guy on the phone. I guess there was no actual crime there. So what's this all about with the F.B.I. then?"

"I think Walker is also a Bonesman."

"What the heck is a 'Bonesman'?"

"In New Haven, Connecticut, at Yale University, there's a secret society called 'Skull And Bones' and it's been the power behind the throne, so to speak, in politics, finance, banking and industry for about a hundred and fifty years. Can you guess the name of one of the guys who founded it?"

"Walker?"

"Herbert Walker — that's right."

"Why does that name sound familiar?"

"It should. There have been a number of his descendants who have been members of this secret society over the years, all having the name 'Herbert Walker' in some configuration or other."

"Including George Herbert Walker Bush?"

"And his son, George Walker Bush."

"Damn Republicans. I knew it."

"Don't get so judgmental, my liberal friend. John Kerry is a Bonesman, too."

"Really?"

"Oh, yeah, they know no parties. They're all about power and control and really don't care about political parties or religions or any of that sort of thing. They're big in banking and international finance; one thing the Bushes and John Kerry all have in common is being multi-millionares."

"Well, if this is such a 'secret' society, why is it that you know so much about it?"

"I did a lot of research on them for one of my books, *The Picadilly Revolution*. It's amazing what you can find on the internet. This organization exists out in the open right there on the Yale campus, masquerading as a fraternity. It has its own building and they own various properties around the country, in Canada, all over the world. I wouldn't be surprised if this hotel was owned by the Skull And Bones. They don't keep their existence a secret and many of their members over the years are a matter of public record. With a little digging you can see just how strategically these guys are placed. But there is so much more that isn't public record. Some things that they just don't talk about and take a death-oath to protect."

"That's disturbing."

"That's why I think we need to be particularly careful with this guy, Walker. I still don't understand why either the F.B.I. *or* the Skull And Bones are interested in all of this."

"Maybe they want the journals, too?"

"Yeah. But for what reason?"

"Beats me. Does it really matter?"

"I suppose not, but I'd really like to understand what's going on so I know when to duck."

The barmaid returned with our coffees and set them down on the small table top, placing a check next to Jacob with a pen. He quickly jotted down our room number and signed the bottom of it, adding a very generous tip. She smiled and took the slip back with her and left the two of us alone.

"So, Jacob, whose name did you sign?"

"George Bush."

"Which one?"

"Does it matter?"

"Ha, ha, ha, ha! No, I guess it doesn't."

"Listen, at dinner, you two were talking about the Illuminati. I've read a few novels about these guys. They're a scary group. Do we need to be worried about them, too?"

"I don't know which novels you've read, but generally speaking, I've noticed that most authors relate the Illuminati, and the Templars for that matter, with the Freemasons. There are organizations that use those names who are associated with the Masons, but we're talking the original, Jesuit Illuminati that Ignatius DeLoyola started. They became the hit squad for the Vatican. They administered the Spanish Inquisition, initiated the massacres in France and Ireland and organized the Ustashi during World War Two. Their goal is to force the expansion of the Vatican's power and influence in the world and crush anyone and anything that might get in the way."

"Including us."

"I imagine we're near the top of their list right about now."

"You know. I ordered decaffeinated coffee because I thought the caffeine was going to keep me awake tonight. Now I'm thinking that that wouldn't have made any difference."

"I think you can sleep okay tonight. If I'm right about Walker, this place is probably a pretty safe place to be for us right now."

"Still, this is a lot to process. Tell me, would it be so bad if we just handed over the books to one of these guys?"

"I've read them. Believe me, what's in those pages will rip the Vatican apart. They don't want these books to ever be seen in public and, no doubt, don't want us out there talking about them, either. The Templars are trying to protect a secret that they've been keeping for over a thousand years. Who do we give them to? And who wouldn't kill us to keep us quiet?"

"I haven't read them."

"They don't know that."

"True. Guilt by association. I knew you were trouble the day I first laid eyes on you."

"You should squint some when you say that, get that Clint Eastwood thing going on."

"You think so? I was going for Bogart."

"Oh. That didn't work either." I looked down at my watch, "look it's getting really late and our bodies are still on eastern time. I just wanted to tell you some of this and with all the noise here in the bar, I figured we'd be safe to talk without being overheard. So much has happened so fast and I didn't want you to think that I was just towing you around through all this confusion, keeping you in the dark."

"Well, I appreciate that, Jack. I hope that, when all this insanity is over, you and I can spend some quality time together. This could be the beginning of a beautiful friendship."

"That's a better Bogart, Jacob."

"Yeah?"

"Oh, yeah, much better."

* * * * *

"Here they come now." A young man sitting at a computer monitor in a dimly-lit hotel room announced as he watched a video feed from a camera in the hallway on the fifth floor of the U.S. Grant hotel.

A few doors down the hall from where Jacob and I were staying, were rows of tables crowded with video screens and computer monitors which were being watched by a pair of F.B.I. agents in polo shirts, their hands jittery from copious amounts of caffeine and too little sleep, and their faces pasty-white from sunlight depravation. Agent Walker gravitated toward the screen that showed the two of us walking toward the door to our hotel room.

"Everything back in place?" he asked without taking his eyes off of the screen.

"Yes," the other man in the polo shirt replied. "We re-packed their bags and put them exactly where they had left them. There wasn't anything else to search; they'd only been in there a couple of minutes before they went down to the bar."

"Good."

They watched on the screen as Jacob reached into his shirt pocket and pulled out the key-card and then swiped it through the slot on the door. A red light lit up on the computer monitor in the surveillance suite as they watched us push the door open and walk into the room. Another monitor watched as we walked into the living area and speakers played our voices picked up by microphones spotted all around the suite as we commented on how tired we were and anxious to get to bed.

The various cameras in the room gave a clear view of the two of us as we took turns in the bathroom brushing our teeth, flossing and gargling before returning to the bedroom and climbing into bed. Finally, when we shut off the lights, the video screens turned green as the cameras transitioned to night-vision and infrared images.

"Okay, gentlemen," Walker announced as he stood back upright and stretched. "I'm going to catch some z's myself. Gotta meet these two knuckleheads for breakfast tomorrow morning at eight. Somebody make sure to wake me by six if I'm not up by then. Okay?"

"Okay, boss. G'night."

"Good night."

Bob Pierce

June eighth, 1791

Bro. Vadim told me this day that his religious order
is called The Poor Knights of Antioch. They are
what remains of the Knights Templar of the Crusades
— very curious. The monastery should be completed
by late summer, other Templars shall begin arrival
in the fall.

October twenty—third, 1791

Hired crew to clear and till garden on North Hill for next season. Templars planneth be mostly self-sustaining. Met a few other Templars today, did not know they had arrived as of yet. Nary a name was volunteered me.

HOW MUCH DO YOU WANT THIS TO HURT?

An attractive, young brunette woman in a white ruffled blouse and crisp maroon blazer sat at the elegant burled wood front reception desk of the U.S. Grant hotel. The early morning sun streamed in through the big, glass doors and bathed the wide open space with warm, golden California sunshine. She had just checked out a businessman who was headed out the front doors to catch the shuttle to the airport as she filed away the papers for his stay with them and entered the information onto the computer terminal on the counter in front of her. As she concentrated on the work at hand, she could see the bustle of the busy lobby out of the corner of her eye, brightly illuminated by the strong early-morning sun streaming in through the ornate windows, always attentive and ready to assists any of her guests.

She was interrupted by the fleeting sight of two men approaching her desk and then looked up to greet me and Jacob with a broad smile.

"Good morning, gentlemen. May I help you?"

"Yes," Jacob said as he subconsciously stroked his brushy mustache. "It's our first time here in your fine hotel and we're supposed to meet someone for breakfast. Could you tell us where the dining room is?"

"Oh, certainly," she got up from her stool and walked around the end of the counter, then pointed down a corridor behind us. "Just down there, you'll see it on your left."

We peered down the hallway that she was pointing to and I looked back at her and said "thanks," before we began walking away.

She acknowledged us with a perky smile, "have a sparkling day, gentlemen!"

We walked down the hallway and found the dining room. As we entered, we found a long buffet table along the left wall with a man in a tall, white chef's hat standing at a carving station at one end with ham and roast beef ready to slice and serve and, a little farther down, another man at an omelette bar, poised to prepare omelets to order. The rest of the length of the table was arrayed with platters and large bowls filled with pastries, cereals, fruits, bagels and breads (with a toaster beside them for self-served toasting). There was even a tourine filled with steaming-hot grits with small bowls and special grits spoons in a rack beside them.

As Jacob surveyed the spread before us, I scanned across the sparsely-filled dining room to see if Walker was there yet.

"I think we beat him down," I mused.

"Do you think it would be rude for us to start without him?"

"I don't think our relationship stands on any such etiquette."

"So you're saying, it's okay?"

"I'm sayin' 'go for it'."

"Good, 'cause I was gonna anyway."

"I figured."

We walked up to the omelette station and ordered omelets for each of us and then, as we waited for the chef to prepare them, we filled our plates with ham, bacon, fried potatoes, grits and pastries. When our respective omelets were ready, we gathered up our breakfasts which, for each of us, filled two plates, and found a table by the window. As soon as we sat down, a young waiter stepped up to our table and turned our inverted coffee cups upright and began to fill them.

"Can I get you anything else?"

Jacob looked around the table and then up at the waiter and asked for a tall orange juice. When the waiter looked at me, I just smiled and said "I'm good."

As the waiter walked away, Jacob's view of the buffet table was suddenly unobscured and he thought he'd spotted Special Agent Walker waiting for the toaster near the platters of bagels. He had his cell phone up against his ear and seemed to be engaged in a very serious conversation.

"Is that Walker over there?"

I turned around and looked back over my shoulder at the buffet table. "Yeah, that's him."

Just then, Walker's gaze panned across the room and, when he seemed to be looking in our direction, Jacob waved to him. He smiled and held up an index finger signifying that he'd be right over (as soon as his bagel popped up out of the toaster).

In a few minutes, with his cell phone still pressed against his ear and his toasted bagel on a plate in his other hand, he approached the table just as the waiter brought Jacob's orange juice. He held the chair out for Walker and asked if he'd like coffee.

"Yes, please."

I couldn't hear much of the hushed conversation that he was carrying on but, just as he approached the table, I heard him say, "okay, just keep me posted. Thanks," and he turned off the phone and slipped it into his belt pouch, folding the velcro flap over it.

He set his plate down on the table top as the waiter walked away. Jacob looked down at the nearly empty plate with two halves of a single toasted raisin bagel laid open on it, smeared with butter and orange marmalade.

"That's it?"

Walker looked down at his plate and then back up at Jacob, "that's what?"

"Mom always told us kids that breakfast was the most important meal of the day. You're just having a bagel?"

"Coffee," I interrupted as I sliced into my ham steak. "Don't forget the coffee."

"I guess I picked up some bad habits being stationed in the Big Apple. Running in and out of the office, breakfast is usually a bagel and lunch is often just a hot dog from a street vendor."

"And pizza for dinner."

"Yeah, something like that."

As we ate our respective breakfasts in the elegant surroundings of the U.S. Grant dining room, the conversation began lightly with topics like sports and the weather and sights in and around San Diego. But, eventually — and inevitably — the conversation came around to that of our situation.

"So what's next?" Jacob bluntly asked.

"Next?" Walker replied.

"Yeah, what's next? We spent a night in your protected hotel room and now it's another day. We're not going to be living here forever, right? What happens next?"

"Before you answer that question," I injected, "it sort of begs another question: How did you find us? We travelled as far across the country as one can go; from New England to San Diego. Another couple of inches and we'd all be in Tijuana. We even changed our flights midway to throw off any trail. To, frankly, shake you off. How did you follow us?"

"Well, you two international espionage types aren't exactly Michael Westen."

"Who's Michael Westen?"

"I think he plays for the Cowboys."

"Rodeo rider?"

"No, the *other* Cowboys."

"For cryin' out loud," Walker interrupted. "Definitely *not* Michael Westen, more like Freebie and the Bean."

"Oh, that was a great flick!" Jacob jumped in. "I love the ending, in the ambulance, 'I want a taco!' Priceless. I think Alan Arkin won a Tony for that!"

"Oscar."

"Who's Oscar?"

"Never mind."

"Look, gentlemen, we have some serious things to discuss here. Do you have any idea just how much potential danger you both are in?"

"A pretty good idea," I replied soberly. "You still haven't answered me. How did you follow us?"

"You two geniuses used your credit cards all day yesterday. You left a virtual trail of bread crumbs from Vermont to California and everywhere in between. When you changed planes in New York, I knew where you were going so I just grabbed a direct flight and waited for you at the airport here in San Diego. You made it pretty easy."

"So if *you* could track us..."

"*They* can track you. That's probably how they caught up with you at the ball park. You even used your plastic for your game tickets and hot dogs." He took a bite of his bagel and then a sip of his coffee and, as he set the mug back down on the table, he continued. "I was just on the phone with my contact at the N.S.A., it seems you boys have become an international sensation overnight."

"What do you mean?"

"They've been monitoring cell phone, e-mail, land-line and social media traffic since just before you two left Vermont yesterday morning and there is a big spike in chatter from the northeastern U.S., the U.K. and much of western Europe. A lot of talk about 'the package' and 'the item.' Presumedly, the 'package' is you two characters and the 'item' is your journals."

"I'm sure glad they called us the 'package'," Jacob said. Both Walker and I turned to look at him.

"You don't want to be the 'item'?" I asked.

"No, we're just friends, Jack, we're not an item."

"You're afraid that people would get the wrong impression?"

"Aren't you?"

"Just because we're from Vermont?"

"Well, this *is* California."

"The 'land of fruits and nuts'."

"You don't want people to think we're fruits, but you're okay that they think we're nuts?"

"Sometimes you just *feel* like a nut, Jack."

"And sometimes you don't."

"Can you two please get serious here," Walker was becoming impatient.

"Yeah, see what I mean?" Jacob asked. But, frankly, he had already lost me with the whole 'fruits-and-nuts' thing.

"Look, guys, my contact told me that there is a lot of chatter coming in and out of San Diego, clearly they know you're here."

"Well, after our 'bout at the stadium last night, I think that's pretty much a no-brainer, Special Agent Walker."

"Yeah, but we still don't know who 'they' are yet; not for certain, anyway."

"That is true, and the N.S.A. analysts are still trying to sort that out. There seems to be a lot of traffic between here and Rome, southern France and New Haven, Connecticut."

"Not sure what's in France, but Rome and New Haven say 'Vatican' to me."

"The Knight of Columbus aren't the only ones in New Haven, you know."

"Yeah, I know, but I figured you wouldn't be telling me about anything the Skull and Bones are up to, so that just leaves the K of C."

"You may well be right. They're still trying to pinpoint locations right now and put some of the pieces together. There's one center of high traffic that they are really having a hard time figuring out."

"What's that?"

"Somewhere in Northern Ireland. There's someone there that they've been monitoring for years who uses some sort of untraceable burner phones and only ever receives calls, never sends out any. He keeps changing phones and phone numbers so they keep losing track of him until they can track him down to the new number again. There tends to be a fairly consistent stream of these calls that are always in some sort of code and always called in from pay phones from all over the world. Totally untraceable."

"But yesterday this guy's phone has suddenly been ringing off the hook?"

"A *huge* spike in traffic, but they still can't make heads or tails of it. The timing, though, is too much of a coincidence to not be about you two and your books."

"I don't believe in coincidences, I think you're right."

"Right now, we've got the D.S.T. in France keeping an ear out from their Sigint listening station in Domme. Hopfully, they can fill in some of the blanks. In the mean time, you two had best stick with me."

Jacob looked over at me with an uncharacteristic look of grave concern, "what are we going to do, Jack? How we gonna get home?"

"I don't know, man. We'll figure something out."

"That's part of why I'm here, guys. From here on out you'll be flying on Bureau aircraft and staying in places like this until this whole thing is over. We've got to keep you two off the grid."

Jacob laid his knife and fork down across his empty plate and then leaned back in his chair, gently stroking his distended belly and brushing the crumbs off of his plaid shirt. He reached for his coffee and took a sip and then, as he set the cup back down, announced that he needed to find a men's room.

"Back out to the hall and take a left," Walker directed.

"Thanks." He got up and brushed the crumbs off of his shirt and jeans and then shuffled off across the dining room to the hallway.

I leaned in to talk more seriously with Special Agent Walker. "Before we go any farther, you have to level with me."

"Level with you? About what?"

"When I saw your name on your I.D. card a big red flag went up in my mind. I'm thinking that 'George Herbert Walker' is not a coincidental combination of names that your mom picked out at the hospital when you were born. It's an old family name. Am I right?"

Walker sat silently for a moment, cradling his coffee cup in his two hands and looking down into the dark reflections in the ripples. Without looking up, he began to answer. "When I joined the Bureau, I thought I should change my name. I thought it might be a problem in some circumstances. But my dad insisted that the family name was too important a legacy and that I should proudly use it." He looked up at me. "I thought you may have suspected something when I first introduced myself."

"I did. Your I.D. card just confirmed my suspicions."

"Yeah, I thought so."

"So now, the big question. Are you or are you not a Bonesman?"

"Hmmm, I thought that's where this might be going."

"Well, *are you?*"

"Yes, Mr. Walsh, I am."

"So what's your interest in all of this? What do you want the journals for?"

"I'm really not at liberty to say."

"Are you prepared to kill us for them?"

"Kill you?"

"You've been telling us that you're trying to keep us safe from everyone else. I'm thinking we might need to be kept safe from you, too."

Bob Pierce

"Whatever else I might be, Mr. Walsh, I am still an agent of the F.B.I., sworn to uphold the laws of this nation and defend the Constitution. I assure you, I am not going to kill either of you."

"So what's your angle? Leverage? That's what I'm thinking. Two of the major players in all of this hold enough economic power that they could topple countries and alter the entire economy of the world. If Skull And Bones could control the Vatican Bank and the Templar Trusts, there would be no limit to what you could do. Blackmail, am I right?"

"Again, I'm not at liberty to comment."

"Comment or not, I can see it in your eyes."

"My job right now is to keep you two out of trouble and out of harm's way. That's it. That's all."

"If you pull this off, they'll probably make you czar or something."

"Where's Goodspeed?" Walker asked partly to change the subject and partly because Jacob hadn't yet returned from the rest room.

"He's old. He takes a while."

"This long?"

"You're making me nervous here, Walker. You think something's happened to him?"

"I think we'd best go check on him. Better to embarrass him in the head than to sit here blissfully ignorant and find out later that something's up."

"Yeah, good thinking."

We set down our coffee cups and rose to our feet, tossing our cloth napkins onto the table as we did. We walked quickly out of the dining room, trying not to appear distressed, trying not to alarm any of the other guests. When we reached the hallway, we turned and ran to the doors to the rest rooms and barged into the men's room.

"Jacob?!" I called out. The men's room attendant standing next to a table of clean towels and miniature soaps looked at the two of us and asked if he could help us.

"Did you see a tall, thin, gray-haired man with a big, bushy mustache and wire-rimmed glasses come in here?"

"Why, yes," the man replied with a Philipino accent. "He was here just a few minutes ago."

"Did he say where he was going?"

"No. A man met him at the door when he left and they walked that way," he pointed in the direction of the lobby.

We rushed out of the rest room and ran down the hallway to the lobby. I paused in the middle of the big, open space and looked around while Special Agent Walker ran out through the front doors to Broadway and scanned up and down the sidewalk.

In a panic, I ran to the desk where the young brunette woman in the maroon blazer had been so helpful to us just a short time before and asked if she'd seen him.

"Yes, sir. He left out the front doors with two other gentlemen."

"Did you see where they went?"

"They got into a cab. When they pulled out, they headed west."

"Toward the airport?"

"In that general direction, yes."

Walker jogged back into the lobby and met up with me at the reception desk. "No sign of them."

"The young lady here says they got into a cab and headed west."

"They've got a pretty good head start on us."

"Can you call anyone at the airport to stop them there?"

"It's a crap-shoot. I can try. But they have their own planes. If they have one fueled up and ready to fly out when they get there, they could be in the air before we get down the street."

"Well, you're the F.B.I., you're Skull And Bones, can't you get someone from the F.A.A. or the T.S.A. or something to stop them?"

"I'll call the tower, but they can be out over international waters in a matter of minutes and then there's nothing anybody can do about it."

"So *call!*"

* * * * *

Special Agent Walker and I ran out to the street in front of the hotel, Walker called out to the valets standing at the valet stand to bring his car around. The man standing behind the stand picked up a walkie-talkie and called out for Walker's car to be brought to the main entranceway. While we waited for it, he frantically made phone calls to try and stop Goodspeed from being flown out of the city, but by the time the car rolled up to the curb, it was obvious that his efforts were futile. He handed the valet a tip and then we both got into the car and drove off in the direction of the airport.

"I'm sorry, Mr. Walsh, I think they're already out of the country."

"So that's it? He's gone? Just like *that?*"

"Well, no, that's not necessarily it. The Carl Vincent is in port right now, they're scrambling an A.W.A.C.S. into the air to do a radar search. My people are tracking on-line and phone chatter too, hopefully we'll get someone blurting out where they're headed. Hopefully we'll get something quickly."

"'Hopefully'? I'm sorry, that's not good enough."

"What more do you want me to do?"

"Is any of that chatter coming from San Diego? Somewhere we can get to?"

"Well, yeah. In fact, *most* of it is."

"From where, exactly?"

"From that Jesuit campus in Old Town; Santa Rosita."

"Okay, let's go."

"Go? What are you thinking?"

"I hate waiting — for anything. We don't have any time to

waste here; I think we should use the direct approach."

"I'm not comfortable with this."

"I really don't care what you're comfortable with, Walker. Turn this car around and let's get over there, *now!*"

"Alright. I guess. But I still don't feel good about this."

"We don't have a lot of options, here; let's go!"

Special Agent Walker turned his rented Hyundai down the next cross street and headed across town to the Old Town neighborhood. As we turned up the central street that enters the district, we could see the towering twin spires of the Santa Rosita cathedral at the end of the street with the buildings of its Jesuit campus clustered around it.

I was losing my patience with all of this. What started out as an interesting genealogical search in a quiet little rural town that most people probably had never heard of before, had blown up into a kidnapping and our two lives were on the line. Ironically, we were in the middle of one of the biggest power struggles in history and absolutely nobody would ever hear about it. If Jacob or I died in this fracas, noone would ever know. I was determined to do whatever I could to at least try and keep that from happening.

We parked in front of the main entrance at the sidewalk at the foot of a cascade of granite steps that led up to an imposing pair of carved oak doors hung on massive black, iron hinges, framed in a sculpted arch of stone and metal. We climbed out of the car and I waited on the sidewalk for Walker to walk around from the street side of the car to join me and then we walked briskly up the stairs to the doors together.

I pressed ahead, grabbing the big iron and brass door handle and pulled the door open enough for the two of us to walk inside. We stepped into a cavernous space vaulting thirty or more feet above our heads with stone walls reminiscent of the medieval castles of Europe with tall stained glass windows interspersed with vertical tapestries hung between each one depicting the stations of the cross. It took a moment for our eyes

Bob Pierce

to adjust from the brilliant southern California sunshine outside to the dimly-lit interior of the cathedral.

From where we stood, we could see rows and rows of wooden pews on either side of an aisle across a ceramic tiled floor with a bright red carpet runner loudly splitting the space in two and leading to the raised altars at the other end of the room. To the right and the left of the altar were alcoves in the masonry set with large statues of the Madonna and Child with racks holding hundreds of flickering candles in translucent red glass cups in neat, inclined rows.

The room was silent save for the quiet voices of the smattering of people scattered around in the pews whispering their prayers. A few small clutches of three or four carried on hushed, echoing conversations around the periphery. In one of those groups stood a priest; a middle-aged hispanic man with wavy dark hair that receded from his forehead. He had a neatly-trimmed mustache and was dressed in the traditional black shirt with a high, starched collar that let show a prominent white rectangle just below his adam's apple. He wore a black frock coat, pants and shoes and carried a rosary wrapped around his left hand with the crucifix dangling from his index finger and smiled as he carried on a conversation with two other people.

I motioned to Walker to follow me and then walked with a purposed gait around the back of the pews and down the open aisle along the side wall to enjoin the priest and break him away from his conversation. As I approached, the priest held his hand up to the couple that he was talking with, looked toward us and asked with a smile if there was something he could do for me and my companion.

I dispensed with any pleasantries or etiquette and simply demanded, "where's Jacob Goodspeed?"

"Who? I'm afraid I don't know the person you're talking about."

"Jacob Goodspeed who flew out here with me yesterday,"

I stepped up toe-to-toe with the priest, completely ignoring the young couple that he was engaged with and repeated my edged demand, "where is he?"

Special Agent Walker looked at the couple and smiled and said something about my having had too much caffeine that morning and then asked that they excuse us.

The couple walked off as the priest once again insisted that he was clueless of what I was talking about and insisted that I lower my voice as there were people there at that moment in prayer and that I might disturb them.

"Disturb them?" I picked up a hymnal from a rack in the pew next to me and hurled it across the room. It came crashing down on the top rim of a pew across the aisle and bounced into a couple of others with each impact echoing loudly and reverberating around the room. "How's *that?*" I shouted. "Now tell me where Jacob is!"

Trying to defuse the situation, Walker opened up his jacket and produced his identification folder and showed the priest his badge. "I'm Special Agent George Walker from the F.B.I., Father....?"

"Rodriguez, Emile Rodriguez. Is he an agent, too?"

"No, he and the man we are looking for are partners in a venture that the Bureau is looking into," he said as he closed up his leather folder and returned it to his jacket pocket. "They're not criminals, they're witnesses in an investigation and I'm trying to keep tabs on them."

"It would seem, sir, that you have failed if what this man says is true, as one of your charge seems to have disappeared. I wish I could help you."

"Disappeared?" I barked. "Your henchmen grabbed him not more than a half hour ago from the U.S. Grant!"

"I don't have any 'henchmen,' sir. I'm sure I don't know what you are talking about," Father Rodriguez was getting more insistent with his assertions, but at the same time, he was beginning to show some signs of deep-seated uneasiness. Agent

Walker could read the man's discomfort and thought it would be a good time to move the interrogation along.

"Father, do you have someplace more private that we could go to so that we could talk without disturbing your parishioners. I'm afraid my friend here is quite agitated and I don't think we're going to get anywhere without him causing a scene."

"I don't know what more you may want to talk about but, in respect for my flock, why don't we retire to my office upstairs. We can talk there without being interrupted or bothering anyone here in the sanctuary."

"That sounds fine. Shall we?" Walker waved to me and we followed the priest's lead to the front of the room and to a side door near the altar platform that led to a hallway and then to an ornately carved oak and mahogany stairwell that led up to the second floor of an adjacent building, taking us to a hallway lined with mahogany paneling and evenly-spaced doorways leading to a half dozen offices on either side.

"My office is right down here," Rodriguez stated as he turned to lead us down the hallway. As we walked, I noticed that each door had a small oak nameplate on it with gold leaf lettering identifying to whom each was assigned. When we passed a door whose sign simply read "Holy Church Office," I stopped dead in my tracks in front of it.

"What's in here?" I asked.

Walker and the priest stopped and Father Rodriguez turned and hesitated as he tried to quickly fabricate a plausible answer. He was clearly distressed by my question, but after a brief but awkward moment, he replied, "oh, that's just the secretary's office in there. Come along, my office is just down here."

He turned to continue down the hallway, nervously trying to draw us away, but I remained in front of the door. "Not buyin' it. Sorry."

Father Rodriguez and Special Agent Walker stopped and turned back. The priest walked slowly back to where I was standing while Walker followed closely behind — he sensed that something wasn't right and he wanted to be right there, just in case he needed to intervene. He had his right hand out in the open and ready to grab the priest or quickly retrieve his Glock from the concealed shoulder holster under his tweed jacket if necessary.

But the priest didn't give him any cause to feel that he'd need to step in as they approached where I was standing in the dark hallway in front of the door.

"This is a Jesuit campus, am I right?" I asked the priest in a decidedly kurt tone.

"Yes, it is. The cathedral and the school."

"The 'Holy Church Office' is a euphemism at the Vatican for the Illuminati; for the inquisition, is it not?"

"Oh, Mr. Walsh, that's the talk of a conspiracy theory dating back hundreds of years."

I lunged out at the priest and slapped my two fists against his chest, gripping the lapels of his black coat, and then slammed him up against the opposite wall. "I never told you my name," I growled.

Rodriguez, looking rather terrified as he looked wide-eyed at me, our faces no more than an inch apart.

"Oh, sure you did," the priest nervously replied, feeling the weight of my forearms pressed against his body, pinning him to the wall.

"Actually, no, he didn't." Special Agent Walker interjected with a cold regard as he stepped closer, keeping an eye on the priest's hands. "I showed you my I.D., but neither of us said his name."

"Yes...yes you did. You introduced yourself when you walked up to me downstairs."

"You lying sack of worms," I shot back as I pushed myself off of the man's chest. I turned and looked at the door again, "'Church Office' means the Vatican's Church Office, doesn't it? The Illuminati. Look at the security on that door: motion sensors, a keypad on the door jamb. None of the other doors in this hallway are so protected. Why is that, do you think?"

"The...the church secretary keeps some very sensitive files in there," Rodriguez quickly fished for a viable response, still trying to maintain the rouge.

"Who is in there?"

"Nobody. Our secretary is only part-time, she doesn't work today."

"You're unbelievable. You don't give up, do you?" I turned and raised my right foot and then bashed it against the door right beside the lock to kick it in. The sturdy wooden door quivered from the impact but remained in place. I stepped back and rammed it again and the door flung open with a spray of splintered wood and brass lock-work scattering across the lush carpet inside.

I barged into the office to find a heavy-set, white-haired man sitting behind a large, imposing wooden desk. The dark walls were paneled with smooth mahogany much like the hall-way outside and the room was furnished with robust and or-nately-carved Victorian furnishings. The desk faced the door with the white-haired man sitting behind it with his back to a large window. He wore a red satin cap and was dressed in a red shirt with a white priest's collar similar to Rodriguez's. He rose quickly to his feet as I burst into the room with Rodriguez and Special Agent Walker following behind. Walker had his pistol drawn and had it trained on the priest; with all of my talk about international conspiracies and his own knowledge of what these groups were capable of, he wanted to be ready for anything that might be waiting for us on the other side of that door.

"Get out here!" I ordered the man behind the desk. I waved at him and repeated my command, "out here, out from behind the desk *now!*"

The man held his hands up at his sides to keep them in view as he walked slowly around the side of the desk to a space between two upholstered chairs placed facing the desk for those he would meet with in his office. I pressed in face-to-face and asked him for his name.

"Monsignor Janick," the man replied.

I grabbed the man's red shirt with my left hand, balling up the fabric in my fist and pulling it up taut, and demanded, "where is Jacob Goodspeed?"

He looked over at Rodriguez who just looked down at the floor and shook his head, then he looked back up at me and stated defiantly, "I don't know."

He grabbed my wrist and twisted my grip off of his shirt and shoved me back. I spun back around with my right arm and struck him in the face with the back of my fist, sending him reeling back a couple of steps. With a bright red face and fire in his eyes, the monsignor came back at me, but Walker shouted, "I don't think so!"

When Janick turned he saw Special Agent Walker standing with the Glock pointed at him, he froze. Walker lurched the gun to direct him to back away from me and he lowered his fists and eased his combative posture.

"Sit down," I ordered.

Janick looked behind himself to see one of the chairs not a foot behind his knees and then looked back at me and I repeated my demand. He still did not capitulate so I shot my two arms forward and slammed his chest with my palms, shoving him backward and making him flop awkwardly into the chair.

"You!" I turned to Rodriguez, "tie him up!"

The younger priest looked at Walker as if to plead against my perceived insanity but Walker, still holding the pistol trained on Janick in the chair, just nodded his head toward the desk, urging him to do as he was told.

I grabbed the phone off of the desk and ripped the chord out of the back of it and then pulled it with both hands and tore the other end out of the wall. I gathered it up in a loose coil and then tossed it to Rodriguez, "wrists and ankles," I directed, "just like in the movies."

As the younger priest tied up the monsignor, whispering his apologies as he did, I drifted over to the wall where there were a number of large, framed photographs and a ceremonial Knights of Columbus sword and dagger hanging with a bright red sash draped across them.

"Ever heard of *Fox's Book of Martyrs*? I've been doing some research on my genealogy recently and reading up on my ancestors from Ireland. You know what I found out? That you animals tortured and murdered hundreds of thousands of innocent people in Ireland in the 17th century. My ancestors fled south to Cork to escape the massacre."

"Conspiracy theories. It never happened."

I ignored his denial and continued, "I've also read about the inquisitions in Scotland, France and Spain — millions horrifically tortured and killed. Drawn and quartered, their internal organs torn out of their bodies while they were still alive, screaming in agony, all before a crowd in public displays. Pregnant women having their unborn babies cut from their wombs and then both burned together alive. All in the name of the church!"

"Lies. Paranoid rantings of godless anti-papists."

"Paranoid? Maybe. But so far you've given me plenty of reason to be."

I yanked the sash down and balled it up in my hand and stuffed it into the monsignor's mouth as Rodriguez finished securing the man's right ankle to the chair's corresponding leg.

"I think that will do the trick, padre" I said, dismissing Rodriguez who returned to stand beside Walker by the door. I walked back to the display on the wall and took down the sword. It was a particularly and uniquely ornate example. It had an ivory handle with a carved scrimshaw cross centered on it, encircled by a crown. The detailed metal pommel and hilt were thickly plated with gold and an appendage at the center of the hilt protruded over the heel of the blade with an enameled, triangular blue symbol of the all-seeing eye. I held the sword by the blade and turned it as I inspected the various symbols in the design hearkening to the Roman See, the Crusades and the inquisition.

"Very interesting," I commented. Then reached out and yanked the wadded-up cloth out of the monsignor's mouth and asked him again, "where's Jacob Goodspeed?"

He shot back "I don't know!"

I shoved the sash back into his mouth and then turned and swung the sword like a baseball bat and swept everything off of the desk, sending it all scattering and crashing onto the floor. Then I swung the blade and smashed all of the various framed photographs on the walls — photos of Janick posing with popes, politicians and various movie stars and dignitaries — smashing the glass and sending the twisted frames and remaining shards flying across the room. Rodriguez lunged forward to try and stop my rampage but Walker grabbed his arm and held him back.

I sat up on the cleared desk top and began carving doodles into the dark wood with the sharp point of the sword, then I turned to the trussed monsignor whose face was turning red with rage.

"You know, the N.S.A. has been monitoring your phone calls and e-mails out of here. They *know* you have him." I leaned forward and grabbed the end of the red sash and yanked it from his mouth again and, again, demanded to know where Jacob was.

"I don't know. You can do whatever you will, but I still won't know!"

I back-handed him across the face and stuffed the wadded-up sash back into his mouth. I lifted the sword up with both hands wrapped around the handle, gripping it tightly as I rested the point of the blade against his thigh. Then, very slowly, I began to apply pressure. Janick's face turned an even brighter red as he anticipated what would come next. Veins began to protrude from his forehead and neck as beads of sweat began to form and run down from his temples. The pointed tip of the blade tore through the black fabric of the man's pant leg and then dimpled the soft skin underneath until it began to give way and the gleaming steel began to penetrate; blood began to pool around the wound until it started running down either side of his leg. The man could feel the cold steel push into his skin and the warm, wet rivulets of blood run around either side of his thigh. He groaned with the pain, closing his eyes with a distorted grimace and arched his back as the blade ever-so-slowly sank into his flesh.

"Jack, what are you doing?!" Walker shouted.

"I'm going to get the truth. If you don't have the stomach for it, you can wait out in the hall!" I continued to press the blade deeper and deeper into Janick's leg.

"I can't be a party to this, Jack!"

"Then go! Get out of here!"

Walker ushered Rodriguez reluctantly back out into the hallway. The blade was, by then, about an inch into the man's leg as I continued to slowly press it deeper and deeper. Finally the old monsignor's moans began to turn to cries of pain through the muffling cloth jammed in his mouth. With a couple of inches of the blade sunk into his leg, I paused. I reached out and yanked the cloth out of his mouth and asked again, "where is Jacob Goodspeed, you son-of-a-bitch?!"

Through gritted teeth, the he just repeated "I don't know!" and then spat at me.

I wiped the saliva off of my cheek with my sleeve and then stuffed the cloth back into his mouth and then, in a quick motion, twisted the blade and yanked it out of his leg. He let out an agonized howl muffled by the wad of fabric. I slapped him across the face and then wrapped my fingers around the man's jaw and held his beaming-red, sweat-drenched face up to my own and snarled, "you're going to tell me the truth, that much is for certain. How much it hurts, though, is entirely up to you!"

I released his face and, with the back of my hand, slapped

him once again, leaving a red mark — a row of red splotches corresponding with my knuckles. I then gripped the sword's handle again with both fists and repositioned the tip of the blade against his thigh, a few inches from the bleeding first hole, pressing it through the fabric of his pants until the point of the blade pressed against his bare skin underneath. I shouted my demand once again "where is Jacob Goodspeed?!" but the elder man just howled defiantly through the muffling fabric.

Special Agent Walker, waiting outside in the hallway, heard the bishop's screams of pain, even through the fabric stuffed in his mouth and through the closed door. He pushed the door open and stepped part way into the room. His pale face and gaping mouth spoke the horror he felt as he saw the image of the old man, bound to the chair, and me standing in front of him with my hands wrapped around the handle of the sword, ready to once again drive it into the man's leg. He was squirming and lurching in the chair, pulling against the restraints. Walker yelled out again, "Jack! What are you doing?!"

I turned to look at Walker and then looked back at the monsignor, "these monsters have murdered millions over the years. Tortured, maimed and killed," I looked down at Janick and grabbed his face to pull it up so that I could look eye-to-eye with him. "Haven't you!?"

The man rolled his eyes toward Walker, hoping for some sort of reprieve, but no such rescue was imminent. Father Rodriguez pushed past Walker and rushed into the room. He froze halfway between the doorway and the trussed monsignor. The blood was by then running down the man's leg and pooling on the floor at his heels, as superficial as the wound I had inflicted may have been, I had apparently struck an artery.

"Jack!" Walker called out from behind the advancing priest, "you hate these people for what they've done throughout history — for all the evil they stand for — for what they've done to your people; am I right?"

"Damned straight!"

"If you do this now, you will become what you hate, you will become them. Are you prepared to sink into those depths?"

"Jacob — they took him."

"I know, but are you willing to compromise your morality for him? To sink to this level of depravity? Jack; these people have tortured and killed people all over the world, are you prepared to mimic that evil for hate's sake?"

"For hate's sake; no. For Jacob; till the cows come home." I knew that Walker was right, how could I lose control like that? How could I debase myself by sinking to their tactics of torture and violence and a complete disregard for the value of life? But I couldn't stop, they believed that I would follow through and I had to keep up the rouge, even though I no longer had intention of continuing with my own personal inquisition. I had to give Walker some sort of a sign that I'd gotten his message loud and clear and that whatever was to follow would all be just theater.

I stopped Rodriguez on his way to a feeble rescue attempt of the monsignor with my flat hand slapped against his chest. Walker rushed up behind him and grabbed his coat to hold him back. I looked over his shoulder at Walker and just winked, with a nod of his head, I knew that he understood where I was going. I raised the blade of the sword, coated with Janick's blood, and rested the tip into the hollow of the priest's chest against his solar plexus.

He looked down at the glistening blade dimpling his black frock and then up at me, "what do you want to know?" he whispered in a panicked voice.

"You know what I want to know: I want to know where you've taken Jacob Goodspeed! *Now!*"

The priest looked at the monsignor who, with wide, tear-filled eyes, vigorously shook his sweat-beaded head as if to signify "no". Father Rodriguez, horrified by the sight of his senior Jesuit brother trussed to a chair with his face flushed and blood running from a gash in his thigh to a small, gathering pool around his heel, frantically looked back at me and then again at the old man.

He pulled away from Walker's grip and looked up at me and said, "okay, I'll tell you. But stop this torture!"

Janick screamed through his gag at the priest to try and stop him from telling me what I wanted to know, but he continued despite the man's protests.

"He's on a plane. He's on his way to Dublin."

"Dublin? Ireland?" I asked.

"Trinity College."

The old monsignor screamed his protests all the louder, but once the information had been uttered, it was to no avail. He slumped in the chair as the bright red color in his face began to drain away. Looking over my shoulder, I noticed Janick's newly relaxed posture and turned to look at Rodriguez again, still gripping the handle of the ceremonial sword in my right hand pressed against his chest. Clearly, they were both still buying the ruse.

"Are you telling me the truth?"

Father Rodriguez frantically crossed himself with his right hand and insisted, "yes, I swear, it is the truth!"

He was convinced that I would not hesitate to jam the blade right through his heart which was, at that moment, pounding with fear. I directed my next question over my shoulder at the monsignor, "is he telling the truth? Is Jacob on his way to Dublin?"

Panting, Janick replied, "you'll never see him again if you don't surrender the journals. It doesn't really matter where he is or where he's headed."

"I don't give a rat's butt about those damned journals, do you understand?"

"You should. You hold an unbelievable amount of power in your hands right now. The ultimate bargaining chip. We aren't the only ones eager to gain possession of them."

"I don't care! Is this man lying or is he about to die?! *It's your call!*"

"No! No! He's telling the truth! Goodspeed is on a plane to Ireland. Right now!"

"That's more like it." I turned back to Rodriguez and just glared at him for a minute or two.

"Jack!" Special Agent Walker shouted, still standing behind the priest.

I just leered at the monsignor who scowled back at me. My right fist closed tightly around the grip of the sword as I stood in a moment of decision with one foot in the world of light that I'd come from and the other in their dark world of vengeance and evil.

I know what these people have done over the centuries, how hundreds of thousands of my own ancestors were killed by them in Ireland so many years ago. How ruthless and power-mad they are to this day; how much blood is on their still-unrepentant hands even now. I could feel the flood of hate rise inside me like a fever. A dark part of me wanted so badly to just split that man's heart into pieces.

Agent Walker quietly stepped up from behind me and gently grabbed my arm, slowly but firmly pulling it away, "come on, Jack, let's go! You got what you wanted. Let's get out of here!"

I pulled away from the agent's grip but stood still for a moment as the priest rushed to Janick's aid. I stood there and looked at the two of them, feeling dirty, like I'd been soiled from head to foot. It was an overwhelming feeling. How close I had come to doing something so reprehensible because I could not see through the red lenses of hate. I just thrust the point of the sword into the wooden floor and we walked out of the room together.

Walker tried to urge me to run out of the building before the police arrived (certain that someone must have heard the old monsignor's cries and dialed 9-1-1), but I just walked with a determined, but measured, gait down the hallway and the stairs leading back to the sanctuary. As we walked past the people sitting in the pews and racks of lighted candles, all eyes were upon us. My face apparently just emanated a scowl of disgust as Walker ushered me down the long aisle and out through the front doors.

* * * * *

The phone on the massive desk rang somewhere in Rome, echoing around the stone-walled room. A tall, thin man in a red priest's blouse reached for the receiver and lifted it to his ear. He spoke in a thick Spanish accent, "sí?"

"Your eminence," the voice on the line greeted, sounding stressed and breathless.

"Is he on his way?"

"Yes. Headed for Dublin."

"Excellent. We have people in place who will be able to stop him there."

"Walker is with him."

"Walker? *George* Walker?"

"Yes. He showed his F.B.I. identification to one of my priests. It's definitely him."

"That may complicate things."

"I'm not sure we should be so concerned about him. Mr. Walsh went totally psychopathic here."

"Oh?"

"He tortured me for the information."

"Torture? How?"

"He drove a sword though my leg."

"Hmmm, he's a studied man, no doubt. Knowing the methods of the Inquisition."

"I'm sure he is satisfied that the information he received is reliable. He and Walker should be on their way to the airport right now."

"You know what to do."

"I do."

"The Holy See is grateful for your anointed service and your faithfulness to the order. You can be assured of your eternal, heavenly reward."

"Thank you, your eminence. I am honored."

"Blessings to you, my son."

"Thank you."

Monsignor Janick hung up the phone on its receiver and handed it back to Father Rodriguez to return to his desk.

Rodriguez had wrapped his belt around the Janick's thigh and tightened it as a makeshift tourniquet, but he could see that his strength was, nevertheless, waning. He had released the man's bindings but weakened, he remained seated in the chair.

"Is there something I can do for you, Holiness?"

Janick looked up at him, thus far he had refused the priest's insistence that he allow him to call an ambulance and get him to a hospital. "On the wall, behind me, the dagger. Please get it for me."

Not knowing what the elder monsignor wanted with it, Rodriguez rushed to the display on the wall from which I had earlier taken the ceremonial sword and retrieved the ornate, matching dagger and stood by Janick's side with it cradled in his hands.

"Thank you," he said as he took it from the younger priest. "Do you have your prayer book with you?"

"No, but I can get it quickly."

"Do, please, Father."

Rodriguez rushed out of the room and ran down the hallway to his own office. On a shelf behind his desk, in a row of books held vertical by a matching pair of heavy, brass bookends, was his prayer book; a small, hard-covered volume with a dark leather cover. He pulled it out from the neat array and quickly returned to the monsignor's office.

"Thank you, Father. Please, stand by me and read me my

last unction."

"Unction? No, Holiness. Please let me get you to the hospital."

"My service is finished, Father. Please indulge me, I pray."

Reluctantly, the young priest leafed through the book until he found the correct page and then, in a wavering voice, he began to read.

> *Asspérges me, Dómine, hyssópo, et mundábor; lavábis me, et super nivem dealbábor, Miserére mei, Deus: secúndum magnam misericordiam tuam. Glora Patri, et Filii, et Spiritui Sancti.*

As Father Rodriguez spoke, Janick unsheathed the polished steel blade, setting the scabbard down on his bloody lap.

> *Intróeat, Dómine Jesu Christe, donum hanc sub nostrae humilitátis ingréssu, aetérna felicitas, divina prospéritas, serena laetitia, cáritas fructuósa, sanitas sempiterna effúgiat ex hoc loco accessus daemonum: adsint Angeli pacis, domumque hanc déserat omnis maligna discórdia. Magnifica, Dómine, super nos nomen sanctum tuum; et bénedic, nostrae conversatióni sanctifica nostrae humilitátis ingréssum, qui sanctus et qui pius es, et pérmanes cum Patre et Spiritu Sancto in saécula saeculórum.*

The monsignor wrapped his two hands around the grip of the dagger and pointed the blade toward himself. Rodreiguez continued speaking, reading the sacred Latin words as he watched Janick rest the point of the blade against his chest. He could barely speak for the lump in his throat nor see the pages through the tears welling in his eyes, yet he pressed on, sensing the gravity of the moment and the urgency of his task.

Bob Pierce

Dóminus noster Jesus Christus, Fílius Dei vivi, qui beáto Petro Apóstolo suo dedit potestátem ligándi atque solvéndi, per suam piissimam misericórdiam recipiat confessionem tuam et restituat tibi stolam primam, quam in Baptísmate recepísti: et ego facultáte mihi ab Apostólica Sede tribúta, indulgentiam plenáriam et remissionem omnium peccatorum tibi concédo. In nomine Patris, et Fílii, et Spiritus Sancti.

Janick closed his eyes and turned his face heavenward. He heaved a deep breath and then, suddenly, jammed the blade of the knife deep into his chest and, with his last ounce of strength, yanked the blade to his left, making certain that his heart was irreparably bisected by the razor-sharp steel. He let out with one last, long breath as he slumped forward in the chair limp and lifeless.

Rodriguez gasped and could barely continue, but he pressed on reading through to the end of the monsignor's last rites and then quietly whispered "amen."

May third, 1794

Asked Bro. Vadim about his order again this day,
sayeth they are sworne to a singular mission in the
name of God, to serve and protect a holy secret which
he would not divulge me.

SURE, ALL YOU SPOOKS KNOW EACH OTHER

The chartered F.B.I. jet landed at Dublin's international airport after a very long flight. Altogether from San Diego to New York and then, finally, to Dublin, we were in the air for almost fifteen hours. We had no luggage, we'd gone right from the Jesuit campus to the Naval Air Station in San Diego to get our flight. The F.B.I. and the N.S.A. kept tabs on phone and internet traffic to confirm that our destination was, at least most likely, where Jacob was being held. Special Agent Walker got occasional updates on his phone as we flew across the country and then across the Atlantic. The priest had mentioned Trinity College; that's somewhere in the city but I don't know my way around Dublin, we would have to rely on some local help.

The cab from the airport brought us to the part of the city south of the River Liffey known as Temple Bar. It's a popular gathering place after dark for both the local residents and tourists alike in that it's an historic center of pubs, restaurants and the arts. Tourists consider it to be the quintessential Irish experience, the locals, however, consider it to be pretty lame and overpriced. Nevertheless, many Brits cross on ferries like lemmings to take in Dublin's night life and the cobblestone streets of Temple Bar are typically crowded on any given evening.

On the narrow street that bears the name of the quaint quarter of town, one street down from the Liffy, is situated O'Reilly's Of Temple Bar, a popular and most authentic Irish restaurant and pub — even by local standards. Its simple entranceway is flanked by tall, Celt-inspired portraits painted on panels on either side of the door with a copy of their menu on an ornate sandwich board sign standing on the sidewalk at the curb.

The cab from the airport, having crossed virtually the entire city from north to south, deposited the two of us at the corner of East Essex Street, a couple of blocks from our destination, the driver respected the local discouragement of extraneous traffic on their ancient cobblestones. We got out of the back seat of the car, Special Agent Walker paid the driver with American dollars (the driver knew the exchange rate, or so he said, but Walker expediently trusted him anyway) and then we walked down the narrow streets to O'Reilly's. At that time of the morning it was pretty quiet, the revelers from the night before had all dissipated by then, the big crowds would start to gather at lunch hour, mostly the tourists at that time. Later the pubs and bars would begin to fill up again and the streets would become choked with people.

On the one hand, we could easily blend in and disappear into such a mass of humanity but, on the other hand, someone with nefarious motives could get to us easily and there would be no way to see them coming or going until it was too late. With the streets so empty as that morning though, we may well be able to see someone coming, but they wouldn't have any problem seeing us coming, either. The paranoid mind just reels; there seems to be no scenario that isn't fraught with potential dangers.

Unbeknownst to either of us just then, the people whom we were headed to meet with had their own sentries posted throughout Temple Bar, watching and monitoring the foot-traffic on the sidewalks and in the streets within a perimeter of several blocks in every direction. They had their eyes on both of us from the time we'd gotten out of the cab.

Bob Pierce

Men and women in aprons and work clothes went about the normal early-morning activities of cleaning and setting things up on the sidewalks, some tourists were gathered in small groups near the shops which were just then beginning to open their doors for business but none of which seemed to pay much attention to two Americans walking past them on the cobblestones. We threaded our way along the sidewalks, past the pubs and bars and other businesses. An art gallery, a barber shop and the Temple Bar Pharmacy. I followed Agent Walker (he seemed to know where he was going; I didn't have a clue) as he stepped up to the black-enameled door of O'Reilly's Restaurant and grabbed the large brass handle to push the door open. As he did, the smells of very old wood that lined the space and the aromas of the chef's expert preparations wafted over us along with the sounds of two old men, both dressed in white shirts and tweed jackets, playing a tin whistle and a bouzouki completed the sights, sounds and smells of the classic Irish establishment. I guess it just brought out the "Walsh" in me, but there was nothing I'd have rather done at that moment but to sit down at one of the tables near the musicians by the big fireplace with a pint and just soak it all in.

But there was still that dark weight that had to be dealt with — perhaps some day I'd be back to do just that, but for the moment, that was not why we were there. A distinguished-looking man with a white gotée and a black tuxedo stood behind the maitre'd podium and met us at the door as we entered. The small oak podium held his reservation book opened across the top of it with a brass lamp illuminating the pages with a soft glow. We paused as the man asked if we had reservations for dinner.

"Yes, we do," Walker replied. "Tell them that 'Mr. Smith' is here, party of two."

"Very good, sir. Please wait right here."

The man waved to another man in a similar tuxedo who stood by an unmarked door just beyond a massive stone fireplace. He walked across the dining room and past the crowded bar to the front doors and spoke quietly with the maitre'd, then turned to me and Agent Walker and, in a thick Irish brogue, instructed us to follow him.

It was approaching the lunch hour and the restaurant was only sparsely attended. Despite us both having caught quick naps on the long flights that brought us to Dublin from San Diego, the lengthy trip and the numerous time zones that we'd passed through in the process were taking their toll, I for one, was really starting to drag and finding it hard to keep up as we threaded our way back through the dining room to the back of the restaurant.

The man in the tuxedo led us to the same unmarked door that he had been posted beside and, producing a key on the end of a long chain from his vest pocket, he unlocked it and ushered us ahead of him through the opening, following behind and locking the door again from the inside. Before us was a narrow passageway about eight feet long that ended at the foot of a stairwell that would then lead us on a winding climb to the third floor of the building and another locked door. Again, the man in the tuxedo produced his tethered key and opened the door to allow us to pass.

Once beyond the door, we found ourselves in what looked like the waiting room of a very modern office building. Distinctly different from the traditional and warm look of wood, stone and brass that we'd seen since stepping off onto the cobblestone and brick streets of Temple Bar. The man left us there and locked the door from the outside as he returned down the stairwell to his post in the dark, rear corner of O'Reilly's dining room, I could hear the sound of his footfalls fade as he descended the stairwell on the other side of the door.

The gray walls and charcoal-colored carpet were spiked with the cold, bluish light of L.E.D. illumination. A row of leather-upholstered chairs with chrome-plated steel tube frames were arrayed against the opposite wall. It was all so sterile

Bob Pierce

looking. To our right and to our left were wooden doors in steel frames with large, chrome hardware on them (probably locked, I presumed).

"We're being watched," I whispered.

"You think?"

"Cameras in every corner. Don't look."

"The dining room, too, and out on the sidewalk. They've been watching us since we rolled into town."

"The airport? Probably."

"The F.B.I. surveils their own areas, but you know that MI5, Scotland Yard, D.G.S.E., D.S.T. and God only knows who-all-else are watching everywhere else."

"Creepy."

"You don't know the half of it."

The door to our left slowly swung open and a handsome forty-something woman with red hair in a smart, gray business suit and white blouse stepped into the room.

"Gentlemen, we've been expecting you."

"Yes, we know," I replied with an edge of sarcasm.

"Jack," Walker injected, "this is Agent Meagan Flynn."

"You know each other? Of course you do; all you spooks know each other."

"We worked together in the D.C. office for a while when we were both still stationed in the States."

"Mr. Walsh, it's a pleasure to meet you," she reached out her hand to shake mine, I reluctantly complied and was surprised at the strength of her grip. "George, it's good to see you again. Come, gentlemen, this way."

Agent Flynn then led the two of us through the doorway and down a short hall to an open door on the left and waved us by to enter; she was very professional and came off to me as being quite competent and confident. The room she led us to was a large bullpen-like space with a cluster of desks in the center separated into cubicles with short dividing walls. Six computer monitors were lined up back-to-back across a row of desks with six work stations near a wall festooned with white boards, plasma screens and papers which seemed to be the focus of activity in the room. All of the stations were being manned at the time, two of the agents so intently fixed there wore headphones as they focused on whatever it was they were working on. There was a flurry of activity as agents fielded phone calls and messages on their computer terminals and updated the large video screens across the back wall with new information and runners brought documents and notes to the six agents from all around the room like worker bees swarming around a hive.

As we walked into the room, I made note of Flynn's thick Irish accent; I smiled and commented, "you're definitely not American."

"Oh, but I am, Mr. Walsh. Born in Minneapolis, I was."

"But you have such a brogue, you sound so much like a local, like you were born right here."

"Took me years to master that, to fit in."

"And the red hair? The freckles?"

"Hair dye and tattoos, Mr. Walsh. I take my job very seriously; I can go anywhere and do anything in this country and remain completely anonymous. A sort of camouflage."

We all stopped as we reached the middle of the room and watched as a woman wrote notes on the large white, dry-erase board mounted on the wall that was braced with various papers and photographs taped to its periphery. I noticed that Jacob's and my photos were taped up there, as well.

When Flynn noticed my attention to the big board she commented, "you see, Mr. Walsh, we've been keeping track of your little adventure for a few days now. We knew you'd end up in Europe sooner or later."

I turned to her and smiled. "You're not F.B.I. are you? State Department? No. You're C.I.A., aren't you?"

Agent Flynn turned and looked at Walker who shrugged his shoulders. She then walked toward the big white board and addressed me over her shoulder. "Are you always so suspicious,

Mr. Walsh? Aye, of course you are. Noone could write the novels that you write without being a devoted conspiracy theorist and at least a little bit paranoid." She stood beside me and panned her gaze across all of the notes on the wall, "we started keeping tabs on you a few months ago when you started doing your genealogical research in the Montgomery Historical Society's vault. We knew the journals were in the area somewhere and were hoping you'd discover them, especially since they originally belonged to one of your ancestors; we were certain that you'd want to take particular attention and read them over thoroughly. We've known about those journals since they'd been written, they're one of the nation's greatest secrets."

"The President's Book of Secrets," I mused.

"Not an urban legend, Mr. Walsh — but don't tell anyone."

"Oh, your secret is safe with me."

"Aye? A novelist? Not bloody likely."

"But then, nobody would believe me anyway, right?"

"Misinformation, Mr. Walsh. You writers and all those U.F.O. nuts and conspiracy theorists out there keep the real information as incredible as the false information. Nobody knows what's true any more and what isn't so they tend not to believe any of it."

"Yeah, I know, and we're all labeled as crackpots and dweebs."

She turned from the board and looked at me, "aye, a system that has worked very, very well for a couple hundred years so far and you've been able to sell truckloads of books because of it," she grinned at me, then turned again toward the note-strewn wall. "When you two were contacted by the Illuminati and the Templars in Montgomery, we became concerned, and when your friend, Mr. Goodspeed, was abducted in San Diego, we started working around the clock here, and at other posts around the world."

"So you know where he is?"

"Well, so far, we only know where he *isn't*. He isn't in

Dublin," she turned to look at me, crossing her arms across her chest as she did. "Aye, we don't even think he's here in Ireland or the U.K. at all. The N.S.A.'s Echelon station in Bude, France's Sigint station in Domme and our own stations in Edinborough and Kent have been on alert and, so far, come up with nothing concrete." She turned back to the white board and pointed to some hand-written notes. "We think, when they left San Diego, they flew to Vancouver. Then they flew to Montreal and, from there, across the Atlantic." She turned back to me, "from there, we have nothing."

I studied the white board, drifting closer to it as I pondered. Beside it were a few large maps, one of Ireland and the U.K., one of France and another one that showed all of Europe, all hung on the wall with various colored pins and post-it notes attached to them (none of which relevant, it seemed, to my search for Jacob). I looked around the room at the video postings on the various flat screens and saw some puzzle pieces that looked like they should fit together, but so far, too many pieces were still missing; still, I couldn't help but wonder.

"Hmmm," I mused as I turned back around and shuffled from the white board to the various maps and back again.

"What are you thinking, Mr. Walsh?" a young man sitting at a computer nearby asked as he rose to his feet.

I was oblivious to the man's question at first. Walker and Flynn stood back behind me as I scrutinized the information spread out before us all along the walls. Without taking my eyes off of the map of France, I asked the man, "do you know what kind of plane they flew out of Montreal on? And how far they could get on a load of fuel?"

"I can check," the man turned back around and sat at his computer and clacked on the keys, bringing up one screen after another on the big video screens on the wall behind him.

Agent Flynn stepped up beside me, studying the white board and the maps that I was looking at, trying to ascertain what it was I was homing in on, and repeated the young man's question, "what are you thinking, Mr. Walsh?"

Without turning from the white board, I replied, "in most circles, a lot of what I might say about secret societies and conspiracy theories would just be written off as the rantings of paranoia." I turned to look at the red-headed woman standing next to me and then up at the video screens across the room and continued. "I have a feeling that, in this room, people might just take me seriously."

"Hmmm, aye. To a degree, Mr. Walsh. I've read *The Twelfth of Darkness* and, frankly, I don't buy most of it and, the rest of it, I wonder about how you got the information you contained in there."

"Much of it is the logical extension of what I know is already going on in the world. Maybe we need to look at this whole thing, for a moment anyway, through the eyes and imagination of a novelist and not the eyes of professional intelligence agents. To me, a lot of it just makes sense."

"When this is all over, Mr. Walsh, I think we need to talk about you coming to work for us."

"Now *that's* funny!"

"Mr. Walsh?" The man at the computer interrupted.

I turned my attention around to him, "yes. What did you find out?"

"Well, they're on a long-range Gulfstream; at least that's what the pilots put on their flight plan when they left Montreal. Their flight plan said that their destination was here in Dublin, but we know for sure that they did not come here, anyway. They would have had enough fuel to get to any western city in France, Spain, maybe even Lisbon or Brussels, if they played their cards right."

"Could they make it to Bilbao?"

"Bilbao?" Special Agent Walker injected. "Where the heck is that?"

"It's in the north of Spain; in Basque country," Agent Flynn answered as she stepped up beside me again to look at the large map of France which, at the southwestern-most corner, showed Biscay Bay and the northern parts of Spain just below the border. She reached out her finger and put it on a spot near the coast where the map showed the city's location along the French border, "right here."

"Why in the world would they fly to, what did you say? Balboa?"

"Bilbao, Agent Walker; aye and honestly, it's starting to make sense."

"Yes, they could easily make Bilbao," the man at the computer announced, turning around and looking up at the map.

I turned to Walker and explained, "it's the biggest city in Basque country and the only really large, international airport in that part of Spain. More importantly, it's just a short drive to San Sebastian."

"And you think that's where Jacob is?"

"Ignatius DeLoyola was born in Basque country. He founded the Jesuits there. The various Illuminati inquisitions and massacres were administered from there. The Basque are known to be a hard people who live by the vendetta. In San Sebastian there is a cathedral and a Jesuit college that he also founded that bears his name and a cliffside residence called the Mans DeLoyola that was the family residence and the historical headquarters of the Illuminati. If I were a bettin' man, I'd bet that we'd find Jacob somewhere in San Sebastian, probably at the college or in the mansion."

"That actually makes sense, Mr. Walsh," Agent Flynn mused.

Special Agent Walker looked to the man sitting at the computer and asked, "can we confirm any of that?"

"Well, that's the Spanish air administration. I could find out through the Centro National, but I don't know if I can, uh,"

"If you can do it *legally?*"

"Well, yeah. I mean, I *could* hack into their system and

find out."

"Then why don't you?"

The man just looked up at Flynn. She looked at me with a contemplative look on her face.

"Mr. Walsh. I heard a rumor — unsubstantiated, of course — that you beat up a Jesuit monsignor using his own Knights of Columbus ceremonial sword to torture him for information. Any truth to that rumor?"

"Hypothetically speaking?"

"Aye, hypothetically speaking."

"Not one of my proudest moments, I'll have to admit, but let's just say that I'm the sort of man who, when he's pushed too hard, could resort to some, uuummm, *unique* tactics."

"Don't you think that torturing a man of the cloth is a little extreme?"

"If you had asked me that yesterday, I would have said that I'd have categorized it more as being expedient. And, too, I wouldn't categorize these monsters as being men of the the cloth."

She leered at me for a moment and then began to smile a sly, Cheshire Cat sort of grin. "I like you, Mr. Walsh. I really do." She turned to the man on the computer and said, "do whatever you have to do and find that plane, Mr. Bryce. Whatever it takes."

"Yes ma'am," the man smiled broadly at the prospect of such a challenge and the official permission to break any number of international cyber laws to meet it. He quickly turned back to his computer terminal and began working.

Agent Flynn turned to the other three men sitting at computers in the room and tasked them to begin checking N.S.A. and other chatter from the Basque region, southern France and northern Spain; to contact the field office in Barcelona and get them on the hunt. They each turned and busied themselves on their computers and phone lines in their new quest.

"Coffee, gentlemen? While we're waiting?"

"I don't know about Walker, but I could use a drink."

"Ha! A man after my own heart. Why don't you two join me in my office."

＊ ＊ ＊ ＊ ＊

Leo Bryce knocked on the office door, "aye, Mr. Bryce," Flynn called out. He opened the door just wide enough to stick his head inside and announce that he and the other analysts had tracked the plane and had the information for us.

"Good, thank you. We'll be right out." Bryce closed the door and returned to the main office. Agent Flynn swallowed down the last bit of her whiskey and announced to us, "gentle-men, it seems we have some answers. Won't you join me."

I, likewise, swallowed the last of my whiskey and Special Agent Walker set down his unfinished coffee on the corner of Agent Flynn's desk and the three of us went out to see what Bryce and his team had discovered.

"Mr. Bryce! Regale us."

"Ma'am," Bryce walked over to the white board and had already added a column of notes which he then summarized as a bullet-item list. "They flew out of Montreal with a crew of three and three passengers, one of which a medical patient."

"Drugged," I mused.

"Yeah, probably," Walker agreed. "That way they didn't raise any suspicions."

"Please, Mr. Bryce, continue."

"They filed a flight plan to Dublin. We knew that much already. They flew into Barcelona, took on fuel, and made the hop to San Sebastian. The plane is on the tarmac there right now."

"I thought the airport there was too small for international flights," I asked.

"For bigger jets like 747s and such, but a Gulfstream like the one they were flying would have had no problem, it's even big enough for a DC-10. They probably flew into Barcelona to clear customs or something — it is a much bigger airport."

"So now what?" I asked.

Agent Flynn turned and looked at me and considered for a moment before answering. "I'm not sure how to reply to that, Mr. Walsh."

"Agent Flynn," Walker interrupted.

"Aye."

"Look, if you're entertaining any thoughts of trying to hold us back on this, I'd forget it right now. Jack has already proven that he's prepared to do just about anything to rescue his friend. He's deeply invested in this, he knows who the players are and knows what they're capable of. Instead, if you could render any assistance..."

"I know. I've gathered from what you've done so far and the very fact that you're even here in Ireland that you're pretty determined and don't really stand on diplomacy. Mr. Walsh, what's next is apparently finding a way to get us to San Sebastian without being detected."

"Us? What do you mean by 'us'?"

"If the Agency is going to be involved in this, I'm coming with you."

"Oh, I don't know about that."

"Could be a good move, Jack," Walker argued. "Agent Flynn knows where all the short cuts are and has resources and connections here in Europe that we could never hope to have, besides, it doesn't look like we have much of a choice."

"And what about the journals? That's what this is all about, isn't it?"

"I'll be honest with you, Mr. Walsh. We would be a lot more comfortable with those books in our custody so that things like the situation we have now can't happen again. Aye, I'd like to recover the journals and ensure the status quo."

"Not gonna happen."

"If you want our help, Mr. Walsh, you'll have to be willing

to hand over the journals when this is all over."

"Well, first of all, they're not mine to hand over. I don't even know where they are right now."

"They're not in the vault at the Historical Society in Montgomery?"

"That would be pretty stupid, don't you think? Where is the first place you, or anyone else, would look? No, before we left, I told Jacob to hide them somewhere. He didn't tell me where — in fact, I wouldn't let him. He's the only one who knows where those books are. How's that for motivation."

"If we don't have a deal, then, I'm afraid I can't help you."

"That's fine, I don't really need any help; don't need any more spooks on the trail with me. I'm the one who figured out that they were in San Sebastian. You might have figured it out eventually, but it would be too late. You really aren't all that much help, anyway."

Bryce looked up at Flynn and just smiled a broad smile. She shook her head and walked slowly away, brushing the tails of her suit jacket aside and slipping her hands into the pockets of her slacks. About halfway across the main office floor, she stopped and stood for a few moments. All eyes and ears were on her at that moment. She turned and looked at Walker with penetrating green eyes and said, "I can't have a loose canon running around Europe doing God-knows-what to God-knows-who, either. Are you going to be able to rein him in, Special Agent Walker?"

Walker, too, grinned broadly as he took a couple of leisurely steps toward Agent Flynn. "In the interest of inter-agency cooperation, what do you say that we work together on this one? Isn't that part of what the Patriot Act was supposed to be all about?"

"That was for dealing with terrorists."

"Do you have any idea what sort of damage the Illuminati could do with the information in those journals? The leverage they'd have on the Templars? They could control economies around the world."

"The 'one-world government,' like in the Bible?"

"It's a heartbeat away, Meagan. If we could all put aside our personal and agency agendas for little while, we may be able to stop it."

Agent Flynn looked down at the floor with a pensive expression and heaved a long sigh; everyone else in the room hung on her as we waited for her response. After a few minutes that seemed to linger forever, she lifted her face and relented,

"there is much more at stake here than just rescuing one man from the Illuminati, Special Agent Walker. You're right, though, those journals in the wrong hands could crash the whole world system. Alright, I'm on board with you — no deals, no agendas. Mr. Bryce..."

"Ma'am?"

"Call Duncan; have him bring my car around. We're going to the airport."

April fourth, 1796

Attendeth graveside ceremony at North Hill, one
of the Templars succummed to pneumonia during the
winter, the first to be interred in their familie plot.
Counted a dozen men in all, first time seeth all in
one place together. Among them a patriarchal man with
long gray bearde also dressed in black. Bro. Vadim
would not introduce me. The deceased Templar will
be replaced from a list of recruits. Bro. Vadim
said they are an ancient order and each one sworn to
serve for life. I asked again bout the bearded man
but to no avail.

Jacob's Troubles

Jacob Goodspeed slowly became aware of his surroundings as the knockout drugs began to wear off. At first, he thought he was lying snug in his own bed back in pastoral Montgomery, Vermont, but as the fog lifted more and more from his brain, he noticed the droning sound of jet engines and realized that he was, in fact, far from home. He forced his eyes open and looked around and saw that he was in a private jet, belted into a seat with a view out the window. He groggily rolled his head to look outside to see if he could make out any landmarks, but all he could see was blackness spread out to the horizon in every direction.

He also became aware of certain aches and pains from having been immobile in that seat for a time and began to stir in an effort to find a more comfortable position. As he did, he groaned quietly to himself, but just loudly enough to attract the attention of those riding in the cabin with him. As he strained to sit more upright, he stroked his mustache with his left hand and saw that he seemed to be the only passenger on board and noticed a man approaching him out of the corner of his eye. He didn't look much like any sort of airline steward. He had short black hair and a mustache and wore a black shirt and tie.

"Hey, pal, where are we? Who are you people?"

The man stepped up to Jacob and raised his hand to slap him across the face. Jacob flinched but, just as the man was about to let his hand fly, another man came up from behind him and grabbed his arm, "no!"

The man turned and looked at the second man and then lowered his hand and took a step back, then walked away toward the front of the plane. The second man stepped up to Jacob and said in a thick, Spanish accent, "señor, apologies for my, ah, associate."

"Uh, thanks. Maybe you should put that boy on a leash. So, who are you people and where are we going?"

"We are, señor, here to see to your comfort. We have been in the air for many hours, if you need to use the baño, ah, the rest room, you may. It is at the rear of the cabin."

"Thank you, I do feel the need. Still, I'd like to know where you all are taking me."

"You will see very soon. We will be landing shortly, we are on final approach right now so, if you need to, please go now."

"You're the two guys from the baseball park, aren't you?"

"Sí, Señor Goodspeed. An awkward encounter."

"My first time as a chicken, but I clocked you guys pretty good, eh?"

"What you Americans would call a 'sucker punch'."

"If I was the chicken, then you know what that makes you?"

The man just sighed and impatiently said, "señor, if you need to use the rest room, I suggest you do so now, we will be landing soon."

Jacob yanked his lap belt open and got to his feet. He was still a little unsteady from the drugs so the man standing by him helped him up and out into the aisle.

"Do you require some assistance, señor?"

Jacob braced himself against the top of the seat and took a moment to gain his equilibrium, "from chicken poop like you?

No, thanks, I think I'll be just fine," and then made his way slowly to the back of the moving plane, holding onto each seat to steady himself as he passed.

The man in the black suit whispered "gringo," as he watched him walk away.

Returning to his seat a few minutes later, his head was a lot clearer of the effects of the drugs and he was able to make it back without any problems and sat down. The man reminded him to fasten his lap belt as they were just about to land.

Looking out the window, over the ocean, everything was black. Suddenly, the sandy shore flashed past, illuminated by campfires and the lights of tourists' cabanas and seaside parties. Then lush, green foliage with occasional clearings filled with illuminated red-roofed buildings. In just a few minutes, the thick canopy gave way to open green expanses with roads and buildings that grew increasingly more urban as they continued.

In short order, he could feel the rapid descent of the plane and then saw the lights at the end of the runway flash past and the sudden lurch of the plane's landing gear hitting the asphalt with loud, all-familiar chirps. The pilots engaged the reverse thrusters and the engines began to yank the plane backward as the forward inertia still pulled everyone on board forward until the aircraft slowed enough at the end of the short runway and everything regained a sense of normalcy.

Jacob peered out the window to see if he could recognize anything, perhaps find a sign or something that looked familiar. As the plane taxied toward the terminal buildings, he could see large, glowing letters on the side of a white building that simply said "Aeroporto Internacíonal Agusto C. Sandino" with no other signage that might suggest where they actually were. Behind the building, he could see the tops of palm trees protruding above the roof line as the plane continued to roll past.

He could see a long building with other planes pulled up to it with portable stairwells rolled up against their sides. The terminal, he presumed, but the plane he was riding in continued past. Beyond the white terminal building, he could see they were approaching a row of three white hangars with rusted, corrugated steel roofs. As they neared, a group of armed men in camouflage, wearing fluorescent green vests with a black stripe across the front of each one, emblazoned with white letters labeling them as "Policia," walked out from the center hangar and approached the plane as it rolled to a stop.

"Hey! Somebody!" Jacob called out to get the attention of one of the others on the plane. The man with whom he had earlier spoken unfastened his seatbelt and walked back to where Jacob was seated.

"Señor, please get up and come with me."

Jacob noticed that the man was then holding a handgun and started getting even more unnerved by his situation.

"Guns? Police? Am I being arrested?"

"Arrested? No, señor, they are just a precaution; for your protection."

"You think an old man like me is some sort of threat?" He thought for a moment, "I guess I should be flattered by that."

"If you wish, señor. Porfavór, come with me now."

Jacob got to his feet and stepped out into the aisle in front of the man with the gun and then the two of them walked to the front of the cabin to where the other man had opened the door and lowered the steps to the runway. He paused at the open threshold and looked out at a dozen armed paramilitary police standing in a semicircle at the foot of the steps with their AK47s braced across their chests.

Without his glasses, he had a difficult time on the steps in the shadows. He held tightly to the thin metal railing to his right as he carefully stepped down, one step at a time, until his feet were on the asphalt. The man with the gun stepped down behind him and then directed him toward the hangar. The police encircled him as he walked slowly to meet whatever fate might be awaiting him inside.

Once in the hangar, he was greeted by a somewhat older

and very distinguished looking gentleman in a black suit. He smiled at him and reached out his hand, "Mr. Goodspeed, I imagine you will be needing these." He then handed Jacob his wire-rimmed glasses.

Jacob reached out and gently took the spectacles from the man's hand, slipped them onto his face, set the earpieces in place and adjusted the way they sat on the bridge of his nose as the man placed his hand against his back and waved his other hand to guide him inside. He was a very serious-looking man with a ruddy, pock-marked face, dressed in a black suit over a dark gray shirt. He wore rectangular, very European-looking eyeglasses. Once Jacob was finished adjusting his own glasses on his face, the man introduced himself.

"Señor Goodspeed; my name is Emilio Moretti. I am sorry about the sedative, but we heard that you were afraid to fly so we thought this would make things easier for you, especially considering the length of our flight."

Jacob rubbed the back of his neck with his right hand and asked, "where are we? Who are you people?"

"We are in Managua, in Nicaragua. It is a stopover as we prepare to fly to our final destination in Europe."

"Nicaragua? Who *are* you people? What do you want?"

"Who we are is of no consequence, suffice to say that we are none to be trifled with. As for what it is we want — you know full well what we want. We want Elijah Browne's journals, Señor Goodspeed. You know where they are; tell us and you'll be on the next plane back to Vermont."

Jacob smiled for a moment, but then his face took on a more grim expression as he replied to Moretti. "I'll tell you just what I told your Knights of Columbus friend back in Montgomery — those journals are part of the town's historical collection and are not available to be taken out of the library. You may make an appointment to examine them there if you like, but you may not borrow them."

"You are truly an amazing man. Devoted to your calling,

one cannot fault you for that. But are you willing to risk your life and, perhaps, that of your traveling companion for a few dusty old volumes?"

"Those 'dusty old volumes' are the property of the Montgomery Historical Society, so back off, pal."

"Clearly, you have no concept of how grave your situation is. As long as you are with me, I can offer you your life and a safe return to your little town. Do you realize that there are any number of people in this world who would not hesitate to kill you for those journals?"

"You sound like Jack with all that stuff."

"Secret societies, ancient orders and conspiracy theories? Señor Goodspeed, your friend is not too far off the mark." Moretti stopped the two of them in the middle of the hangar, the armed men held back, lingering near the large open doors to the airfield. "There are those who are awaiting our arrival in Europe who will stop at nothing to extract this information from you, Señor Goodspeed. You will, eventually, tell us what we want to know; I am offering you the opportunity to do so painlessly." He then turned and looked at Jacob and continued, "as soon as the plane touches down there, that opportunity will end. Do you understand?"

"I understand — do *you* understand? Jack tells me that the information in those journals could change the course of history if they fall into the wrong hands — yours, presumedly. I'm seventy-four years old, my man. I've reached a point in my life where I think a lot about legacy, about what I might leave behind. If I hand over those books, I would be betraying the trust that the people of my town have placed in me as steward and I would be a part of all of your evil. No, those books belong to the Montgomery Historical Society. They will remain secure in the vault in Pratt Hall and available to anyone in the public who cares to examine them. They belong to the people of Montgomery. If you'd like to make an appointment..."

Moretti sighed and put his hand on Jacob's shoulder, "I

cannot tell you how much I respect you, Señor Goodspeed. Your commitment is commendable. I will be sad to hand you over to the inquisitors. I promise you that I will light a candle for you and plead with the Blessed Virgin for your soul, that your pain would be brief and your reward in Heaven swift. In the mean time, as you are my guest," he directed Jacob's attention to a table spread with trays of fresh fruits, meats and breads, "please feel free to indulge. The plane will be ready to leave in half an hour."

Jacob smiled, it was just past midnight and he'd not had a bite to eat since breakfast. He then turned to Moretti and asked, "what's the movie on this flight?"

The man just smiled and began to walk away, but suddenly there was the sound of gunfire from out of the darkness and three of the Policia standing guard outside the big hangar door fell to the ground while the others scattered for cover. Moretti ran back and grabbed Jacob, pulling him down, behind the tables of food for safety.

As the fire fight raged outside the front of the building on the airport tarmac, the rear door from the hangar's parking lot burst open and a trio of camouflage-clad Honduran mercenaries rushed inside and searched for Jacob, finding him hiding with Moretti. One of the mercenaries butt-whipped Moretti with the stock of his AK47 while the other two grabbed Jacob by the arms and ran back toward the door with him in tow, leaving Moretti sprawled out on the floor unconscious with a bleeding mouth and a few loose teeth.

Attempting to retrace their steps back out through a large hole in the chain link fence behind the row of hangars, they were cut off by Policia reinforcements. Entrenched behind concrete Jersey barriers and empty steel drums stored along side the building, they were pinned down by gunfire from in front of them and from either side. Trying to avoid becoming completely surrounded and cut off from their escape route, the mercenaries left two of their number with Jacob behind the relative safety of the concrete barriers and fanned out around the buildings to attempt to flank the Policia and effect their escape.

As they crept around through the dark maze of stacked up crates, dumpsters and small storage sheds, two vans filled with more Policia reinforcements arrived, rolling up to the front of the hangar. The occupants threw the doors open and rushed into the fray, taking fire from the mercenaries from several directions, forcing them to find cover amongst the aircraft parked along the apron in front of the row of buildings.

Moretti opened his eyes and struggled to get to his feet. He rubbed his jaw with his palm — everything seemed intact save for a couple of suspect teeth. Once he got upright, though still a bit unstable, he looked around and saw the open back door from whence the mercenaries had come to grab Jacob and a fallen Policia officer on the concrete just inside the big door up front. He grabbed a fist full of napkins off of the buffet table to press against his split lip and yanked his Taurus 92 from its holster and ran back to the back door.

He paused just inside the door frame and peered outside in quick glances, trying not to expose himself for more than a second or two at a time. In the darkness it was hard to tell if it was safe to venture out, but he took the chance and found that all of the mercenaries had fanned out beyond where he was in an attempt to get the jump on the Policia, so he quietly worked his way along through the labyrinth of junk and obstacles until he found Jacob, crouched down behind the barriers with two mercenaries on either side of him quietly waiting for their opportunity to make a break for the fence-line.

In the melee and the noise of the ferocious gun battle all around them, Jacob and the two mercenaries never heard Moretti approach. He was able to get within arm's length of them and, when he did, he quickly pressed the muzzle of his pistol against the back of one of the men's heads and fired a shot through his skull and then, before he could react, he turned and shot the other one and then grabbed Jacob's arm and quickly led him back out the way he had come from the hangar.

"Out of the fire and back into the frying pan," Jacob mused. Moretti told him to be quiet as they crept around behind the hangar. When they reached the back corner on the opposite side, they could see the big DC-10 out on the apron near the terminal building; its engines were spun up and the lights were on — it was ready for take off.

Moretti led Jacob closer and closer to the plane, cognizant of the swarming combatants and the crossfire from the fire fight that he was hoping to put behind them. Finally, he saw their chance and the two of them ran for the plane. As they approached the steps to the door at the side of the plane, he shouted and waved to the ground crew telling them to pull the wheel chocks and detach the cables and pull away the ladder as soon as he and Jacob were on board. As he ran up the steps he shouted to the plane's crew to get the plane in the air immediately.

The steward pulled the door shut as the pilot pushed forward the throttles and the plane began to slowly roll toward the taxiway leading to the leeward end of the runway. Two of the mercenaries noticed the plane rolling away and broke away from the gun fight, ran out to one of the Policia vans left running in front of the hangar and quickly turned it around and drove out toward the runway with several of the Policia in futile foot pursuit.

Without clearance from the airport's tower, the big plane turned out onto the end of the runway with the protests of the air traffic controllers shouting in the ears of its crew. Two troop transport trucks arrived with paramilitary troops on board to put down the battle raging among the hangar buildings. Monitoring the radio traffic of the Policia already on site, they were alerted as they'd arrived that one of their vans had been commandeered by the mercenaries and was racing out toward the runway.

Jacob and Moretti each planted themselves into seats and

strapped themselves in, cinching up their lap belts as tightly as possible as the pilots pushed the throttles and the plane began to roll down the runway, picking up speed quickly.

The paramilitary trucks drove across the lawns to the taxiway parallel to the runway and saw the van at one end of the runway and the plane at the other both rushing toward one another in a deadly game of chicken. The big jet engines roared louder and louder as the plane picked up more and more speed and the van raced head-on toward it.

The troops rushed out of the truck and several of them began to fire on the van, but it was getting too close to the plane too quickly. Then two of them ran out to the grass and knelt down with an R.P.G. and leveled it at the careening van. A streak of yellow flame drew a luminous line in the air across the grassy strip and across the tarmac of the runway. The van driver saw the projectile coming toward them and swerved to avoid it, but it was not enough. The missile struck the van just behind the door pillar on the driver's side and the vehicle exploded in a fireball of flying shrapnel and flaming debris, the momentum of the forward-moving van spreading it all forward and across the runway toward the oncoming plane. The pilot of the approaching aircraft could see the explosion and the spray of fire and twisted metal flying toward him. His only hope was to get the plane in the air before the two overtook one another.

He slammed the throttles fully forward and began to pull firmly back on the yoke to get altitude, but they weren't moving quite fast enough yet.

A few seconds later, with the help of his copilot, he tried again and the nose wheel began to slowly rise from the ground.

The flaming debris was fast approaching.

They pulled back a little farther. As the nose lifted up, they lost sight of the twisted, scattering wreck, knowing that if it should slash a tire or fly into the fuel-engorged engines the plane would most certainly crash and slam back onto the run-

Bob Pierce

way in a ball of fire.

They could feel that soft cushion of air firmly lift the plane from the ground and then the sickening sound of a metallic thud as some part of the tumbling wreckage on the ground slapped into the belly of the fuselage, but the plane continued to lift off of the ground and quickly fly out of harm's way. The air crew inspected each and every gauge and did a visual walk-through of the cabin and determined that whatever it was that they heard didn't do any damage that would cause the flight to be unsafe. They circled the plane to the east and headed it into the sunrise.

Jacob breathed a sigh of relief and released his seat belt. He got to his feet and announced to Moretti that he had to use the rest room. As he walked the length of the cabin to the back end of the plane he felt grateful that he'd survived that ordeal and that they were safely in the air — but to what end? What awaited him at the end of that flight when he'd be delivered into the hands of the Illuminati's Grand Inquisitor?

October thirtieth, 1799

Bro. Vadim cometh hither to the boarding house this day. I asked him, since he was away from eyes and ears at the monastery, who the old man is. He told me only thus, the man is the apostle whom they serve. Tis his secret they are sworn to preserve to the glory of Christ Jesus.

A BRIDGE TOO FAR

Agent Flynn's driver, Duncan, brought the big Mercedes sedan around from the parking garage a block away behind Temple Bar, to the curb in front of O'Reilly's Restaurant. It was just about lunch time and the crowds on the street had just begun to build. The man in the tuxedo at the foot of the stairs escorted Agent Flynn, Special Agent Walker and me through the dining room to the front door. The maitre'd held it open for us as we rushed out to the sidewalk toward the car where Duncan waited with the front and rear passenger-side doors open at the curb.

As we walked briskly out to the sidewalk, Agent Flynn paused as Walker and I continued toward the car; before climbing in, we looked back at her and I asked, "is something wrong?"

"I don't know, Mr. Walsh," she replied as she peered up and down the length of the street. Duncan, alarmed by her hesitation, began to look around as well and then, realizing what it was she was noticing, he urgntly ushered the two of us into the back seat of the car as Agent Flynn quickly slipped into the front passenger seat, drawing her pistol from its holster as she sat down and pulled the door closed. The driver ran around the car and climbed in behind the wheel and we were off, rolling down the bumpy wet cobblestone streets as fast as we reasonably could.

"What's going on, Meagan?" Special Agent Walker asked from the back seat. I suddenly became very concerned when I noticed that then both agents had their side arms drawn, holding them with their muzzles pointed toward the headliner of the car, poised to fire at any threat we might encounter.

Agent Flynn's head turned left and right and, occasionally she'd duck down to get a view of the passing rooftops as we drove out of Temple Bar and out to Wellington Quay, a major thoroughfare that paralleled the River Liffey along its south bank. "My people on the street, Agent Walker. None of them were in sight when we came out of the restaurant."

"Maybe they're off getting coffee or something," I was hoping for some sort of benign, harmless explanation.

"No, Mr. Walsh, these people are dedicated agents and would not leave their posts until they'd been relieved. They would have heard the call for Duncan to bring the car around, too, and would have been particularly vigilant. Aye, something is amiss."

On the broader, smoother Quay, Duncan was able to put the pedal down in the big Mercedes and race to the bridge over the Liffey that would lead us into the center of the city. Walker instructed me to keep a wary eye out for anything that might look suspicious, out of place.

"I've never been here before in my life — how would I know if something were out of place?"

"If you see someone with a gun in their hands, just sing out!"

"*That* I would definitely notice!"

We reached the intersection of Church Street South and took the right onto the bridge. There wasn't another car on the bridge, I thought that seemed odd at that hour of the day. Duncan quickly accelerated up the slope of the bridge's arch, only to suddenly slam on the brakes when we reached the apex of the bridge and saw a car parked across both lanes just beyond.

"Not good!" Walker called out as the squealing tires brought the car to a quick stop and we were all thrown forward, bracing ourselves on whatever we could reach out and grab.

We heard a loud popping noise from somewhere in front of us, Walker and Flynn knew instinctively what that sound was, I wasn't sure, but I had a pretty good idea that someone up ahead was shooting at us.

"Get us out of here, Duncan!" Agent Flynn shouted as she leaned on the button to lower her window. Duncan threw the big Mercedes into reverse and she reached around the A-pillar and fired a few rounds toward the car that was blocking the bridge. In a moment, we were back far enough that the apex of the bridge's arch protected us from the roadblock ahead, but again, Duncan had to slam on the brakes as a large truck had rolled up from behind us, boxing us in.

"This is it!" Walker shouted. He reached across in front of me and grabbed the three-pointed chrome logo moulding on the seat back in front of me and yanked open a panel revealing a Cobray M/11 submachine gun and a pouch full of extra magazines. "Do you know how to use one of these, Jack?"

"I wrote about them once in one of my books. Sure, I know how to use it!"

"Good, grab it and when I say 'go', you roll out your door and get behind it for cover!"

"I'm not sure I can do *that*, though! I'm a writer! I do all my shooting with a keyboard!"

Once again we heard the distinctive popping sound of shots being fired in our direction, that time from behind and that time a few of them slammed the big car's sheet metal. As we both tried to keep our heads down inside, Walker leaned into my face and snarled, "are you not the same guy who smacked around a priest in California just yesterday?"

"Yeah, but that was *different!*"

"I know, the man was tied to a chair and couldn't fight back. Nobody was shooting at you. Now it's time to see if you really have the gonads that you posture. Are you ready?"

"I don't know..."

"Are you *ready!!?*"

"Yes! No...I mean..."

"Dammit, Jack! *Go!*"

I gripped the door handle and, as if in slow motion, I yanked it up and shoved the door open with my shoulder and rolled out onto the pavement. As I did, the two agents did likewise. By then, the shooters from the blocking car ahead had moved up the bridge toward us, taking cover behind large, decorative metal light poles along the bridge's railings. We were taking fire from both the front and the rear.

I lay prone on the asphalt, firing short bursts of nine millimeter rounds to the rear, toward the truck that blocked our escape, trying to determine where the shots were coming from and where the shooters were hiding. I felt a tug on my pant cuff and looked back at Agent Flynn who shouted to me to get with her between the two open doors for cover.

As I turned back around, I caught a glimpse of Special Agent Walker across the open expanse of the Mercedes' back seat just as a spray of red exploded from his back and he flew backward against the open door and then slumped down out of sight. My eyes instantly widened in disbelief. I'd written a dozen novels over my career about detectives, spies and gangsters and so often had written into the stories the various characters being killed in any number of ways — sometimes including all of the gruesome, bloody details. But never had I actually experienced the intensity of a real gun battle or witnessed the reality of someone I knew being shot in the street.

I was momentarily frozen in fear, but almost simultaneously was gripped with the instinct for self-preservation and quickly crawled under the open door to join Agent Flynn in the

Bob Pierce

relative safety of the space between the two open doors.

"Not like the movies, is it Mr. Walsh?!" She shouted as she tried to pick off one of the men working their way along the bridge railings as he ran from the cover of one lamp post to another.

"This is ridiculous!" Cornered and pinned down on the bridge, I then looked over across the front seat and saw Duncan sitting slumped in the driver's seat and shouted out to Flynn "Duncan?"

"First shot got him through the windshield."

"He was already hit when he backed us out of there?"

"He got us this far and that's it! Why do you even care?!"

With the sound of gunfire all around us and the echo of bullets slamming into the sheet metal of the big sedan, I just looked at Agent Flynn and, as I did, my countenance morphed from fear and self-preservation, to rage. I pulled out the partially-emptied magazine from my gun, jammed in a full one and yanked back the charging handle, then I looked over at Flynn and growled, "I'll be right back."

I darted out from behind the cover of the doors and into a cavity next to a lamp post on the bridge railing. Agent Flynn yelled out to me "are you insane?! Get back here!" I ignored her and then just charged the truck behind us, yelling at the top of my lungs and firing as I ran forward. A man standing behind the passenger-side door of the truck was intent on the occupants of the car, presuming they were all clustered in or around it for cover and did not see me approach until it was too late. I fired a burst through the door's glass, shattering it and perforating the man's chest. He fell from his perch on the cab's doorsill onto the pavement. But I didn't stop, the task wasn't done yet, the danger hadn't been squelched. I kept running forward and, when I reached the truck, I fired across the inside of the open cab and caught the other man completely by surprise, cutting him down; he fell to the ground and disappeared from view on the other side.

I could still hear gunfire and knew that Agent Flynn was still pinned down at the car. I ran back to join her in the cover between the open doors that I'd just left her in.

I poked my head up to see if I could see much of what was in front of us and then quickly squatted back down.

"That was reckless, Mr. Walsh," she chided.

I just ignored her chastisements as I continued to size up our options.

"Do you hear me, Mr. Walsh?! Your recklessness is going to get us killed!"

I turned to her with my face just an inch from hers and snarled, "it's just a matter of time if we just stay here. What's your plan? Just shoot it out till we run out of bullets and then wait for them to come and finish us off?!"

She was dumbfounded and couldn't reply. I turned back and looked at the lifeless driver slouched in the driver's seat. The car's engine was still running, Duncan had managed to put the car's transmission in "park" before he expired.

I sat back down on the pavement and then rose up quickly to assess the threat in front of us. I squatted down again, then reached out and grabbed Agent Flynn's sleeve and yelled, "get in!"

She began to shout something to me to try and stop me from doing something stupid (or suicidal) (or both), but I was lunging across the console of the front seat before she could stop me. I shoved Duncan's lifeless body out onto the bridge and swung my own feet around to the pedals, keeping my head ducked down below the level of the dashboard. Agent Flynn had no sure idea of what I was up to, but, with lead raining down on us and the distant sound of wailing sirens getting louder, she climbed back into the passenger seat and pulled the door shut. I jammed the accelerator down to the floor and the car raced forward, spinning its tires and leaving stripes of rubber behind. I pulled my own door shut as we raced forward and cleared Duncan's body. Sorry, Duncan.

The two men hiding behind the lamp posts fired at us as we ran the gauntlet between them. Flynn fired at the one on the passenger side of the car as we approached him and then, leaning out the window as we passed by, she continued shooting behind us. I reached out and grabbed her jacket and pulled her inside, yelling "hang on!"

She planted herself back in the seat and braced her hands against the dashboard as I rammed the big, diesel sedan into the rear quarter panel of the car blocking the road in front of us. The airbags exploded in front of us and the blocking car was shoved sideways, spinning it partly out of the way — but not quite far enough.

With the deflated airbag hanging from the steering wheel, I thew the car into reverse and pegged the pedal, backing up ten or twenty feet. As I did, Flynn leaned back out the window. The two men were running toward us from behind, I could see them approaching in the mirrors. She fired a few shots in their general direction which caused them to duck and weave to try and avoid getting hit. I grabbed her coat again and she quickly got back into the car as I jerked the gearshift back into "drive" and shoved the accelerator back down onto the floor.

The car roared forward and, again, slammed into the rear quarter of the car in front of us, that time shoving it far enough back for the bullet-riddled Mercedes to squeeze and scrape past. The open rear doors were twisted and squashed shut and the car's sides were gouged from head light to tail light on each side.

The car raced across the remainder of the bridge onto Church Street North, toward the heart of Dublin's city-center.

We had each lost a comrade in arms on the bridge, having to leave them behind. But there was no time for sentiment, I just drove as fast as I could, north through the Smithfield neighborhood of Dublin.

"Do you have any idea where you're going?" Agent Flynn called out from the passenger seat.

"Not a clue! I figure we'll start seeing signs for the airport sooner or later and I'll just follow those."

"They know we're coming, Mr. Walsh! We can't go to the airport, they'll be waiting for us!"

"Then what should we do?"

"Turn here! Left! *Now!*"

I quickly tapped the brake pedal and turned the mangled Mercedes left at the next intersection. I had no idea where we were or where we were going but I knew that the steaming, rattling car was not going to get us very much farther.

As we drove, I became aware of a car that seemed to be tailing us; looming larger and larger in the rear view mirror.

"Meagan, check out behind us."

"Aye, I see them. Could be nothing."

"Let's keep a good thought."

I kept one eye on my mirrors and the other on the road ahead, trying to drive as steadily as possible, keeping my speed below the posted limit, to avoid any complications with local law enforcement (though I'm sure that if a police officer took one look at the bullet-riddled car and the trail of steaming fluid it was leaving behind, he'd stop us in a heartbeat anyway). The car behind us got closer and closer.

"I've got a bad feeling about this," Agent Flynn whispered as the car got within a few car lengths. And then a flash from behind us and the sound of a bullet slapping the Mercedes' trunk lid.

"They're shooting at us!" I called out, still trying to keep the car — and myself — under control.

Agent Flynn leaned out the window again and trained her pistol at the car behind us and squeezed off a couple of rounds, not knowing if either of them hit the mark, the car was still on our tail and getting closer. I pushed the gas pedal down and the big sedan sped along faster, but still not entirely able to pull away from our pursuers. She dropped back into her seat and looked around.

"Next intersection, turn right!"

I looked ahead and saw a turn just about fifty feet ahead, not much time.

"Don't telegraph it, let them get closer then take a sharp right across the lane!"

"There's traffic coming! Are you sure about this?"

"Aye, get ready!" She reached around again with her side arm and fired her last two shots toward the chasing car behind us and then with a sudden lurch, I yanked the wheel to the right and the big car slid sideways through the intersection. Instinctively (after having lived for decades in northern New England and negotiating ice and snow-covered roads), I spun the steering wheel around, turning into the slide and swung the rear end of the car back around like a pendulum and then, again, sawed the wheel back the opposite way and regained our lost traction without lifting my right foot from the accelerator.

The car that pursued us tried to make the turn, but ended up sliding sideways and into the barriers at the corner, rupturing the large barrels of sand and water and twisting the car to a state of undrivability. They came to rest with the car teetering on a gathered pile of dirt and shattered plastic barrels, its wheels dangling uselessly in the air.

We had lost them, but I was totally lost in Dublin. Agent Flynn directed me through a series of turns and we finally found ourselves on a major roadway headed north out of town.

"Where are we headed?" I asked.

"Coloraine."

"Coloraine, where's that?"

"It's on the north coast, above Belfast."

"We're never going to make it, this ride is toast!" I could hear the engine making some very disturbing metallic noises under the hood and I knew those were the big Mercedes' death groans.

"There's a big lory station up ahead. Let's pull in there and we can figure out what to do."

"That's a great idea." I drove about another ten minutes

and I could see the big facility up ahead on our left. I pulled into the busy parking lot and between the rows of idling trucks to park somewhere out of sight. I slid the gearshift into "park" and then turned key to shut the engine. The noise it made when I did that made it pretty clear to both of us that the big car was never leaving that parking lot again under its own power. I released my seat belt and took a deep breath and then turned to talk with Meagan and that's when I noticed that she was clutching her right hand around her upper left arm and wincing in pain.

"What's the matter? Are you hurt?"

"Aye, I just got winged. Nothing to concern yourself with."

"Winged? Let me see that."

"No, it's fine."

"Take off your jacket, let me take a look at it."

"Really, I'm fine."

I grabbed her hand away from her arm and I noticed that the gray fabric of her jacket had a sizable tear across it that was stained with blood. I then demanded that she take off the jacket and, when she did, the white blouse she wore underneath was streaked with red from the site of the bullet wound down to her wrist.

"We have to deal with that. We have to get you to a hospital."

"No hospital; they have people everywhere."

"Then we're going to have to take care of it ourselves, here."

"Here? With what?"

"You sit tight, I'm going into the truck stop and see what I can find."

"Lory."

"Lory?"

"You're in the U.K., Mr. Walsh. Not trucks, Lories."

"Right. You just stay here, I'll be right back."

I climbed out of the car, pushing the deflated airbag down

behind the steering wheel to get by, and jogged across the parking lot to the store. Much like the truck stops in the States, there were rows of gas pumps and diesel pumps and a store that carried snacks, drinks, cigarettes, groceries, truck parts and various other necessities and, around the corner, a fairly large diner. I looked around the store shelves and found a first-aid kit, a sewing kit, a bottle of rubbing alcohol, a roll of duct tape (the handyman's secret weapon) and then grabbed a couple of bottles of Coke and a bag of something that appeared to be baked and probably sweet — sugar and caffeine to keep us going a bit longer.

When I returned to the car with my bag, I opened the passenger side door and told Meagan to get out and come with me to the rest rooms. She hesitated, but got out of the car anyway. I hung her gray jacket over her shoulders so that it would hide the bloody sleeve of her blouse lest we attract any undue attention.

When we reached the doors to the rest rooms, I pulled the door to the ladies' room open a couple of inches and called in "housekeeping! Anyone in here?" There was no response so I ushered her in and then locked the door behind us.

"Here, sit up on the counter and take off your shirt," I instructed her as I began taking things out of the bag and opening up the first-aid kit. I looked up after a few minutes and noticed that she hadn't yet even taken the jacket off of her shoulders. "Come on, Meagan, I can't do this through your clothing."

"I'm not comfortable with this."

"Not *comfortable?* What are you talking about? You've been *shot.*"

"I'm sorry, I just don't feel comfortable taking my clothes off in front of you."

"You're kidding. We've just been through a life-or-death shoot out and a car chase through the city of Dublin and now you're turning into...a girl?!"

"I don't care, Mr. Walsh, I have my convictions."

"Look, since I met you I've got to admit, the thought of seeing you naked has occurred to me. Actually, it's occurred to me several times, especially after seeing you hanging out the window of a speeding car shooting at the bad guys like that. Maybe it's just all that adrenaline, but that's some kinda hot. But this is serious and I've gotta just deal with the here and now."

"Great, so now I'll be wondering if you're undressing me in your mind?"

"You're a strange woman, Meagan, you know that?" I just sighed and then turned to open up the sewing kit and the bottle of alcohol to sterilize the needle and thread. "Do you remember the American Civil War? We had an amazing number of casualties in that war, but not all of them were killed on the battlefield. The big, slow-moving bullets would tear through a soldier's uniform and drag bits of fabric into the men's wounds. Many of them who were found to have minor, non-life-threatening wounds were just patched up and sent on their way without another thought. Even though they might have gotten the bullet out, the bits and pieces of dirt and fabric in the wound would cause infections and they'd lose the limb or, if they didn't amputate in time, the wound would get septic and the soldier would die."

"That's a frighteningly stark bit of history, Mr. Walsh, but it doesn't change my mind."

"Look, Meagan, I'm not looking for a cheap thrill here, I want to keep you from losing your arm — or your *life*. I only care right now whether you might live or die. Can you trust me just *that* much?"

"I don't know. Can I?"

"I've got an idea. That blouse buttons up the front, right? So, I'll turn my back and you unbutton it just as far down as you need to to slide the sleeve off of your left arm, then take the fabric and wrap it around yourself. When you're ready, let me know and I'll turn back around. How does that sound?"

"Actually, Mr. Walsh, that sounds like a pretty good idea. But don't let me catch you looking until I say it's alright to turn around; don't forget, I've got a gun."

"Yeah, but you don't have any bullets left."

"I can still pistol-whip you with it and leave a nice crease across your skull."

"True that. Okay." I turned around and walked over to the other side of the room near the stalls and waited to hear the all-clear.

I could hear the fabric of her clothing rustling with her restrained groans of pain as she rearranged her bloodied blouse to expose her wounded arm and keep herself covered to retain her modesty.

"Alright, Mr. Walsh, you can come back now."

When I turned back around, I saw her sitting on the counter with her bloodied white blouse wrapped around her, clutching it with her right hand. Her left shoulder and arm were exposed and a prominent gash was clearly visible about midway between her elbow and her shoulder. The bullet had ripped the skin and torn through the fleshy part of her arm on the back side. Thankfully, the bullet just ripped a nasty trench and kept on going so all I'd have to do is clean it out, stitch it up and cover it until we could get some professional help.

I tore off a few paper towels from the dispenser on the wall and picked up the bottle of alcohol, pouring some into a folded up wad of paper.

"This going to hurt, I'm sorry. I'd suggest you bite down on a bullet but, it seems, we're fresh out of them."

"It's okay, just do what you have to do, I'll be fine," she tightly gripped the edge of the counter with her left hand and instinctively stiffened in preparation.

"So, uhhh, you're still a virgin?" I asked a nuclear question to get her mind engaged — for better or worse — as I slapped the alcohol-drenched paper towels against her wound and poured the burning liquid out of the bottle to flush it out.

"Aaaaahhhhhgh!" clearly it was really painful. She twisted and flinched, but tried really hard to keep her left arm as still as possible by clamping her fingers more tightly to the edge of the counter.

"I don't know, Meagan, a bad-ass chick like you, it just sort of follows to me that you'd be the female version of James Bond. You know, love 'em and leave 'em." I blotted off the blood-tinged alcohol that was running out of the gash and down her arm with a dry paper towel. I bent down a little to get a closer look to make sure I'd gotten all the foreign matter out of the wound that I could. It looked clean. I applied some pressure to get the bleeding to stop.

"You're a real bastard, you know that Mr. Walsh?"

"Yeah, I hear that a lot. So are you?"

"Am I what?"

"A virgin. Are you?" I knew that I was running the genuine risk of causing her to hate my guts (and/or punch me in the face) but I'd rather that she'd focus on me than on the pain.

"Not that it should matter to you, but I'm saving myself for marriage; if ever a man would be interested in the life that would come attached to being married to a woman with a career like mine."

"Oh, don't sell yourself short, Meagan. I already told you that I think you're pretty hot; I'm sure I'm not the only guy who has thought so," I took the tube of antibiotic cream out of the first aid kit and squirted some into the wound. I knew that, at some point, we'd still have to get her to an emergency room and get it dealt with by real doctors. I'd hoped that the antibiotic would help keep things from getting infected in the mean time.

"Are you proposing, Mr. Walsh?"

"Oh, I don't know, it gets pretty lonely up there in St. Albans — especially in the winter. I think it might be nice to have a hottie like you to keep me warm, especially a hottie who knows how to handle a machine gun. Might just take up deer hunting; we'd definitely have an advantage!" She shook her head and groaned a little bit. I couldn't think of anything more outrageous and engaging to say before I pinched the wound closed and started sewing. All I could think to say was "Meagan, get ready, this time it's *really* gonna hurt."

It did.

She bit her bottom lip and moaned loudly through her clenched teeth as I passed the needle through her skin. I could feel the muscles in her arm tighten and see her knuckles turn yellow-white as she gripped the edge of the counter even harder. I tried to be as gentle as I could and work as quickly as possible to get it over with. The gash was about two and a half inches long, it needed about a dozen stitches, I probably put in eight or nine, I just couldn't torture her any more than that. She sucked in a deep breath with each stab of the needle. She arched her back and stiffened with each penetration of the needle and the drawing of the alcohol-soaked thread through her raw skin. When I finished with the last stitch, I announced it to her and she just exhaled a long breath of relief. I tied off the thread and tossed the needle back into the open sewing kit.

"There, that wasn't so bad — was it?"

She just leered at me, "are we done now?"

"Not quite, I just need to put some antibiotic gunk on it and wrap it up. It'll just take another minute or two. But, hey, the worst is over and you're not going to lose your left arm. You can use it to slap me across the face when we're done if you like."

"I may just do that, but I'm grateful that you coerced me into this. I don't know when we'll be able to get to any sort of medical facility."

I smoothed a slathering wad of white cream all over the wound as gently as I could and stuck a couple of squares of gauze to it and then taped it up with the white medical tape from the first-aid kit. Finally, I took a roll of gauze and wrapped it all around her arm to keep it covered and as protected as possible.

"There, we're done. I'll go stand over there again while you get your blouse back together."

She looked up at me over her exposed shoulder and said, "it's okay, Mr. Walsh, I trust you."

Nevertheless, I knew she was uncomfortable with me standing there, I turned away and started packing up all of the stuff I had scattered all over the counter and tossed them into the trash. I was really hoping that we would not need them again. I then reached down into the bag and pulled out the two bottles of Coke and the package of pastries and set them down on the counter. After I had tossed out the bag, I turned and saw her just re-buttoning the last button of her blouse near her throat.

"Look, I want to apologize for the things I said to you just now. The one thing that I couldn't buy in the truck stop was any sort of anesthesia and I knew that this was going to really hurt. I wanted to get your mind off of the pain and, hey, if your mind was focused on being pissed at me, that was fine."

"I appreciate that, Mr. Walsh. I'm a very private person, I don't normally talk about these things."

"Well, let me just say one last thing; in this world that we live in and the way we're barraged with sex-soaked advertising and media, it's a really awesome thing that you still hold true to your values and virtue. I can't tell you how much I respect that."

"So you're not going to be undressing me in your mind any more?"

"Well, I can't make any promises about that, but you know I'll respect you in the morning."

"Aye, and you're a sick puppy Mr. Walsh. But since we're being brutally honest with each other right now — not that I'm trying to set any sort of precedent — what I told you about my hair and my freckles and such...not true. I was born outside of Londonderry, I went to college in the States and that's where I was recruited by the Agency. After college and some training at Langley, I was sent out into the field back here in Ireland. I worked my way up the ladder to become station chief in Dublin and I've been there ever since."

"So that's your story?"

"Aye, and I'm stickin' to it."

"Works for me. Come on, let's go."

* * * * *

We sat on a picnic bench around the side of the truck stop building to munch our pastries and sip our sodas. Despite our very-necessary diversion, we still had the mission of rescuing Jacob ahead of us. Meagan was convinced that we'd get some help from some friends in Coleraine that she'd done some work with in the past. We just had to figure out how to get there. In the movies, the good guys would just steal or commandeer a car and nobody would care because they had a grander purpose. But in the real world, they call that "grand theft auto" or whatever its Irish equivalent might be; so that wasn't an option.

I picked up another one of the bite-sized pastries and commented, "these are really good, I could eat the whole package. What do you call these over here."

"'Munchkins'."

"Seriously?"

"Don't you have Dunkin' Donuts in the States?"

"Yeah, we do. I just thought that there would be some other name for them over here like calling trucks 'lories'."

She picked up one of the Munchkins and bit off half of it, "you know, Mr. Walsh, I'm really concerned that I might have a leak back in my office."

"I was thinking that, too. Who would have known that we'd be on that bridge at that moment? Someone tipped them off. Do you have any idea who your leak might be?"

"It will take some investigation, but I have my suspicions," she dropped the other half of the Munchkin into her mouth and then brushed the white powdered sugar off of her hands. "Bryce seemed to be quite engaged in our little discussion, don't you think?"

"He was awfully interested, but to be fair, I'd never met any of you before so I don't have anything to compare to."

"Hmmm, I guess that makes sense. Well, we have bigger fish to fry right now, do we not?"

"One thing I was wondering was just who those guys on the bridge were. I'm still not clear who all the players are in this, we seem to stumble on more of them all the time."

"I'm reasonably sure those men were Sons of Erin."

"'Sons of Erin'? Can't say I've ever heard of that group. Who are they?"

"Technically, they're I.R.A., but in recent years the I.R.A. has been more engaged with diplomacy and deal-making through Sin Féin. The Sons of Erin are a splinter group that still thinks that firepower is more effective than dialogue. The I.R.A. has a really hard time keeping them reigned in."

"Loose cannons."

"Aye, that's a good analogy, Mr. Walsh; and they are vehemently loyal to the Vatican. If I were pressed to make an educated guess, I'd say that we've got the Sons of Erin now in the mix. If we can make it to Coleraine, though, we have some friends up there."

"Yet another secret society to add to that mix?"

She smiled and took a sip of her Coke and then looked at me and said, "aye, Mr. Walsh, Lámhdearg. Besides, Eamon O'Neill owes me a favor or two."

"Good guys?"

"Neutral, Mr. Walsh. They're major players here in Ireland with influence just about everywhere, but I know that they don't want those journals to end up in the hands of anyone who might upset the status quo — especially the Illuminati. They'll help us."

"Well, that's encouraging…a little bit anyway. But first we have to get there; any ideas?"

"Don't look, but had you noticed the lory driver sitting a

couple of tables to our left?"

I looked off in the direction of the gas pumps and tried to get a glimpse of the man in my peripheral vision, "brown leather jacket?"

"Aye, that's him."

"Do you know him?"

"No, but he's going to give us a ride, I believe."

"How do you know? How do you even know that he's going where we're going?"

"I don't, not for sure anyway. But if we don't ask, we'll never know, right?"

"I suppose. Hey, I've been shot at today, destroyed a car in a chase through the city and played doctor with a bad-ass C.I.A. babe. How could this day get any better? Get popped in the face by a truck driver if I was lucky, maybe even get my nose broken — that should just about put a bow on it."

"Lory, driver, Mr. Walsh. Lory driver."

"Whatever."

When the man had finished eating his sandwich and gathered up his trash to throw into the nearby receptacle, Meagan got up and picked up her bottle of Coke. I didn't know what she was up to so I just got up and grabbed my bottle and followed along behind her. The driver walked out to the yard where the rows of trucks were parked idling. We followed behind at some distance, the busy traffic of vehicles and people made it easy to keep a little behind and avoid being noticed.

Eventually, he approached a blue semi-truck cab and reached up for the door handle, that's when we approached him. Meagan, in a very conservative gray suit, was not a typical truck-stop-girl so she'd clearly have a lot more credibility than most.

"Pardon me, sir."

"Aye," the man pulled the door of the truck open and then turned to see Meagan stepping up to him with me trailing behind. "Is there something I can do for you, lass?"

"My friend and I are experiencing some car trouble and were wondering if you were headed north and might we catch a ride with you?"

"North? How far north?"

"We're headed to Coleraine, but we'd be grateful for any distance you might be willing to take us."

The man stroked his hair back and looked down at me. I was pretty disheveled, I guess. After having rolled around on the bridge and getting various peoples' blood all over me, I was a mess. "What happened to you?"

"Oh, I was trying to fix the car and got a little banged up for my trouble. Not much of a mechanic, I guess."

"Aye. A bloody Yank, too."

"Literally."

The driver smiled and then offered, "I can take you as far as Belfast. I'm headed there to make some deliveries. I can drop you off at the Grand Parade, maybe you can catch another ride to get you the rest of the way. Would that be alright?"

"Aye, that would be most generous."

"Then climb in, one of you can ride up in the sleeper."

We walked around to the passenger side of the truck and climbed up the steps. I crawled into the sleeper and then Meagan got up into the seat. Her bloodied left shoulder would be hidden from the driver's view so we weren't very concerned that he might be suspicious of anything.

He released the air brakes with a loud gush and hiss of air and we rolled out of the parking lot and onto the broad, northbound thoroughfare, on our way to Belfast, we should be there in just a couple of hours.

I took an uneasy deep breath and thought that, hey, maybe it just wasn't my day to die.

But then, it was barely past noon.

Bob Pierce

February twenty-sixth, 1804

Visiteth Duncan Lamoille to make order of two more caskets. The Templars loseth two more of their number over the winter. It was a particularly harsh season, both of the deceased were quite elderly. Ground should allow for burial in a few weeks. Bro. Vadim cometh hither by the boardy house this morning and tolde me that old man on North Hill wanted to meet with me and inviteth me to come yon to the monastery to visit with him. He still would not tell me who the man is, but sayeth that, when I meet him, all shall be made clear. Am excited to meet the man who is so handsomely paying me to be his liaison and concierge here in Montgomery.

November twenty-fifth, 1809

I met the old man this day. I still cannot believe the experience. We sat in a room filled with books and papers, he toldeth me his name was John. He then toldeth me a most amazing story. Sayeth he was living in Antioch with a handful of disciples after having left city of Ephesis some years past. That is when he meeteth Helena Constantius who was on a tour of Judea seeking relics for the Roman church. She considered taking him captive to return with the ultimate relic (unclear what he may have meant by that). Instead, she posteth guards in Antioch to protect his secret and appointeth an order of warrior monks to his protection. Years later, as Saracens were advancing northward, a rebel band of Templar Knights came through Antioch, discovered John there, and evacuated him to a mountain fortress in the north.

enter the red hand

The truck driver was not much of a talker and his taste in music was a little odd, but still, it was far better than walking a hundred-and-fifty miles to Belfast. Every once in a while, he'd pick up the microphone from the ever-chattering C.B. radio and make a few remarks. With my paranoia on high-alert, I listened intently to everything he said, but it all sounded like pretty generic trucker-talk to me. Meagan kept a weather-eye out the big windows for anything that looked the least bit suspicious, but the trip turned out to be refreshingly boring and uneventful.

I noticed a sign as it passed us that announced our arrival in the outskirts of Belfast. "How much farther till you have to drop us off?"

"That intersection up there is Grand Parade. I have to make my first delivery at the Grand Parade Service Station; I'll drop you there. About ten minutes or so."

So, true to his estimation, I could see the red canopy of the Grand Parade Station up ahead on the left. He slowed the big rig down and pulled up along the curb right in front.

"Thank you so much for the lift, we really appreciate it," I said as we climbed down out of the cab.

"You're welcome, glad that I could be of service."

I closed the door and the driver pushed the gearshift into first and slowly pulled away from the curb and drove off. Meagan and I stood on the sidewalk and looked around. I could see that she was being very studious of our surroundings.

"What's the matter? Do you see something?"

"Didn't the driver say that he had to make his first delivery here at this station?"

"Yeah, you're right. He just drove off."

"Aye, and that seems awfully suspect, don't you think?"

"I do. And we're in Belfast — behind enemy lines, so to speak."

"Hmmm, that's probably a much better analogy than you may have thought. Sons of Erin could be behind every building and lamp post."

"Obviously the driver expected someone would meet up with us here at this gas station. He must have made better time than he thought he would or whoever it is who was supposed to be here is running late. We'd best keep moving before they figure that out."

"Aye, this way," she pointed up the street, still going in a generally northward direction, and then stepped off. I followed along and caught up with her after a few paces.

"So what's the plan? We still have to get to Coleraine."

"Right now, let's just keep walking. The first thing to do is just stay alive, then we can figure this out."

We continued along the sidewalk, headed north. The area reminded me of a lot of the towns in northern Vermont with a mix of two and three story commercial brick buildings mixed between two story homes, some of which had offices and storefronts at the street level. I noticed that Meagan seemed to be hunching her shoulders up and keeping her head turned slightly toward the street, it made me wonder what it was she was looking for.

"Is someone following us?"

"Dark blue Vauxhall."

Bob Pierce

"We've gotta get off of this sidewalk."

"See that lory parked up there along the curb? Looks like he's making a delivery to that store."

"Yeah, I see it."

"When we get there, stop walking and get up close along side it. We'll see if that car is following us or not."

We kept walking, not changing our gait at all. As we neared the truck, we drifted out toward the curb and when we came up alongside it, we stopped and pressed up against it. I could hear the blue car roll slowly past us and roll to a stop.

"Quick, get behind the lory," Meagan shoved me back and we ran around the back of the truck and watched the blue car. It had stopped in the lane, paused for a moment until another car came behind it and was blocked. The second car's driver began blowing his horn so the blue Vauxhall pulled up to the curb and cleared the narrow street to let him pass. A man in a faded blue denim jacket got out of the passenger side door and began walking quickly up the sidewalk toward us as the driver backed the car up closer to the front of the truck. "Now, across the street and down that alley," she directed, "run!"

We dodged the traffic and ran to the other side of the road and then quickly ducked into an alley between two brick buildings. I looked back to see the man come running around the truck and stop next to it in the street looking around and then run back to the blue car. He stood there next to the car and looked all around them; I didn't hang around to see what they did next, we just kept running.

When we got to the back yard of the building, we grabbed a couple of trash cans and put them up against the fence and then used them to climb over into the next yard and were able to make our way all the way, yard by yard, fence to fence, to the back yard of a small store on the cross street. We cautiously crept out to the corner of the building at the sidewalk and took a quick look around. I don't know Vauxhalls from a hole in the ground so I was just looking for anything blue. A blue car drove past us but it didn't look the same to me. Just to be safe, we ducked back into the shadows until it was past. While we stood there, I could hear the loud rumble of a train not too far away.

"Does Belfast have a subway system or an elevated train?"

"No, but there is a train station just about a mile from here," she turned to me and smiled a broad grin. "It goes all the way to Londonderry."

"Londonderry? But I thought we were going to Coleraine."

"It's one of the stops along the way."

"Do you think we can make it?"

"Frankly, Mr. Walsh, I don't know how we've been able to get *this* far. You must be charmed or have a guardian angel with you or something. We're in the back yard of the Irish Republican Army and their evil offspring, the Sons of Erin. They know every brick, every street, every lamp post in this city and they have more guns and explosives than most banana republic armies. Normally I'd answer your question, no, I don't think we have a prayer. But for some reason, right now, I'm feeling lucky."

"We should go, then, before you change your mind."

"Aye, before I come to my senses. This way!"

We crossed the street and walked up the block until we came upon a street vendor selling all sorts of dubious fashion accessories. We each bought hats, sunglasses and scarves — not much of a disguise, but hopefully it would be enough to get us to the train station unnoticed.

We continued down the sidewalk when I heard the tires of a car approaching from behind us slowing down. My paranoid radar was on high alert so I reached out and yanked on Meagan's sleeve and led her into the front door of a coffee shop. Just as we walked in the door, I could hear running footsteps approaching from behind us on the sidewalk.

"Run!"

We ran into the dining room of the cafe and around the counter to the back room. I heard the front door slam and people shouting as at least two men pushed furniture and people out of their way to try and catch up with us. When we got into the back room I was thinking that, we could just run out the back door, but who knows what might be waiting for us out there or if there was even a way out at all, so I grabbed a large cast-iron frying pan and pulled up behind a cabinet. A man came running down the narrow corridor into the kitchen and I just swung the frying pan with both hands just as hard as I could and caught him right in the face, crushing his nose and splattering blood all over the walls of the narrow corridor. He fell backward onto the floor like a wet sack of cement.

The second man, still standing behind the counter, leveled his pistol at me and took a shot; I quickly raised the frying pan and with a loud clang, it deflected the bullet, sending the ricochet into the ceiling. I didn't think I'd get that lucky twice, so I threw the pan at him and we ran for the back door.

We found ourselves in an enclosed yard with a high fence on all sides. The only way out was a gate that led to an alley back out to the street — the one direction we didn't want to go in. I figured that we were trapped, but I wasn't going down without a real scrap. I found a piece of ragged lumber that I could use as a club, Meagan picked up a piece of galvanized pipe, and we stood ready to fight it out with the second man that was chasing us.

We waited — and waited — and then, to our surprise, a man with a stained white apron calmly walked out of the door and onto the concrete step outside. He just stood there for a moment, wiping his hands with a towel. I suspected that he might have a gun under that towel, so I was poised to take a swipe at him before he had a chance to use it.

Nobody said a word, it was a classic stand-off, each waiting for the other to make the first move.

But then he just turned to Meagan and asked, "Agent Flynn?"

She seemed surprised, and then braced herself, raising the

pipe to be ready to wield it like a jo stick, "aye, who's asking?"

The man slung the towel over his shoulder, revealing his empty hands. "My name is Braniel, I own this little cafe."

"What about those other two?" I still wasn't comforted by his presence.

"Oh, we took care of the second man. A rolling pin to the back of the head can ruin one's whole afternoon. We'll keep them both on ice until dark; someone should find them in the harbor in the morning. 'Gang violence' the papers will say. Nasty stuff."

"Why?"

"Why, you ask? Well, I got a call this afternoon telling me that you had run into some Sons of Erin back in Dublin and that you might possibly be headed for Coleraine. If you couldn't avoid Belfast, we were asked to keep an eye out for you. Such a happy accident that you just happened to run into my cafe!"

"Yeah, quite the coincidence," I said sarcastically, still holding my stick at the ready.

"Your guardian angel, Mr. Walsh?" Meagan mused and then turned again to the man in the apron and asked, "Lámh-dearg?"

"Aye, Eamon called me."

"Eamon? How in the world did he hear about all of this?"

"You have to ask?"

"No, I suppose not."

"Who is this 'Eamon' guy?" I asked.

Braniel looked around for a moment and then said, "we should talk inside, it may not be safe out here."

Meagan put down the pipe she was holding and I reluctantly lowered my piece of lumber and then dropped it onto the ground and the three of us went back into the cafe. We followed Braniel into a back office, closing the door behind us.

He looked at Meagan and asked, "is this the writer?"

"Aye, he's alright. He may even live through this."

Braniel leaned up against his desk and looked at me as he crossed his arms across his barrel chest, "Eamon O'Neill is the heir-apparent to the throne of Erin."

"The king of Ireland?"

"The family has enormous control of politics and finance throughout the U.K."

"'The family?' Sounds like the Mafia."

"The O'Neill family were the first royal family of Ireland. Have you noticed the symbol of a red hand all over the city?"

"Yeah, now that you mention it."

"That red hand is the symbol of the O'Neill royal line. The people of Northern Ireland still honor the family to this day and respect the throne."

"In fact, Mr. Walsh, the name Lámhdearg means 'red hand' in Gaelic tongue."

"So how can I help you two?"

"Well, before we ran into your cafe, we were trying to make it to Sydenham Station to catch the train to Coleraine. Would you help us get there and make sure we get on our way safely?"

"That's it?"

"Aye, that's it. And just let Eamon know when to have someone pick us up at the station at the other end."

"I thought you were going to ask for something really hard or dangerous. My car is parked in the alley," he reached around behind him to untie his apron and began lifting it up over his head. "Let me make a couple of phone calls to get some extra muscle to meet us at the railway station."

"Thanks, that's great."

"Before we go, let's put a bag of something to munch on the train together for you," we walked out of his office and he called for one of his employees, "Semus! Bag up some scones for these folks and a couple of bottles of iced tea, please." The man nodded and returned to the front of the cafe to gather what Braniel had asked for. It all seemed so surreal that he was talking about iced tea and scones while a couple of his other employees were dragging the corpses of a couple of Sons of Erin thugs into their walk-in freezer as though it were just business as usual.

"Do we know when the train leaves?" I asked, trying to ignore the grisly activity at my feet.

"Not for a while," Braniel said, looking down at his watch. "You've got some time yet. I'll bring you to the station and have some of our people keep an eye on you while you wait in the security office. I'll have a couple of our people ride along with you just to make sure. How's that sound?"

"You guys are definitely the 'good guys'."

"I'll be sure to tell Eamon just how accommodating you have been."

"Oh, yeah, public transportation," a concerning thought came to my mind. "She has a gun on her. Is that going to be a problem?"

"No, we'll take you in through the security entrance."

"She doesn't have any bullets left for it, though."

"That's not a problem, either. What do you need? Forty caliber? Nine millimeter?"

"Forty caliber."

"Come on back into my office, I have a floor safe that should fix you right up."

* * * * *

We made it safely to the train station and were led in through the security entrance. We had to wait about a half hour for the train to roll in, so we were allowed to stay in the security office rather than out on the platform where we'd be exposed. When it did arrive, we waited for all of the arriving passengers to get off before we headed out from the office to the train so that there would be the least possible chance that we'd be spotted boarding. Two of the men who met and waited with us at the station boarded with us; they weren't very cheery but what they lacked in personality they more than made up for in their professional carriage. I felt just a little more comfortable with them around us.

Perhaps due to my edginess, I watched every face and every hand of every passenger on the train and, as we rolled along the route toward Coleraine, every face on every platform at every stop on the way. I saw a potential threat in every one, but the two Lámhdearg guys sitting next to us didn't seem too concerned so I tried to relax.

Well, I tried anyway.

The train finally pulled into Coleraine. Before we were allowed to disembark, one of the two guards with us got off and took a quick look around the busy platform then, when he was satisfied that all was safe, he waved the rest of us to follow. When we got out to the street, there was a car waiting for us that took us directly into town to a central square they call "the Diamond" where their historic Old Town Hall is located within a closed off square, rimmed with shops in equally-aged and meticulously-preserved three and four story stone and brick buildings. This is home turf of the Lámdearg so, even though the Diamond is closed off to vehicles and we'd have to walk the equivalent of a couple of blocks, we were completely safe. Still, there were a lot of tourists and shoppers around at that time of the evening so I was still somewhat on my guard.

The two men we were with (they never told us their names) led us to a gray stone building that faced one side of the Old Town Hall. As we approached the door, someone inside opened it for us. The interior was reminiscent of the warm stone and oak interiors that I'd seen in Temple Bar. That all went down just that same morning but it seemed so long ago that I was there with Special Agent Walker; so much had happened in such a short amount of time — little wonder why I was feeling so exhausted and a bit overwhelmed.

We were standing in what appeared to be the reception

area of an office building. Any offices that might have been in that building had long-since closed for the evening. The man who had let us in was a night watchman, apparently he was expecting us. Before I could ask an undoubtedly stupid questions, a man dressed in a suit and tie emerged from a hallway that led beyond the lobby and asked us to follow him. Meagan and I went along with him while our two traveling companions from Belfast stayed behind.

The man in the suit led us down the corridor to an elevator which was waiting for us with its doors open. When we all three stepped inside, he pressed the button for the third floor, the doors closed and the car rose for the short ride up two floors. When we stopped and the doors opened again, we were led out into a hallway of wooden panels hung with framed oil paintings; portraits of various vintage with small brass plaques attached to the lower portions of the frames identifying the faces above.

At the end of the hall was a pair of carved wooden doors with polished brass hardware. The man in the suit stopped us and then went inside, leaving us in the hallway. I just looked at Meagan and whispered, "what's going on?"

"Don't worry, these people are very cautious. That's Eamon's office in there, shouldn't be a minute or two."

Just as she finished saying that, the door opened again and the man in the suit beckoned us inside. As we stepped through the doorway, he slipped back out into the hall and closed the door behind us. The office reminded me of a museum with imposing floor-to-cieling bookshelves, paintings and even a coat of arms with a red cross, a crown and prominent red hand in its center and a pair of crossed swords behind it hung on the wall behind the desk.

A dashingly-handsome man of fifty years or so in a crisp, silk suit, with a ruddy, chiseled face and a brush of white trailing back from his temples came out from around the desk, buttoning his suit jacket closed and called out, "Meagan! It's been too long!" He embraced her and she wrapped her arms around

Bob Pierce

him, I could hear her make a quiet wince of pain and he immediately released her and apologized, "I'm so sorry, I'd forgotten that you'd been injured." He stepped back and continued, "the left arm? I can have my people look at it for you."

"No, no, Eamon. I appreciate it, but Jack patched me up pretty well and I'll be fine."

"Jack Walsh, yes, the author!" He walked over to me and shook my hand vigorously. "I have several of your books but, unfortunately, I have very little time for recreational reading. I read a very positive review of your latest, *The Twelfth of Darkness*, a couple of weeks ago and ordered it from Amazon but, alas, there it sits on my desk, still unopened."

Sarcastically, considering the guy is supposed to be the King of Ireland, I offered to autograph it for him, "would you?! I'd be so honored." He turned to his desk and grabbed the book and a pen and handed them to me. I was trying really hard not to laugh out loud as I personalized it to "my friend Eamon, the King of Ireland," and then signed my name. He was thrilled as I handed it back to him — so bizarre.

He then offered us a couple of chairs and then mindlessly unbuttoned his jacket as he sat down on a leather sofa facing us, dispensing with the formality of his desk despite his own personal sense of outward formality and propriety. He set the book down on the table beside the sofa as we all sat down, "Mr. Walsh, I know you'll be pleased to hear that your friend Walker is going to be alright."

"Calling him my friend would be a stretch at best, but I am very happy to know that he's okay. We thought for sure he was dead back on the bridge."

"The bullet went completely through his chest. He had a collapsed lung but, after surgery, the doctors in Dublin are confident he'll have a full recovery. As for your driver Duncan," he turned his attention to Meagan, "I'm afraid the news is not so rosy, he was found deceased at the scene. Were you close?"

"Not close, but he was a very good and loyal agent. I'm

sad to hear that he's gone, he'll be sorely missed."

"I'm sorry to bear you bad news."

"Aye, thank you."

Just then, the door from the hallway opened up and the man in the suit came back in. He was carrying a tray with a an ice bucket and three glasses. As he set it down on a table beside the leather sofa, O'Neill opened a drawer in the front of the table and, inside, were rows of soft drink cans. "I didn't know if either of you would be interested in any sort of liquor as you're both sort of 'on duty' on your way to Spain, so I thought I'd offer you something really special from my personal supply," he reached into the drawer and produced a dark maroon aluminum can with the name "Dr. Pepper" emblazoned across it. "I have them flown in from New York."

Really? The guy smuggles Dr. Pepper into Northern Ireland?

So we each poured ourselves a nice stiff drink of Dr. Pepper — this was the hard stuff, not that diet stuff — on the rocks, and sat back to savor it for a moment.

I was certain that I'd be waking up soon.

But no, this was no dream.

Nor was it a movie — that would be too easy.

Suddenly, things got serious. O'Neill set his glass down and leaned forward with his elbows on his knees and looked up at me. "As much as I'm pleased to see the two of you in my humble office, your trip to Dublin was a ruse, Mr. Walsh."

"What do you mean?"

"The monsignor in San Diego let you beat him up so that the information that he ultimately revealed would be believable, but it was all a lie. Your friend, Mr. Goodspeed, was never coming to Ireland."

"Yeah, we sort of figured that out in Dublin."

"The Illuminati has vast resources — you probably know that already. They flew out of San Diego, filing flight plans to Canada and scattering red herrings all over the world to put you off the trail. I'm amazed that you figured out that they're headed for San Sebastian; our people on the ground there confirmed that just this past hour."

"You have people in Spain?"

"The Lámdearg has people everywhere, Mr. Walsh," Meagan grinned as she sipped her drink.

"By the way, did you know that the monsignor is dead?"

"Dead? I didn't kill the guy! I just slapped him around some and trashed his office!"

"He was stabbed through the heart with a ceremonial dagger. Another priest there said you did it."

"I poked him with a sword a few times, but I never stabbed him. Am I wanted for murder now?"

"Oddly, the police found only the priest's and the monsignor's fingerprints on the dagger. They're relatively sure that the man committed suicide. We're working with some friends from Interpol to clean things up for you. In the mean time, you two need to get to San Sebastian."

"Are you sure that's where Jacob is being taken?"

"He was flown out of San Diego to South America and, as we speak, a plane is flying to Barcelona. We believe they'll be changing planes there; the airport in San Sebastian is too small to handle the large plane that they'd need to fly across the Atlantic."

"How do you know all of this?"

"We watch everything and everyone, Mr. Walsh. You're just going to have to trust me."

"Why? I don't know you, I've never heard of your organization before."

"Ireland is rife with secret societies, Mr. Walsh. I'm not surprised that an American, even one so versed in conspiracies and such skullduggery, would be ignorant of some of them. But, really, that's what the whole idea about 'secret' societies is — am I correct?"

"I suppose so."

"Jack, you know that I'm C.I.A.," Meagan interrupted. "I've worked with Eamon and the Lámhdearg on several occasions. If I didn't think they could be trusted, believe me, we wouldn't be here."

"There, Mr. Walsh, a glowing endorsement and, as an author, I know you can appreciate a good review."

"A review, eh? Alright, I'm on alien turf here. I have to trust someone; I trust Meagan and if she says I can trust you and your people then, okay, I'll trust you. But I'm still unsteady in these waters so forgive me my trepidation."

"Understandable."

"So, Eamon, my friend. Will you be able to get us to San Sebastian?"

"We've already made arrangements. I have one of our jets getting prepped on the tarmac at Derry Airport as we speak. We'll fly you to Barcelona and have a car waiting there for you. You can then drive to San Sebastian from there; the G.P.S. will be programmed for you, it should take you about three hours to get there from the airport."

"Why not fly right into San Sebastian?" I asked.

"San Sebastian is a pretty small resort town, Mr. Walsh. The airport has but one runway. There is no way you would be able to fly in there without being found out and your mission would be over before it ever began. It's bloody difficult to keep an eye on street traffic in such a congested area, though. Just stick to the speed limits and don't do anything to attract the attention of the local police and you should be able to roll into town unnoticed."

"Can you get us any help on the ground, Eamon?"

"Basque Country is pretty closed, really tight, we don't have a lot of influence there I'm afraid. I do have a lot of intel that I can get to you. I'll have it delivered to the plane. We were able to find the floor plans for Mans DeLoyola, hopefully that will be a help."

"So, what you're saying is that, we're basically on our own."

"Aye, Mr. Walsh, I'm afraid that's what I am indeed saying."

"We'll be alright, Jack, your guardian angel has gotten us this far."

"I sure hope you're not being serious about that."

"I'm just trying to think positive. But if you think about it, with a good plan of attack, a team of two could get in and out before they ever knew what hit them."

"It had better be a *really* good plan."

"How about logistics, Eamon. Supplies?"

"I've got a man in San Sebastian who will meet you there to help you size up the mission. He'll have MP5s, vests, rappelling harnesses and other gear and plenty of ammunition available, take whatever you think you'll need."

"Thank you, that will be very good."

"In the mean time, if you two would like to clean up a bit, we have showers down the hall. Mr. Walsh, with all due respect, you look like someone had kicked you off of the back of a speeding turnip truck."

"Yeah, thanks. I kind of feel that way, too."

"I have tactical clothes for each of you. You can throw a jacket or a shirt over them until you're ready so you don't attract any attention."

"How about some first aid stuff? Meagan should really redress that bandage on her arm before we head back out."

"Aye, I'll have some bandages and supplies brought up for her."

He stood up and we did likewise. We shook hands and then he raised his glass of Dr. Pepper and we all toasted a hopeful mission.

* * * * *

"I have to use the rest room," Jacob announced.

"Again?"

"I'm old. I have to pee. Get over it."

"Alright, just make it quick."

Jacob released his seatbelt and walked to the rear of the cabin to the rest room. As he did, his captors reported to Emilio Moretti who was seated near the front of the cabin, attempting to get some sleep on the long flight across the Atlantic. He groaned and then got to his feet and watched for Jacob to emerge from the back of the cabin and return to his seat.

After a short wait, Jacob came back out from the rest room and made his way forward through the narrow aisle toward his seat. Moretti was sitting on the arm of one of the seats nearby waiting for him and stood up with his arms crossed as Jacob approached.

"Señor Goodspeed, we will be landing in Barcelona in about an hour. From there you will be boarding another, smaller plane to fly to your final destination. I want to give you one more chance to tell me where those journals are hidden before we land to save you the ordeal of being interrogated for the information."

Jacob just stood in the aisle with his elbow resting on the top of the seat to his left. With his right hand, he reached up and adjusted his wire-rimmed glasses and then, almost subconsciously, he stroked his mustache before finally slipping his hand into his pocket.

"Mr. Moretti, as I've told you before, those books are not mine to give to anyone; they belong to the Montgomery Historical Society and you are welcome to come and examine them any time you like, just call and make an appointment."

"I know you are no fool, Mr. Goodspeed. You understand the gravity of this situation. The people I work for are determined and will do whatever they feel is necessary to extract the information from you."

"Torture?"

"You could call it that."

"And you might kill me?"

"It may well come to that."

"And what about my family? Friends? Are they in danger, too?"

"If you continue to refuse to cooperate, that is a real possibility."

Jacob just smiled and again stroked his mustache and then leaned forward a little to look eye-to-eye with Moretti."

"I'm seventy-four years old, Mr. Moretti. I'm a cancer survivor in remission, that means that I'm on borrowed time right now. I buried my wife over a decade ago and almost all of my friends and old war buddies are gone. I am the last one left. If you torture me you'll likely kill me and, if you kill me, you'll never find those books," he just smiled and then stood back upright. "I have to tell you, Moretti, that I've never seen so much of the world as I have in these past couple of days. I've eaten at a great restaurant in San Diego, got to wear the Chicken costume and goof around on a Major League Baseball field during a game, I've read a really good novel — well most of it — and spent the night in an amazing hotel. And now I'm flying to Barcelona with you. I know you're paid to be a real s.o.b., but I have a feeling that, under different conditions, you and I could have a real blast together," he side-stepped into the space in front of the seat next to him and then lowered himself down. "Mr. Moretti, I live in a tiny, quiet, rural town where nothing much ever happens, and we like it that way. Right now though, I'm having a great time and if I die tonight, well, I die. I've had a really good run."

"Mr. Goodspeed, you confound me."

"You know, we have a saying in the U.S.: 'you can catch more flies with honey than you can with vinegar'."

"What do you mean?"

"Try to bribe me, of course! Offer me a fancy car, piles of cash a new Harley!"

"And you would tell me where the journals are hidden?"

"No, of course not, but it would be fun to try, don't 'ya think?"

November twenty-eighth, 1809

A troubled night, could not sleep. Could not stop
pondering what the old man on North Hill toldeth
me. The more I considereth his words, the more it
seemed to suggest that he was claiming to be none
other than John the Apostle — the Revelator. But
that would be impossible, he would have to be nearly
two thousand years olde.

i kinda like the music

Eamon O'Neill was gracious and accommodating, but something about him just didn't sit right with me. Meagan and I were both given the opportunity to shower and she was able to get her wound redressed while we were still in Coleraine. O'Neill's people provided us both with black tactical clothes including long-sleeved jerseys, black cargo pants, boots, gloves and balaclavas and, to complete our ensembles, bullet-proof vests. I have to admit, when I saw the vest, the real possibility of being caught in a hail of bullets again hit me like a brick. I wasn't anxious to repeat the scenario on the bridge in Dublin any time soon.

To blend into the civilian tourist scene at San Sebastian, I also had a green Hawaiian-style shirt with big olive green palm trees against a lighter green pattern of gigantic leaves and stripes - kind of brash, but subdued enough to keep me from standing out very much in a crowd. A pair of aviator shades and a dark gray Irish tweed flat cap completed the resort camouflage. Meagan, too, had some stylish camo to help blend into the scene; a long mauve shirt with a belt around her waist, a raspberry scarf tied around her neck and big, rectangular sunglasses with faux-tortise shell frames.

Just before we left, Eamon met with us one more time in

his office and told us that a man would meet us on the tarmac at the Barcelona airport with the keys to the car that we would drive to San Sebastian where we'd meet our contact who would help us the rest of the way. A quick hug for Meagan and a shake of my hand and we were off.

A car picked us up at the street end of the Diamond and drove us out to the A2 highway and northwest toward Londonderry. It was late, nearly midnight, and I was getting seriously tired but the adrenaline that was fueling my paranoia kept me peering out the windows from the back seat at every pair of headlights that passed us, suspecting any one of them to be another potential attacker. By my count, at that moment anyway, we had at least four or five different secret organizations looking for us: the Illuminati, the I.R.A. and their evil cousins the Sons of Erin, the Skull and Bones and the Templars, not to mention who-knows-how-many intelligence and law-enforcement agencies from the F.B.I. to Scotland Yard, MI-5, Interpol (although I thought that if I had become most-wanted by Interpol it could double the sales of my next book) and I'm sure that our own State Department was curious about what was happening along with the N.S.A. who no doubt was keeping close tabs on our communications which, I assumed, is why Meagan left her cell phone in the mangled Mercedes back in Dublin. And we hadn't even left Ireland yet — who knew what or who might be waiting for us in Spain.

And there I was in a car owned by the Lámdearg with a C.I.A. agent riding up front. So it would seem that I had plenty to be paranoid about.

The ride was a little less than an hour long, but it seemed to take forever. Time tends to drag when you're spending it looking over your shoulder. With my radar on high alert, everything that we'd pass and every vehicle that went by was suspect and I still wasn't all that sure of Eamon O'Neill and his driver in whom we'd had to put our trust. Eventually, we came upon the lights of the airport as we neared it. We drove around to a gate

Bob Pierce

that was marked as "CoDA Aviation Centre" which is the area of the small airport that serves private and corporate aircraft. O'Neill's Gulfstream was standing by on the tarmac near one of the hangar buildings and we drove past the terminal building and across the parking area, past rows of multi-million-dollar private jets, to a plane that was a bit larger than most with oval windows along its sides, its door open and steps folded out to the pavement. As we approached, a man came out from the plane's interior and climbed down to greet us as the car turned around and stopped parallel to the plane.

Our driver climbed out and walked around to open Meagan's door while the man from the plane pulled my door open and let me out. He grabbed the gear bag that was sitting on the back seat beside me and carried it to the plane and we followed behind across the windy tarmac. I heard the car pull away and had a sinking feeling of having passed the point of no return as I watched its taillights recede back toward the gate and disappear out to the street. I guess in reality, I'd passed the point of no return back in San Diego when Jacob was kidnapped and I determined to rescue him at all costs, even to the point of slapping around a priest. Clearly there was no turning back so I just heaved a big sigh and climbed the aluminum steps up to the plane's door and found myself a seat.

About midway in the cabin were a pair of seats that faced each other across a small table. Meagan and I each dropped into the soft, leather-clad seats and buckled up for take-off as the steward pulled the door closed and the plane taxied out to the runway.

I just watched out the window as the lights of the Irish countryside whisked past the windows until they fell far below us and then drew away leaving the stark view of the black ocean waters of the north Atlantic as my only view out the window. I turned to Meagan and just smiled.

"What?" she asked suspiciously.

"I don't know, I just suddenly feel this sense of relief. With the plane in the air I don't feel so much like I have to keep looking over my shoulder."

"Aye, I know what you mean. But those vests aren't just fashion accessories; we've still got a ways yet to go."

I sat and just looked at her as she looked down at a folder that O'Neill had given her and opened it up on the table. She read some of the information and flipped over each sheet as she absorbed information that would certainly be needed when we reached our destination. For me, though, I was just too exhausted to even attempt. I just sat there, looking across at her flame-orange hair, the collar and cuffs of her black jersey showing from behind the neck and sleeves of her touristy shirt and thought about the fire fight on the bridge and the way she hung out the windows of the speeding car shooting it out with the bad guys that were chasing us through the streets of Dublin. I just smiled to myself when the thought occurred to me of her as a young girl playing with her Barbie dolls — probably dressed them in cammies, Barbie's "Dream House" was probably a fortified bunker and she opted for a Hummer in lieu of the pink Corvette. I'm sure her Barbies' ensembles were smartly accessorized with plastic M-16s slung over their shoulders and diving knives strapped to their plastic ankles.

She looked up from her reading and caught me grinning at her.

"What?"

"Oh, nothing. I was just thinking that you reminded me of absolutely none of the girls I grew up with as a kid in my old neighborhood."

"What are you talking about?"

"Never mind."

"You're obviously tired and you're a writer which means you don't think like normal people do. Why don't you just find somewhere to stretch out and get some sleep."

She was right, of course. I was incredibly tired and she certainly wasn't the first to accuse me of being a little, well, strange. I like to think, however, that it works for me.

As I continued to sit there across the table from her, I just couldn't help but wonder about her; now I'm not a very religious person, in fact I guess one might say I sort of hover between agnostic and atheist if one were to try and put a label on me, but I've always had a sense that there was some sort of higher power, God perhaps, however one might define him — or it. Meagan seemed to be quite an enigma in my mind, such a staunch moral code that she seemed to adhere to just filled me with questions.

She looked up from her papers again and I guess she once again saw a look on my face that drew an expression of annoyance from her,

"Now what?"

"I was just wondering…"

"Aye? Wondering what, Mr. Walsh?"

"Are you a religious person? I mean, with this strict morality that you adhere to, I have to wonder if it's based on some sort of religious conviction."

"No, not really. I just have a deep-seated ideal of what is right and wrong. I guess I was just brought up that way."

"So, I wonder then, and please excuse my clumsiness, I'm really tired, but without some sort of benchmark for morality — no God to answer to — what's the point?"

"What do you mean?"

"Well, if you aren't accountable to anyone, why not eat, drink and be merry? Why not sleep around when the spirit moves you, so to speak?"

"The Bible says 'thou shalt not murder, thou shalt not steal,' right? But even the most secular of governments have laws against such things and even without those laws, people just know that killing and stealing are wrong. Don't have to be religious to know that; don't need God."

"Hmmm…that's deep, really deep. I've never been married. I guess I always thought that it could happen some day, but never really looked for it; you know? But I haven't exactly been celibate in the interim, either."

"So I presumed."

"So, if mankind is somehow instinctively aware of what is right or wrong, would it not follow that he was endowed with that awareness by his creator? God, perhaps?"

"So what you are saying, Mr. Walsh, is that the very fact that man has the capacity for moral judgement without the need for God just proves that there is a God?"

"It does sort of make sense, eh?"

"Can we change the subject, Mr. Walsh?"

"You're a tough broad, Meagan."

"Aye, and you're the embodiment of the 'ugly American'."

"Ha, ha, ha!" I leaned forward over the table and dropped my voice, "okay, change of subject: tell me, in all honesty, do you trust this guy, O'Neill?"

"Aye, Mr. Walsh, as I've told you, he and his organization have worked with me and the C.I.A. on many projects. I trust him — mostly."

"It's odd that he didn't ask anything about the journals. Why is he doing all this for us, what's in it for him?"

"Eamon O'Neill is a man of high moral character, but of very little principal. Generally speaking, if there is no profit in a particular endeavor, he has no interest in it. He won't gain anything from helping us out today, but I can assure you that one day I will get a phone call in Dublin and he will look to cash in this favor."

"Yeah, and that reminds me. When Jacob and I first hooked up with Special Agent Walker, he told me about all the agencies around the world that were monitoring phone calls and e-mails and stuff, and he told me that there was somebody, somewhere in Northern Ireland who was getting a constant flow of phone calls to an untraceable burner cell phone from pay phones all over the world. Always calls coming in, never any calls out; seems pretty strange. Could this be your friend Eamon?"

"I don't know. He is a man with financial holdings around the globe, I wouldn't be surprised if he were getting reports from people far afield who might be managing them. Nothing illegal in that."

"Yeah, but Walker said that, when Jacob and I got on the plane in Vermont and began heading west, this phone in Ireland was getting a huge spike in traffic. If that's O'Neill, then he's clearly interested in those books."

"Perhaps he is, but don't you think he'd have asked you something about them when we were with him in Coleraine?"

"That's the really strange part — one would think so."

"My advice is to just keep one eye open, but otherwise, don't worry about Eamon O'Neill, Lord knows there are plenty of other things to worry about."

"My concern is that he may be helping us to rescue Jacob just so that he can get his own hands on him."

"I think you're really just being paranoid now. Believe me when I tell you, I don't ever trust anyone one hundred percent, and I never trust anyone at all until they've earned it. I know what Eamon is capable of and I respect him for it. Besides, he's embarrassingly rich, he's biding his time maneuvering himself politically to finally split off Northern Ireland as an independent state and reinstate the Irish monarchy. That's his passion, but he's in no rush. He's really enjoying life with his big homes, exotic cars and black-market Dr. Pepper; he has no desire to risk losing it all."

"I guess that makes sense."

"Look, Mr. Walsh, I'm really tired and we've still got several hours left until we get to Barcelona. I'm going to go to the back of the cabin and stretch out on one of those lounges to get some sleep. You'll excuse me."

"Certainly. Would you like some company?"

"May I remind you that I still have my gun and I now also have bullets."

"I was just kidding! You go ahead and catch some z's, I'll

just tip this seat back and close my eyes. I can never sleep on planes anyway."

She flashed a quick half-smile and then got up from her seat at the table and walked down the aisle. A cabin steward approached her and brought a couple of pillows for her as she kicked off her shoes and laid down on the cushions, he then spread a blanket over her and turned off the light. I pushed the button on the arm rest and pushed my seat back as far as it would go and then reached up and switched off the overhead light. I must have been far more tired than I had thought because, before too long, and to my surprise, I actually dozed off and slept through much of the flight.

✻ ✻ ✻ ✻ ✻

The big DC-10 from Managua taxied to the terminal annex building at the Barcelona airport, by far the largest aircraft among the other private planes parked along the sides of the runway. A man in a reflective green vest directed the pilots to a parking area large enough with a pair of bright orange hand-held cones. He swung the cones to one side with a sweeping, circular motion and the big plane made a ninety-degree turn to the left and then slowly rolled into place and came to a stop.

Immediately, a ground crew rolled a portable stairway up to the side of the plane as one of the crew inside opened the cabin door and swung it back, flat against the side of the fuselage. Other ground crew members swarmed around the plane setting wheel chocks around the tires and connecting various service cables and tubes to ports along its belly.

Emilio Moretti rose to his feet and looked back down the aisle of the aircraft and announced, "we are here, Señor Goodspeed."

"Here? Where's 'here'?" he peered out the window in the early morning sunlight. He could see the main terminal building to the left, white letters spaced across a dark band along the upper half of the long building spelled out "Barcelona."

"We're in Spain? Cool! I've never been to Spain, but I kinda like the music. Ya' know, they tell me I was born here, but I really don't remember."

"What in the world are you talking about, señor?"

"Three Dog Night — did you grow up under a rock somewhere, Moretti? Everyone knows that song!"

"Señor Goodspeed, I am truly going to miss our little talks."

Jacob walked up the aisle toward the front of the cabin where Moretti was standing waiting for him. He stopped him and said, "Señor Goodspeed, once you walk down those steps to the ground, I will have to hand you over to the Grand Inquisitor. He will do whatever he has to do to get the information that our order wants from you. He will torture you and, despite your age and fragility, he will use whatever means necessary to keep you alive just long enough to extract what he wants. He will pump your veins full of drugs and use electrical shock to keep your heart going. When he is finished with you, you will die. I am giving you one last chance, while we are still on this plane and I still have some control over your situation, por fávor, tell me where those journals are."

Jacob just smiled and looked around the cabin of the plane for a minute before turning back to Moretti and answering him, "Mr. Moretti, you have been a gracious host and if you and your pals are ever in Montgomery I'd love to have you look me up. You can come by the Historical Society and look at those journals — with an appointment, of course — and spend all the time you like reading and studying them. But those books are the property of the Montgomery Historical Society and they are not allowed out of the building. While you're in town though, we can go get a couple of Reubens at Dino's, if you like."

"I truly do not understand you, Señor Goodspeed; your life is at stake and still you insist. I grieve for you."

"Oh, don't worry about me, Moretti, I'm having the time

of my life!"

"Sadly, there is not much left of it."

"Live fast, die young and leave a beautiful corpse, I've always said."

"You live in a sleepy, rural town, you're seventy-four years old and, no offence, señor, but you are no Sean Connery."

"Obviously, I've been saying that one for a long, long time."

Moretti just smiled and then picked up a folder from his seat and led Jacob to the door and out of the plane with a pair of his guards following behind. At the foot of the stairs stood a severe-looking man wearing a black suit and black fedora. His white hair tufted out from under his hat and was matched by a white goatee on his deeply-creased face. He wore a pair of black-framed glasses with circular lenses and gripped a silver-tipped cane with hands sheathed in black leather gloves. Standing around him were three men in black suits and three uniformed para-military police armed with HK submachine guns. Jacob was flattered, he'd never thought of himself as being so dangerous, but it would appear that those folks did.

Moretti held his hand up to stop Jacob at the foot of the steps, then walked farther forward and handed the folder to the man with the cane. They spoke for a moment while Jacob waited with his hands in the pockets of his jeans.

After a short wait, Moretti motioned for Jacob to join them and introduced him to Cardinal Innicus de Recalde and explained that they would be boarding another, smaller plane that would then take them to their destination. Jacob reached his hand out to greet the stern-looking man but, as he did, another man clamped a pair of handcuffs on him and roughly grabbed him by his upper arm.

"Adios, Señor Goodspeed. May God speed your soul," Moretti placed his hand on Jacob's shoulder as he turned and walked away.

Two of the men in black suits gripped Jacob's arms and led him to a smaller corporate jet parked nearby, following de

Recalde who walked before them, leaning against his cane with each purposeful step.

As they walked along the tarmac near the building, the Gulfstream that Meagan and I were riding in was taxiing toward an open space along the runway past the big DC-10 and, as we passed, I looked out the window and saw Jacob in handcuffs being ushered into another plane.

"Jacob!" I shouted out, helplessly unable to be heard.

"Where?!" Meagan asked as she turned and rushed toward the window.

"There, with those men in black, they're getting onto another plane!"

In a moment, we had rolled past and the view of Jacob and his captors was blocked by the other planes parked along the line. I turned to Meagan, "can we stop that plane? Can you call someone?!"

"No, Mr. Walsh, I cannot. The C.I.A. can't interfere with the Spanish air traffic control without a court order. They'll be in the air before we even get off of this plane."

"I can't believe it, we've come so close!" I was unspeakably frustrated. If but for a few minutes — if we'd just showered a little faster, if the driver who took us to the airport just drove a little quicker, if the plane just had a stronger tail-wind — we'd have arrived soon enough to catch up with Jacob. But Meagan made a very good point to me, the only sort of firepower we had was the one pistol she carried and the men who had Jacob were armed with machine guns; we wouldn't have had a chance.

"Best to stick with our plan," she encouraged. "Eamon's people will meet us here and we will mount a rescue fully prepared. We'll have a much better chance."

"Yeah, but here at the airport there were just a few of them with no sort of cover, by the time we catch up with them at the Mans DeLoyola they'll be burrowed in like termites and armed to the teeth."

"I'm sure Eamon has gathered an enormous amount of intel for us and made arrangements for us to be well equipped for the mission."

"I'm sorry, I still don't trust the guy."

"Aye, but it's the best we've got, Mr. Walsh. Let's try and work with it."

The plane rolled into its assigned parking space and came to a stop. The turbines whined down to a lower and lower pitch until they finally became silent. We each grabbed out gear bags with our bulletproof vests and other tactical gear in them and made our way to the door and out to the pavement of the Barcelona airfield. The air was much cooler and fresher than I had anticipated but, then, we were pretty much on the Mediterranean beach so despite all of the jet exhaust and other odors all around us, the gentle sea breeze made the air seem clean and inviting.

When we got to the end of the steps, I wasn't sure where we were supposed to go from there, but a man in a polo shirt and khakis walked out from between the building and the plane we had parked beside and introduced himself. He was O'Neill's man there in Barcelona.

"Hóla, Señor Walsh, Señorita Flynn," he extended his hand for us to shake and then motioned for us to follow him. "I have a car for you in the parking area just outside the gates."

I knew the plan was to drive across to San Sebastian, but I was worried that I didn't have any sort of papers with me, no passport or anything, just my Vermont driver's license in my wallet in my back pocket.

"No worries, señor, there is an envelope in the glove box for each of you with American passports and all the documents you will need."

I turned to Meagan as we walked toward the gate, "so I guess Eamon has friends with the State Department."

"Eamon has friends everywhere."

"Friends who owe him favors."

"That's how it works, Mr. Walsh; that's how it works."

The little Spanish man in the polo shirt led us between the rows of parked cars and to a dark silver Jaguar XJR and then he stopped and turned around with a grin on his face, reaching into his pocket for the keys.

"Wow, this is not what I was expecting," I was impressed.

"Aye, not what I was expecting, either. I thought we'd be driving something much more pedestrian."

"San Sebastian is a resort town, señorita; a playground for the rich. A plain automobile that would blend in in Barcelona, would stand out in San Sebastian."

"I suppose that's true," I mused as the man handed me the keys. I looked at Meagan, "I guess you're going to owe a *really* big favor to O'Neill."

"Don't forget, Mr. Walsh, you're with me. You're accumulating a debt as well."

"I autographed a book for him."

"That may not be enough."

"Well, I'll overnight him a case of Dr. Pepper when I get back to the States."

She smiled a broad grin and said, "knowing Eamon, that might just do it, Mr. Walsh."

We put our bags into the trunk and the man in the polo shirt bade us a safe trip and excused himself saying he had to check in to report that we'd arrived safely and were on our way to San Sebastian.

"Do you need a quarter for the phone?" I asked.

"Señor?"

"Never mind. Just say 'hi' for me."

"Si, señor Walsh, I will do that. Adiós!"

"Adiós."

We got into the front seats of the car and I found myself looking at a dashboard that more resembled that of the plane we had just come in on than anything I'd ever seen in a car before. I held the key in my hand and realized that it wasn't a key at all, just a small plastic box with a Jaguar logo on it. I sat there, staring at the dashboard and tried to figure out what to do.

"How do you turn this thing on?" I asked rhetorically.

Meagan leaned over and pointed to a round button on the dashboard near the steering column. I pushed it and the big Jag came to life. Then I looked down at the shifter on the floor. Even that was complicated. I pulled on it and moved it to the first notch that made the car go forward — "drive" I presumed — and we were on our way.

Meagan got the GPS gizmo in the dashboard working to guide us and even got it to speak English for us.

San Sebastian lies almost directly west, across the narrow northern portion of Spain just below the French border. Our route would take us parallel to the border from the Mediterranean to the Atlantic. The drive took just a few hours and we found ourselves rolling into the valley where the town was nestled between rising mountains on either side and the glistening Biscay Bay beyond. We made really good time, perhaps I was motivated to press a bit harder on the accelerator after having glimpsed my friend being led away in handcuffs back in Barcelona. Thankfully, we didn't arouse any unwanted attention from local police.

Getting ever closer to San Sebastian and the goal of our mission, I was becoming increasingly more uneasy and fully expected to end up trashing the big Jag just like we did the Mercedes back in Dublin in some sort of rolling gun battle. But all was quiet, though I had no doubt we were being watched and reported upon all along our westward progression.

"Why do you suppose noone has tried to stop us?" I asked Meagan as we neared our destination.

"It's a trap."

"A trap? You say that like it's something routine, like going to the grocery store."

"Think about it, Mr. Walsh. Who knows about all of this outside of the Vatican and the Illuminati? Just you and me. They could chase us all over Europe, but why bother?"

"Jacob is the bait."

"That may not be a bad thing, at least for now."

"Why do you say that?"

"If your friend were dead, what motivation would we have to ride right into the belly of the beast to try and rescue him?"

"So until we either rescue him or die trying, they won't hurt him."

"Exactly."

"That means we have one chance to get this right. Yeah, no pressure."

Until that moment, despite all that I'd been through, I hadn't actually felt any real fear. Things that had happened just sort of happened and I just reacted to them; I hadn't had time to think about them. But on this drive to San Sebastian, that's all I could think about. But I knew that saving Jacob was only half of our mission, getting him away from the Illuminati would keep the journals away from the Vatican. That was more important than Jacob's own life. But should we be successful in that, who next would swoop down on us? The Templars? The Skull and Bones? To me, it didn't seem that this would ultimately end well.

I felt like I had to throw up.

Writing novels about this sort of thing is pretty safe. I go to the library, I visit various locations and poke around on the internet and do all sorts of research and then in the safety of my rural Vermont home, I put all the pieces together and write the chapters that take my characters through hell and back. And if they don't survive it, it's no big deal, they're just fictional characters whose lives exist only as black marks on white paper and the only thing that really matters to me in the end is how many copies I can sell.

But riding into San Sebastian on that otherwise beautiful

day made me realize the enormity of these sorts of situations that I had so cavalierly written about in my books. In real life, this stuff is really, really scary and the upshot of a failed mission isn't just that I won't be on the next page, it will be my funeral (presuming my body is ever located).

O'Neill's programming of the GPS device led us to a sidewalk cafe on a very busy street in the heart of the tourist-filled town. We drove past a short way until I could find a parking space large enough that I felt comfortable pulling the big Jag into without hitting anything else. It was late morning, nearly noon, and the streets were congested with rich tourists and their ridiculously-expensive cars. The guy back at the airport wasn't kidding that a plain Toyota or Chevy would stick out like a sore thumb. I had parallel parked the Jag between a Maserati and a Bentley. We got out and I pushed a button on the plastic fob and heard a loud "click" which made me assume that the doors were locked (I didn't want to check lest I not appear to be the legitimate owner of the car).

I was trying to blend into an environment totally alien to me. I kept trying to emulate Robert Culp in "I Spy," he'd fit into this San Sebastian lifestyle like a chameleon. I was wishing that I had a white tennis sweater to tie around my neck to complete the ruse.

We walked back to the cafe and looked around through the crowd for anyone who might be trying to catch our attention and/or anyone who might be looking to kill us (who may well be one and the same). As we looked around through the shifting humanity, Meagan gently tugged on my sleeve to get my attention without drawing anyone else's. She nodded to our left and I looked through the passing bodies but couldn't see what she was pointing out to me so I just trustingly turned and followed her as we threaded our way along the crowded sidewalk. As we neared the wrought iron railing that defined the cafe from the rest of the sidewalk traffic, I suddenly spotted what had caught her eye: a middle-aged man, looking very British dressed in tweed from his flat cap to his jacket patched on the sleeves with ovals of suede that he had draped over the back of the chair next to him. He had a scraggly mustache and a gap in his teeth making him look reminiscent of Terry Thomas, the British comedian. He was sitting by himself with a can of Dr. Pepper on the table in front of him.

Of course.

As we walked up to the table, the man noticed us approaching and stood to greet us. He had a decidedly British accent and invited us to sit and join him at the table.

"American tourists, and I see you've been to the Emerald Isle on your tour to Europe."

"Huh?"

"Your cap, mate. You no doubt got that in a gift shop somewhere in Ireland."

"Oh, right, yeah. Nice place. Lots of green stuff in that store," I was obviously feeling pretty awkward.

"My name is Moses Jones, most blokes just call me 'Jonesy'."

"Pleased to meet you...Jonesy. I assume you know who we are."

"Indeed."

"We are in a hurry to mount this little project and I don't know what you have planned, but we also haven't eaten anything substantial in over twenty-four hours. I'm famished. Do we have time to order some lunch?"

"Certainly! Must keep up our strength, you know. Luck favors the prepared as they say!"

"Uhhh — if one were prepared, why would they also need luck?"

"Hmmm...jolly good observation. You're the writer I take it. Work with words do you?"

"My stock and trade, assuming I survive the next few days to continue doing so."

"Well, let us start with a hearty luncheon!" He rose from

his seat and waved to a waiter to come with menus. When he sat back down he turned to me and added, "San Sebastian is famous for its epicurean delights. The town draws disgustingly-rich foodies from all over the world. I'm sure you'll enjoy whatever catches your fancy."

"Can I just get a burger and fries?"

He turned to Meagan and asked "where did you find this Neanderthal?"

She smiled and looked over at me "You'll have to excuse him, he's an American, I don't think they use words like 'epicurean' where he comes from."

"And where is that?"

"My dad used to call it 'the sticks', Mom called it 'God's country'."

"'God's country'? Where is that, I must ask?"

"A mythical land called 'Vermont'."

"I must visit this 'Vermont' one day. It sounds positively charming."

"Much of it is; just don't read the local papers, they'll make the 'charming' part wear off pretty quickly."

"Indeed."

* * * * *

After a positively amazing lunch, the three of us got back into the Jag and, following Mr. Jones' direction, we found our way to the Amara Plaza Hotel near the beach. When we got into his room, there were folders full of papers on a table with rolled up plans which he unfurled, using an ashtray and the television remote to hold open at either end to keep them flat. He leaned over the table and began pointing out features on the plans.

"This is the Mans DeLoyola," he announced as Meagan and I leaned over and followed along on his two-dimensional guided tour. "It has three floors above ground, the lower level opens in the rear to the patios overlooking the bay. It's built at the edge of the cliffs that drop about seventy-five feet to the rocks below, the only way to approach is from the front."

"There's not a lot of cover once you get past that outer wall."

"Aye, it's a no-man's land until you get to the terraces and the porches."

"A night time approach would probably be best," I mused.

"The open yards are criss-crossed with infrared sensors and there is a laser grid all around the building, about twenty feet from the walls. The infrared would see you in an instant in the cool of the night."

"And the lasers?"

"Not much you can do about them, once you break the beam it sets off the alarms inside and a bunch of blokes with guns come runnin'."

"And you believe that Jacob Goodspeed is somewhere inside."

"Don't you?"

"I was mostly sure until we got to Barcelona. But when I actually saw him there at the airport with that nasty-lookin' guy with the black fedora, I was certain."

"Nasty-lookin' bloke in a black hat? Did he have a cane?"

"Yeah, how do you know?"

Jones stood back upright and folded his arms across his chest, "that man is evil incarnate, mate. His name is Cardinal Innicus de Recalde, he's the Grand Inquisitor for the Holy Church Office. Bad news."

"So all the more reason to move fast here," I insisted.

"Yes, Mr. Walsh, but not foolishly. We need a good plan before we do something stupid."

"You mean like charging a couple of guys with machine guns and crashing a car through a road block through a hail of bullets."

"Aye, exactly."

"Well, *that* all seemed to work out."

"I know I'd said that I believed that a guardian angel is hanging around you these days, but I'm not really willing to bet my life on that."

"Are you two done? You sound like an old married couple, you do."

"I believe in the direct approach."

"There's 'direct' and there's 'foolish', Mr. Walsh."

"You know, Meagan, you're supposed to be the bad-ass C.I.A. agent here. Why is it that you're the one with cold feet?"

"Not cold feet, Mr. Walsh. I just think we should take a few minutes and see if there is some way we can actually be successful and, if it's not too much to ask, perhaps even survive this operation."

I turned to Jones and asked, "is there any way to shut down these security gadgets? Can we create a power failure like they do in the movies?"

"We could, I suppose. The Mans is supplied through underground cables. All we'd have to do is find an access point and drop in a small charge of C-4."

"There, Meagan, problem solved."

"Not entirely, mate. The Mans has backup generators. As soon as the power from the street is cut, those generators will kick on."

"How long would that take, do you guess?"

"Well, they'd trip automatically in less than a second, but would have to spin up to speed before the Mans would have full power again. Maybe half a minute or so; and then they'd likely only power up essentials like heat, air conditioning, lights in stairwells and hallways. They probably wouldn't power up the security systems or, at least, not all of them."

I studied the plans laid out on the table in front of me and did some quick calculations in my mind.

"What are you thinking, Mr. Walsh?"

"On either side of the driveway, just inside the gates, there are a pair of big trees. If we could get over the wall or through the gate and duck behind those trees, we could remain undetected until the power line is blown. Then we would have about thirty seconds to get inside the perimeter of the lasers before the power comes back on."

"Good point. We wouldn't have to actually get inside the building in thirty seconds, just inside the sensors."

"But who is going to blow the power lines up, mate? There's only two of you."

"No, Mr. Jones, there are three of us. That will be your job."

"My job?"

"What's the matter, Jonesy? This getting too dicey for you?"

"Well, I wasn't really expecting to go in on this mission. I'm not a field agent, I'm just an intel guy."

"So here's your big chance to be a hero, you up for it?"

"Aaahhh...I suppose."

"Good, now, do we have any idea just where in this building they might be holding Jacob?"

We spent a few more minutes looking through the pages of the floor plans of the Mans and figuring out the most logical places that they might be interrogating Jacob. Such a big mansion and so many unknowns, we made a few educated guesses based on what information we had, but they were still just guesses.

There wasn't much more discussion, it appeared that, once we got inside the building, we would have to mount a search from room to room. Assuming that we were not detected or we were able to subdue anyone that we might come across, it would be time-consuming and the Illuminati would be hunting for us as much as we would be hunting for Jacob. I think we all three knew deep down that this was likely going to be a suicide mission. The one thing that remained unspoken, but we all three knew it, was that the journals could never fall into the hands of the Vatican at any cost. If that meant that we had to kill Jacob before he could divulge their location — and die ourselves in the effort — we four were all expendable for that greater purpose.

Oddly, under the gravity of that revelation, the fear that I had been harboring had lifted from me. I was ready, psychologically, anyway. I really didn't think about it but somehow I was okay with killing an innocent man and sacrificing my own life at the same time. Funny, they didn't teach this in college in my English major, preparing to become a famous author.

Despite the somber and unspoken realizations, we still had work to do to get ready. I asked Jones if he could direct us to do a drive-by of the Mans so that we could get a first-hand look at it while it was still light out.

"Sure," he grabbed his jacket, "gets bloody windy up on those cliffs."

We left the hotel room and took the elevator down to the lobby. As we walked across the open space of the ornate Spanish/Basque decor, I noticed a couple of men sitting by themselves reading newspapers who seemed to be somewhat out of place and was immediately reminded of a scene from "The Maltese Falcon." As it turned out, that analogy was pretty accurate. As we neared the doors to the street, the two men put down their newspapers and got to their feet, following us at a distance. I'd hoped that we could get out through the doors to the car quickly, but as soon as I pushed the door open and stepped out into the sunlight, another man stood there with thick, curly black hair and wrap-around sunglasses and the other two from the lobby stepped right up behind us, just outside the hotel doors.

"Mr. Walsh, Miss Flynn, please do not make any unnecessary disturbances. You must come with me."

It seemed that destiny had taken a hand; the trap had been sprung.

March fifteenth, 1811

Was invited to spend time with John again, so left
my work at the liv'ry stable and eagerly joined him.
Today he told me that he had been eye—witness to
the crucifixion of our Lord, was the only one of the
remaining eleven who dared to be present. He later
visited the empty tomb with Peter and had to explain
events to others hiding in Jerusalem. After day of
pentecost, he took Mary, the Lord's mother, and a
small band of other disciples and went to Ephesis
where Mary dieth years later. He sayeth she always
wanted to be buried in Jerusalem so he brought her
bones back to the city.

John also sayeth, when he had left Ephesis, rumors spread of his demise. Truth in fact, a tomb there was presumed to be his and many pilgrims came worshipping there. He took the opportunity to go into hiding and travel from city to city and even'lly return to Antioch. Said he remembered the Baptist who once told him to follow Christ Jesus instead of himself, saying that he had to decrease that Christ may increase that he, too, needed to decrease. Since he'd been promised to remain til Christs return, hiding in faith that he would not be exposed, was to be his strategy.

VERY STRANGE
BEDFELLOWS

Meagan and I were gathered up into a plain white van that pulled up in front of the hotel and were told to sit together on a bench seat in the back. A man sitting inside waiting for us pulled black cloth hoods over our heads making us unable to see anything as we heard the sliding side door slam shut. On the ride from the hotel, I tried to listen for background sounds, count the number of bumps in the road and the sound of the tires on different road surfaces. Not as easy as they make it out to be in the movies and rather futile, frankly, since I didn't know anything about San Sebastian and no idea where we were going. But then, what else did I have to do in the dark in the back of a van on the way to who-knows-where?

I asked Meagan "Who are are these guys?"

"I don't know."

"They're not Eamon O'Neill's people, for one thing, they're definitely not Irish."

"Aye, that would not seem likely."

A voice from the front seats of the van called back to us "please, no talking."

"Why, what are you afraid that we might say?' I asked with my usual jaded aplomb.

"Please just do as you are asked."

"Or else, what? You're gonna kill us anyway, right?"

"No, Mr. Walsh, we are not going to kill you."

"So why the black hoods? Are you guys really all that ugly that you're afraid we might ralph on your carpets in here?"

"You'll have to excuse his crude talk," Meagan explained, "he's American."

"Yes, Miss Flynn, we know."

"And that's another thing — how do you guys know our names?"

"We know a lot of things about you, Mr. Walsh. Please do not be alarmed."

I was, of course. Alarmed, that is. First Jacob got kidnapped by the Illuminati and then I found myself in the same sort of circumstances. In the back of my mind I was thinking that we should have just taken those old journals out into the back yard of Platt Hall, doused them with gasoline and tossed a match on them. At that moment I could have been sitting in my favorite booth at Jeff's Seafood with a nice broiled talapia and a glass of fine, white wine worried about nothing. Instead, I was riding in the back of a van in Spain with a bad-ass C.I.A. babe and a bunch of scary-looking guys with curly black hair and halting English.

Oddly though, they didn't handcuff us or in any way restrain us. I suppose that, if we'd given them any grief, they might have. After a while, I felt the van stop and then I could hear a sound like some sort of mechanical whirring and high-pitched rumbling from in front of us, when it stopped, the van rolled forward — slowly for a short distance — and then stopped again. I heard that same mechanical sound again but then it was coming from behind us. A garage door, I thought; it sort of made sense. That meant that we were inside a building somewhere.

I heard the two front doors of the van open and could hear the shuffling of the men's clothing against the fabric of the seats as they climbed out and shut the doors behind themselves. A

Bob Pierce

moment later, the sliding door on the passenger side of the van slid open. I heard a voice from outside announce that we had arrived and that it was time for Meagan and I to get out.

"You first, Miss Flynn," the voice said. I could feel the bench seat that we had both been sitting on shift as she rose to her feet. "Careful, a step down," the voice said as she reached her foot down to the concrete floor and then climbed completely out of the van.

A voice from behind me announced then that it was my turn. I felt his hands grip my upper arm firmly, but not too aggressively, and guide me to my feet. I began to stand up, but he pulled back on my arm "mind your head, Mr. Walsh." Still inside the van, the ceiling was not high enough to stand completely upright so, somewhat hunched over, I inched my way toward the open door. Voices from outside the van directed me to step off from the van's floor and step down to the ground. The man's hand on my arm helped me keep my balance until I had both feet on the ground.

I could hear several voices all around me and a lot of activity. The voices and other noises echoed as though we were in a large, open space. The men who had abducted us from the sidewalk in front of the hotel spoke English to us, but with a very thick accent that I had a lot of trouble placing. The voices that I heard inside that building around us spoke in another language which I assumed was the native language those other men spoke when they weren't addressing American tourists. I'm really not fluent in any other language but English, but I have a pretty good ear for the sound of certain languages such as French, Spanish, Chinese, Canadian and German, but the sound of the speech of these men (and they were all male voices that I was hearing) I just couldn't put my finger on. The accents, though, that I was hearing were reminiscent of some that I'd often hear whenever I'd visit New York City, particularly the Bronx or Queens; some of the shop owners and street vendors came to mind. I had never paid much specific attention to them before, it was all just sort of the background sound of the city and its many integrated cultures.

We were led to a room somewhere off of the large-sounding space where all of the activity was, and once a door was closed behind us, the sounds were almost completely muffled. We were guided to a couple of chairs and directed to sit down. I heard the door open and close again and someone come into the room.

"Gentlemen, it is alright to remove the hoods," another voice I'd not heard yet with the same thick accent directed.

In a moment, the black cloth hoods were lifted from our heads. We found ourselves in a room about twenty by twenty feet across with a pair of large steel tables in the center and a few chairs scattered around. There were some rack cases with all sorts of electronics in them and cables hanging out of either end at one end of the table and a man with a pair of headphones sitting in front of them, studying the screen of a laptop computer off to one side and making notes on a pad at the edge of the table top. Behind him was a large chalk board that looked as though it had been there for many decades. The walls were otherwise stark and blank and looked like they had served this facility for many, many years without having been repainted or cleaned.

I looked up and one of the men grabbed an empty chair and carried it over to where Meagan and I were sitting side by side. He turned it around so that the back of the chair faced us and he sat down straddling the seat.

"My name is Gideon Erdan. I am so sorry to have had to bring you in here so abruptly, but you really gave us no choice." I recognized his voice as the man who had last entered the room after us.

"Gideon, an interesting name. Obviously, you already know who we are," I observed. "Why are we here? What did we do that gave you no choice but to kidnap us off the street?"

"Kidnap? No, no, Mr. Walsh. We just saved you."

Bob Pierce

"Saved us, from what?"

"From yourselves, from doing something so amazingly — what's the word?"

"Stupid?" Meagan offered.

"Eh, 'stupid' — yes."

"What are you talking about?"

"Did you honestly believe that you two would be able to charge into the Mans DeLoyola by yourselves and rescue your friend?"

"And live to talk about it?" Another man standing behind Gideon chimed in.

"We knew it was dangerous," I argued.

"Was foolish, my friend. You would never have come out alive."

"So you kidnapped us to save us — why?"

"Because, if we let you go ahead and kill yourselves in this futile effort, you may well have compromised our plans."

"Your plans? Who *are* you people?"

"We are a specialty team that was put together to rescue Jacob Goodspeed and keep the secret of the journals safe."

"Oh? Put together by whom?"

"We are working with the true owners of the journals — on their behalf."

"My great, great grandfather wrote those journals. If you're working for their rightful owner, you'd be working for me. And, honestly, I don't remember calling in any special teams of any sort to help, I don't have that card in my Rolodex."

"We have a very old arrangement with the Poor Knights of Antioch, I believe you've heard of them."

"The Templars, yes. So who are *you*?"

"Our agreement goes back to the centuries before the Poor Knights, with the warrior order that preceded them. They are a small band with fierce abilities to defend themselves in close combat, but they do not have the ability to handle such tasks as this one. That is where we are called in to help."

"You're not Balkan, that accent of yours, that's not Slavic. You're Israeli, aren't you. Mossad? You've *got* to be kidding me?"

Erdan smiled and then looked up and around the room, then turned back to me and answered, "obviously, I cannot respond to that."

"Or deny it, either."

"Mr. Walsh, we, too, have prepared a plan of attack on the Mans DeLoyola. With greater resources and training, it takes on a much more, uh, dimension, than the plan you contrived in your hotel room; and much greater probability of success. But we also came upon the same problem that you did and I must say that when we heard of your solution, we immediately incorporated it into our own plan."

"You were listening in to our conversation in the hotel room? You bugged the hotel?"

"No, Mr. Walsh, we would not waste such effort and resources when we could just listen in to someone else's devices."

"You mean somebody else bugged the hotel and you bugged their bug like the N.S.A?"

"No, the N.S.A. listens in on you, we listen in on the N.S.A."

"Hmph, some sort of poetic justice in that but, frankly, makes me all the more paranoid."

"There is no privacy in the twenty-first century, Mr. Walsh. It's all just a paper front."

I looked over at Meagan, she hadn't said much of anything thus far, "did you know anything about these guys?"

"Well, of course I've heard of the Mossad, but I wasn't aware of this operation, no."

"So you think these guys are Mossad, too, then?"

"I can't say for sure."

"You're C.I.A., don't you spooks all know each other?"

"We don't have a lot of contact with the Mossad, nobody

does. That's why they're so good at what they do."

"But it looks like we don't have much of a choice but to cooperate with these guys then?"

"Aye, it would seem."

I looked back up at Erdan, "I want to go in with you guys. I want to be there to help rescue Jacob."

"That is actually part of our plan, for both of you to join us. Certainly, Miss Flynn is a capable agent and should be able to handle herself in such an operation and you, well, from what I heard about you on that bridge in Dublin, I have no doubt you'll be alright. Just don't go running off on your own."

"Fine, I'm good with that."

"Miss Flynn, this is far from your jurisdiction. You can opt out or come along; it is entirely your choice."

"Aye, you can count me in. This creepy American has saved my butt more than once, I suppose I owe him one."

"'Creepy American'? After I patched you up and bought you Munchkins?"

"Aye, but I'm always thinking that you're undressing me with your mind. That's creepy."

"Right now though, it's workin' for me."

She just shook her head in disgust and turned to Erdan and asked, "so what exactly is your plan and how do we figure into it?"

"Our strategan has been reworking our plans after we'd heard your idea, Mr. Walsh, and everyone will be gathering in here shortly for a briefing. You'll hear the whole plan then."

Just then there was a knock on the door, one of the men standing behind Erdan opened the door and spoke quietly with the man who was standing outside. They spoke for just a minute or two and the man outside walked away. The man by the door then told Erdan that the other team leader was ready to make his presentation and was gathering the others together to join us in the room.

"Excellent," Erdan replied, then turned to me and Meagan, "we will have to make some room."

We got up from our chairs and pushed them to the walls and then drifted to the back of the room as the other (presumed) Mossad commandos came in. Altogether, there were eight of them. We'd hear later that there were two teams of four. The last man to come into the room carried an armful of papers and a large roll like a map. As he came in, Erdan steered him over to where Meagan and I were standing to introduce him.

"Mr. Walsh, Miss Flynn, this is Moshe Levin, he's the leader of Team Two who will be making entry at the rear of the building."

We shook hands and I asked, "from the rear? It's a sheer drop to the ocean back there."

"Yes, it is, Mr. Walsh," Erdan interjected. "Please be patient, all will be explained."

"It was a pleasure to meet both of you," Levin graciously said as he turned and walked to the other end of the room and set down his papers on the end of the table next to the racks of electronics. He took the rolled up paper and hung it on the chalkboard, it was a plan of the Mans showing the layout of all three floors and the basement.

The other seven men gathered around either side of the table to get as close a look as possible as Levin began to explain.

"As you already know, we have two teams here for this operation. Team One will be entering from the front, Team Two will enter from the rear. At midnight, Team Two will be brought to the beach just east of the canal, here," he stood next to a large blow-up of a satellite photo of the area and pointed to a crescent-shaped beach to the right of a long, rectangular channel that cut through the eastern portion of the city. He zeroed in on what looked like a sea wall at the eastern end of the beach, just before the steep hills and cliffs rose up around the clusters of red-tile-roofed buildings in the valley.

"From there, we will paddle out and around this peninsula, which should give us good cover until we come into a small cove on the other side. The white water breakers just behind the Mans will put us onto the rocks at the base of the cliffs. It will be tricky, but the tides will be ebbing so the breakers will be at a minimum. Our intelligence tells us that there is little or no security back there until we reach the top of the cliffs and the patios behind the building. We will hold our positions at the precipice until we get the 'go' order at dawn."

He then pointed to Erdan and continued, "Team One will arrive about an hour before sunrise. Van one will drop off Uri at the cable vault, here," he pointed to a red circle on the winding road leading up the mountain that appeared to be about half a mile from the Mans, "and then continue to the gates of the Mans and drop off Reuven so that he can take up his position behind the wall to lay down cover fire for Team One when they enter. The van will circle back around and pick up Uri and bring him, with the rest of the team, to the wall near the gates.

"Uri," he looked at a man with a close-cropped black beard standing across the table from me and Meagan, "you will then fix the charges to the gate to blow the mechanical opening arms away. In the mean time, Team One will find cover among the trees and foliage around the wall and across the street from the gates."

"At dawn, Gideon will give the signal. The power cables and the gates will be detonated simultaneously. In the short window before the generators restore power to the building, Team One will rush in the front gates and find cover wherever you can to make your way to the building. Reuven will take out any hostiles on the porch, the portico or anywhere else he can while you work your way forward. At the same time, Team Two will come over the cliffs and enter from the rear. We will have charges to blast through the doors if we need to — do not take time to pick locks. The windows have iron grating behind them so we cannot simply smash the glass and enter.

"Team Two will sweep the first floor and eliminate every hostile that we encounter. As we spread out, the attention should be removed from the front of the building and Team One can come up the steps to the portico and enter from the front," he pointed to the front and rear entrances on the floor plan of the first floor. "From there, you will rush to the back of the great room to the stairwell to the second floor; that is where we believe the target is located. Team Two will have your back as you go up the stairs.

"Once on the second floor, Team One will spread out and do a room-by-room search for the target. Any hostiles encountered are to be eliminated, we will take no prisoners. Team Two will secure the back stairwell from the kitchen area to prevent any escape from the second floor," he pointed to a cluster of small rooms in the northwest corner of the first floor plan.

"Once the target is secured, everyone returns to the main stairwell to make our escape. Any questions?"

I raised my hand.

"Yes, Mr. Walsh."

"What about me and Meagan?"

"Mr. Walsh, it will be your job to identify Mr. Goodspeed. Our intelligence has not been able to produce any reliable images of him, so we will be relying on your eyes. You will follow Team One through the front doors and up the stairs to the second floor. I will brief you and Miss Flynn on the specifics when we're done here."

I nodded my agreement.

"Any additional questions?" No response, it seemed that everyone knew just what they were expected to do. "Alright then. Let's get everything ready and then get some sleep. Team Two rolls out in," he pulled back the sleeve of his shirt to check his watch, "in just over seven hours."

And, with that, the other six members of the team got up and walked back out into the big warehouse space to complete their preparations, the one man who was obsessively focused on the computer screen and other electronics at the table, remained at his task with his headphones wrapped over his scalp (presumably snooping in on the N.S.A. or Interpol or some-one). Meagan and I stayed where we were standing in the back of the room as the crowd thinned out.

Levin lagged behind and then walked up to us, "Mr. Walsh, do you have any tactical experience at all?"

"Well, I did shoot it out with some bad guys on a bridge in Dublin and then drove a big ol' Mercedes full of bullet holes in a pretty wild car chase through the streets. Does that count?"

"Not really. Why don't you two come with me, I'll give you a quick primer."

He led us out into the warehouse. This was the first good look I had of what was going on in there. On several folding tables were rows of guns, black canvas packs of various sizes and a lot of other gear that I'm still not entirely sure how to identify (except that most of it was black). Several of the other men were busy at these tables. Parked beyond were two vans, the white one that we had been brought in and a blue one. The blue one was lettered to look like it belonged to the local water company and the white van was in the process of having letter-ing added to it to make it look like something the local power company would be using.

Levin led us to one of the tables. Laid across it in a neat row were a number of identical machine guns laid side by side. He picked one up and held it so that I could see it clearly as he explained, "this, Mr. Walsh, is a Heckler and Koch MP5 sub-machine gun."

"I expected you guys to be using Uzis."

"We do still use Uzis, they have certain characteristics that make them best applicable to certain scenarios. For this opera-tion, however, the MP5 is a better choice. Among other rea-sons, the MP5 is made in Germany. We will carry nothing into this mission that is made in Israel. Should we lose any gear in the heat of the exchange or if any man is hurt badly enough that he must be left behind, there is nothing to tie us or this operation to Isreal."

"What about the credo: 'no man left behind'?"

"We do not adhere to such sentiments. Every man on this team knows that he is not more important than the mission. If we can, we will bring everyone home, but if we have to, we will leave men behind to assure a successful mission."

"That's cold."

"Our people have survived as a nation for many thousands of years. We all know what a sacrifice may be necessary for us to remain as a nation. Israel is not just a country, Mr. Walsh, it is a people."

I was taken aback by the dedication that these men have to their mission; success at all costs and each was willing to lay down their own lives for it. It was an ideal that, frankly, I could not understand. My sensibilities, perhaps, are too grounded in western values and individualism to be able to wrap my mind around it. I was just hoping that I wouldn't be the one to make any of those guys have to make that sacrifice and, even more so, that I wouldn't be expected to.

He held the weapon in his right hand by its pistol grip, "the models we use have a collapsible shoulder stock, laser sights and silencers. Many of our team do not use the laser but, Mr. Walsh, I want you to use yours," he depressed a pressure switch on the pistol grip and, across the room, a small, bright red spot of light appeared on the wall. "The MP5 is not a target rifle that you would take careful aim with before firing. It is a point-and-shoot weapon. These men are highly trained with it and instinctively know how to point and aim. You will extend the shoulder stock, plant the weapon against your shoulder and point it at your target. Whatever that red dot appears on is where the bullet will hit. Understand?"

"Yes, I got it."

"Miss Flynn, I assume you're checked out on the MP5?"

"Aye, just had my annual quals."

"You will excuse me, then, if this is all redundant for you." He turned to me and handed me the gun with the right side of it up. "Do you see this switch on the side? That is the selector switch. It will set the gun to a safe condition, single-shot semi-automatic mode, a three-shot burst and then full automatic. Because of the high cyclic rate of this weapon, you can easily fire all of the rounds in the magazine in a matter of seconds. For that reason, Mr. Walsh, I want you to only use the three-shot burst mode. Grip the weapon as you would to fire it," I grabbed the tapered fore-stock and pressed the butt of the shoulder stock against the hollow of my right shoulder and then gripped the pistol grip with my right hand. "Good. Now reach out with your trigger finger alongside the receiver and feel for the selector." I stretched out my finger and could feel the thin tab on the switch. I then pushed it and pulled on it to rotate the switch around as he told me what position it was as it clicked from one to the next. It was really pretty idiot-proof, though I knew full well that I could likely disprove that.

He took the gun away from me and set it back down on the table and then we walked over to another table where there were a number of bulletproof vests stacked up. He handed one to me and then picked up another one and held it up to Meagan and commented that it could be adjusted to be a bit smaller for her. She was familiar with these vests and just took it from him and began pulling in the various tabs and straps to fit it to herself as Levin began his explanation to me.

"This vest is made of Kevlar which is essentially bulletproof but, for safety's sake, there is an additional steel plate here in the center of the chest to protect your heart. On the outside are a number of pockets and pouches; you won't be using most of them except for these two rows here along the chest. The upper row will be for extra magazines for your sidearm and the lower row will be for magazines for your primary — your MP5. The pouch below that on the left is for your radio."

I turned the vest around and looked at the front of it and saw what he was referring to and then he helped me get it on and began adjusting the side straps and the back to get it to fit best.

After we had finished fitting our respective vests, we carried them with us as he continued to explain the use of the handguns that we would be using and the radio gear with a small earbud in each ear. When we were done, I was beginning to get this foreboding feeling of just how grave this whole business was and the potential for really bad, even deadly, mistakes to be made.

"Can I ask you a question?" I queried.

"What is it, Mr. Walsh?"

"Well, as you've noted, I'm not really experienced at this sort of thing. Meagan here is a pro, but I'm not much more than a tourist with a gun. What if I accidently shoot one of your guys?"

Levin leaned back against the table and folded his arms across his chest, "you need not concern yourself about that. My team is not only highly-trained in their specialties, but also sworn to their service. They are fully accepting of the possibility that they may have to sacrifice their lives for the mission — whatever that mission may be. I don't want you to hesitate for a second, Mr. Walsh. You point your weapon and you fire; don't take time out to ponder if it's a good guy or a bad guy if you're confronted. The vests that we all will be wearing should be a great deal of protection and, besides, I'm not all that confident of your marksmanship so I believe our chances are still pretty good even if you do fire on one of us."

Not exactly a Yogi Bera-style pep-talk.

"One more important point, Mr. Walsh: do not go off on your own. When we get inside the building, it will be chaotic and there will be shooting and running all around you. You will be in constant contact with the team on your radio, if you find yourself separated, tell someone where you are and then stay there until someone gets to you. When you hear the order to evacuate, you stay with the group and follow them out. Do you understand?"

"Yes, I understand."

"Good. There are some foam mats over there behind the vans. Why don't the two of you try and get some rest. Team One will be gathering to head out at around three o'clock."

"Thanks," I said as he turned and walked away toward the blue van to help the others load up. I turned to Meagan, "what do you think?"

"What do you mean?"

"What do you think? About all of this? You're C.I.A., you've done this sort of thing before. Do you think this is a good plan?"

"From what I can tell, aye, I do believe it's a good plan — far better than what we had come up with."

"I have to tell you, I'm still not comfortable with these guys. Your friend Eamon seemed a little sketchy to me but these guys actually scare me."

"If they *really are* Mossad, I don't think you have anything to worry about. Their mission, for which they are all willing to lay down their lives, is to rescue your friend Goodspeed."

"Yeah, but then what?"

"I don't understand."

"What is their motive? Why are they doing this? I have to wonder — I mean — Jacob is the only person on the planet who knows where those journals are hidden. Are they rescuing him just to be able to squeeze him for the information just like the Illuminati who have him now are trying to do? Are we going to have to rescue him from his rescuers when this is all over?"

"I think you're being paranoid, Mr. Walsh."

"So far, 'paranoid' has been working for me."

"Is that the name of your guardian angel?"

"All kidding aside; I don't trust these guys any farther than I could throw any of them. But I trust you."

"What are you saying?"

"When I was a kid, I took the Red Cross swimming course and one of the things that they told us to do was never go swimming without a buddy and make sure that, when we were in the water, to keep an eye on him and always know where our buddy was. When we get in there, would you be that buddy and stick with me? Help me find Jacob and make sure we get out okay?"

"Under one condition."

"Condition? What condition?"

"That when you're keeping your eye on me, in your mind I remain fully-dressed."

"I'll try, really I will."

✵ ✵ ✵ ✵ ✵

Pope Linus II stood in his office speaking with a pair of his cadre of inner-circle cardinals when there was a knock at the door. An aide announced that Cardinal Giulio Medici was outside waiting to speak with him.

"Gentlemen," the Pontiff announced to the two men in his office, "Cardinal Medici and I need to speak on a matter of great importance. Would you be so kind as to excuse us," he extended his hand so that each man could kneel before him, kiss his ring and then bow as he left the office.

The Pope walked to the windows across the room from the door as it opened and the cardinal, dressed in brilliant red robes, entered the room. He paused just inside the door and bowed, waiting for Linus' signal to approach in the extension of his hand. Medici walked to the Pope's presence, genuflecting onto a trapezoidal patch of sunlight projected across the carpet from the windows beyond and kissed the Papal ring.

"Rise, my son. What have you to report?"

"Your Holiness. We have the historical society director, a Jacob Goodspeed, in custody. The Grand Inquisitor, Cardinal de Recalde, is preparing to question him in San Sebastian at this hour."

"He has not volunteered any information as of yet?"

"No, Holiness, he has not."

"Please be sure to impress upon the good cardinal the gravity of this situation. It is imperative that those journals be found."

"Señor Goodspeed is an elderly man and appears to be in frail health. I am certain that Cardinal de Recalde will be judicious in applying his methods lest we lose this opportunity."

"The integrity of this church is not worth the life of a solitary man."

"But, Your Holiness, if Goodspeed should die before divulging the whereabouts of the journals, we will have lost our opportunity altogether. Before leaving his home in America, he hid the volumes. He alone knows where they are hidden."

Pope Linus turned toward the window, "come, look out and tell me what you see."

The cardinal stepped up beside the Pontiff, taking care to stand just a half step back from where he stood, and gazed down from the window at the sun-drenched expanse of St. Peter's Square spread out before them.

"I see the square, alive with the milling of people. Some in small groups, some two-by-two and some alone."

"Yes, people. Tourists, pilgrims, all believers. They come to St. Peter's because they believe. For the sake of this church, we must not allow them to stop believing for, if they do, this institution will fall as a house of cards."

"Sí, Holiness."

"The journals are but bread crumbs on the trail to our true goal."

"John."

"John. The Templars who protect him and his secret are also actively seeking those journals. If you are able to get the information out of the American, do not recover the journals. Wait and watch. Allow them to search, give them clues to help, even allow them to find, that is your opportunity to trace them back to wherever they have secreted John away. You are to recover John and return him here. He belongs here — with us."

"And what of the Templars?"

"They'd outlived their worth centuries ago."

"I understand."

"Very well. I look forward to your next report. You may go."

"Thank you, Holiness."

A very long night

Even though I hadn't had a whole lot of sleep in the previous couple of days, there was no way I was going to be able to drift off lying on a two-inch-thick rectangle of foam rubber on a concrete floor — it was going to be a long, long, night.

The Mossad guys had shut off most of the lights, but there was always someone milling about working on something or other, trying to be as quiet as they could. At about eleven o'clock, the four commandos on Team Two opened up the back doors of the blue van and stuffed in the rubber boat that they planned to paddle around the rocks that night. I wasn't sleeping anyway so I got up and lent a hand. We had to get it in kitty-corner which created a triangular void just large enough for them to slide in their gear bag, four paddles and two commandos before swinging the doors closed.

One of the other men got into the driver's seat and Moshe Levin was headed toward the switch to open the overhead door, but I told him to go ahead and get into the van and I walked over and waited by the wall beside the door. Once they were ready and gave me a nod, I pressed the big green button and the door began to roll open. I was certain that the loud, clattering noise would wake up everyone else in the building but nary another soul stirred. These guys seemed to be able to sleep on the edge of a fence in a thunderstorm. When the van was completely outside of the warehouse, I pressed the red button and the door rolled back down with an equally obnoxious noise.

In the dim light, I found my way back to my foam rubber mat behind the white van. As I sat back down on the hard floor I could hear Meagan ask me quietly, "was that Team Two heading out?"

"Yeah, go back to sleep. We don't have to be up for a few more hours."

"Sleep? Have *you* been able to sleep?"

"I think I may have dozed off a few times but, no, I haven't really been able to sleep."

"I was just falling asleep when that big door opened up. I don't think I'll be able to sleep any more tonight."

"Sorry. That door made a huge racket. I don't know how those guys could still be sleeping."

"Their training. They can control their melatonin and adrenaline at will. When it's time to sleep, they sleep. Their body clock will start pumping adrenaline when it's time to wake up again."

"That's weird. That's like some kind of Frankenstein flick or something."

"Maybe, but it works. They'll be nicely rested when it's time to go."

"Well, I'm gonna just stretch out again and, even if I can't actually fall asleep, I can close my eyes and get a couple of hours' rest. That's gotta be worth something."

"Aye, good idea. Good night, Mr. Walsh."

I laid out on my back and tried my best to get comfortable with my bulletproof vest under my head as the worst substitute for a pillow that I'd ever experienced, "good night, Meagan."

* * * * *

The four-man Team Two drove the blue water company

van in a peripheral route around the busy heart of the city. San Sebastian is, among other things, a very popular tourist destination that's known for its sophisticated epicurian fetes. The streets throughout the core of the city are dotted with restaurants and pubs while the streets and sidewalks are often packed with people and traffic. Midnight was still early for most of the revelers who venture there from all over Europe and the world, so a circuitous route actually saved time.

The commandos drove through the darkened streets to the western end of the town and the foothills of the steep mountains that abruptly surround the city and drove a lonely road to the eastern end of the broad beach that lines the sheltered eastern cove. The van pulled up in the darkness to a chain stretched across between two steel posts, keeping those not authorized from using the access road reserved for emergency and rescue vehicles leading down to the water's edge. Moshe Levin climbed out of the passenger seat with a pair of bolt-cutters in his hand and approached the end of the chain that was padlocked to a large ring welded to the steel post. He cut the padlock and then walked the end of the chain across to the other post and allowed the van to pass through, then using a duplicate padlock that he had brought with him in his pocket, secured the chain again so that anyone passing by on the road would not see anything out of place.

When he got back into the van, they drove along the narrow, sand-swept, crumbling asphalt down the hill along the eastern end of the beach toward the water. Just before they reached the high-tide line, they drove the van into the bushes at the foot of the steep hillside and shut off the lights and the engine. Levin and the driver walked around to the back of the van and pulled open the two doors, then helped the two men who were squeezed into the narrow void space beneath the rubber boat out onto the sand.

The four men then grabbed hold of the boat and pulled it out of the back of the van and set it down onto the beach.

While Levin and the driver pulled out a camoflage net and began to spread it up and over the roof of the van, the other two
men lashed their gear bag into the center of the boat and set
the paddles inside it. When the van was well-hidden by the
net, all four men donned night-vision goggles and pulled black
balaclavas down over their heads and faces, then each grabbed
a corner of the boat and carried it to the water, wading out into
the surf until they were about waist-deep and then, one-by-
one, they climbed in and began paddling out from the beach to
round the end of the rocky peninsula.

Because the surf coming into the shore would swirl and
break over the jagged boulders along the shoreline, they kept
their boat out at a safe distance in the cove to keep from being
tossed up and onto the rocks. It was slow going, paddling by
hand against the in-rushing surf, but they eventually rounded
the tip of the peninsula and began paddling toward the cliffs
below the Mans DeLoyola. From their vantage point, they
could not see the building itself, but could see a glow from the
security lights at the top of the cliff which was all the more
discernable with their goggles. The tricky part was to keep the
boat stable and allow the breakers to swell and lift the boat
up and over some of the largest boulders at the foot of the
rock face until they could maneuver themselves to a narrow
strip of rocky sand and gravel along the base of the nearly-
vertical cliffs. As they deftly pushed and strained against the
swirling tide, they paddled through the rocks and made it to
the narrow beach.

With a rope in his hand, one of the men perched in the
bow of the little boat, climbed out and steadied the craft as
the other three men climbed out and onto the beach. Once the
boat was secured between some of the rocks to keep it from
being seen or washing back out into the cove where it might
be discovered, they removed the black gear bag and attached a
long rope to it which was then tied around the waist of one of
the commandos. The heavy bag contained all of their prima-

ry weapons, explosives and other specialty gear which would make their climb up the cliffs awkward if any of them were to try and carry it with them. They would climb up in stages and draw up the bag whenever they had reached a logical place to move up from. It would be a free climb, they could not risk attracting attention with the noise of hammering in pitons and running climbing ropes up the side of the cliffs. It would be dangerous, especially at the beginning. The high ground where the Mans was built curves away quickly to a steep hill that then is violently eroded into deep crags until finally falling away to a sheer, rocky drop to the water's edge. From the base of the cliff to the point at which they could conceivably walk virtually upright would be a precarious climb of about one hundred feet and then, from there, about another hundred feet to the terraced plaza and porches at the rear of the building. Somewhere near those porches, they would need to find a secure place to stay hidden until getting the "go" sign over the radio from Gideon leading Team One.

The sky was beginning to brighten and they had climbed as far as they'd dared and held up just below the crest of the rise behind the Mans at the top of the cliffs. The ground was steeply sloped, but not sheer, so they could settle in to wait out of sight for the radio call. They pulled up their gear bag and distributed the MP5s, magazines of extra ammunition, bullet-proof vests and other gear and then tossed the empty bag down the embankment to get it out of view. Once they had themselves totally prepared there was nothing left to do but wait.

* * * * *

Jacob Goodspeed was led into a dimly-lit room by two men in white shirts and black slacks. They each held onto his upper arms, one on either side, and walked with him gently guiding him to a chair that sat in the middle of the sparsely-appointed room. The plain, metal chair belied the opulent appointments of the richly paneled walls and ceiling and the intricately par-queted floor beneath. The chair stood on a rectangular plastic tray about three feet square with a raised lip all around its pe-rimeter of about two inches height. The chair and the tray sat upon a well-worn, patterned carpet that extended several feet in each direction.

Jacob sat in the chair and just rested his hands on his thighs as he watched the two men go about their tasks around him. From the shadows to his right, he could hear the sound of a cart of some sort being rolled toward him. As it got closer, he could see that it was a wooden table, about waist high, and about two feet across and three feet wide. The man who pulled it toward him, rolled it onto the carpet and arranged it at a per-pendicular angle to the chair a couple of feet to Jacob's right.

As he turned to walk away, the other man appeared with a stainless steel tray that he set down on the table and then re-moved a white cloth that covered its contents. When he did, it revealed an assortment of gleaming stainless steel and chrome surgical instruments of virtually every imaginable description. Jacob's eyes widened at the sight.

"What are these for?" he asked, but got no response. "Hey! Buddy! I'm talkin' to you!" Still he got no response as the man walked away.

In a few minutes, the man returned carrying a stack of neatly-folded white towels which he set down on the table be-side the tray. Jacob was getting nervous. Up to that moment he had been having an interesting, if not somewhat strange, ad-venture of a vacation. But things were starting to look serious. He started to get up from the chair but, as he did, two hands clamped down on his shoulders and pushed him back down.

"Señor, must I bind you to the chair?"

"Huh? What?" he looked around him and saw the other man in the white shirt standing behind him with his hands still on his shoulders. "Uh, no, I guess not."

"Bueno," the man removed his hands and then disappeared into the shadows once again, only to return with a large overhead surgical lamp on a tall, rolling stand. He wheeled it up to a place directly in front of Jacob, just at the edge of the carpet and then angled the big reflector head so that the cluster of lights faced directly at Jacob's face. The lamps, thus far, had not been turned on but he got the idea.

The first man returned and the two of them stood at the edge of the carpet near the large lamp stand and talked quietly to each other. Jacob couldn't understand what they were saying; he knew a smattering of Spanish but what little bit he could hear of their hushed voices was quite different, though still similar. The two men were Basque and spoke a dialect that was common to that region. But he didn't have too much time to muse about the men's conversation before the door from the hall opened again behind him and he heard limping footfalls approach accompanied by the rhythmic wood-on-wood "click" of the tip of a cane against the parquet floor.

"Señor Goodspeed," a gravelly voice spoke from behind.

Jacob swiveled his head around but didn't see the man dressed in all black until he was almost upon him.

"Oh, it's you," he said with a tone of apprehension.

"Are you comfortable?"

"No, not really, but I'm not dead so at least that's something."

The dark man in black smiled as he hung the crook of his cane on the edge of the table, "yes, well, we shall see about that."

"Who the heck are you?"

"I thought I had introduced myself on the airplane."

"Yeah, Cardinal something or other. But who are you really, and what were you before? What did you do and what did you think?"

"You ask a lot of questions for a man in such a dire circumstance."

"I'm rambling. I do that when I'm nervous."

"You have been the picture of calm and composure thus far. I cannot believe that you are nervous," he turned to the two men in the shadows and nodded and then, suddenly, the big surgical lamp came alive, assaulting Jacob with its blinding lights. He squinted and shaded his eyes with his hand, ducking his head to try and keep some sort of view of the sinister cardinal.

"This isn't helping."

"Oh, but it is," de Recalde said with a sneer. He moved to stand in front of Jacob and cast his own shadow across his face to relieve him of the blinding glare. Jacob lowered his hand from his eyes to see the cardinal standing before him with a black leather zippered pouch in his hands. "You have seen the instruments I have at my disposal to work with already. You may have noticed the plastic tray under your chair, that is there to catch any blood or other bodily fluids that you may shed as we proceed. You are an intelligent man, Señor Goodspeed, I believe you understand what is about to happen here. So I ask you, to save yourself from all that you may be imagining and so much more: where are the journals hidden?"

"Are you going to kill me?"

"No, Señor Goodspeed, I am not. On that tray are pre-filled syringes of adrenaline for your heart, local anesthesia to deaden the pain in certain areas, tourniquets to stop profuse bleeding and a soldering iron to cauterize wounds to keep you alive until you are ready to tell me what I want to know. I even have a defibrillator to restart your heart should the need arise. You may yet die in this exercise, but I will not kill you."

"And all I have to do is tell you is where the journals are and you'll let me go?"

"You shall be on the next airplane back to America."

"Really?"

"Yes, really."

"I would have to be some special kind of stupid to believe that, wouldn't I? I mean, you can't afford to kill me and *I know* you can't afford to kill me so you're gonna try and scare me into telling you?"

"Do you know who I am, Señor Goodspeed? I am the Grand Inquisitor of the Holy Church Office. I am expert in the ancient art of convincing godless souls such as you to divulge information and I am anointed by the Holy See in the name of God to this task."

"So, what you're saying is that you torture people for God?"

"You are trying my patience, señor."

"I've told your buddies on the plane and back in Vermont that those journals are the property of the Montgomery Historical Society and cannot be removed from our archives. Like anyone else, if you'd like to make an appointment..." de Recalde swiped his black leather-clad backhand across Jacob's face, snapping his head to one side with the impact, the sound of the leather striking Jacob's skin echoed in the wood-sheathed room.

"That is enough, Señor Goodspeed! You leave me little choice." He unzipped the leather case in his hands and spread it open like a book, laying it on the table on top of the glistening tools. Jacob watched intently as he removed a small glass bottle filled with clear liquid from a pouch inside and shook it and set it down on the table. He then removed a syringe and peeled off its sterile plastic wrapping. He lifted up the bottle and held it inverted as he stabbed the rubber cap with the needle and drew out a small dose of the drug inside.

"Truth serum?" Jacob asked.

"Very good, Señor Goodspeed. This is a very special serum, it's called SP-117. You see, the human brain will naturally respond to any question with the truth, we cannot help it. But we learn to mask the truth by crafting lies and diversions. If I were to ask you what color the sky was, for example, your brain instantly responds with 'azure', 'blue', but if you wanted to tell me something different you would have to consciously create a different answer. This drug blocks that ability in your brain so that, once it takes effect, you will no longer be able to avoid telling me the truth."

"Drugs, great, I can use the sleep."

"Sleep? No, señor, this drug will put you into a sort of twilight state, it will increase your adrenaline as your brain slips into a soft state of panicked calm. If you thought you were nervous earlier, you will become a quivering, paranoid — how do you Americans say? — basket case. You won't be sleeping for a very long time."

One of the men in the white shirts came up from behind Jacob and wrapped his arms around him, pinning him to the chair, while the other man grabbed his arm, pulled back his sleeve, and held it out straight so that de Recalde could find a good vein to inject the drug into. He quickly tied a rubber strap around Jacob's bicep and pulled it tight. He yanked off the black leather gloves on his hands and then slapped the soft flesh on the inside of his elbow joint, pausing to feel for a pulsing vein until he was satisfied that he'd located one. Then, with the syringe in his right hand poised to stab his arm, he asked Jacob one last time, "where have you hidden the journals?"

"No dice, pal! You gotta make an appointment like everyone else."

"Wrong answer, señor," he turned and positioned the point of the needle against Jacob's skin and then penetrated it into his vein. Slowly he pushed the plunger down to flow the drug into his body. The liquid burned in his flesh and Jacob gritted his teeth as the searing sensation spread up and down his arm. He arched his back as the fluid filled his vein and writhed in the chair, straining against the men who held him place.

Finally the last of the drug had been pushed out of the clear plastic cylinder and into Jacob's arm and de Recalde removed the needle, yanking off the rubber strap and daubing the drop of blood from the site with the corner of one of the white towels. The burning sensation subsided and Jacob relaxed his posture. The room was beginning to almost inperceptively feel as though it were moving around him, the blinding lights shining in his face just intensified the psychedelic effect.

"The drug takes about thirty minutes to take full effect, señor," the cardinal set the empty syringe onto the table and retrieved his cane, pulling his black leather gloves back onto his hands. "I will return and we shall begin in earnest."

Jacob hung his head and felt his body slowly going limp as he heard the cardinal walking away.

❋ ❋ ❋ ❋ ❋

I guess I had actually dozed off that night because I was awakened by a hand shaking me by my shoulder and calling out "Mr. Walsh, it's time."

I sat up on the thin foam rubber mat and rubbed my eyes. The lights were on in the big warehouse and there was a constant din of activity all around us. I looked over and saw Meagan standing, buckling the straps of her bullet proof vest. She looked down at me sitting on the floor, "Mr. Walsh, it's time to get ready. Get your vest on and gear-up."

"Yeah, yeah," I stretched out my arms as I yawned with a gaping wide mouth. I got to my feet and then bent down to pick up the vest that I'd been using as a pillow. I'd never put one of those on before so I examined it to see if I couldn't figure it out without asking for help, but Meagan saw my perplexity and came over to give me a hand. It was a lot simpler than I was thinking it would be and, once it was on, it seemed to fit pretty well although it seemed awfully stiff and I thought it might restrict my movements but she assured me that I'd get used to it and, besides, it well might save my life.

Good argument.

Reuven Stern, the team's sniper, came over to see how we were doing.

"I think I've got this thing on right, Meagan seemed to know what she was doing so she gave me a hand."

"Aye, he's all set."

"Excellent. Please come with me to get outfitted."

As we began to follow him around the van to the tables of guns and gear, Meagan asked if he might be able to find a rubber band for her hair.

"And I could use a breath mint," I added.

"I'm sure I can find a rubber band, I'll see what I can do for a breath mint."

He led us to one of the tables where Gideon was standing with two groupings of gear laid out for each me and Meagan, "good morning Miss Flynn, Mr. Walsh. I hope you got some rest last night."

"Some," I replied.

"Good. Mr. Walsh, would you please come around this side of the table." I walked around to where he was standing; he grabbed me by my vest and turned me to face him. Then he picked up a handful of steel magazines filled with 9mm bullets, "these are for your primary weapon, your MP5." Then he reached out and yanked open the velcro flap on a narrow pocket on the left side of my chest and inserted one of them and closed the flap over again. He then repeated the routine four more times. I was doing the math in my head, with those five magazines and the one that would be in the gun when we headed out, with thirty rounds in each one, I'd have a total of a hundred and fifty bullets and with five other members of our group going in the front door, we'd collectively have nine hundred shots. I was hoping that would be enough.

Gideon then reached down and picked up a smaller magazine, "these are for your sidearm, you have fifteen rounds in each one," he handed it to me and then yanked open another pouch on the front of the vest in a row just below the ones that he'd just filled, "they go in these, you have five of these, also." He then turned to Meagan, allowing me to stow away my own magazines and told her, "we were able to locate some magazines for your Sig, Miss Flynn. Finding forty caliber bullets was a little more challenging here in Europe, but we were able to locate one box, so I'm afraid we were only able to fill three magazines and part of a fourth."

"Aye, I'm sure that will be sufficient," she said, as she began picking up the magazines and inserting them into the pockets of her vest.

"As experienced as you are, I thought that you might not need as many bullets as your civilian partner might."

"Partner? No, he's not my partner."

"I thought we made a pretty good team," I protested, trying to add a little levity to the moment.

Meagan just leered at me as she continued putting away her magazines of forty caliber pistol rounds.

"You two remind me of my uncle Uri and aunt Aliza."

"I'm not sure how to take that," I commented as I slipped the last of my pistol magazines into its pocket.

"Married for forty-seven years. Bickering and joking with each other the whole time. You two remind me of a couple who have been married for many years — like them."

"Banish the thought," Meagan grumbled as she picked up the gear belt nearest to her on the table and began adjusting its length.

"It's less of a symbiotic relationship than it is an ambivalent one," I added.

Gideon looked at me for a moment with a gaze of confusion, but then just shrugged his shoulders and grabbed a belt similar to the one that Meagan was preparing for herself. He pulled out the nylon strap from the buckle and then instructed me to lift up the crotch flap in the front of my vest. When I did, he reached around me from behind and clipped the plastic buckle closed in front of me, wrapping the belt around me just below the bottom edge of my vest. I watched Meagan as she was getting hers positioned around herself to see how this thing was supposed to go. There were so many appendages and dangling bits on the belt that I was unclear just how it was supposed to attach to my body. Gideon came around in front of me and grabbed the buckle with his right hand and the end of the nylon strap with his left and pulled on it to cinch the belt up to fit me as tightly as it might be comfortable to move in.

"How is that, Mr. Walsh?"

I wiggled my hips a bit like a hula dancer and announced that it seemed to fit just fine.

He then showed me how to tie down the holster for my pistol by strapping it to my thigh and another pouch on the other leg. I didn't have anything to put in that pouch, but since it seemed to be permanently attached to the belt, if I hadn't strapped it down, it would have been flapping around loosely and, I guess, that would have been a bad thing.

He handed me the pistol and showed me how to load the magazine, rack the slide to load one round into the chamber and then click on the safety, then insert it into the holster strapped to my right leg.

Then he handed me the MP5, Moshe Levin had checked me out on it the evening before, but Gideon showed me how to load it, work the charging lever to arm it and then reminded me of how the selector switch worked so that I could set it to the safe position. The sling that went over my shoulder allowed the gun to be swung around pretty freely and would keep it always at the ready and prevent me from losing it.

When Gideon was done I looked up at Meagan, she was all fitted out and was tying her bright orange-red hair back with the rubber band that Reuven had found for her. We'd be wearing balaclavas when we would be going in, having her hair tied up would make it a lot easier to pull the fabric over her head without having to fumble. She'd clearly done this before.

When she was done I walked up to her, the two of us looking like some sort of S.W.A.T. team from the movies, "I see they found a rubber band for your hair."

"Aye, and someone had this," she nodded down at the table while she still had her two hands behind her head to a

Bob Pierce

small metal tin of Altoids mints.

"Oh, great," I reached down and picked up the package and flipped open the lid. I reached it out to Meagan; she smiled and took one of the mints and then I picked one out and put it into my mouth and closed the cover. I began to put the package into my pocket, but she stopped me, "oh, sorry, he wanted it back?"

"No," she took the tin container from me and gently shook it, it made a very noticeable rattling sound.

"Oh, right," I took out a second one and put it into my mouth, then just left the package on the table.

Gideon then walked out into the middle of the room and called everyone together. We joined with the other three men — all of us in black tech gear and armed to the teeth — and formed a circle. "Is everyone ready?" We all nodded and quietly replied that we were. "We will be heading out in just a few minutes." And with that announcement he and the other commandos closed their eyes, tipped their faces up toward the ceiling and held out their open palms. They were praying.

Now, I'm not a praying kind of guy. I wouldn't go so far as to categorize myself as a pagan, but if there's a god up there, somewhere, I wasn't really sure it would be very well received that we should have been praying to him to help us kill other people.

Meagan, however, went with the flow. In more of a western posture, she closed her eyes, bowed her head, folded her fingers together and let her hands hang down in front of her. I thought it best to do likewise, even if I was just doing it for show.

Gideon began by praying something in English, probably for my and Meagan's benefit. He prayed a few sentences about keeping us all safe, to help us see through the mission and to do God's will to keep the great secret intact. And then he prayed for a few minutes in Hebrew, some of it kind of lyrical, while the others joined in. After a moment or two, they all chimed in "amen" and we turned to load up in the van.

Gideon and our demolition expert, Uri Shelah, pulled on baggy, light blue work shirts over their vests. They would be riding up front and would be in view. The truck was lettered for the local electric utility so two men in blue work shirts would look normal to anyone who might see us out there. Gideon got behind the wheel, Uri stood by the door to push the buttons to raise and lower it to let us drive out, the rest of us got into the back. There were no windows, we couldn't see anything outside the van from there; I could hear the big door open and then, after we'd driven out and stopped, I could hear it roll closed again behind us. Once Uri was back inside, we were off.

It was still dark out, I could see that much out the windshield through the grate behind the front seats. We had to drive some distance from the city to get onto one of the long, winding roads that climbs up the steep hills back toward the sea and the cliffs where the Mans stood. Once out of the city's intersecting streets, it was a long ride devoid of any stops or turns. We drove for what seemed to be a much longer time than it actually was (those vans were not built for luxury or comfort), but eventually I could feel the van slow precipitously and pull off to the side of the road and then we came to a stop. We had reached the power company's cable vault. Gideon called back for someone of us to give Uri a hand getting the vault open. I needed to stretch my legs so I volunteered.

I climbed out of the van and followed Uri to a small enclosure fenced in with chain link. The headlights of the van helped illuminate the scene for us. He handed me a black canvas bag to hold while he cut the lock off of the gate and then swung it open. I followed him inside. He took the bag from me and set it down on a concrete slab and unzipped it. He then pulled out of it an L.E.D. head lamp that he strapped on across his forehead.

We stood on a raised slab of concrete, it was about twenty feet long and ten feet wide and the top of it was about two feet off of the ground. At one end were a pair of large, gray

Bob Pierce

metal boxes with rounded tops and some assorted labels on their sides. Before us was a diamond-plate steel panel about eight feet square set flush into the concrete with a hatch in the center of it. The door, I presumed.

He shone his light around the edged of the hatch and found what appeared to be a handle. It had a lock on it under a rubber cover that kept it from the elements. He had me fold the rubber flap back and hold it open for him while he picked the lock. It only took a minute or two and the lock was opened. We both then grabbed the heavy steel door and pulled it up and open, the hinges allowed it to be opened all the way until it laid flat on the concrete. He shone his light down into the opening and then looked up at me, "I'll climb down and then you hand me down the bag."

"Okay."

"And be careful with it, it's full of C-4 and detonators."

"Oh — right." I suddenly had a much greater respect for the rather plain-looking black canvas bag.

The plan was to let Uri set up to work his magic underground while we drove on to get Reuven Stern, our sniper, to his post so that he could get himself into a prime location to cover our advance across the front lawns and driveway to the entrance doors. I climbed back into the van and we drove on up the road toward the cliffs and the Mans DeLoyola. We drove past the gates to a slight bend in the road just beyond where we stopped and Reuven got out. He just shut the door behind himself with his sinister-looking sniper rifle in his hands and that was the last I would see of him for the next few hours.

We drove a little further up the road to a wide place where we could turn around. The plan then was to go and retrieve Uri and return to the Mans to get into position for the raid.

When we returned to the cable vault, there was a police car parked along side of the road and the officer standing there by the open gate talking with Uri. When we pulled up, the cop turned and looked at the van which (especially in the dark) looked very official. He walked up to the driver's side door and talked with Gideon who asked, "is there a problem, officer?"

"We received a notice from the alarm company that this facility had been opened, I was dispatched to come and check it out."

"Sí, we too got that notice. Seems we got here just before you. I dropped off our specialist to inspect the site while I drove up the road to inspect the switchers up there. Everything seems to be fine up the hill so we should be able to fix the problem right here, should not take very long."

With the officer's attention on Gideon in the van, Uri quietly moved around behind him and slowly approached.

"Well, I'm just doing my job," the officer said.

"And we do so appreciate it."

The officer didn't notice Uri creeping up on him from behind until it was too late, he quickly pressed a stun gun against the officer's neck and in a flash of electrical bolts, dropped him to the ground. Gideon called out again for some help and I again jumped out to lend a hand. We loaded the cop into the back seat of his car and then came back to the van.

"Are you ready?" Gideon asked Uri.

"Almost, the officer interrupted me. I need about ten more minutes."

"Alright, Mr. Walsh, you drive the officer's car back down the hill until you find somewhere that you can park it off the road. I'll follow you and bring you back. Hopefully, Uri will be ready when we return."

Uri immediately turned and jogged back to the hole in the ground where he had been working and I nodded to Gideon and ran to the patrol car. I climbed into the driver's seat, turned it around, and headed back down the hill.

I didn't have to go very far until I found a wide part in the road. I backed the car in to make it look like he might be doing a radar trap, though a very unlikely place to do so. When I had parked the car, Gideon helped me get the officer out of the back seat and prop him up behind the wheel. We handcuffed his wrist to the steering wheel and cut the wire to the microphone on his car's radio. I put on the parking lights and found a clipboard on the passenger seat.

"What are you doing?"

"I used to work for a newspaper many years ago and I wrote a story about a cop who used to park in a remote parking lot on the night shift and do his paperwork when things were quiet in town. I got him in a lot of trouble with a picture I shot of him. But it gave me an idea."

I put the clipboard on the dashboard and a few papers up there next to it so that they'd be visible to passers by. I found a pair of reading glasses in the glove compartment so I put them on the cop's face. Then I pulled the keys out of the ignition and tossed them into the woods.

"Very nice, Mr. Walsh. People driving by might think that he's fallen asleep while parked here doing some homework."

"That's the idea."

We climbed back into the van and returned to the cable vault. Uri had finished setting the charges underground and was waiting for us, hiding behind a clump of bushes nearby. I helped him close the big steel trap door again and lock up the chain-link gate, then we ran back to the van.

Driving from there to the Mans was an excursion of absolute silence. Except for the road noise of the engine and the tires on the asphalt beneath us, not a sound could be heard. Everyone was deep in thought or, perhaps, prayer. Me, I was contemplating two things: having to deliberately shoot another human being and the distinct possibility of being shot myself. There was a startling possibility that I may not survive the next few hours. I reminded myself of the advice that Gideon and Moshe had given me: don't hesitate to shoot, don't worry about friendly-fire, and don't wander off by myself. Stay with the group, these guys are trained commandos, they'll take point and cover our backs.

A piece of cake.

A walk in the park.

A day at the beach.

Right.

In just a few minutes, we pulled off the road and it was time to get out and get real. Those of us in the back of the van climbed out and stood out of sight of the road between the van and the bushes, each one adjusting and straightening their gear from the ride bumping along in the back of the van.

Gideon joined us and Uri left to go and set the charges on the iron gates in front of the Mans' driveway.

"Alright, we all know what to do. Find some cover to sit tight until the 'go' signal. When I call it out over the radio, Uri will blow the power and the gates simultaneously, that will be our signal to rush in from the front and for Moshe and his team to come in through the back. By the time we reach the front doors, he should have the first floor pretty well cleared, but expect to take fire. Reuven will keep us covered as best he can from the wall. The key is to keep moving and stay together. Are we ready?"

"Ready."

"Ready."

"Good, may God go with us. Shalom."

"Shalom."

We followed Gideon in a column along the edge of the foliage. It was dark and we didn't have night-vision gear, but the sun was just beginning to put a glow into the sky which was just about enough light to keep us from tripping around in the dark. Well, most of us. Actually, everybody but me, I was not doing well and was really hoping and praying to whoever up there might care that that would not be the harbinger of things to come.

ΠΟΕ LiKE
in the movies

Meagan and I had found a dark hiding place behind a large tree and a clump of foliage directly across the street from the steel gates at the end of the driveway. Except for the real possibility of me not living to tell about it, it was like hiding in the bushes as a kid on micheif night before Halloween, preparing to "egg" the neighborhood carmudgeon's house. Strange what comes to mind at moments like that. Others had likewise found similar cover but, from where we were, I couldn't see them in the dark — I just knew they were there, somewhere, all around me. I could hear some hushed chatter on my radio coming in through the earpiece; everyone was poised and on the edge, ready to run when the signal would come.

The sky was brightening behind us. We all knew that we were waiting for the very crack of dawn so that we'd have at least a little bit of light to find our way. Team Two in the rear, had night vision goggles and were only a few yards from the back doors but we had to get through the front gates and make our way down a broad driveway that was about half the length of a football field. We wanted to have enough light to find our way but not so much that we'd be easy targets for the Illuminati guunmen posted at the front doors.

We watched the eastern horizon.

And waited.

And then, suddenly, the first bright yellow flash of sunlight broke over the summit of the eastern mountains.

"Go! Go! Go!" Gideon's voice called out over the radio.

Just as we all broke out from behind our hiding places I saw all the lights in the building and all the lamps that lined the driveway instantly go dark, then at the same moment I saw a small flash and the two big iron gates in front of us slowly swing free. Gideon ran up to the gate on the right and pulled it open and we all followed him inside.

I could hear pops and noises coming from the building, the guards firing wildly into the darkness, knowing that they were under attack. I knew that they couldn't possibly see us, but just shooting randomly down the driveway like that, well, they could get lucky, so I kept finding trees, bushes, lamp posts, whatever I could to stay behind, hoping my luck was better than theirs.

Occasionally I'd hear a somewhat louder "bang" from behind us. It was Reuven with his sniper rifle covering us as we worked our way forward. He had a starlight scope on his gun so he was able to see the guards on the big, granite portico in front of the building in the dim light and pick them off whenever he could. It wasn't an absolute surety that we'd be free and clear to run up and into the building, but it was way better than nothing. I could hear Gideon calling out on the radio for us to take a few shots to keep the guards engaged, but not to waste ammunition (it was pretty unlikely that we'd be able to hit anyone anyway). The red spots of the lasers wove and swirled across the building's granite and marble facade. We were in the thick of a fire fight that would only get more intense as we'd get closer to the building and nearer to more concentrated defenses.

As we got nearer, Gideon told us to aim for the glass in the doors and windows. I, thus far, hadn't fired a shot, but when I got that word, I leaned up against a metal lamp post and

Bob Pierce

braced the MP5 against it. I could see the red dot from my laser sweep slowly across the front of the building until it reached the doors, when it disappeared I figured it was shining through the glass, so I pulled the trigger. I could hear the glass shatter and saw the shards reflecting in the emergency lights shining from inside the doorway.

Just then, I heard a loud "clang", a bullet fired out from the Mans had ricoched off of the lamp post just a foot or so above my head. I instantly dropped down to the ground. My heart was pounding — that was way too close.

✳ ✳ ✳ ✳ ✳

Cardinal de Recalde stood in front of Jacob who was sitting, drooling, in the metal chair with the bright surgical spot lights trained on his face. He regarded his interrogation subject over his shoulder as he pulled on a pair of latex surgical gloves and then leaned over and grabbed him by his chin and pitched his head up. Jacob looked up at him through half-closed eyes.

"You look funny. Not funny 'ha-ha', but funny. You know? Like weird. Or is it just me?"

"Tell me where the journals are, Señor Goodspeed."

"Journals? What journals?" He began to giggle like a school girl and his speech was getting increasingly slurred.

"Elijah Browne's journals."

"Oh, *those* journals. What about them?"

"Where are they?"

"Oh, they're the property of the Montgomery Historical Society. If you'd like to make an appointment…"

The cardinal released Jacob's face, then slapped him across his left cheek and then back again across his right, "I'm losing my patience with you, Mr. Goodspeed. Either you tell me right now where you've hidden those journals or I am going to be forced to employ more direct methods!"

Jacob shook his head and stroked his brushy mustache. He

then looked up at de Recalde and smiled. Then he beckoned him closer as if he was about to divulge his great secret for the cardinal's ears only. He leaned over closer until his dark, chiseled face was just inches away. Anticipating the answer to his questioning, he looked Jacob in the eye and Jacob just snickered and then blew raspberries into the cardinal's face, "sssppppppppxxxxxxssss!"

Cardinal de Recalde snapped back upright, and spun around and away from Jacob who sat laughing hysterically in the metal chair. He snapped up one of the folded white towels to wipe his face off with and then raised his hand to strike Jacob across the face once again...

...and suddenly the room went black.

"What is going on?" he shouted out.

A moment later, a loud "bang" echoed through the Mans and a man ran into the room as the emergency lights came on in the hallway, "we are under attack! They are coming in through the back doors!"

"Get some men down there and take care of it! Now!"

* * * * *

By the time we had reached the massive portico at the front of the building, the generators had kicked in and the lights were coming back on while Moshe and Team Two had blown open the back doors and were sweeping through the first floor. I could hear gun fire from inside, obviously they had met up with some of the Illuminati guards and were flushing them out.

I hung back while Gideon and some of the commandos from Team One rushed up the granite steps to the patio at the front doors, they paused and waved the rest of us on. I ran up the steps behind them and, as I reached the top step, saw three of the guards lying on the terra-cotta tiles, sprawled in their own blood, each with a devastating wound to the head. It was a sobering scene just like in the movies except that it was for real. Reuven's deadly precision was clearly and graphically evident.

I'd never realized that blood had such a unique smell. I'd only ever been around blood in small amounts — a cut to my finger or even while I was patching up Meagan's shoulder — but in enough quantity, it has a very metallic smell. It reminded me of the smell of copper water pipes when I was doing plumbing work in the basement of my house in St. Albans. I don't think I will ever do that sort of home repairs without the smell of the metal bringing back the horrific images of those men sprawled across that porch.

I was suddenly paralyzed. I could not take my eyes off of the dead men grotesquely lying at my feet.

I stood just outside the doorway with my back pressed tightly against the carved marble frame, trying to make myself as narrow as possible to be the smallest target that I could be. My heart pounded in my chest and I could feel beads of cold sweat forming on my forehead and running down in rivulets from my temples.

I didn't know why I was so reticent all of a sudden. I was hearing gun shots all around me, but I'd made it across the lawns and up to the porches without getting shot. Even so, there were a number of close calls; maybe that guardian angel that Meagan kept talking about had something to do with it.

I don't know why it was so easy to go charging after those gunmen on the bridge in Dublin; maybe it was the passion of the moment or maybe I just didn't think about it before I did it. I thought that, maybe that was the answer, maybe I just needed to stop thinking about things at that moment in that doorway but, nevertheless, I was paralyzed. I was pressed up against the door frame with my eyes fixated on the dead Illuminati gunmen sprawled in spreading pools of their own blood to my left and to my right. Just inside the door, a few feet from where I was standing at that instant, raged a running fire fight. I could hear the shooting and the agonized screams of those inside who would become like those that I was looking at outside on the porch.

"Are you alright?!" Meagan's voice penetrated my frozen moment. I snapped my head around to see her pressed up against the wall right beside me. She had come out of nowhere, I never heard her coming. I took a moment to gather my wits.

"Aaaahhh, yea. I mean, I guess so."

"Come on, Mr. Walsh, we need to find your friend!"

She was right, of course, that was what we were there for, to find Jacob and get him out and those commandos were counting on me to help them locate and identify him. I kept turning and looking down at the bloody scene on the porch, she grabbed my face and pulled me around, "eyes on me, Mr. Walsh, eyes on me!"

I took in a deep breath and nodded nervously.

"I'm your swimming buddy, remember?" I nodded again, her fingers still wrapped around my jaw. "Undress me in your mind if you have to, Mr. Walsh, but keep your eyes on me and stay focused!"

I know that she was trying get my mind off of the horror of the moment with that comment, but the levity was totally lost on me just then. I had never been so scared before in my entire life, but I looked into those green Irish eyes and found a little something inside to get me back on track; I just sucked in a deep breath and pulled my face away from her hand, then nodded to her again and turned toward the open doorway.

We peeled away from the wall and followed the last of Team One as they rushed in through the door. As we did, a couple of members of Team Two ran past us toward the kitchen. In our briefings the previous night it was stressed the critical need to secure the kitchen and a second stairwell, a service stairwell, that could hide some of the Illuminati guards and allow them to get around us and ambush us on the second or third floor. I heard gun shots echoing from all directions. The hardwood walls and the proliferate marble and polished floors reflected the sound making it difficult to tell from what direction they might be coming. I just kept my head down and followed the leader across the great room toward the broad, stone stairway that curved up to the second floor.

Gideon and two of the other commandos ran up the stairs, keeping themselves behind cover as best they could. As they neared the top at the second floor, they drew fire from a couple of directions. They crouched down behind the granite balusters until the commandos who were working their way up the service stairwell could flank behind the Illuminati guards that were keeping them pinned down and catch them by surprise.

Midway up the stairwell, Illuminati gunmen who were hiding behind the stone railings along the balcony's rim above kept firing down on them, trapping them on the stairs, tucked under the ornate stone and iron bannisters. Gideon and the other commandos trapped there with him kept firing up at the gunmen above to keep them engaged, waiting for Levin's team to circle around.

Meagan and I crouched down in the big, open entrance-way with the rest of Team One and watched every tense second. Even though I was just a spectator at that moment it was definitely not like in the movies. Sometimes real life sucks and this was a perfect example. Somebody was about to die, it was just a matter of who was going to kill whom first.

With each loud, echoing crack of gunfire, my body instinctively recoiled; and then I watched helplessly as Gideon stretched up from behind the safety of the stone cover that protected him to take a shot at one of the gunmen above and, in an instant, I saw his head jerk around to his left and a spray of red arc out from under his chin. He fell backward against the bannister with one hand clamped tightly against the right side of his neck. Before he completely crumpled to the steps below him, a flurry of gunfire from above echoed down from the second floor and then, when it suddenly stopped, two commandos from Levin's Team Two leaned over the railings to give the all-clear signal.

On that cue, the commandos that we were hunkered down with rose to their feet and began running for the stairwell, Meagan and I followed.

As I ran up the steps, I came across Gideon, sitting slumped and limp, his blood-coated hand lying at his side. He was red from his neck, down his shoulder and across his chest. The bleeding had stopped, however. Gideon was dead.

I felt nauseous but someone coming up from behind me pushed me to press on up the stairs. I had to pull it together. Dazed and confused that I was, I turned away and slowly took the next step up and then the next and finally got back into the pace of the rest of those who were with me.

When I reached the top, the rest of the commandos had fanned out into the various hallways and rooms to the left and the right. Moshe Levin stopped me at the top and reminded me to keep from getting separated, to stay with someone. I knew that Meagan was watching my back, but he seemed to sense my anxiety and eagerness to find Jacob and wanted to put a damper on that before something bad happened — like me getting blown away. He shouldn't have worried, I was laser-focused at that moment with a combination of determination and sheer terror. I assured him that I had no desire to get shot and I'd be particularly careful. His words were graphically punctuated by the sound of more gun shots echoing from down the hallways and the genuine danger was clearly apparent.

I walked past Levin to a door off to the left of where we were standing. The commandos had fanned out to the farthest ends of the hallway to search room by room, leaving the rooms closest to the center, closest to the top of the stairwell, for last. The door was closed, it seemed that noone had yet explored that room. I stood in the hallway to one side of the door and reached around to the door knob and tried it — it wasn't locked. Meagan came up alongside me and I looked back at her.

She nodded.

I pushed the door open with a back-handed shove and pulled myself back for a second, then the two of us rushed inside. I'm not sure if I was disappointed or relieved, but there was noone in the room. There was another door across the room that seemed to lead to yet another room beyond. It wasn't in the right place to lead back out to the hallway, so I ran to it and we braced ourselves on either side of the door way and, again, I reached around and shoved the door open.

That time we received a much different reception. Shots rang out from within the room, the bullets striking and ripping up the wood of the open door as we both recoiled beyond the door frame. Meagan watched carefully the direction from which the bullets were coming. She motioned to me with two fingers, and then pointed one toward the right and one almost dead in front of us. She pointed to herself and motioned that I should take out the gunman to the right and that she'd take the one in front of the door. Then, on the count of three, we spun around the door frame and, before anyone inside could fire a shot, I planted the red dot of my laser on the man in the white shirt to my right and fired, dropping him to the floor. But I didn't hear Meagan fire or any gun fire from my left. When I looked around I saw an arresting sight. A tall, thin man with white hair and beard dressed in black was holding Jacob in front of himself as a human shield, pressing the muzzle of a pistol against his temple.

"Jack!" Jacob called out, obviously not himself, quite inebriated on the truth drugs that he'd been injected with. "You look awful!"

"Yeah, I haven't slept much lately," I just replied as I crept closer, trying to get my red laser dot on the man behind him, but not having much success. The man was the same one that I had seen from the plane in Barcelona strong-arming Jacob. Gideon had told me all about him. Being that he was the Vatican's Grand Inquisitor, much of what he'd told me was not very surprising. For the moment, though, the only thing that I was concerned with was the fact that he'd blow my friend's brains out in a heartbeat and I was not about to let that happen if I could in any way stop it.

I had my MP5 trained on him, but I was afraid to fire. He moved slowly backward toward another door on an adjacent wall, a door that would lead back out into the main hallway. With his arm wrapped around Jacob's shoulders, he kept him in front of himself making it impossible for me to take a shot. Frankly, at that moment, I wasn't so concerned about being able to punch the Inquisitor's ticket as I was about keeping him from killing my friend.

I shouted to him, "let him go!"

"No! Back away or I will kill him!" He reached behind himself and unlatched the door handle.

I looked around and realized that I was alone in the room — exactly what I had been warned against doing. Where was Meagan? What should I do? I was feeling quite unsure of my situation and vulnerable, but I couldn't walk away.

He shoved the door open with his heel and began to back out into the hallway. I moved in closer as quickly as I could as he disappeared out the door. All of a sudden, I heard a chorus of voices shouting at him from out in the hallway. Levin and the others had heard me shouting at de Recalde and were waiting for him outside the door. When I reached the door, I saw him backed up against a wall with Jacob still pulled tightly up against his body for protection and the pistol aimed at his head.

I moved out into the hall, just outside the doorway. I was to his left, three of the other commandos were gathered directly in front of him. He was trapped.

I slowly moved in closer, still trying to get the red dot of my laser sight to settle on him long enough to take a shot.

De Recalde turned to his left and aimed the pistol at me. I raised my MP5 to my shoulder and aimed it right at his head (still not daring to pull the trigger for fear of missing and killing my friend in the process).

"Back away! Back away!" he shook the pistol in my direction.

I stopped moving, pausing about fifteen feet away. I could tell that Jacob was getting more and more affected by the drugs. His eyes were beginning to roll back in his head and he was getting increasingly limp and more difficult for de Recalde to hold up.

The air was thick with the tension of the potentially deadly standoff.

I felt myself beginning to hyperventilate. I knew that I had to keep my calm. I forced myself to breathe normally, taking long, slow breaths.

De Recalde quickly turned his glance to the encircling men in black vests and balaclavas and snapped his right arm around to pan the muzzle of his pistol in their direction. They were totally unintimidated. I took the momentary distraction to move in just a step closer.

He quickly snapped his head back, turned toward me and shouted again "back away!"

Then a loud report and I felt the stinging pain of the impact of a bullet against my chest.

He'd shot me!

I couldn't believe it!

I'd been shot!

"Back away!" he shouted again as I fell backward. The next few seconds went as a crawl. Like some people describe being in a car wreck. It all seemed to be in slow motion. Instinctively, I slapped my hand against the point of pain as I landed butt-first onto the hard floor.

Almost immediately after, I heard another single gun shot, then I saw Jacob fall to the floor. I thought de Recalde had shot him, but when he fell, I could see Meagan behind him with the slide of her Sig just returning from recoil. She had left me to sneak around through the service stairwell from the first floor to come up behind the Inquisitor. When he had turned to shoot me, he exposed himself from behind and she took the shot.

As Jacob slumped to the floor, every gun in the room opened fire and Cardinal de Recalde, the fearsome Illuminati Grand Inquisitor, flew back against the wall in a hail of bullets. As his body slid to the floor, he left a broad, red vertical smear of blood on the walnut paneling until he laid in a ungangley heap on the floor.

I quickly got to my feet. I noticed that my hand that I'd been pressing against the painful strike against my chest was surprisingly bloodless. The vest had stopped the bullet, but I felt a searing pain nevertheless.

I ran to Jacob to get him to his feet. The bullet had hit my left chest and it was incredibly painful to use that arm so, with my right hand, I grabbed his upper arm and tried to get him up. He looked up at me with half-closed eyes and smiled, "I want a taco!" he slurred.

I couldn't help my self, in the scene of such death and violence I just couldn't keep from chuckling a little as I struggled to raise him from the floor. Levin rushed up to me and grabbed Jacob's other arm and, together, we got him to his wobbly feet.

One of the Team Two commandos rushed up the stairs from the first floor and announced that reinforcements were just then arriving and coming up the driveway fast.

"Reinforcements? Who's that?"

"Jesuit Guard, from the monastery."

"Were you expecting them?"

"We were about eighty percent sure they'd be coming."

"So, you have a plan 'B'?"

"Plan 'A' took this into consideration, Mr. Walsh. Quickly, we have to move."

We each wrapped one of Jacob's arms around our shoulders and headed for the stairwell but, instead of turning down the stairs to the first floor to make our escape, Levin steered us to the stairwell leading up to the third floor.

"Where we going?" I asked with an urgent sense of confusion.

"Up the stairs, Mr. Walsh. Up, quickly!" There was no time for questions, I turned with him and we ran toward the stairs.

Jacob's feet were barely taking steps as we moved him, mostly they were just dragging on the ground and snagging on the steps. Another commando ran up behind us and grabbed his ankles and the three of us rushed Jacob, then totally suspended, up the stairs as he shouted out, "faster than a speeding bullet, more powerful than a locomotive, look, it's a bird! It's a plane!"

As we reached the top steps at the third floor I heard a burst of gunfire from below. The Jesuit Guard had rushed in through the front doors and a few of Gideon's commandos were keeping them pinned down at the foot of the stairs from cover behind the big, granite balusters on the second floor.

As the fire fight raged on behind us, we raced across the third floor hallway to the door leading to the service stairwell. In my mind, I was thinking that we were going to go down and get out of the building behind the Jesuits but, no, instead we continued *up* the stairwell.

The service stairs were far narrower and enclosed and we could not walk side by side with Jacob between us so he took hold of him with his arms wrapped over his shoulders and around his chest while the other commando kept hold of his ankles and we climbed the stairs as quickly as we could. Men in the stairwell below us kept any of the Jesuit Guard from coming up from the kitchen entrance on the first floor, others raced on ahead of us to make sure it was clear above us as we made our way up. As we did, the rest of the commandos retreated into the narrow stairwell and followed us up.

When we reached the top of the stair, I could see daylight shining in through the open door to the roof and I could hear a deafening roar from beyond. As we ran out onto the roof, I saw a Blackhawk helicopter hovering with its wheels just kissing the flat surface of the roof and Ruven in position with his sniper rifle inside the open side door, ready to cover our escape.

"A helicopter?" I shouted over the noise to Levin as we ran across the rooftop.

"Oh, did I forget to mention the helicopter?"

"I guess it just slipped your mind."

"See, Mr. Walsh, plan 'A' is still working just fine!"

When we reached the helicopter, Meagan was waiting to help get Jacob's limp body up on board, by that time he was completely unconscious. A couple of commandos inside grabbed his arms and helped to hoist him up and get him strapped into a seat as quickly as they could. We all then clambered up and found places to sit down and hang on. When the last of the commandos came out of the rooftop door from the stairwell, he waved a signal to Ruven to let him know that he was the last one out and then the sniper kept the Jesuit Guards pinned down inside the doorway until everyone was on board and the chopper lifted off from the roof.

"Hang on tight!" someone called out, and the helicopter made a sharp bank to the right and dove down past the cliffs toward the water and then flew out away from the shore, far out of range in a matter of seconds. Once a safe distance away, the pilot turned northeast and headed for the French border.

The vibration and jostling of the helicopter antagonized the pain in my chest. I rubbed my hand against the place and felt an indentation in the Kevlar fabric of the vest and then I felt something come loose and fall into my hand. When I looked down, there was the mushroomed bullet that had been stopped by the vest in my open palm.

"A souvenir!" Meagan shouted out to me.

"I suppose so! Never been shot before; I think I'll frame it!" All joking aside, I was in a lot of pain. I could feel something shifting around inside and was sure that I had at least a couple of broken ribs. The stiff bullet proof vest kept my rib cage more or less immobile so I wasn't too concerned about any further damage, even on the rough ride in the Blackhawk. I was much more concerned about my friend.

Levin crouched down in front of Jacob and planted his palm against his face, lifting his eyelid with his thumb, "we're going to have to get some fluids into this man immediately."

"What's the matter with him? Is he drugged?" I asked. Almost a rhetorical question.

He reached into his pocket and pulled out a half-empty glass vial, "I found this in the room on the floor. I think they shot him up with it."

"What is it? A truth serum?"

"The label says 'SP-117.' It's Russian, nasty stuff. I think he's too old to metabolize it completely, we need to try and flush it out of him as soon as possible."

Just as he finished saying that, one of the other commandos crab-walked over to Levin and handed him an I.V. bag which he reached up and hung on a hook on the ceiling. The other man inserted a needle into Jacob's elbow and taped it over, then he adjusted a plastic valve on the tube to allow a fairly steady drip to descend from the bag. Levin looked back over at me when it was all set up, "saline solution, Mr. Walsh. It will help his kidneys to process the drug out of his system."

"There's no antidote?"

"Not for this drug, I'm sorry. He seems to be a pretty tough old bird, though, I think he'll be fine."

I was somewhat relieved to hear that, but still concerned. Jacob just hung in his seat, flopping back and forth like a rag doll with every bump of air turbulence we rode along on. A couple of the commandos who sat next to him on either side kept ahold of him to keep him upright in the seat. He really looked quite pathetic and fragile at that moment.

I looked over at Meagan; she was sitting on the nylon bench almost directly across from me. Out of the corner of my eye, I noticed the commando sitting next to her handling what looked like a black Magic Marker. I didn't pay much attention to what he was doing, I was going to make a wisecrack at Meagan when all of a sudden I saw her sitting bolt-upright and her eyes widen. I glanced down and saw that the man sitting next to her had pressed the end of what I had thought was a marker into her thigh. As he pulled it away, I saw the tip of a short needle at the end of it. An epi-pen; she'd just been injected with something. Before I could say or do anything, I felt a sting in my own thigh and looked down to see the man sitting next to me with his hand pressing the tip of an epi-pen into my leg.

I looked back across at Meagan and she was staring across at me with her mouth open and her eyes closing. I could see her body quickly relaxing and beginning to slump and slouch. The man sitting next to her reached his arm across in front of her and then she went totally limp, he held her up in her seat while the man on the other side of her reached across with a strap to hold her in place.

I was beginning to feel my own body feeling profoundly warm and relaxed. I felt an arm press against my chest and then everything went black.

Bob Pierce

October fourth, 1877

Bro. Vadim passed today. I ordered another coffin.
John sent me a note to tell me and to be certain
that I would be at the funeral ceremony in a week
hence. Truly a sad day.

January thirtieth, 1821

John told me a disturbing story today. Of a journey
he took to Babylon in ancient days. He had gotten
word of Peter's frail condition, that he was failing.
Peter was the eldest of the twelve, John the youngest.
Peter had been living in Babylon for many years
after razing of Jerusalem and the temple with an order
of Jewish believers called the Magi. John arrived in
time to spend few weeks with his friend before his
passing. Peter was buried in Babylon with his
people. I had always believed that Peter had died
a martyr in Rome, but John insisted that Peter had
never set foot in Rome. It was now clear to me
why John needed to be kept in hiding, there are
those who would silence him lest this truth destroy
the Roman papacy.

the revelator

It was dark; my eyes were closed and I became aware that I was lying on my back on something cushioned. It was quiet. I felt sleepy, but not a natural sleepiness, it was a somewhat unfamiliar sensation, but then I remembered the helicopter and the stab to my leg.

The drug.

Apparently, I was coming out of that drug-enduced state of unconsciousness.

After a while, as my mind began to clear, I began to recall some of the horrific sights, sounds and smells that I'd just recently experienced — not by design but rather my mind seemed to be so filled with the enormity of it all that it just overwhelmed my consciousness as it slowly returned to me. I could not but recall my initial, gut-wrenching reaction to seeing those Illuminati gunmen shot dead and lying on the ground as some sort of grotesque parody of all that I'd so cavalierly incorporated into my life's works without the understanding of the cruel reality.

I opened my eyes for a moment just to see if I could and then, when I closed them again, the images were still there. I just opened them again and looked straight ahead — straight up.

I found myself looking up at a pattern of three-dimensional squares made of some sort of dark, polished wood. A ceiling, a very ornate one divided into square panels with intricately-carved moldings that descended four or five inches from the square panels that they encircled which, themselves, rose to a slight pyramidic point in their centers.

How long had I been out? I found it an effort to move my head, I still felt very foggy and somewhat disoriented. For a moment I thought I was in my own bed back in St. Albans and the strange texture that I was seeing above my head was just a waking dream.

But, no.

The searing pain in my ribs was a testament to that cruel fact. I raised my hand up to my side and felt something under my shirt. Trying not to apply any pressure so as not to antagonize the pain any more than it already was, I felt around and discovered a band about as broad as my hand and apparently encircling my entire body. A bandage, I presumed. Someone had checked out my wound while I was still under. The knock-out drug seemed to have worked as some sort of anesthesia because, at that moment as the drug was wearing off, the pain was getting more intense.

I forced myself to roll my head slightly to my right and I caught a glimpse of a chandelier hanging from the panels at some distance. Looking around, I saw that there were four identical chandeliers hanging in an evenly-spaced array around the room. Just then I heard a groan and I turned my head farther to my right, panning my eyes down the wall opposite from where I was and I saw an elegant sofa braced with intricately-carved legs, arms and frame around a bright blue velvet cushion and, lying on that cushion was Meagan, still in the black tactical garb from the raid in San Sebastian, sans the bulletproof vest, gun belt and balaclava.

"Meagan!" I called out, trying to force my beleaguered body to sit up on my own blue velvet cushion.

She groaned again and asked, "is that you, Mr. Walsh?" She still hadn't opened her eyes.

"Yeah, are you okay?"

"I think so. I think I've been drugged."

"On the helicopter. They shot us both with some sort of pens, like kids with severe asthma carry."

"Aye, epi-pens, I remember. I still can't open my eyes."

"Don't worry, it's wearing off," I pushed myself up from the cushions with shaking arms and got to my similarly-shaking feet. I shuffled across the parquet floor spread with a large oriental rug with my arms spread out wide to try and maintain my balance, the posture also helped to mitigate the pain in my side just a little bit, too. When I reached the other side of the room, I bent down and grabbed her shoulders to lift her up, but she was still limp as a wet noodle and completely dead weight.

"Ow!" she winced when I lifted her.

"Oh, I'm sorry. I forgot," I had forgotten about the bullet wound to her left arm. I moved my hand behind her and lifted her up, the exertion pulled on the bruised muscles down my side and I grit my teeth from the pain, trying not to let on. I sat down and just supported her for a few minutes with her back leaning up against my shoulder while she regained her senses.

"Do you have any idea where we are, Mr. Walsh?"

"Not really, but it looks a lot like the inside of the Mans de Loyola."

"Same decorator perhaps, but not the same place. It smells different."

"*Smells* different? Really?" I took a couple of sniffs but, frankly, I didn't notice any appreciable odors, but the wood had a smell; and we were surrounded by wood. Perhaps it was the polish that they (whoever "they" might have been) used on all of that wood to keep it so clean and glossy.

"Aye. The Mans had the smell of the ocean. Above the cliffs with all the spray that must rise from those rocks, the whole place smelled of salt water."

"Hmmm, I'd never thought of that," I took a couple more sniffs. "You're right. So where do you think we are?"

She leaned forward and rubbed her eyes, trying to bring the world back into focus again. "The windows — have you looked outside yet?"

"No. It was all I could do to drag my flopping feet over here," I tried to stand up again and found that I was a bit more stable than I had been just a few minutes earlier, still, I held tightly to the arm of the sofa for support. "Let me see if I can get over there. Do you think you can walk?"

She tried to get to her feet. I reached down and grabbed her wrist to help pull her up, but I wasn't all that stable myself and the pain from her pulling on my arm was unbearable; we both started to fall back onto the couch again.

I let go of her wrist and just said, "I'll go check it out."

I shuffled across the room to the large windows. The ceiling was about twenty feet high and the windows rose from their sills at about waist high to within a few inches of the ceiling, coming to a point much like the stained glass windows one might find in a cathedral. There were hundreds of diamond-shaped panes bound together with lead strips causing almost a kaleidoscope effect when viewing the world outside. When I reached the wall with the row of windows, I braced myself against the wooden frame of one of them and peered out on a sunny day below.

"I don't recognize anything," I reported. "I see an awful lot of very old-looking buildings with some more modern ones in between. There's a trolley system, I see tracks in the streets." I leaned in closer to the wavy glass panes to see more clearly, "lots of red roofs and steeples. I see some skyscrapers in the distance and there seems to be a river snaking through the city — I can see glimpses of it between the buildings and a couple of bridges. That any help?"

"Aye, maybe," she rubbed her forehead and then gripped the blue velvet upholstered arm of the couch to help lift herself to her feet. Slowly, she made her way across the floor to join me. She braced her hand against the window frame across from

Bob Pierce

me and looked out the window with me. "Aye, Prague. We're in Prague."

"You've been here before?"

"Aye," she pointed out a few landmarks, "that's St. Nicholas Church over there and, over there, is the National Theatre and, down there," she pointed to an area just a couple of blocks from where we were, "that's the Old Town Square. I recognize it but I don't know why we're here. The Mossad is Israeli, why are we in Czech Republic?"

"You know, Meagan, I've stopped trying to make sense of a lot of this stuff early on. Consequently, nothing surprises me anymore. We've just gotta roll with it and be ready for anything."

"I guess you're right, Mr. Walsh."

I turned around and leaned back up against the window frame and just looked at her, "you ever seen anyone shot before?" I asked.

She braced her hands against the window sill and lowered her head and quietly answered, "aye, I have. Many, far too many."

"Is it always like this?"

She turned her head to look over at me, her mane of flame-orange hair shifted and fell onto her other shoulder, "like what?"

"Frightening, haunting."

"No, not always."

"What about the first time?"

"The first time — aye, I may not be the best person to ask about that. For me, I was in Derry during the 'troubles.' I was a girl, walking along the sidewalk heading to the bakery to buy bread for my mother who'd sent me on an errand. A moment after I'd walked past a shop, the entire front of it exploded out into the street. A bomb had killed four people inside the shop and several more outside and the shattered glass that sprayed out across the sidewalk and the street shredded dozens more. So much blood, so much blood."

"What about you? You must have been terrified."

"I don't know; no, not terrified. When you grow up in an environment like that, Mr. Walsh, you just learn to function in it. I just instinctively dropped to the ground and pressed myself up against the bakery building, covering my face and head with my arms. Still, pieces of glass sliced my arms and one struck me in the face. An inch to either side and I'd either have lost my eye or would have cut my temple and I'd have bled to death there on the sidewalk. People covered in blood were screaming, running in every direction. Soon all that were left were the dead, the dying and those too badly hurt to run."

I was speechless. She just turned her head again and looked out the window onto the ancient streets of Prague and heaved a deep sigh.

"I was a girl, just a girl. You ask if this sort of thing haunts a person — aye, it does. It does."

"Even to this day?"

"Even to this day," she turned to look at me again, "one may get used to the mechanics of a deadly mission, shrouded in tactics and painted with righteous purpose and duty but those demons are still there. When it's all over and you lay your head down at night, they're still there."

"You've been doing this for a long time, a whole lot longer than me. You must have some mechanism to cope with it; no?"

She turned and leaned her hip up against the window frame and looked down at the floor for a moment. Then she looked up at me again, "Mr. Walsh, you asked me if the first time was the hardest. Were you asking if the first time one might see a man killed would be the hardest or were you asking if the first time one *kills* a man would be?"

A deep and disturbing question which caused me to pause for just a few seconds, "I suppose both. But you just answered the first part of that question."

"Aye, and believe me when I tell you that my experiences growing up in the midst of the troubles didn't prepare me for what my duty would later call on me to do. You know, there are cold-hearted killers in the world, some who have some sort of purpose and others who just kill for the joy of it. For them, devoid of conscience, there seems to be no ill effect. But when a person with some sort of moral base is tasked to kill for their country or to keep the peace as a police officer might, the first time is actually easy."

"Easy?"

"Aye, the first time you go into a situation and you think about all of your training, you're mentally checking off all the boxes and not really thinking about the reasons for pulling that trigger. Not until afterwards, when the reality and weight of having taken another person's life settles into your psyche do you begin to deal with the emotion and horror of it. The second time, Mr. Walsh, the second time is the hardest."

"I'd never thought of it that way before."

"When we were on the bridge in Dublin, you just ran out like a fool and charged those two men in the truck without thinking. Tell me, were you frightened?"

"Uuhh, no, it never occurred to me to be scared."

"You killed two men out of self-preservation and to save the rest of us. Your mind was fixated on your mission and not on the consequences. When you rushed in through those gates in front of the Mans and ran from pillar to post along that driveway being shot at, those consequences were *all* you could think about."

"I suppose you're right; in fact, I'm sure you are." I looked away for a moment, the motion of a tram on the street below caught my attention for just a second as I thought, "I can't help thinking about Gideon, seeing him dead on those stairs. I had just been talking with him a few minutes before. His voice was still in my memory from the ear piece, calling out directions and there he laid dead. And we just ran past him and left him behind. We left him! I don't know what's going to haunt me more, killing another man, seeing Gideon killed or the guilt of leaving him behind."

"I don't have any words for you, Mr. Walsh. We succeeded in our mission, we recovered your friend and preserved an ancient secret. A cause larger than any one of us — or even all of us put together. I think you should be consoled in that, anyway."

"Did we?"

"What do you mean?"

"Where's Jacob? Why isn't he here with us? Did these Mossad — or whoever they were — just use us to find him and then dump us off in Prague while they went and gathered up the journals? Heck, he was already drugged full of truth serum by the Illuminati, their job was half done when we found him!"

"That is curious."

"Curious, yes. I want to find some answers. Can you walk okay yet?"

She stepped away from the window, "aye, not a hundred percent yet, but I believe I can."

"Let's get out of here and see what we can find out."

"Do you have any sort of a plan, Mr. Walsh?"

"Plan? No, I figure we just wing it, what have we got to lose?"

"Aye."

Just then, before we had a chance to begin exploring for Jacob, we heard the echoing rattle of the lockwork of the large, carved door at the other side of the room and watched as it slowly swung partly open. A man dressed in a black suit, black shirt and tie stepped into the room and paused part-way inside. He looked around and then saw us over by the windows and smiled, "I thought that I had heard voices. You are awake — that you are?" He stepped into the room, closing the door behind him, and walked toward us, stopping halfway across the room.

I stepped in front of Meagan and asked kurtly, "who the heck are you?"

"I heard you talking," somehow his smile seemed quite

disingenuous to me.

"You haven't answered me. Who are you and where are we?"

"My name is not important. I am here to see to your well being."

"Your voice sounds familiar," I was having trouble placing it, but the tone of his voice and the accent were eerily familiar — but from where?

The phone. It was the voice that had called me at home when this whole thing started, "Gregor Ivonovich."

The man's fake smile melted, "you know my name, Mr. Walsh?"

"Someone I bumped into in San Diego told me about you."

"Yes, that would be Special Agent Walker; of course. Bonesman, he was. His mission, of course, failed."

"What mission, to protect me and Jacob?"

"That is what he told you? Yes, part of it that was, but only until you led him to the journals. Then he'd have abandoned you and disappeared with the books, back to the Tombs."

"You had him shot."

"No, no; that was just a convenient coincidence. Your C.I.A. friend correctly deduced that those men were I.R.A., the Sons of Erin. The Illuminati already had your friend Goodspeed and tried to stop you from looking for him. That is why they lured you to Dublin. It was a trap. However, I do not believe that they ever counted on you connecting with Agent Flynn."

"You seem to know everything."

I walked across the floor and stood inches from the man. I remembered how Walker had told me what a bad guy he was and how dangerous he could be but I didn't care, I was ready to go toe-to-toe with him — I was just that angry. I looked him in the eye and snarled, "where's Jacob Goodspeed, you son-of-a-bitch?" I had had enough of this little adventure, of people lying to me and secret orders and religious terrorists taking shots at me. I just wanted to gather up my friend and get on the next plane to Vermont.

"Your friend is doing well. We have been giving him fluids and drugs to counteract those that the Illuminati had administered. A man of his age is not able to tolerate such a dose of such a powerful drug. The past few hours have seen a remarkable return to health. He will be joining us in just a short while."

"You're lying. What did you do to him?"

He ignored my accusation and continued, "we helped him to process the Russian drug out of his body. The effects are now almost completely gone."

I dialed back my ire a bit and backed away from him, drifting back across the room toward the windows where Meagan was standing. I wanted to believe him so I thanked him for taking care of Jacob, but then asked, "so where are we?"

"You are in Prague."

"We figured that out just by looking out the window."

"You are in one of our estates here in the city, I cannot explain in any more detail than that."

I glanced out through the window at the old city and recalled some of the things that I had read in Elijah Browne's old journals and a revelation came to me. I looked over at Meagan and smiled, "John's house," I said quietly.

"What?" Meagan asked. "What are you talking about?"

"John's house. This is where John lives," I turned to Ivonovich, "am I right? This is the monastery du jour. You Templars are here in this big house hiding John from the world. You must be getting ready to make another move or you'd never have brought us here. Right? Am I right?"

Ivonovich's back straightened and he looked around the room with his arms folded in front of him. Finally, his eyes settled on me and Meagan standing together by the windows, "you will be meeting with the master in a short time. I would suggest you take some time to prepare yourselves. There is a lavatory through the doors at the end of the room. I will come and retrieve you when it is time; your friend will be joining you then."

Without another word, he turned and walked back out the door, closing it behind himself, I could hear the lock being turned, making sure that we two didn't get out and wander about the building.

I stood there in a mild state of shock. I'd read those journals and found myself engrossed in the tale that they told but, even though I understood the story to be true (supposedly, anyway), it never really struck me as reality. It always had seemed like some sort of distant historical account that may have been true once upon a time, but today, no. No way. But Ivonovich contended that we were about to meet John the Apostle, the Revelator, in person.

Couldn't be real. Couldn't be.

Meagan sat back down on the sofa and looked up at me with a look of confusion on her face, "what are you talking about, Mr. Walsh?"

I leaned back against the window frame and stuffed my right hand into my pocket to support it so I could relax the muscles on that side and ease the immediate pain of my still-aching ribs for a little bit.

"This is what this is all about, Meagan. Those journals are a set of three ledger books that my great, great, great grandfather and his son had kept records in while they were acting as liaisons for a religious order that had come to their town in Vermont just after the Revolutionary War. They were an order of warrior knights called The Poor Knights of Antioch, a splinter group of the Templar Knights of the Crusades. For generations they had been guarding their secret, that John the Apostle was still alive."

"That's ridiculous. He'd have to be, what, over two thousand years old by now."

"Right. But there's a few passages at the end of the book of John that suggest that that may very well be the case. Peter was told by Jesus not to concern himself about John, even if he remained alive until Jesus' return. Well, the second coming hasn't happened yet as far as I know which means…"

"Which means he would still be alive."

"And apparently he had some pretty deep conversations with Elijah Browne and told him about being with Peter and Mary when each of them had died and tells a very different story than the traditional yarns."

"Well, I grew up in the Catholic Church, I know all about those things."

"Do you?"

"Aye, sure, Peter was crucified in Rome and was the first Pope. The Virgin Mary ascended to Heaven just like Jesus did after the resurrection."

"What if that wasn't true? What if there was irrefutable evidence and an eye witness to categorically debunk all of that?"

"Well, if those things turned out not to be true, then the basic foundations of the church would just fall apart."

"So now you know why the Illuminati kidnapped Jacob and why so many people want to get their hands on those books."

"And on John, too, I would imagine."

"True that. What if they got the books but John was still out here somewhere. There would always be the danger that he might make some sort of public statement or some other historical documents like the journals might surface."

"They'd have to eliminate him."

"Or, short of that, imprison him until the end of time. The Vatican could do that."

"Aye, lots of dark catacombs and underground vaults in Rome to hide a lone prisoner."

"That's why the Templars shuffle him around from one part of the world to another. They've been doing it for a thousand years."

"That's what you meant when you said that they must be

ready to move again."

"Even if we knew exactly where we are right now, if we ever came back here they'd be long gone. Thousands of miles away, set up again anonymously in some other city or remote village somewhere."

"That's amazing."

"It is, isn't it. I couldn't have imagined such a story for any of my novels. It's just mind-boggling."

"Indeed."

I stepped away from the window and walked over to the couch, I wanted to sit down to take some of the strain off of my throbbing ribs, "why don't you go and freshen up first?"

"Aye, we don't know how long we have until he comes back. I want to take a look at the wound on my arm, too. It may need some cleaning up by now."

"Okay, go ahead. I'll just hang out here," I parked my butt down to wait for her while she made her way to the lavatory.

Once I sat down, I realized that the drugs had almost completely worn off by the fact that just about every muscle in my body ached. I'm a fifty-something year old writer. I work each day sitting at my computer. I take walks in the fresh air once in a while and do a little fishing on Lake Champlain — that's the extent of the rigors that I put myself through on a normal basis — this aging body was not prepared for commando raids. I was a hurtin' puppy.

* * * * *

I came out of the lavatory after washing up as best I could. I found a comb in there and straightened out my do just a bit. I also found a bottle of acetaminophen and slugged down a few of them to help with the muscle aches and the painful ribs. Ivanovich didn't make us wait very long. I found Meagan standing by the windows looking down at the city as I emerged, just about the time that he came back into the room to lead us to meet "the master," to meet John.

Still, I was concerned about Jacob. He had assured me that he was doing well and was being nursed off of the truth drugs that the Illuminati had given him, but was anxious to see him for myself. He was a septuagenerian historical society director, even less adapted for this sort of adventure than I.

Ivanovich led us down a corridor as ornate as the room we had just woken up in, to a pair of doors, one of which was ajar and I could hear Jacob's voice from beyond. Ivanovich pushed it open and led us inside.

The room was large and lined from floor to ceiling with shelves which were stacked with books, papers and scrolls. Light coming in from the leaded glass windows beyond silhouetted a man with white hair sitting at a large table with massive carved legs. In front of the table were three plushly-cushioned, tall chairs arrayed in a row, Jacob was already seated at the one to my left as Meagan and I approached.

He rose to his feet and looked back at me, then whirled around from the front of the chair and grabbed me in a big bear hug. I groaned in pain, but tried not to make too much of a fuss because I was so glad to see him. With my left arm, I returned his embrace. He let me go and held me by my shoulders and, with a broad grin that curled that big old bush of a mustache of his up at either end, he said, "I can't tell you how happy I am that you are not dead!" Another movie quote; a good sign that he was himself again.

He stepped back from me and looked at Meagan and asked me, "so, who's the redhead, Jack?"

"Agent Meagan Flynn from Dublin," I announced, waving her over to join us. "Bad-ass C.I.A. babe," she just leered at me with that all-so-familiar look of amused disgust (at least I think she was amused — a little bit, anyway) as she extended her hand to Jacob, "Meagan, this is Jacob Goodspeed, director of the Montgomery Historical Society."

"I am pleased to make your acquaintance, Mr. Goodspeed."

"Judging by the matching black outfits, I'm guessing you were with Jack when he came and rescued me?"

"Aye, I was."

"Who were all those other guys in black?" he asked, stroking his mustache.

"Mossad," I replied.

"They never actually said that," Meagan interjected.

"Yellow or brown?" Jacob asked.

"Grey Poupon."

"But, of course."

"Do you guys do this all the time?" Meagan asked.

"All the time?" I asked.

"No, not all the time," Jacob added, "we do have to sleep occasionally."

"And eat."

"Which reminds me, I had this awesome smoked fish thing in Managua, at the airport..."

I interrupted Jacob's undoubtedly riveting account, I could see that Ivanovich was becoming impatient and wanted to break up our impromptu reunion and get us seated, so we quietly walked between the chairs and stood in front of the table where the white-haired man patiently sat facing us across its width strewn with books and papers. He looked up at the three of us and smiled.

Ivanovich stood to one side as the man rose to his feet, "Mr. Jacob Goodspeed, Mr. Jack Walsh and Miss Meagan Flynn, I would like to introduce you to John."

The man behind the table walked around the end of it to the side where we three were standing. One by one, he embraced us, and we sat down. He was not very tall, perhaps five foot six or so, but nevertheless imposing (partly because of who he was supposed to have been, I suppose). He carried an air about him — an aura, some would characterize. His face was shrouded in a snow-white beard that extended to his collar bones and his short-cropped hair was equally devoid of color.

He wore a simple, dark blue linen shirt and dark gray slacks over which was a long, black coat that reached to his calves. On his feet were sandals, though he did wear them over a pair of dark-colored socks; no doubt the centuries-old house was a bit drafty.

He walked slowly around the end of the table with his hands folded in front of himself and his face tipped down toward the floor clearly engrossed in thought. When he reached the center of the table, directly in front of me in the center chair, he turned and leaned back against the table, resting his palms against it at either side of himself with his fingers curled around its intricately-carved edge.

The room was silent. Ivanovich and a couple of other Templars, all dressed in black suits, stood imposingly nearby for security. I'm not sure what they thought we three might do, or were even *capable* of doing as two of us were in great physical pain for having been shot prior to that meeting and the third was coming down off of a drug-enduced, near-death experience, but nevertheless they stood guard.

The white-haired man panned across at the three of us, particularly me and Jacob, and finally faced me directly, smiled and asked, "are you Jonathan Bartholemew?" He knew my real name. I hadn't heard anyone actually verbalize it in many years.

"Yes," I hesitantly responded. "These days, though, I go by 'Jack Walsh'."

"An author. A nom du plur."

"It was my publisher's idea a long time ago."

The man's voice was slow and laced with an indiscernible but thick accent. If he was who we were all expected to believe he was, then he'd have lived in so many countries and in so many cultures that it would make complete sense that he'd have learned numerous languages and absorbed various accents over the centuries culminating in a sort of Mulligan stew of dialects.

"I see," the man continued, and then introduced himself,

Bob Pierce

"my name is John, son of Zebedee of Galilee. I knew Elijah Browne in America."

"He was my great, great, great grandfather."

"He was an honorable man. He served our order excellently and saw to all of our needs while we were there. I enjoyed his company immensely when he would come up to the monastery to visit with me. We would talk for hours. As you might imagine, living the way I need to, I do not often get the opportunity to converse with people outside the walls of my quarters."

"Did you know about the journals that he kept? Notes about his conversations with you?"

"Yes. In fact, he told me about them himself."

"And you were not alarmed by that, knowing that what you had told him and what he might have recorded could cause world-wide upheaval?"

"Not at all. People will believe what they wish to believe, Mr. Bartholemew. The journals can only effect those who rest any belief on what they say."

"You know that, if they ever got out into the public, they would rip the Roman church apart?"

"And that frightens you?"

"I know the church's history, what they've done and what they're capable of. Does that frighten me? You bet it does."

"Are you a student of Scripture, Mr. Bartholemew?"

"A student? I know a good deal about it, if that's what you mean."

"Yes, but not a believer I understand."

"The jury's still out, to be honest."

"At the end of the Gospel that bears my name, I record a comment that our Lord says to my friend, Peter. Do you recall?"

"Something like 'never mind about him, you just follow me'?"

"Indeed."

"So you don't care what happens to this world as long as you can hide behind these walls with your Templar buddies and stay insulated and safe?"

Ivanovich stepped forward, presumedly to respond to my perceived insolence, but John raised his hand to him to stave him off. When the man in black backed off, he lowered his hand and looked back at me with a smile.

"Do I not care? Certainly I care, Mr. Bartholemew. We all have our pursuits, however, in His service. I cannot allow the evils that conspire around me to distract me from that. One can care and one can even contribute to some form of relief, but one cannot allow themselves to be removed from their righteous duty. My duty is to occupy until His return, living out the promise of His own prophecy."

"Convenient," my sarcasm was rising.

John then looked over at Meagan and asked, "Miss Flynn, you are a soldier, of sorts."

"Of sorts, I suppose."

"Not engaged in battle on a traditional battlefield, but engaged in battle nonetheless."

"The forces of evil have many weapons, take many shapes, not all of them are tangible."

"Yes, electronics, computers, internet. I must admit, so much of it eludes me. I've seen the rise of human invention over many centuries but not until the past seven or eight decades have I seen to much advancement so quickly. I am lost to keep up with it. I understand that books these days now come on electronic slates."

"They're called tablets. Many people like to read books on them, but there are still plenty of people who read — even prefer — ink-on-paper books that they can hold in their hands."

"You see around you, Miss Flynn, the evidence of my own writing efforts. Over the centuries I have endeavored to write down all of the things that my Lord has done and said that I'd been witness to..."

"All the libraries in all the world..." Jacob whispered.

John turned to him and smiled, "yes, Mr. Goodspeed. I suppose that if I had learned the discipline of using a typewriter or one of these new computers I may well be even more pro-liferant, but the volumes that fill these shelves may only be the beginning, should His return be any more delayed."

"This is what you've been doing for two thousand years?"

John smiled that smile again that caused his eyes to twin-kle just a bit as he pushed himself off from the edge of the table and began to slowly step to my left, toward Jacob, "no, Mr. Goodspeed, this is not all that I have been doing for all of these years. To answer Mr. Bartholemew's earlier question, there has been much work done in the communities that we have been visiting. Anonymous, though that work by necessity must be. But living until the end of time, one needs to have a pursuit, a focus lest one go mad over that time. The Lord has given me this task and from my love for Him and for His creation, I put every possible moment into the work He has set me to."

He continued to walk around behind us, and asked Jacob, "do you believe, Mr. Goodspeed?"

"Believe? Believe in what?"

"Oh, to begin with, do you believe in me?"

"Do I believe that you are who you pose to be? In all hon-esty I must say that I'm still not sure. You may well be the prod-uct of something that I may have eaten in the past few days, a bit of spoiled meat, an underdone potato, perhaps..."

"'...there may well be more to you of gravy than of the grave.' Very good, Mr. Goodspeed, Charles Dickens, you quote the classics."

"Albert Finney, actually."

"Of course, I had forgotten your passion for film," he slowly walked around behind me as he continued. "I assure you that there is nothing of 'grave' in me; in fact, I propose only life, as my Lord so often spoke of."

He came around from behind my chair and walked slowly between me and Meagan. As he passed, he rested his hand on her left shoulder. I heard her let out a startled syllable and then suck in a deep, full breath. As John passed by, I could see her sitting in her chair with her back arched, her eyes closed and her arms stiff and straight at her sides. Her mouth was open and her face was flushed red. In a moment, she began to relax and then looked around the room with a look of mixed embarrassment and perplexity.

I snapped my head around to John who was once again standing in front of the three of us, leaning against the table. Before I could say anything, he again addressed Jacob, "you do not believe that I am who I and everyone else says that I am. In truth, that is actually a good thing, Mr. Goodspeed, as I am not important. But where is your faith as it comes to that of the Scriptures? Again I ask, do you believe?"

I looked back at Meagan, she was sitting in the chair with her hands braced against the edges of the seat and panting as if out of breath. What had John done to her? I was beginning to get angry and it seemed to show as I saw Ivanovich stepping forward again. John and Jacob, however, continued their conversation seemingly oblivious. I held my tongue and looked back at Meagan, then attended to the conversation at hand.

"I grew up in the church," Jacob began. "I went to Sunday School as a kid and, until I graduated high school, I went to church with my parents and all the years of my marriage, I attended with my wife. But after she passed I guess I just sort of drifted away, though."

"But that is not what I asked, Mr. Goodspeed. I did not ask if you attended church. Many people attend church but don't believe. They attend weekly meetings, perform a variety of rituals but remain far from God. Where are you, sir? Where is your heart?"

Jacob was dumbfounded. I'm not sure he understood the question or, maybe more likely, how to relate to it. He sat in silence. John turned his attention to me, "Mr. Bartholemew, I ask you the same question: Do you believe?"

"I'm an author. I write detective novels so I read up on conspiracy theories and secret societies and such and I know that there is an awful lot of deceit and deception out there in the name of so-called religion. People have been killing and torturing one another for thousands of years in the name of God and, frankly, I've become quite jaded. I have to be honest. You'll have to go a long, long way to convince me that you are who you say you are or to prove to me the reality of an all-powerful God like in the Bible."

"So, your answer then is 'no'."

"That's right."

"Indulge my curiosity for a moment, Mr. Bartholemew. What, then, would it take for you to believe?"

"I don't know."

"A miracle, perhaps?"

"Maybe."

"What of the many miracles recorded in the Scriptures? Do they not bode with you?"

"Made-up stories. There's no corroborating proof that any of those things ever actually happened."

"You would need to witness something miraculous in person, then."

"I suppose; yes, I would."

"That would make you believe?"

"Maybe."

"After all that you've experienced over the past few days and all of those who have given witness to the fact that I am exactly who I am does not prove to you at all that I am, in actuality, John the Apostle of Jesus."

"Secret societies often have deep-seated and bizarre spiritual traditions that, quite honestly, defy intellect and rationale. The Illuminati, the I.R.A., the Skull and Bones, the Lámhdearg, the Masons and all of the others; they all could be laboring under their own self-crafted belief systems that just so happen to embrace you as being John the Apostle. Or perhaps, they may not actually believe that but, barring the possibility that it may be correct, were hedging their bets by getting in on the hunt. No, their obsessions do not offer any veracity to what has become the legend of John the Apostle."

"So, a *legend*, I've become? How fascinating. So you are telling me that you would need to not only witness, but *experience* some sort of a miracle and, even so, you may well still not be convinced."

"Try me."

"Ha, ha, ha, ha — no, Mr. Bartholemew. You see, belief is borne of faith. Without faith, you can never believe. I could turn Mr. Goodspeed into a frog or cause the sun to reverse its course and you still would not believe because you have no faith. Your heart is cold as stone and you are far, far from God."

"Or He is far from *me*."

"No, He stands beside the door ready to respond to your invitation. Anytime, anywhere, in any circumstance. When you are ready to surrender to Him, He will be there. But then, that is the issue is it not?"

"What's that?"

"Surrender. You cannot embrace that, you cannot let go of your grasp of the world."

"I suppose that may be true."

Out of the corner of my eye, I saw Jacob raise his hand like a schoolboy seeking to be called upon by the teacher. John turned his head and smiled at him, "you know, in Jack's defense, the world has become a very dark and cold place. The Bible isn't looked upon with the sort of regard that it once was. Very few people believe any more that it's God's own word, and so don't give much credence to what it says."

"That has become quite apparent."

"But what if you, John, assuming you are who you say you are, what if you went public. What if you got out into the world and vouched for the Bible, encouraged people to read it and live by it. You could help bring the world around to God again."

"Yeah," I added, "you could do all of the talk shows, make the rounds. Jimmy Fallon, Wolf Blitzer, Sean Hannity, David Letterman, and tell them who you are and make your case."

"Right, tell the world. You could even write a book."

"Write a book?"

"Well," Jacob quickly glanced around at the encircling shelves of John's writings, "write *another* book. It could be *huge*, like Oprah."

"Oprah?"

"Yeah."

"Let me ask you a question, Mr. Goodspeed. If someone like Jonathan Bartholemew is any indication of the hearts of people around the world, and he doesn't believe who I am even though I am standing in front of him, talking with him and asserting my own truth, what makes you believe that a world full of Jonathan Bartholemews would respond any differently — considering that they would not have the same opportunity to meet me in person? No, it would be futile. Besides, I cannot be the one celebrated, I cannot stand in the bright light that might cast a shadow on the Lord. His word is complete, it does not need me to endorse it or argue for it; to add to it or explain it. Without faith, it matters nothing what I might say."

"But if you could convince them of who you are..."

"I am nobody. I have no authority or capacity to convince anyone of anything that they don't come to in their own faith. In the grand scheme of God's plan, I matter very little."

"But you're *John*," Meagan interjected.

He leaned back against the table and smiled broadly at her. I looked over at her and saw that she had a pleading look on her Irish-pale, freckled face. There was a long pause in the conversation, I looked back up at John again and sat back in my chair, ready to become all the more insistent with my point, but he spoke before I had opportunity.

"We have made arrangements for each of you to get home. Brother Ivanovich and his men will get you to the airport and on your way; Miss Flynn, back to Dublin, you two men, back to Vermont. Your sacrifice and zeal have been remarkable over the past several days and you can all feel great satisfaction that your efforts and risks have been for a much higher purpose. I just wanted to personally thank you," he reached out his hand to shake with each of us and then turned and walked back around to the far side of the table and stood by the window and watched us as we got up to leave.

Ivanovich stepped up in front of us and waved his arm toward the door. I was flabbergasted that the conversation had been so abruptly cut off. I felt like calling out to regain John's attention, but I felt a hand in the middle of my back urging toward the door. There was so much more I wanted to say, so much more I wanted to ask but it seemed clear that he didn't want to engage us any farther. I glanced back over my shoulder as we walked out of the door to the hall and saw him sitting at the table, pen in hand, with his head down intent once again on his writing and wondered for how many more years he would be so industried; for how many more centuries?

We were led down the hallway where Ivanovich handed each of us a packet of papers which included passports and other travel documents along with boarding passes for flights out of Prague that afternoon and then led with two of his brother Templars down the stairs to the front door and out to the street. It was a fresh, sunny day in Prague, an ancient and beautiful city that one day I would like to return to and explore. But on that day, there would be no time for tourism. We were ushered into a large, black car and driven across the cobble-stoned streets of the Old Town and through streets lined with gleaming new buildings interspersed with old, stone buildings of all sorts of descriptions, some many hundreds of years old.

We didn't talk much in the car. Meagan rode up front with

Ivanovich, Jacob rode in the back seat with me. We two were fascinated by the sights of the city and watched all of the buildings, the people, the street vendors and sidewalk musicians as we passed by them. Meagan mostly sat stoically quiet in the front seat. Throughout the entire drive, we spoke almost nothing to one another until we had arrived at the terminal at the airport where Ivanovich parked the car and we walked across the sky-walk to the main building.

We checked in at the counter together; we would all three be on the same flight to Paris and the Templars had reserved us seats next to one another. I was taken aback by the very visible presence of paramilitary security at the airport. Uniformed guards with machine guns stood throughout the building. Their T.S.A.-style processing was just as thorough as ours in the States but with armed guards all around. All the travelers walked through the lines silently and self-conscious of their every move lest they give anyone cause to cull them from the herd for closer scrutiny.

I could see Ivanovich watching us from behind the glass wall that separated the unsecured portion of the terminal from the secured area filled with passengers who had completed processing for boarding. He remained there, watching, until the airline announced time for us to board and we walked down the tunnel to the plane. In less than fifteen minutes, we were in the air and on our way from Prague. By the time the plane would land at Charles DeGaul International Airport in Paris, John and the Templars would be gone, as well. Gone to some other city in some other part of the world. Far from those who would seek him out for their own profit; to destroy him, imprison him or just kill him to silence him and the truths that surround him.

June 14, 1841

Was awakened in the middle of the night by the
clamor of the town's fire brigade. The monastery
on North Hill was ablaze. My father had served
the holy order that lived there for many years;
since his passing, I'd come to know many of the
men who served there. I could see the flames from
my back porch, leaping high above the tree line.
In the morning, I walked up the hill to inspect the
damage. I thought it odd that none of the Templars
had come to the house or met me on the road as I
climbed the hill and, once at the property, there
were none to be seen. In the rubble, there was not a
stick of burned furniture, ashes from the stacks
and cases filled of books and papers that I'd seen
inside, no corpses, in fact the graves had all been
opened and the caskets of the dead Templars lay
empty on the grass. The entire order had somehow
vanished in the night to where I know not.

June 16, 1841

Upon seeing off a few of our guests this morning
and returning to my desk, I discovered an envelope
that I'd not seen there before. In it was a large
sum of money and a note thanking me and my
family for our loyal support, and signed, simply,
John.

A REUBEN AND
A DIET DR. PEPPER

I had been home in St. Albans for a few days; safe and sound. I sat in front of my computer, staring at the blank screen as writers in years past would have stared at a blank piece of white paper mockingly protruding from the rollers of their typewriters. The jet-lag not withstanding, my mind was completely captivated by the whirlwind of events that I'd experienced over the previous couple of weeks. What an amazing adventure, who would ever believe it?

But there I sat. Before all that insanity had begun, I was actually about halfway through the first draft of my next novel. But writer's block had a firm grip on me and I was not accomplishing anything.

Nary a keystroke.

Nothing.

I stared wistfully out the window at the lush green surroundings around my home. Down the hill, I could see the rooftops of the city center and, beyond that, the broad expanse of Lake Champlain glistening in the morning sun.

Undeniably beautiful, but I was getting absolutely nothing

done, staring out the window.

Road trip.

I had to get out of there and somehow find the 'reset' button to get myself back on track. I reached over and picked up the phone. Speed-dial number four dialed up the Montgomery Historical Society and, after a few rings, a familiar voice answered.

"Hello?"

"Is this the Montgomery Hysterical Society?"

"Hi, Jack."

"Hi, Jacob."

"How's it going?"

"I've been sitting here staring at a blank computer screen just totally blocked. The same blank screen I stared at yesterday and the day before. I've gotta get out of here. What you doin' for lunch?"

"I guess I'm goin' to Dino's with you for a Reuben."

"Great idea. I'll be right over."

I shut down my computer, got into my car and drove over to Montgomery. From where I live in St. Albans, it's a drive through a few sparsely-populated towns with clusters of homes and farms along the way. A warm spring morning, I rolled the windows down in the car and enjoyed the fresh air that blew through along the way and the sun coming in through the windows was warm and inviting. A very pleasant trip, a much needed diversion. I took my time to make the experience extend as long as I could.

I rolled into town and pulled up across front of Pratt Hall, the converted church that is home to the Montgomery Historical Society and the office of Jacob Goodspeed. When I walked in, I found Jacob up at his computer at the back of the hall, leaning back in his chair with his fingers laced together, resting on the top of his scalp and staring at the computer screen in front of him. He looked over at me as I walked through the displays in the big room and approached the rear platform where his desk was and smiled up at him. He lowered his hands and removed his reading glasses and set them down on the desk beside the computer monitor.

"Jack, it's great to see you."

"Nice to see you too, Jacob."

"I've been sitting here staring at my own computer, just not feeling very motivated. I've been thinking that it seems just too quiet around here."

"Too quiet? You'd prefer to have people shooting at you?"

"I don't know. I guess it would be okay if they didn't actually hit me."

"You've become an adrenaline junkie — you need some action in your life."

"Oh, I don't know, a little might be nice, I guess," he got up and grabbed his other glasses off of the stack of books on his desk and slipped them on, then stroked his mustache as he stepped down to the main floor where I was standing.

"Lunch at Dino's isn't enough action for you, then?"

"It's a start, I suppose."

"Well, let's see if we can't walk down the streets of Montgomery without getting shot, kidnapped or beat up. What d'ya say?"

"Sounds risky, but I'm game if you are."

Dino's Bar and Grille is in the middle of the village of Montgomery Center, a crossroads in the geographic center of town. A bit too far to walk from Pratt Hall, so we drove up the street and parked in the parking lot beside the restaurant. Despite its small size, the little crossroads is rather busy with a grocery store, Dino's and a couple of other small businesses clustered around the three-sided intersection.

But lunchtime at Dino's is pretty quiet. That's one of the reasons why we so like to frequent there in the middle of the day. The door from the street enters the restaurant at the bar where, at that time of afternoon, we'd normally find Jenny the bartender at work preparing for the evening rush but on that day, the restaurant's owner, Ed, was at the bar, wiping down the shelves and putting away the glasses and silverware from the dishwasher back in the kitchen.

"Good afternoon, gentlemen."

"Hey, Ed."

"Just go on in and sit anywhere you like."

"Sure, thanks. Hey, no Jenny today?"

"Nope, haven't seen her for days."

"Really? Is she alright?"

"Don't know. She just didn't show up one day, never called."

"That doesn't seem like her."

"No, it doesn't. After a couple of days, I drove by her place but she wasn't there. I looked in the windows and the place was empty, all her stuff. She's gone."

"That's weird."

"Yeah, it is. So go find a table, I'll be right with you. What would you like to drink, fellas?"

"A Dr. Pepper, no ice," I replied.

"Diet D.P. for me, Ed. Jenny keeps, er, kept a stash of it under the bar for me."

Ed bent down and peered under the bar and then looked up at Jacob and smiled, "so she did. Okay, gents, I'll bring your drinks right out."

Jacob and I walked down into the dining room and sat down at our favorite table near the juke box, by the window. So much to talk about, but neither of us really knew where to start.

"So, having any trouble with jet-lag?" I asked, trying to break the ice.

"I haven't really slept much in the past few days. Cat-naps now and again either intended or just passing out from total fatigue. How 'bout you?"

"About the same. If I hadn't called you, I'd probably have just dozed off right there in front of my computer."

"If you hadn't called me, I would probably have done the

same."

"Yeah."

"Yup."

Silence.

"Strange about Jenny," Jacob began.

"Very strange."

"She seemed like such a reliable girl. Head on straight, devoted employee. Easy on the eyes, too."

"Yeah, just doesn't seem like her to just up and disappear like that."

"Yeah. Kids these days. Hard to read 'em."

"I guess so."

"Yeah."

Silence again.

Enough shallow small-talk, I thought I'd just dive right in, "so tell me, did you buy any of that stuff back there in Prague. Did you think that that guy was actually John the Apostle?"

Jacob leaned back in his chair and smiled a Cheshire Cat sort of grin while he stroked his mustache, "you know, Jack, some years ago I went to see a one-man play where John Aston — remember him from The Addams Family? — he played Edgar Allen Poe. He was dressed in the right clothes, had the Poe mustache and spoke eloquently and confidently just like you'd imagine Poe might speak. After a few minutes at the very beginning, even though in my brain I knew without a doubt that I was watching and hearing an actor, I was totally buying that I was hearing and seeing Poe himself. Aston had become Poe to me and to the rest of the audience that evening."

"So you think that the guy we met was an actor portraying John?"

"I don't know. It seems unlikely that he'd be a man two thousand years old. If you discount that possibility, then, yeah, maybe he was just an actor."

"I suppose."

"How about you, Jack?"

Before I had a chance to answer, Ed came to the table with our drinks and a couple of menus in his hands, "do you fellas need menus, or do you know what you want?"

Jacob looked over at me with a quizzical look and responded to Ed, "I know what I want, how about you, Jack?"

"Yeah," I looked up at Ed, "a Reuben, please, with an extra pickle slice and fries."

"Very good," he looked over at Jacob.

"That sounds good to me, too. Same thing, Ed. Thanks."

"Thank you, gents, I'll have your orders up in a few minutes."

When he walked back into the kitchen, I turned to look at Jacob again and he refreshed his question to me, "so, Jack, what did you think? Did you buy any of that?"

"I've gotta tell you that I have thought about almost nothing else since we got on the plane in Paris. First of all, I never bought the idea that the guy we were talking to was, in fact, John the Apostle. Like you said, I can't imagine anyone living to be two thousand years old."

"But you gave such an argument for it all before we left town. You cited a bunch of examples of people living that long in the Old Testament. What changed your mind?"

"I guess my mind can't transition from the theoretical to the actual. I mean, I can go to the movies and see a science fiction flick and completely get what's going on and accept all the super powers and futuristic technology, but when I leave the theater and walk back out into the real world, none of it applies. It's just fantasy and there's a decided disconnect in my mind between the two."

"Hmmm, I guess that makes sense. Now that you put it into words, I think I understand my misgivings, too. So, with that in mind, we did meet with an actual person so he would have to be some sort of an actor or, if you will, an impostor."

"Yeah, however you slice it, he couldn't possibly be the real deal."

"But what did you think of what he said? All that stuff about believing and faith and all?"

"I've heard a lot of that before. When it comes to religion, Jacob, I'm probably the last guy you want to ask. To me it's all smoke and mirrors or, as someone once said in a song: 'the smile on a dog'."

"You don't believe in God, even?"

"Oh, I guess I do. Or at least some sort of higher power, some kind of supreme being; you can call it 'God' of you like or 'Allah' works, too or 'Floyd', if that cranks your tractor."

"I don't know, Jack. Maybe because I'm as old as I am. I've buried a lot of friends over the years; I buried my wife a decade ago. It makes one really ponder one's mortality. Don't you ever think of those things? Don't you ever consider your time here and wonder what's next?"

I took a sip of my Dr. Pepper and smiled. Sure, I had thought of those things, but try not to. I honestly just try to keep my focus on the tasks at hand: my next publishing deadline, paying the electric bill, making sure there's enough stuff in the house to make a sandwich for lunch while I work on my next book. My mind is engrossed in the research for my next project, I don't have time to ponder eternity, nor do I care to. I had to be honest with Jacob, "yeah, I've thought about it from time to time, but I'm too focused on the things in my life that I really don't have time to pursue those sorts of things out on the periphery."

"I used to go to church with my wife every Sunday. To that Baptist church across the street there," he turned his head and gazed at the wall of the dining room that faces the church beyond and continued wistfully, "when she died, I just lost my motivation to go, I'd skip a week here and there and then skip weeks and months at a time. These days I just show up on Easter and Christmas, most years." He turned and looked back at me, "after this little adventure, I've come back home and found a big hole in my life. A big hole that I didn't really realize was there before. I don't know if that guy was an actor or the real thing, but to me it doesn't really matter. I've been thinking about it a lot and I think, talking with you here and now, I've become convicted to get back to that little church — to look for all that I've misplaced," he sat back in his chair, picking up his glass of diet soda and looked down at it, "misplaced or, maybe more precisely, set aside and partitioned off." He looked back up at me, "time to get it back."

"Wow, I didn't get any of that."

"Maybe something the guy said about faith has a lot to do with it."

"What do you mean?"

"He said that, before you could believe in something, you had to have faith. He said that you didn't have any. Could that be right?"

"I hadn't really given it much thought before but, yeah, I would have to say that that would be right. I have faith in what I'm able to do for myself, I have faith in my friends, like you. I have faith in what I can see, touch and interact with, but not in some unseen spiritual power."

"What about your friend the so-called 'bad-ass C.I.A. babe'? You have faith in her?"

"She saved my life, yeah, I think it's fair to say that I have faith in her."

"Have you had a chance to talk with her since Paris?"

"No, actually, I'd not heard a word from her. I've thought about picking up the phone and making a call to Dublin more than once, but just never got around to it."

"Friendships are often lost to that sort of thing."

"What sort of thing?"

"Neglect. Relationships need to be fueled with communication. Promise me that you'll call her when you get home this afternoon."

"Yeah, you're right, I think I'll do that. It would be nice to talk with her again."

"Even if she's busy or you just leave a message on her

phone, at least you've made contact, that's important."

"Did you notice that he never really talked with her?"

"Now that you mention it, yeah, I did notice. He confronted both of us about believing and faith, but never really directed anything at her. I wonder why."

"Me too."

"Do you think that maybe he could sense where her heart was, what sort of level of faith she had. I mean, if he could peg you for being devoid of faith, could he have pegged her for being full of it?"

"Full of it?"

"You know what I mean."

"Ha, ha, ha, ha — yeah, I know what you mean. Yeah, maybe. Someday I've gotta tell you the story of when I had to ask her to take off her shirt in the women's rest room."

"What?"

"She had been shot in the arm. We couldn't go to an emergency room so we went to this truck stop and I stitched her up in the ladies' room. She had to take her shirt partly off so I could get to the wound. She was very modest, embarrassed, even."

"Doesn't sound like someone I'd nick-name as 'bad-ass'."

"Believe me, she earned that nick-name in so many other ways."

"But if you think about it, Jack, that would be consistent with someone of faith. Maybe she isn't a church-going kind of person, but maybe she was brought up with some sort of religion and those values are still with her and, maybe, there's a small sliver of that religion in there somewhere, too."

"You know, you might be right. Maybe John — or whoever he was — knew that, could somehow sense that. Why preach to the choir, as it were?"

"And what happened when he touched her? Did you see that?"

"Yeah — I don't know, she never said anything about it.

She acted like something between ecstatic and excruciating, it was really weird."

"But it happened when he walked by her and touched her on the shoulder."

"Yeah."

"You should ask her about that when you talk to her. I'd really like to know what happened."

"Yeah, I will."

Our conversation was interrupted by a couple of perfect Reubens being brought to the table with a couple of plates of fries, crispy and fresh from the kitchen.

"Thanks, Ed," Jacob said.

"You boys enjoy. If you need me, I'll be in the kitchen, just yell."

"Okay, thanks again."

As he walked back to the back room, I grabbed the salt shaker and ketchup bottle and dressed my fries and then took one off from the top with my fingers and bit into the end of it.

"You know, something else strange," I began as Jacob took a bite from his sandwich, "the Templars never asked us anything about the journals. Did they say anything to you?"

Jacob quickly finished chewing and swallowed, then grabbed his napkin and wiped his mouth and mustache, "no, not a word. Those Illuminati guys were all over me about them but the guys in Prague never said a word."

"That's very strange. Maybe they knew that we had them safe and aren't worried about them."

"Maybe, or maybe they just don't care."

"What do you mean."

"Well, remember all that talk about John not mattering, that what he might say or do doesn't make any difference?"

"Yeah."

"Well, maybe they think that, no matter what happens with the journals and who might be effected by them, John is still who he is — or at least, who he says he is — and nothing in their world would change. Maybe they just don't care."

"That kind of makes sense," I said, and then leaned over my plate and quietly asked, "so, Jacob, where did you hide them?" I just had to know.

He just smiled and slyly stroked that mustache of his as he stood up. He looked around the room and then reached into his pocket and pulled out some change, spreading it out in his palm with his index finger and then picked out a penny. He put the rest of the coins back into his pocket and held up the penny with a sly grin to show me.

I had no idea what the coin was all about, but then he walked over to the juke box and squatted down next to it, using the penny to undo the four twist-latches that held the side cover on, "when you called me that night, I drove to Pratt Hall and got the journals out of the vault. As I was driving back, I was trying to think of a good place to hide them where noone would think to look and then I saw a couple of lights on here at Dino's. It was after hours and I knew just one or two people would be here cleaning up after closing so I took a chance and the side door was unlocked. I snuck in and came back here to the dining room. It was all dark, all the lights were off," he released the last of the latches and then started to pull the panel off of the machine, "so I remembered being here once when the service guy from the vending company was here and saw the inside of the machine while he had it open." He set the panel aside, leaning it up against the wall.

"Inside, at the bottom, is a false floor with a finger-hole in one end to get hold of it and lift it out," he stuck his index finger into the hole and lifted the plank of black-painted particle-board up out of its frame, "a space underneath that's just the right size to…"

Suddenly, he stopped and just stared inside the machine.

"What's the matter?"

He didn't say anything for a moment, I got to my feet and he whispered, "they're gone."

"Gone?" I ran to the juke box and crouched down next to him, looking inside. Sure enough, he had lifted out the black plank of wood to reveal an empty cavity underneath. I stared at the void for a moment or two and then it all came together in my mind, I began to laugh.

"What's so funny?" Jacob asked.

I just sat down on the floor, "Jenny!"

"Jenny?"

"Yeah, she's Templar! Don't you get it? That's why they never asked us about the journals — they had them all along."

"She's been missing for days. She probably saw me put them in here that night and grabbed them the next day or something and disappeared."

"She was probably in Prague with us the whole time, somewhere in that big old house."

"You mean, we just went through all of that for nothing? They had the books this whole time?"

"All those groups probably had people here in town for years. I'll bet you'll find a few other folks who just as mysteriously disappeared. Your friend from the K of C who came looking for the journals for instance, and the Skull and Bones, they probably had someone here in town, too. May even have been someone on the Historical Society's board of directors."

"How better to keep an eye on things — sure."

"Yeah, Jenny just got lucky. If you had hidden them somewhere else, who knows who may have gotten their hands on them."

"I'd hate to imagine."

Jacob and I just looked at each other for a minute or two and then just busted out laughing. He set the black board back in place, "here, let me help you get this thing put back together so we can finish our lunches, our Reubens are getting cold."

* * * * *

The stately O'Neill country estate set high on the lush, emerald green hills east of Coleraine, was lit up as guests arrived in expensive cars and limousines for a formal dinner party. Their host for the evening, Eamon O'Neill, was dressed in his black tuxedo and made the rounds of the guests in his home on an unusually sultry Irish spring evening. Dignitaries of all kinds populated the rooms of the sprawling home — politicians, business associates and friends — all enjoying O'Neill's hospitality as more guests arrived and they awaited the announcement that an anticipated culinary masterpiece was about to be served. They sampled caviar, smoked salmon and fine pastries as they sipped champagne and the finest Irish whiskey served by a staff of caterers. A chamber quartet played in the central great room, their lofty strings singing throughout the stately ground floor. The rooms were filled with the voices of dozens of elegantly-dressed people putting on their highest of airs, talking and laughing with measured abandon.

At the height of the evening, shortly before dinner was to be served, Eamon O'Neill was engaged in conversation with a circle of elegantly-dressed and bejeweled women of high society when a young waiter approached him with a message in an envelope on a silver tray.

He interrupted his attention with the women and took the note from the tray, thanking the young man with a nod. He opened the envelope and removed the folded paper from inside, opened it up and read the note. His face lit up with a broad smile. He folded the paper again and returned it to the envelope and announced, "ladies, I must excuse myself. I've just been informed that a very special guest has arrived here at the estate. I do not wish to be rude, but I must go and greet her."

"A woman?" one of the ladies asked, fishing for some dirt and gossip about one of Northern Ireland's most eligible bachelors.

"Aye, she has just arrived from America. Do please excuse me."

"Indeed."

He smiled and then turned and made his way out of the busy room to the stairwell near the front of the big house and ascended to the quiet second floor and to his private library. With great anticipation, he pulled open the door and walked inside. An attractive young woman stood in the room with one of his first editions in her hand, "Chauser? Is this where my inheritance is evaporating to?"

He just laughed out loud and called out, "Gennivere!"

She set the book back onto the shelf and replied, "Papa!"

In a moment they embraced and stood together in the quiet of the library, the noise and bustle of his guests far from their hearing and far from interfering with their reunion. When they finally released one another, he held her out at his arms' length, "my, my, just look at you, lass. Your time in America has certainly agreed with you."

"I enjoyed my time there, but I really missed the isle, all of this — you. I'm really glad to finally be home."

"When did you get in?"

"I landed in Dublin yesterday and took a flight to Derry this morning."

"And the books?"

"Safely locked up in the archives at the Diamond. Semus met me at the airport and brought me round."

"You make your Papa proud."

"Just as you said, Papa, patience will out. Watch and listen and wait and they practically placed them into my own hands."

Eamon stood and looked at his not-so-little girl and grinned a broad grin.

"What?"

"We must celebrate! My girl has come home!"

"Aye, we must toast!"

"Indeed, a toast! Come, I want to introduce you to my guests. Tonight we celebrate; my little girl has come home!"

Jack's Blog Entry: June 2nd

Sitting in the waiting area at Burlington International Airport with my laptop and Starbuck's, waiting for Meagan's plane to land from Washington. She called me a few days ago to tell me that she was at C.I.A. headquarters in Langley, Virginia for some meetings and, when she was done, she'd have a few days before she had to get back to Dublin and wanted to know if she could come and see me. I told her that I had a guest bedroom that she was welcome to stay in for as long as she wanted to and offered to pick her up at the airport — so here I am.

I finished hoeing out that spare bedroom of all the stuff I had stored in there, dusting, vacuuming and putting fresh sheets on the bed. When I bought the house, that extra bedroom had always been intended as a guest room, even has a bed and a dresser and some other appropriate furniture in it but, until this morning I'd never had any guests so it became just a catch-all junk

room but, when she called me, I found that I could transform it once again into a reasonable guest room in pretty short order. I just couldn't imagine making even a bad-ass C.I.A. babe stay at the Cadillac Motel.

When she called, she asked me about what I thought of our meeting with the man who called himself John, presumedly the Apostle. I was kind of surprised by her question since, at that meeting, she barely said two words and he never actually spoke much to her, but apparently she was riveted by it all and came away with a very different perspective than I did.

It's interesting to me that the three of us sitting together in the same room hearing the same words from the same man could all come away with very different impressions. I didn't buy any of it, not that I was talking with a two-thousand-year-old man nor any of the rhetoric that he laid on us. Jacob was intensely engrossed in all that the man had to say, but as far as him being John, well, for Jacob the jury is still out. But Meagan, it seems, bought the whole thing and it seems to be challenging the entire paradigm of her life and that was disturbing her.

She posed a very deep question to me on the phone. She asked me that, if one believed in any part of the Bible, then should they not believe in all of it? If it's all supposedly inspired by God and some sort of contiguous, continuous document, shouldn't any part be as viable as any other part? Me, I read a lot, I know a lot about the Bible from all of my research and studies in my writing, but I've never actually taken any of it any too seriously. There are some pretty fantastic stories in there about giants, floods, the dead coming back to life and I find it pretty hard to swallow as a whole, But I suppose that she makes a very good point, if one were to believe in any one part of it, one would have to accept all of it, giants, floods and all.

And within her point some of the things that John said make a lot of sense in hindsight. He insisted that he, himself, was irrelevant to the veracity of the Bible, it doesn't need any sort of proving, noone to vouch for it to give it any sort of legitimacy; it speaks for itself and stands on its own and that all sort of follows so, if he was right, he doesn't matter a lick any more — hasn't for about two thousand years. Staying hidden would keep those who might use him to their own designs from distorting or diverting any of what the Bible says. If he stays a figment of conspiracy theorists' imaginations, then the world would remain safe — at least it would maintain its status quo.

Although I may have a lot of head-knowledge about the Bible from my reading, I am no sort of theologian so I talked to my neighbor who is the pastor at the Assembly of God church in town and asked him if we could spend some time with him tomorrow. We set up an appointment for ten tomorrow morning in his office.

Meagan wants to talk about what we'd been through which I'm more than happy to do. We'd shared a lot over those few days, thoughts about life and death, killing and dying and living with the horror of it all. I still had a lot that I wanted to talk about and, really, noone here at home to talk to. She understands, she's been through it all, far more than I could even imagine. I look so forward to some long, deep conversations with her when she gets here.

But I think this evening over dinner, we should talk about who we should and should not share that experience with. She's C.I.A. so she knows how important it is to keep secrets and I believe that we should talk with the pastor about the theological aspects of what we'd experienced and leave out all the stuff about the Illuminati, the Mossad, the I.R.A. and all the shooting and beating up priests and stuff. He might get the wrong idea. No, actually, he'd probably get the right idea and that would be worse.

I just checked the video board and saw

that her plane is still listed as being on-time. She should be here in about fifteen minutes or so. Got a refill of my coffee while I was up, too.

I asked her on the phone about what had happened when John had touched her shoulder and she reacted in such a painfully ecstatic way. She said that, when he touched her, she suddenly felt a sense of warmth from inside just flood through her whole body, it caught her by surprise. She felt a strange tingling sensation in her arm that radiated from the area where her bullet wound was and spread all the way down to her wrist and across her shoulder. When it passed, she was out of breath and noticed that the pain in her arm where I'd patched her up was gone. When she got home to Dublin, in her own apartment, she took off the black tactical jersey and found loops of thread tied in small circles fall out of the left sleeve onto the floor. When she removed the gauze wrap and slid her hand over the site of the wound, it was smooth and painless. She checked it out in her bathroom mirror and the wound was entirely gone, no scar, no redness, just gone.

I'm still not buying any of this but, I have to admit, I'm having trouble explaining this one away. I mean, I saw that wound, it was a vicious, ragged tear through her flesh. The way I patched it up with a rudimentary stitching job should have left an absolutely gruesome scar when it all finally healed. It was so bad that I was absolutely convinced that, if I hadn't done something, she would certainly have lost that limb. In less than a week it was completely healed without a trace. The stitches and bandages just fell away. Is this the miracle that John had challenged me with? Did he think that it would make a believer out of me? Well, it sure seemed to work on Meagan!

So, it would seem that we have a lot to talk about with the pastor tomorrow morning.

This evening, however, we have reservations at the Black Lantern Inn in Montgomery for dinner with Jacob. If she's up for it, maybe we'll take in some of the night life at Dino's before heading back to St. Albans. I'm sure she'll enjoy his relating of the San Diego chicken suit story.

They just announced on the loudspeakers that the flight from Ronald Reagan International was landing so I'll have to wrap this up. I told her I'd meet her at the luggage carousel. Shouldn't be too hard to pick her out of the crowd with those freckles and that bright orange-red mane of Irish locks.

Just one last quick gulp of my Starbuck's…

thank you

Thank you to Pastor Charlie Kuthe who convinced me to stop writing this book, write another one first, and then finish this one later. It was worth the delay as I was given so much more inspiration that never would have found its way into this volume if I hadn't followed his advice.

Thanks to my wife, Stephanie, who reads through all of my manuscripts and offers encouragements and fresh ideas.

Thanks to Scott Perry, the real director of the Montgomery, Vermont, Historical Society, for patiently answering my e-mails and phone calls with questions about my own genealogical investigations and this story that grew out of that search (www.montgomeryhistoricalsociety.com).

Thanks to Cliff Daggett for being the inspiration for one of the heroes of this book — and for being such a good sport.

Thanks to Mart DeHaan of RBC Ministries for some tips and guidance in developing the theme of John's relationship with Christ, the Gospel and man — which were instrumental in creating the conversations in chapter thirteen.

Thanks to the Maple City Diner in St. Albans, Vermont for the great Reuben sandwich and fries.

And thanks to the Lord for giving me the ideas for my books, the motivation to write them and the inspiration for the messages they contain. All of which for His own glory.

what if
Author's notes

Admitedly, the premises of what this book is based upon, the things contained in the pages of Elijah Browne's journals, fly in the face of commonly-accepted so-called facts. I say "so-called" because in each case they are based solely upon the claims and traditions of certain established religions and have since become widely considered to be irrefutable, despite having no tangible, Biblical or historical support.

In this book, I put forth three controversial ideas, not entirely my own. First, and probably the easiest to examine, is the idea that John the Apostle may still be alive to this day. I read the conversation between Jesus and Peter at the end of the Book of John some years ago and thought that the possibility certainly existed, even though it defies our common, mortal sensitivities. Looking at the text from the New King James translation, John 21:21 & 22 reads:

> Peter, seeing him, said to Jesus 'But Lord, what about this man?' Jesus said to him, "If I will that he remain until I come, what is that to you? You follow Me."

This exchange took place after Jesus' resurrection while he and several of his apostles and desciples were walking along a road, Peter beside him holding this conversation, John and others following behind. Peter, when he refers to "this man" is essentially pointing over his shoulder and referring to John (the context of the next several passages confirms that). Jesus was frequently speaking to them about His ultimate return which many of the apostles and subsequent church leaders assumed would be imminent but, to this day, He has not yet returned. But then in the next verse, 23, John adds:

Then this saying went out among the brethren that this disciple would not die. Yet Jesus did not say to him that he would not die, but, "If I will that he remain until I come, what is that to you?"

Obviously, John thought it was a fantastic claim to think that he would not die despite that many others in their company did. And why not? That sort of longevity is not without precedent as they were all well familiar. In the Old Testament, there are many figures who lived to be many hundreds of years old, even thousands. Adam, Noah, Melchisadech, just to name a few. That sort of longevity was apparently commonplace at one time. Besides, Jesus never did say that John would not die, just that he'd remain until He would return (though, presumedly, John would be caught up in the rapture and, so, would avoid a physical death).

Commentators and theologians have all essentially taken the same perspective. Halley and the venerable Albert Barnes (*Barnes' Notes*) essentially dismiss the idea of John living beyond a natural lifespan of his day. But Matthew Henry, though he gives a nod to the incredible idea of John living even to his own time, also insists that we must not over-anylize scripture or disregard something just because, to us, it seems impossible. He insists that we must take God's word for what it is, just as it was written and, so, must at least accept the possibility – however remote – that John may well survive to see Christ's return.

If that were true, how then could he have avoided detection for two millenia? He would need to have the support of some sort of network. Surely he would have the protection of angels and God Himself, one could also imagine that Christ might periodically visit him as well. But what would that network look like? It took a lot of research and some deduction and, if you've already read the book, you can see what I had constructed. Granted, it is all conjecture at best and certainly I make no claims to its historical veracity, but maybe, just maybe, some sort of similar mechanism would have to be in place and most certainly, the Lord would orchestrate it and direct it for John's best interest and His own glory.

The second bomb that I drop in these pages is the contention that Peter died of old age in Babylon and not by having been crucified upside down in Rome. This really defies the accepted traditions but, bear with my logic for a moment. The passage that the tradition is entirely hung upon appears right beside the one that I'd previously quoted, in John, 21:18 & 19, with Jesus speaking again to Peter:

> *"Most assuredly I say to you, when you were younger, you girded yourself and walked where you wished; but when you are old, you will stretch out your hands, and another will gird you and carry you where you do not wish." This He spoke, signifying by what death he would glorify God.*

From this, somehow, the traditional story has grown, stating that Peter had gone to Rome and, upon encountering persecution there, he tried to flee the city. But, as he walked away, he encountered he resurrected Jesus on the road and asked Him where He was going. Jesus responded that He was going to Rome to be sacrificed again because Peter was running away from his fate. So, then, Peter turned and returned to the city, surrendering himself with the request that he be crucified upside down as he felt he did not deserve being executed the same way that Christ was.

You may have heard this story before.

The yarn is critically important to the Roman Catholic Church who maintains that Peter was, in fact, their first pope and the first of a lineage that can be traced all the way back to him. But, if Peter had never been to Rome, it would put this entire lineage in jeapordy as their contention is that Peter's authority as one of the original Apostles has been handed down

Bob Pierce

from one pope to the next for centuries. The papal authority would be lost without Peter's initial founding which would, then, link the office to Christ Himself.

But as we examine the origins of this legend, we find that it has its first roots in the *Letter to the Corinthians* by Clement of Rome in 90 a.d. in which he makes a cryptic suggestion that Peter came to his end by execution, however not including a date, location or method. A few years later, in 110 a.d., Ignatius claimed in his *Letter to the Romans* that Peter was, in fact, the Bishop of Rome. Other early Roman Catholic commentators and historians also affirmed Peter's office and his unique martyrdom in Rome. Ultimately, the esteemed historian Eusebius, who was himself a ranking member of the Roman church, included these legends in his Ecclesiastical History and, even though there were no eye witness accounts or any other sort of proof or evidence to support them, they were accepted as historical fact and continue to be so to this day.

The story has some glaring inconsistencies. First of all, throughout Scripture, particularly in Paul's writings that follow the Gospels in our Bibles, the statement is repeated that Jesus had been sacrificed "once for all time." Even human logic would dictate that for Jesus' sacrifice to have been of any redemptive value, it could never be repeated – ever. To suggest that He would offer to take Peter's place in their supposed encounter on the road outside of Rome is simply preposterous. He would never have suggested that He would return to the cross. The ideal, however, supports the basic tenants of the traditional ceremony of the Catholic mass and, with the Vatican's assertion that it's traditions have as much canonical legitimacy as Scripture itself, the entire structure of the church is totally reliant on the legend of Peter being accepted as gospel.

The Vatican also contends that Peter's body (or at least his bones) (or at the very least, *some* of his bones as shown in a recent public display) reside in a crypt below St. Peter's Basillica in Vatican City. Again, we have nothing more than the contention of the Roman church. The story goes that a workman, who was working on some renovations on St. Peter's in the early part of the twentieth century, happened upon a casket with the the phrase "here is Peter" scratched into its side. Inside were a few bones which he spirited out of the crypt and kept in a shoe box in his closet at home until many years later when he surrendered them to the church, telling the story.

But what is most curious of all is that the Gospel of John was written many years after Peter's death. With all of the detail and John's passion for exaulting the Lord for his works and the fulfilment of prophecies, why did he not simply tell us that Peter had been crucified upside down in Rome, rather than include this exchange between him and Jesus that suggests that Peter may well have simply died of old age? Consider again what Matthew Henry said, that we should not over-think Scripture and just take it for what it says, even if it may be contrary to what we might think we know.

Evidence this: In the book of Second Peter, he observes in verse 1:14 he writes:

...knowing shortly that I must put off my tent, just as the Lord Jesus Christ showed me.

Peter was near death, the second epistle that bears his name was written around 66 a.d. which would make Peter quite an old man. His comment about "putting off his tent" was a commonly-used colloquial phrase at the time that he used to refer to his death and the context around this passage, particularly those that follow it, are comments of a man who is trying hard to make his last statements to those whom he had mentored. He knew he was going to die soon and many commentators cite the end of this passage and citing the passages in John 21 that are contentiously referred to as evidence of his martyrdom in the manner of the old Roman Catholic tradition. But consider an elderly man of seventy-plus years (well past the average life expectancy of his day). A proud man who was impetuous and impulsive in his youth; headstrong and maybe just a bit arrogant, reduced to having to have nursemaids attend to his needs by helping him dress and take his outstretched hands to steady him as he slowly walked with feeble, unsure gait.

Also note that the passage in John to which so many refer to as predicting Peter's "martyrdom" in fact does not say that. The Greek word *thanatodz* (*Strong's* ref. 2288) is used in the passage, the generic word for death by any means, as opposed to the word *martus* (*Strong's* ref. 3144) which appears elsewhere in the New Testament specifically referring to a martyrous death.

It makes way more sense than being crucified upside down in Rome.

But add to that evidence, one more thing, In First Peter, the passage of 5:13, as he signs off his letter written just a year prior:

> *She who is in Babylon, elect together with you, greets*
> *you, and so does Mark my son.*

Peter was clearly in Babylon, far from Rome, in his twilight years. Mark, his frequent companion and writer of the second Gospel, was with him. Mark's Gospel was written at about the same time as Peter's two letters, perhaps a few years later, perhaps immediately after Peter's death.

After the Babylonian captivity and the return of the nation of Israel to Jerusalem, a remnant remained in Babylon. The Magi, made famous by the Christmas story many centuries later, were originally established by Daniel during the captivity, after he'd established his credibility with King Nebecheddnezzer. A community of Jews remained there for all of that time, thriving in their land which was, in fact, the easternmost end of God's promised land.

Peter was known to be the Apostle to the Jews as Paul was

known to be that to the gentiles. Paul even had to admonish Peter when he showed favoritism while visiting one of the Asian churchs, snubbing the gentile believers and favoring the Jewish converts. Peter had risen to lead the home church in Jerusalem in the time just after the resurrection, but was soon replaced by James, Jesus' half-brother. Peter's ministry was convoluted at best, nonetheless effective as God clearly had a use for his particular idiosyncricies, but despite his overt personality, Peter was not leadership material. It would make perfect sense that he would head east. Paul and John were making inroads to the north and west, other of the Apostles were venturing to the south and the far east, but where was Peter to go but to his own people. Since he was deposed of his leadership in Jerusalem, the Jewish community of Babylon would be a welcome home for him in his latter years.

So, to compare the legend of Peter's death by inverted crucifixion in Rome versus his much less spectacular passing of old age in Babylon, clearly there is far more credible evidence – Biblical evidence – that he simply died an old man with his people.

And lastly, the final resting place of Mary, Jesus' Earthly mother. At the crucifixion, John (the only one of the Apostles with guts enough to stay around) is given her care by Christ as He hung on the cross. We see glimpses of John taking this charge after that and in Acts, but we are otherwise left to a wide range of historical accounts and legends. The Bible doesn't give us much more to go on than that and legitimate historians have been essentially silent but almost all, at least, agree that she accompanied John to Ephesis when he left Jerusalem. Most of John's writings were penned late in his life and, being the youngest of the original Apostles, that dates most of them in the 80s and 90s a.d. One could easily extrapolate that he may have taken his charge of caring for Mary until her death, after which, he embarked on his broader ministry work, his arrest, his exile on Patmos and his later ministry back in Ephesis when he finally settled down long enough to write. But what became of Mary?

Again, the Vatican weighs in on this question – in a huge way. They contend that Mary remained a virgin throughout her life, even after giving birth to Jesus and several subsequent children. The church claims that she was sinless, as was Christ, was born of immaculate conception, as was Christ, and never experienced physical death, instead was risen to Heaven much as Elijah and Enoch were but, unlike them, she occupies a position in Heaven as the intermediary between man and Christ. Catholics worship and venify her as a goddess, refering to her as "the Blessed Virgin," "the Holy Mother," etc.

Historians and theologians outside of the Vatican paint a much different story. Most agree that she expressed a desire to be buried in Jerusalem upon her death. Whether that actually happened or not is not clear. There is one school that believes that she was buried in Ephesis where she died. Another belief is that, after her death, her body was brought to the Kidron Valley, at the foot of the Mount of Olives outside of Jerusalem, to be buried (probably by John). And yet another thought is a bit of both. In those years, it was customary to inter a body in a tomb to decompose. Once reduced to bones, they would be gathered and cleaned and placed into an escuary – a stone box – that would then be placed in a carved-out shelf in the wall of a crypt. This third line of thought has her passing in Ephesis and her bones brought to Jerusalem to be interred. In any case, it is almost universally believed that she had died in Ephesis. With a name so common as Mary and no reliable historical records, there is no way to verify any of these theories, however. There is a tomb in Ephesis that local tradition holds is hers, there have also been numerous eschuaries discovered in Israel marked with her name (likely by con artists) but without any sort of DNA testing or other means of verifying anything, the final resting place of Mary will always remain a mystery.

Another scenario that has some traction in the historical

record has John and Mary traveling to visit Thomas in India. Along the way, Mary passed away and was buried in a town called Murree in modern-day Pakistan. Another related belief is that, after the crucifixion of Jesus, she fled there and lived out her life and was, subsequently, buried there. The name of the town is a double-entende, a sort of play on words. The name Murree is a local dialect of the name "Mary" and also means in the local tongue "high place."

So there it is, the logic and evidences (however thin) that are the basis of *The Journals of Elijah Browne*. If these were true, or any one of them (and, frankly, who's to say for certain one way or another), it would be a genuine powder keg if they were ever to see the light of day and given any credence.

Bob Pierce

bibliography

All Biblical quotes in this volume are taken from *The Holy Bible, New King James Version*, © 1982, Thomas Nelson, Inc.

* * * * *

The Bad Popes, E.R. Chamberlin, © 1969 E.R. Chamberlin, The Dial Press.

Catholic Doctrine In The Bible, Rev. Samuel D. Benedict, © 1930 Samuel Benedict, The Conversion Center, Inc.

The Crusades, History & Myths Revealed, Michael Paine, © 2009 Michael Paine, Fall River Press.

The Element Encyclopedia of Secret Societies, John Michael Greer, © 2006 Michael Greer, Barnes & Noble, Inc. / HarperCollins Publishers.

Fox's Book of Martyrs, John Fox, edited by William Byron Forbush, © 1954 Holt, Rinehart and Winston (assigned 1967 to Zondervan Publ.), Zondervan Publishing.

John's Story, The Last Eyewitness, Tim LaHaye and Jerry B. Jenkins, © 2006 LaHaye Publishing Group LLC and the Jerry B. Jenkins Trust, G.P. Putnams's Sons, Penguin Group, Inc., Publishing.

Larson's New Book of Cults, Bob Larson, © 1982 Bob Larson, Tyndale House Publishers.

Secrets of the Freemasons, Michael Bradley, © 2006 J.W. Cappelens, Metro Books.

Secrets of Romanism, Joseph Zacchello, © 1977 Joseph Zacchello, Loizeaux Brothers Publishing.

Smokescreens, Jack T. Chick, © 1983 Jack T. Chick, Chick Publications.

* * * * *

Barcelona Airport / Airport El Prat,
www.barcelona-airport.com.

BCW Project, British Civil Wars, www.bcw-project.org.

Car and Driver Magazine, www.caranddriver.com.

Centro National de Inteligencia, www.cni.es.

Central Intelligence Agency, www.CIA.gov.

City of Derry Airport, www.cityofderryairport.com.

Directorate-General for External Security,
www.defense.gouv.fr.

City of Dublin, www.dublincity.ie.

Federal Bureau of Investigation, www.FBI.gov.

Find The Best, www.helicopters.findthebest.com.

Fish Eaters, www.fisheaters.com.

www.Friesian.com.

Google Maps, www.maps.google.com.

IMDb, www.imdb.com.

Interpol, www.interpol.int/en.

Jesuit Conference of the United States, www.jesuit.org.

Knights of Columbus, www.kofc.org.

The Montgomery Historical Society,
                        www.montgomeryhistoricalsociety.org.

Mossad, www.mossad.gov.il/.

National Security Agency, www.nsa.gov.

The New York Times, www.nytimes.com.

O'Reilly's of Temple Bar, www.oreillysoftemplebar.ie.

The Prague Experience, www.pragueexperience.com.

Pubby's, www.pubbys.com.

RailEurope,
            www.raileurope-world.com, www.raileurope.co.uk.

Rotten Tomatoes, www.rottentomatoes.com.

Thought Catalog, www.thoughtcatalog.com.

Today I Found Out About, www.todayifoundout.com.

Visit Temple Bar, www.visit-templebar.com.

United Church of God, www.ucg.org.

U.S. Grant Hotel, www.usgrant.net.

www.Wikipedia.org.

Wired, www.wired.com.

WiseGeek, www.wisegeek.org.

Yelp, www.yelp.com.

aβout the author

Bob Pierce was born and raised in southern Connecticut and has lived in New England all of his life (so far, anyway). He's been a graphic designer for almost all of his adult life and has written numerous articles and promotional copy for clients. This is his fourth novel. He works at a Christian radio network in northern Vermont and plays bass guitar and is lead singer for The Kingdom Blues Project, a Christian blues band that plays all around northern New England.

Other artistic pursuits include painting and illustrating. His paintings have hung in galleries all over the east coast and reside in collections across the country.

He is married and has three married sons and one granddaughter.

Contact him at BobsAwesomeBooks@gmail.com and keep up with the writing process of his future projects on his "Bob's Awesome Books" Facebook page.

Gritty, powerful and clever, The Dakota Chronicle by Bob Pierce second novel paints a sometimes dark and sometimes hopeful picture of a man seeking the happiness he truly believes is attainable in life. The story explores a wide spectrum of emotion, hope, anger and fear in the heart and soul of a man who makes his living killing others. What is the price of freedom? The cost of happily-ever-after?

Serving his country as a C.I.A. surgical assassin during the waning years of the Vietnam war, Dakota believes that he has found true joy and happiness in the midst of the decay and depravity that was wartime Saigon, only to see his family brutally destroyed when the city falls to the communist forces in the spring of 1975.

He blames God and vows to paint the world with blood. For over two decades, each mission becomes a bloody statement of defiance. But years later, when he has lost everything and everyone he had ever cared about, the nightmares begin and in some appears a Plains Indian who had mentored him as a boy, bringing cryptic messages and life lessons.

One day, Dakota serindipitously wanders into a storefront church in Boston where he befriends the pastor who helps him walk away from his life of violence and pain. He fakes his own death, changes his name and disappears into the idyllic, rural White Mountains of New Hampshire to, finally, hopefully, live happily ever after.

But when his dark past suddenly catches up with him years later, he has to decide how to protect those he loves without allowing the beast within to again run wild. What choices will he have to make; what will he have to sacrifice?

Availavble in print on Amazon.com, for Kindle, and at bookstores worldwide.
ISBN-13: 978-1482704983   ISBN-10: 1482704986

"Thanks, Bob for a great tale!
I didn't want to put it down and am still wanting it not to be over."
— Dick Ekwall

"The genius of this novel is that, within the peace offered in Christ,
there is still inevitably a past that rears its ugly head to
challenge even the most committed of believers."
— Rev. Charles Kuthe, Georgia Plain Baptist Church

"A captivating narrative that engages from page one and doesn't let up until the thrilling
climax atop New Hampshire's frigid Mount Washington. This espionage thriller
will have you on the edge of your seat. It will make you think,
and it will make you cry, and it will keep you guessing."
— Author Jacob Grant, The Stormcaller and The Dragon

"It's one of those books that grabs you right off and you just want to keep
reading. I sincerely hope that Bob Is writing another book!"
— Marilyn Prevuznak

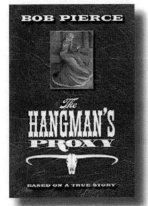

Vanessa McCain grew up as an orphan on the west Texas prairie. Her parents were killed on the trek westward and she grew up from a toddler on the Bar-V Ranch, raised by her uncle. The mid 1800s were a boom time for the western territories and many people migrated from the east seeking their fortunes. One such adventurer was Baldwin Vance whose sprawling ranch and the adjacent town that bore his name, offered unlimited possibilities for thousands. A man of hard will and a pension for quick and brutal frontier justice, it was his passion to build his business and tame the lawless territory by the point of a rifle or the end of a rope.

But among the ambitious settlers to this region, there came those who seethed with hate, obsessed with vengeance. A blood-feud between two families who had both moved west to escape the senseless killings and the ravages of war, had followed them. One man had risen to a position of power within Vance's organization and used that position to hatch a devious plan to destroy his rival and his entire family. Only Vanessa had access to the powerful cattle baron to hopefully save her family from the evil plan. She would have to risk everything — her marriage, her home, even her very life. How much was she willing to sacrifice to put down the nefarious conspiracy?

Based on a timeless true story, The Hangman's Proxy weaves that ancient tale into the familiar time and place of the American west. The story is filled with elements of love and hate, strength of family and faith, vengeance and the desperate price that it can extract from those who seek it. This drama will challenge and inspire everyone who reads it and keep you on the edge of your seat right up to the powerful climax.

Availavble in print on Amazon.com, for Kindle, and at bookstores worldwide.
ISBN 978-1494811082   Title ID: 4590653

"I loved it! Thanks so much for sharing this imaginative new book.
Could not put it down!"
— Marilyn P.

Bob Pierce

Made in the USA
Columbia, SC
04 August 2017